A Dreadful SPLENDOR

a novel

B. R. MYERS

wm

WILLIAM MORROW

An Imprint of HarperCollinsPublishers

A DREADFUL SPLENDOR. Copyright © 2022 by B. R. Myers. All rights reserved. Printed in the United States of America. No part of this book may be used or reproduced in any manner whatsoever without written permission except in the case of brief quotations embodied in critical articles and reviews. For information, address HarperCollins Publishers, 195 Broadway, New York, NY 10007.

HarperCollins books may be purchased for educational, business, or sales promotional use. For information, please email the Special Markets Department at SPsales@harpercollins.com.

FIRST EDITION

Designed by Diahann Sturge

Library of Congress Cataloging-in-Publication Data has been applied for.

ISBN 978-0-06-320983-1

22 23 24 25 26 LBC 6 5 4 3 2

For Mom

A
Dreadful
SPLENDOR

CHAPTER ONE

London, November 1852

I t's good you've finally summoned me," I said. "There's no doubt a spirit torments this house."

Each grief-stricken face turned my way. I stood in the parlour doorway, gripping the handle of my bag. Despite the blaze of the fireplace and the richly upholstered furnishings, there was no sense of comfort. The heavy drapes were closed, shrouding the room in darkness. The funeral bouquets had begun to wilt, but their scent remained strong, saturating the air with a tired misery.

The matriarch, Mrs. Hartford, sat beside the ornate fireplace. The flames flickered, casting shadows that stretched up the walls like gossamer spirits. A sheer black veil obscured her face, leaving only her chin exposed. Even from across the room I could see a few wisps of white hair. Just like Billy Goat Gruff, Miss Crane would say.

On the other side of the room, a younger woman was perched on the edge of a settee, her silk skirt reaching the floor. Her finger was wound around the end of a long string of pearls, and as she looked me over, she gave the necklace a twist. It was a careless gesture, but she likely had more than one set of pearls at her disposal.

The two gentlemen stood as I entered. So silent was the room,

I heard someone's knees crack. The taller man had an ample stomach and a thick grey mustache. The younger was thin and fair, clothed in an elegant jacket that hung shapelessly off his slight frame. I guessed that our ages might be close. When I nodded to him, he dropped his gaze to stare at the floor.

Good.

The servant offered my card on a small silver tray to Mrs. Hartford. She plucked it up with her spindly fingers and held it close to her eyes. Her jeweled ring and matching bracelet glinted in the fire's light.

My knuckles tightened around the handle of the bag. This would be the last one, I promised myself. In my mind, I conjured the picture of a room: a bed with a thick quilt, a hot pot of tea waiting on the table, a door with a lock for which only I had the key.

One more and I'd never have to do this again.

"Esmeralda Houghton," Mrs. Hartford read, the veil fluttering with her breath. "Spiritualist and communicator of the dead."

I gave a quick curtsy. She returned my card to the tray, her eyes shifting up to the portrait hanging above the fireplace's mantel. As if on cue, the rest of the family followed her gaze.

Mr. Hartford, I presumed. The painting portrayed a serious man with grey hair and a strong posture. However, his eyes were focused not on the artist, but off to the side, giving the impression that he was looking over your shoulder. I was almost tempted to turn around, as if the object of his attention would be standing there.

"Shall we get started?" the older gentleman prompted. He looked at his pocket watch and smacked his lips.

You can learn much about the dead from how their loved ones mourn them. I had been called to this noble home for one reason, and I suspected that it wasn't for a last tearful goodbye. No matter, the greedy as well as the grieving still pay for a séance.

I made my way to the round table in the middle of the room. Slipping off my gloves, I opened my bag and began to remove my supplies, setting them up as I had done countless times before. As I prepared, the whispers started behind me. I caught a few snippets.

"Will this work?"

"Is this safe?"

"Can we trust her?"

Standing taller, I took in a long breath through my nose, then held out my hand. "Water," I said, careful to keep the bulge inside my left cheek tucked away. A small crystal glass was placed in my grasp. Such elegance for an object of ordinary use, and such a waste. It could likely fetch enough to afford a full month's rent at Miss Crane's, and enough left over to replace my weathered boots with a new pair, ones with polished leather and thick heels that kept out the rain. I carefully placed the glass on the table, marking my spot. "Come," I said, inviting the others.

Mrs. Hartford eased her thin figure into the chair opposite me first. Then the rest claimed their seats. The young man was the last to join us. A dewy patch of perspiration was breaking out across his forehead. I watched as the older gentleman and the woman exchanged a knowing glance.

Before each seat I had placed a single lit candle with a glass chimney to protect the flame from any shifts in the air. Then I laid a small velvet bag in the middle of the table. "No jewelry," I said, pointing to the empty sack.

The younger woman did not hesitate. In fact, her eyes brightened as she dropped her jewels into the pouch one by one—the pearl necklace, a matching set of earrings, and a simple silver bracelet. Mrs. Hartford slowly turned the ring on her finger.

"Please, Mother," she said. "Metal can interfere with spiritual connections. It's imperative we talk to Father!"

One by one, I turned down the oil lamps around the room until the only light came from my candles and the fireplace. The glow illuminated the sharp angles of their faces, draping everything else in shadow. The space immediately felt smaller, more intimate.

I took my seat in the empty chair between the men. Facing Mrs. Hartford, I motioned to the ghost book I'd laid out on the table before me. The weathered black cover was blank, offering no hint as to its use or value. It was merely several slates bound together inside a book's jacket, but with it I had the power to reveal the message of a loved one from the other side. I caressed the binding slowly like a beloved pet, and then with great care I opened the cover. My palm waved over the blank surface in a smooth, practised motion. "Your message?" I prompted her.

She withdrew a slip of paper from the folds of her sleeve. Her hand reached across the table, but then paused, hovering over the book. I noticed her ring and bracelet had indeed been removed. It was a feat of pure willpower for me to not smile.

The older gentleman beside me stiffened. "There's no point in delaying, dear sister," he said. "We've tried every other possible means. This is our last chance." He attempted to soften his voice, but it was a poorly disguised demand. No one rebuked him, though. Instead, they each pinned Mrs. Hartford in place with their impatient stares. The air in the room was heavy, a bloated sky before a thunderstorm.

She finally dropped the note onto the open book's exposed slate. I gently closed the cover, trapping the paper between the slabs. I kept my palm pressed against the cover and sighed, sending the message with a prayer. Then I sat back, leaving the book in the middle of the table. Next, I picked up the crystal glass and took a mouthful of water, letting it sit for a moment before swallowing. "Hold hands," I finally said, placing mine atop the table.

Mrs. Hartford let out a sharp breath as I accepted the older gentleman's hand without my glove. Still, I kept my face rigid, even as the young man took my other hand, squeezing ever so softly.

"Should we close our eyes?" the daughter asked. Her knuckles were almost white.

"No." My reply was slightly muffled from the bulge in my cheek. It was readily expanding from the recent mouthful of water, but no one seemed to take notice.

I stared at the candle in front of me and breathed from the back of my throat. Everything faded in my periphery until there was only the spot of light.

Then I began, "Oh, beloved Arthur Hartford. We bring you gifts of love from our hearts to reach you in death. Commune with us and move among us."

I repeated the phrase. The young man's palm was damp against mine. A sudden pressure squeezed at my chest. "He is here," I proclaimed. I tilted to one side, letting my head fall against my shoulder.

The daughter whimpered.

"Show yourself," I called out.

Three distinct knocks came from the middle of the table. A collective gasp almost broke the circle.

I kept my eyes on my candle. "With whom do you wish to speak?" I asked.

Silence.

From the corner of my vision, I watched the parlour door silently ease open. I repeated the question. "With whom do you wish to—"

Mrs. Hartford let out a startled cry as her candle went out. A tendril of smoke rose straight up from the middle of the protective chimney.

"Mother! He's here. Quickly, you must ask him."

Mrs. Hartford stared at her burned-out candle.

"Check the book!" The older gentleman released my hand, reaching toward the middle of the table.

At once, my head snapped upright. A low growl began in my chest.

"You b-b-broke the circle," the young man stuttered. His face had gone as pale as his pressed white shirt.

The growl grew louder, burning as it went up my throat. My lips parted, and I spewed a river of ectoplasm into my lap. My body flopped forward, almost splitting my head open on the edge of the table. After a moment, I sat up, gasping for air. The women were still holding hands, staring at me with equal measures of disgust and fascination. As I had anticipated, they weren't the type to leap to someone's aid. I allowed their awkward gawking to continue as I recovered.

"Are you well?" The young man held the glass of water toward me. My hand shook as I drank it all. Then I reached for the book. All four relatives leaned forward in eager anticipation as I slowly peeled back the cover until it was laid open. The note had vanished, and in its place a scrawled message was written across the slate.

The young man tilted his head to see the passage. "'I am at peace,'" he read.

"I don't understand," the daughter said. "Mother, what was your question to Father?"

The older gentleman sniffed. "What about the key?" he asked. "He was supposed to tell us where he hid the key." Bit by bit his baffled expression morphed into anger. He pointed an accusing finger at my face. "You," he began.

I held his stare and silently counted to three. I'd dealt with skeptics before, and furthermore I wasn't finished. "With whom do you wish to speak?" I asked. At once, his candle went out.

"Keep us safe, dear lord," the daughter prayed. Her candle was the next to extinguish.

A ghostly breath blew out the remaining candles, throwing the parlour into near-complete darkness. Screams echoed off the walls.

"Quick! Open the curtains," someone cried.

A chair fell backward, taking the body with it as they collapsed to the floor.

I grabbed the velvet bag and stood up, pushing a thin pair of shoulders to the side as I made my way to the sliver of light coming from the parlour's ajar door. Behind me, the young man yelped. He'd been the only one to show me an ounce of kindness—that should teach him. No good deed goes unpunished.

I escaped to the hallway and spotted the servants' door. I pulled it open and rushed down the stairs and into the kitchen. The staff glanced up in surprise, but I ignored them as I ran the length of the room to wrench open the back door.

"Ouf!" I smacked into the chest of a blue uniform.

"All right, then, Miss Timmons?" the copper asked smugly. His black beard and matching coal eyes were instantly recognizable. I could see the smirk beneath his mustache, which was badly in need of a trim.

"Constable Rigby." I glowered.

He ripped the bag from my hand. "I'll relieve you of those, thank you."

A second officer had handcuffs at the ready and took great pleasure in shackling my wrists.

"And don't even think about reaching up to that pretty hair of yours for pins," Constable Rigby warned. "These here cuffs are pick-proof."

I stayed silent, knowing there was no such thing—at least not for me. But I was stunned by this ambush. How could they have known where I'd be?

Footsteps came clamouring down the stairs behind us. "Thank heavens," Mrs. Hartford's daughter said, out of breath. "An officer."

He tipped his hat, then opened the velvet bag, allowing her to see the contents. "I assume these are yours," he said.

She looked at the jewels and gave a huff, either too embarrassed or too angry to admit she'd been tricked.

Constable Rigby smiled with greasy satisfaction. "All of London's been looking for this one," he said. "Slippery as an eel she is."

"Common swindler," she sneered, handing him my card.

I rolled my eyes at her description. A swindler? Yes. But I was hardly common.

He peered at the card and chuckled. "Esmeralda Houghton?"

I had worked on that card all last night in my tiny room, making sure the ink would be dry for today. Of all the names I used, this one was my favourite. It had been inspired by the heroine of *The Hunchback of Notre Dame*, my favourite book. My only book.

Mrs. Hartford's daughter leered at me, nose crinkling as if I were a rotten carp at a fishmonger's stall. Her earlier ghoulish anticipation had tarnished to a spiteful pride. I shouldn't have felt slighted; it was obvious from the beginning that my presence in her home was a necessary unpleasantness. But I had at least been entertaining, and she had been a true believer not five minutes earlier.

"Take this forgery away at once," she commanded.

Her crass hypocrisy touched my last nerve. "If I'm a fake, then I suppose you'll have no interest in hearing what your father's ghost told me."

She huffed, but stayed in place.

"He whispered into my ear just as your candle went out," I said, leaning my face closer.

"And what did he say?" she enquired, her hand moving to her throat, searching for the string of pearls she was no longer wearing. I knew then that I had her.

The word popped into my mind. "'Fireplace,'" I said.

Her brows came together.

Constable Rigby tugged me back roughly. "Don't let her fool you," he said to the daughter. "Lies come as natural to this one as breathing. You and your lot are lucky. You'll read about her in the paper tomorrow. This here is Genevieve Timmons, wanted for theft, larceny . . . and murder."

She blanched and took a few steps back. By this time the entire kitchen staff and the rest of the family had filled the space behind her, bearing witness to the entire scene. Constable Rigby tightened his grip on my arm and leaned over me, close enough that I could smell the kippers he'd had for lunch. "You'll not slip away from me, you little eel," he hissed in my ear. "I'm making sure you swing from the gallows this time."

I stayed silent as the officers led me to the paddy wagon waiting on the edge of the cobblestone. There was nothing I could say to defend myself. Everything he'd said was true.

CHAPTER TWO

The police station smelled of London's back alleys in the early morning, heavy and full of drowsy desperation. I waited, still in handcuffs, as Constable Rigby took his time scratching an update into my file. I already knew what was written there. I turned my face to the side, blinking away the memory of a motionless body, its head caught at an ugly angle.

"Your days of crime are over, Miss Timmons," he said, not bothering to keep the salacious pleasure from his voice. He was drawing out the process for my benefit; I was usually in my cell by now. "We've set a date for your trial. Hardly worth having, really. There's enough evidence to fill the courtroom. You'll draw a large crowd on hanging day." He dipped the quill in the ink pot, then added his signature with a flourish.

I let out a yawn to show him I was unaffected by his gruesome delight. In truth, I'd known about the particulars of my death for years. I could recite the fortune-teller's warning by heart. I was to die with water in my lungs, not hanging at the end of a noose—at least Constable Rigby wouldn't bear witness to that. At the moment, I was most concerned for my bag. I inched my neck forward, trying to see if it was behind the desk. I hated the thought of Constable Rigby laying his grubby hands on Maman's ghost book.

"I'll make bail," I said. Miss Crane had eyes and ears all throughout London. News of my arrest would have reached her by now. It was Miss Crane who had learned of the Hartfords' fretful state from a regular visitor at the boardinghouse. She had promised I could take enough from those rich fools to keep my room for another three months without needing to entertain customers like the other girls.

But three months' worth of rent was also the last bit I needed to get away for good. A train was leaving from Paddington station tonight, and I still had every intention of being on it. I hadn't been planning my escape all these months only to be blocked at the last moment by Constable Rigby. I could still make it, I assured myself.

I needed to get away from London and her damp alleys; away from Miss Crane and her lipstick smiles that hid a heart of coal; away from all the grieving families; away from all the death.

"Dying is the easy part," Maman used to say, her French accent smoothing the edges of the English words. "It is those left behind that suffer."

The familiar ache rose from the depths of my heart, but I didn't let it linger. I flattened the memory with all the rest, pushing it far down until I couldn't recognize it, like the mucky bottom of the Thames.

There was a rattling cough to my left. Several feet away from me, an elderly man in an elegant wool coat held a handkerchief to his face. I could make out white eyebrows beneath the rim of his beaver hat. His other gloved hand gripped the top of a cane, carved into the shape of a golden serpent's head with two red eyes that could be rubies. A rare item like that would fetch far more than Mrs. Hartford's ring and bracelet.

"I'm sorry, sir, but there is nothing I can do," an officer said to the gentleman.

"You must understand," the old man said. "My lord insists that the case be reopened."

The young officer grimaced. "We have no new evidence." He paused, looking for a moment like he wanted to add something, but remained silent.

Constable Rigby moved down the long desk and muscled the younger officer to the side. He spoke to the gentleman. "The coroner's inquest was thorough," he said. "Unless you have anything new to offer?" The hint in his voice was obvious.

With a sigh that held the whisper of a wheeze, the gentleman produced an envelope from his coat pocket. "I believe this may help convince your superiors to revisit the case." He then placed it into the waiting palm of Constable Rigby. At least the copper had the sense not to count the money in front of everyone. Instead, he nudged the younger officer my way. "Take this one to the holding cell in the back," he ordered. "I'll see to this gentleman personally."

The rounded face of the younger officer seemed to shrink a bit.

Constable Rigby noticed. "Only thing scary about Miss Timmons is the sound she'll make when the noose chokes her."

My back straightened. "I hear the dead," I told him. "They say otherwise. Mark my words, Rigby, I'll be leaving the station tonight before your shift is over."

"Is that a fact?" he said, showing a row of crooked teeth. "What's in my pocket, then?"

"I only know what the ghosts say to me. They care not for what's in your pocket—only what's in your heart, or in your case, the lack of."

"Ghosts?" The younger officer swallowed, but his expression was one I intuitively recognized—reluctant hope mixed with grief.

There was also kindness in his eyes, something I could use to my advantage.

I squinted at him. "I sense someone with you," I said. "A woman."

He stayed quiet, but his cheeks reddened.

"Her hair is"—I paused and tilted my head, like I was trying to focus—"pulled up."

He sniffed. "Is it grey?"

"Stay quiet," Constable Rigby interrupted. "She'll use any information against you."

I continued, "She's older. Someone close to you. Her eyes are—"

"Blue?" the officer offered.

I shook my head. "No, concerned. She worries about you. This is a relative, someone important in your life."

"Mum," he said, the word escaping his lips like a prayer.

"For the love of Christ almighty," Constable Rigby grumbled, now completely ignoring the gentleman in the elegant attire. The rim of the beaver hat inclined my way, but not enough for me to properly see his face.

The young officer leaned closer to me. "She never wanted me to join the police. She was afraid for my safety." His voice dropped. "Can she tell you, well, I mean, is there any way she can warn me if I'm going to . . . you know." He drew an invisible line across his throat with his finger.

"No," I said gently. "But she's so very proud that you always help people when they need it most."

He cleared his throat, suddenly reaching for my file on the desk to tidy the papers. "I always wanted to hear that from her," he admitted.

When I spoke next, I filled my voice with every ounce of supplication I could muster. "Is there anything you can do to help me?"

His eyes grew large.

Constable Rigby pushed him to the side. "Doing your spooky mind tricks, are you, Miss Timmons? Well, tell me, then. What ghost is lurking around me?" He snorted. "Who's my guardian angel?"

"Your guardian angel?" I lifted my chin. "No one," I said. "Absolutely no one."

His grin melted into a hateful scowl. He ordered the younger officer to take me to the cells. Only when I turned my back did I let the smile creep into place.

"Hang from the gallows, Genevieve Timmons," Constable Rigby called after me. His voice bounced off the stone walls, echoing his words like a promise.

I stood in a familiar cell. My hair hung halfway down my back; the officer had removed all my pins. It would be tricky to pick a lock now.

Tricky, but not impossible.

There were several other women here. I recognized Drusilla from Miss Crane's boardinghouse. Her voluptuous pink dress stood in stark contrast to the grey walls. I sat down beside her on the cold bench. It didn't take much imagination to know why Drusilla had been arrested.

Her glassy eyes, ringed with heavy black liner, stared back at me. "Miss Crane said you'd get caught for good this time." She slurred her words. I couldn't quite tell if it was the result of too much opium or simple exhaustion.

"She didn't give me much choice," I replied. "She raised the rent again."

Drusilla sighed. "After everything that happened with yer mum, I wonder why she let you stay in the house at all." She touched a finger to my chin, angling my face up toward her. "But I can see why she'd want to keep a pretty thing like you around. You'd be good wages, at least the first while."

My stomach twisted at the thought. I stayed quiet, knowing my mother and Miss Crane had made an arrangement some time ago. The men who frequented Miss Crane's were hardly a parade of suitable beaus. And even if they were slightly handsome, the hunger in their eyes as they sized up the girls was enough to relieve them of any human decency. But when Maman died, her agreement with Miss Crane died with her. Now my séances included a little robbery on the side if the family had anything worth stealing. So far, I'd earned enough to keep my bed to myself, and save a bit too.

Miss Crane wouldn't let me rot in a jail cell for long. Yet I felt a flutter of panic in my heart. I only trusted that woman when I could see her, like a snake charmer with its cobra. "She'll come and get me," I said more to myself than Drusilla. "She always does."

Someone clanged on the bars. A gruff officer unlocked the cell door and motioned to Drusilla. "Get up, you sordid thing."

I rolled my eyes. I had, in fact, seen this very officer come to Miss Crane's on various occasions. If he paid to be with "sordid" women, what did that make him?

Then I heard the sharp clicks of Miss Crane's heels on the stone floor. My eyes searched for the source of the sound until she appeared from around the corner. If her large bosom and red lipstick didn't catch your eye, her choice of attire would. Her large hat was the most flamboyant shade of violet I'd ever seen. The coat with the fur trim was new as well.

Still, no amount of money would restrain respectable women from crossing the street to avoid sharing the same space as her, no matter how fashionable her shoes.

She took Drusilla in her arms and pulled her close, nearly suffocating her in the ample cleavage. Even if Miss Crane considered us property, the gesture was maternal enough to evoke a thankful sigh from Drusilla. A strange heaviness settled around my heart.

I started to follow, but the officer shut the bars in my face.

"No, Jenny," Miss Crane said. "Not this time."

I scowled at her pet name for me. Surely, she was teasing me. Did she want me to beg or cry?

"Drusilla and the others can't pick up your slack in the rent any longer," she said. "I gave you as many chances as I could afford. I can't keep you safe anymore. Do you know how many people in the city would turn you in just for the reward money?"

I watched her red-stained mouth as the harsh understanding swept over me. No small wonder where the money for the new hat and coat had come from. "You set me up?" My throat went dry. "How could you?"

"Don't play me for a fool." She smiled, but her tone was knife sharp. "I know what you've been hiding from me. I found your secret purse hidden in the mattress."

No, no, no, my mind screamed. I gripped the bars so I wouldn't collapse. My eyes stung.

"You made a costly mistake. And hiding money from me is the last one you'll make." A wickedness played across her lips. "Oh, now, don't give me them dark pools of fake tears. You'd sooner cheat a dying man than give him a drink of water."

Then she and Drusilla turned away, the echoes of their footfalls growing softer until they disappeared around the corner. The copper tapped his billy club on the bars, making me jump back. As monstrous as she was, Miss Crane had been my best chance at escaping this cell. Then I realized that the money I had saved was now in her hands. I listened intently for the click of her heels, hoping that she might still come back and tell me the scare was on purpose.

My heart was racing. This couldn't be it. I had to catch that train! I fell to my knees and scoured the floor for anything, a dropped hairpin I could make use of, but that only proved entertaining for the officer. Hopelessness began to take hold of me, sapping what little energy I had left.

I started to make a braid, trying to recall what Maman's hands felt like in my hair. "Remember, *ma petite chérie*," she'd tell me in her thick accent. "The only one you can count on is yourself."

"But we have each other," I'd said, turning around to look at her.

"Not forever." Then she'd add, "Think of all those tortured people who ask us to speak to the dead. That's what loving someone else gets you—deep, unending grief. If you never want to feel that pain, protect your heart."

I fell asleep curled up against the stone wall of the cell, dreaming of a fireplace and a key blackened with soot.

"Timmons!" It was the officer's brusque voice that woke me. "Your lawyer's here."

"Lawyer?" I rubbed at my eyes, feeling the grit of a fretful sleep.

The officer made no motion to unlock the door, but I saw that he was holding my bag. I stood at once, fighting the urge to grab it from his hands.

The man in the beaver hat was watching me from the other side of the bars. He was pale, with drooping eyes that crinkled at the edges in a knowing smile, and a neatly trimmed white beard. He held his weight against the serpent cane. "Mr. Lockhart, at your service," he said, giving a little bow of his head.

Tentatively, I made my way closer. I wasn't used to polite gestures from strangers. Even more suspicious, the guard stepped away to give us privacy.

"I've arranged bail," Mr. Lockhart said. "You'll be in my care until your court date."

I thought I had misheard him. There was no scenario in my imagination that would allow Constable Rigby to agree to this. "You must be a powerful man," I said.

"I'm not," he replied. "But the man I work for is, and he desperately needs your services."

My shoulders slumped. *How unoriginal.*

He must have read my thoughts. "No, nothing like that. My lord is an honorable man." Mr. Lockhart leaned forward, framing his thin face between the bars. "Your talents with the young officer caught my attention. I know you're a fake," he said. "But you're a good fake, remarkable really. I especially liked the personal touch with the message of support from his mother. When I saw the look of absolute relief on his face, I knew you were the answer to my prayers."

"I don't understand," I said.

"I need you to perform a séance to contact the late lady of the estate and ease the suffering of my lord." He pulled out a pocket watch and frowned at the face. "However, if you agree, we must leave at once. Somerset Park is several hours away. I can explain more on the journey."

I should have felt an enormous amount of gratitude toward Mr. Lockhart, or at least relief at what he was offering, but it did not come. Instead, there was only a persistent unease. "But you must know of the nature of my arrest, sir," I said.

He snapped the watch closed and tucked it away. "The constable was kind enough to familiarize me with the many charges in your file," he said. "I wouldn't agree to take you on as my client unless I was certain. The case against you is questionable, and from my experience, Miss Timmons, women are most often the ones villainized in these circumstances. You wouldn't be the first to be wrongly accused." He paused and gave me a long glance. "Am I wrong?"

"No," I lied.

Anything that seemed too good to be true usually was, but it would be foolish to turn down this opportunity. He was only a frail old man; I could wrestle that cane from his grip and use it as a weapon. Maybe bruise his knee so he couldn't run after me. It would fetch more than a tidy sum at the pawnshop. The pocket watch had potential as well. With either, I could sleep in my own private berth on the train that very night.

I finally nodded. "I accept your offer."

He put a hand to his chest and performed another small bow. He seemed to have more grace in his whiskers than there was in all of Constable Rigby's soul.

The officer unlocked the door and handed me my bag. I checked inside and saw that my supplies were all accounted for, including the ghost book. I already felt more secure with it back in my possession.

As we were led back through the front office, Constable Rigby's eyes bore into me—an alley cat watching a mouse. I could have sworn a grin pulled at the corner of his mouth. Anything that gave him pleasure would surely be at my expense.

A sharp pang pressed against my ribs, but I hid it with a smirk. "Have a safe shift," I called out.

Outside, a black coach waited for us. An insignia was painted on the door in gold, and velvet curtains were drawn down behind the polished windows. Had anything so grand ever graced these drab London alleys? Who was this lord?

The coachman helped me step inside. Next came Mr. Lockhart, wheezing as he collapsed into the seat opposite me. The cushions were a deep blue satin trimmed with golden cord, so plush that I feared I might dirty the upholstery just by sitting. Brass lamps burned above our heads, casting a soft glow.

With the crack of a whip, we were in motion.

"Somerset Park is a half day's journey to the coast," Mr. Lockhart informed me. He laid the cane against the door. "We'll make it by midnight."

"Midnight?" I'd never been outside of London.

We hit a bump, and the cane tipped closer to my side. The ruby eyes caught the lamplight and winked at me. In that moment, I gave up my plan of escape. If the carriage was this beautiful, I could only imagine how grand the estate was. The Hartfords' home was impressive, but I had a feeling Somerset Park would make it look like a servant's cottage. It had taken me half a year's worth of séances to amass enough for one train ticket. I could get that much back in one night, and maybe more.

Somewhere in the city, church bells struck four times. I pictured my train preparing to leave the station without me. Outside the carriage, the murky streets of London sped past. Good riddance, I thought.

Mr. Lockhart yawned. "I'm sure you have many questions, but it's best if I take a brief rest." Then he gave one last cough and shut his eyes.

Just as well; I needed time to plan. I watched the rise and fall of his chest. He soon slipped into the rhythmic breathing of a sleeper, dead to the world.

CHAPTER THREE

The jostling motion of the carriage had been rattling my bones with each mile for the last hour. At first, I enjoyed watching the dirty smokestacks of the city slowly fade into wide pastures. But as the sun set and darkness descended, the window eventually offered nothing but a reflection of my own face. It seemed like the coach could drive right off the edge of the earth and into the night sky.

Rain began to tap on the roof so heavily it startled Mr. Lockhart awake. He righted himself from his slumped position. "My apologies, Miss Timmons," he said, checking his watch again. "I've been a terrible host, haven't I?"

"I thought you were my lawyer," I said, trying not to let my eyes linger too long on the gold chain attached to the watch.

He chuckled dryly, but it collapsed into a cough. He pressed a handkerchief to his lips. "You're all business, I see. Very good. And since we're closing in on our destination, I'll tell you exactly why you're so desperately needed at Somerset. My lord, Mr. Pemberton, is a most honorable man. Wretchedly, though, he was widowed six months ago." His shoulders hunched as his voice took on a melancholy tone. "His bride was young, beautiful, and in love. He's never gotten over the tragedy. Every month he writes a letter to the police, which I then make the journey to deliver in person, and personally beg for them to reopen the coroner's enquiry."

"Enquiry? How did she die?"

His face blanched. "Her death was peculiar in circumstance, but the evidence left behind was conclusive. Suicide."

I had not anticipated that. If a coroner had concluded suicide, I didn't see what bribing the police would accomplish. "I take it Lord Pemberton is convinced otherwise."

His lips pursed in confusion. Then an apologetic expression softened his features. "No, my dear. Pemberton is his surname, but since inheriting the title of earl, he is now Lord Chadwick." He sagged against the seat. "Suffice to say, Somerest Park has seen its share of tragedy. Regardless, his grief over this latest calamity has made him inconsolable and obsessed. He refuses to let her rest and therefore has sentenced himself to an early grave for all the life it's draining from him."

I nodded. Inconsolable grief was something I understood.

Mr. Lockhart continued, "My lord will not let his grief subside until he knows his dearly departed love is at peace. I want you to use whatever talents and trickery you possess to give him the closure he craves and end his suffering."

He phrased it romantically, like this task would be a kindness. But I needed to be certain. "You want me to perform a fake séance to convince your lord I've contacted his dead bride beyond the grave?"

"And in return I'll represent you in court." He spoke with such simple conviction, almost unrealistically so. Constable Rigby's smile pulled at the hairs on the back of my neck.

"It's rather deceitful," I replied. "Surely, there must be a less elaborate way to ease his pain."

He touched his beard. "My anguish is authentic, Miss Timmons. I'm ill, very much so. I only wish to help my lord find peace before I part from this world." His eyes pleaded with me, brimming with a genuine misery I wasn't expecting. I felt a spasm of guilt for considering hurting him with his own cane.

The carriage took a sharp turn as something brushed against the outside of the window.

"We must have turned down the drive," Mr. Lockhart said, squinting into the darkness. There was a nervous hitch to his voice. "One last thing before—"

He was interrupted by a deafening clap of thunder, followed by a deluge of rain that stomped against the carriage's roof like a million boots. I imagined the driver was soaked to the skin.

At last, we came to a halt. I cupped my face and pressed it against the window, but the night afforded no hints of what lay outside.

Mr. Lockhart's expression was grave. "No matter what you hear or see at Somerset, you must remember, you are the only person capable of giving my lord the one thing money cannot buy him—peace."

Before I could ask him to elaborate, the door of the carriage opened, bringing in a torrent of water. A footman stood before me, shivering as he held out an umbrella. Another clap of thunder shook the ground. I stepped into a puddle, feeling the water soak through the worn heels of my boots.

I blindly walked forward, head down to shield my eyes from the wind. A gust caught the umbrella, whipping it back just as a bolt of lightning illuminated the scene before me. For a moment I thought it might have been a trick, but then a second flash brought the colossal estate into view once more. One set of eyes could hardly take in the entire building at once. The front façade had more windows than I could count. A pair of stone lions flanked wide palatial steps that led to a massive front door, open and ready to swallow us whole, carriage included.

Mr. Lockhart and I were ushered inside by the soaked footman.

A gentleman in finery greeted us with a slight bow. The entrance hall was larger than Miss Crane's entire parlour. My attention jumped from vase to statue to gilded artwork. Was this a museum or a home? I hugged my bag against my chest for fear that I'd turn and knock over a priceless work of art. Farther inside, a staircase extended upward, the newel post carved in the likeness of an angel.

The man whom I assumed was the butler took Mr. Lockhart's coat and hat, addressing him by name. "Your message arrived an hour ago. His lordship awaits you in the study." He motioned to a doorway over his shoulder.

"Thank you, Bramwell," Mr. Lockhart said tiredly. He turned to me. "I'll leave you in good hands." I watched him hobble away with his cane, wishing I could go with him.

A stern woman in a black dress stood off to the side, holding an oil lamp. Her greying hair was secured into a bun so tight it might have been made of iron. She looked down at my boots, and I imagined she was tallying the amount of mud I would track inside. I hoped the lighting was dim enough to hide the frayed edge of my cape. Bramwell then said to me, "Mrs. Donovan will see you to your room."

The woman's expression was so hard she could have been one of the statues. I followed her quietly, uncertain if I should reply with a thank-you, worried my voice would echo in the vastness. I took in the grand staircase, looking up at the balcony that ran along the second floor. My fingertips smoothed over the dark walnut railing, enjoying the smell of fresh polish. I had done séances for the wealthy residents of London, but the scale of Somerset Park was unlike any place I'd ever been. I wondered if I should leave a trail of bread crumbs. I could easily turn down the wrong hallway and be lost for years.

As we reached the upper landing, there was the distinct sound from below of someone raising their voice. Mrs. Donovan paused, turning halfway so I was looking at her sharp profile. "His lordship is not happy to have a spiritualist in the manor."

The argument continued beneath us, muffled by the closed door to the study. I caught the sounds of the first voice, raised and impatient. Then I identified Mr. Lockhart's calmly hesitant response.

Mrs. Donovan continued, "Mr. Lockhart ventured to London to bring back a police detective. You can imagine how his returning with you instead would be disappointing."

"You obviously haven't met many coppers," I said. "I've found most of them are disappointing too."

Mrs. Donovan clicked her tongue in disapproval, then continued walking down the long hallway. She stopped in front of a door that looked identical to all the others we passed; I doubted I'd be able to find it again on my own. After pulling out a ring of keys, she unlocked the door, then held up the lamp as she went inside.

"My apologies for the staleness of the room, Miss Timmons," she said, lighting the sconces by the fireplace. Above the mantel was a large painting of a schooner sinking in the stormy waves. The sails were tattered, as if it had been wrecked in battle and lost to the sea. I turned my back on it.

"I would have properly aired it out but for the rainstorm," she explained. Then she glided across the room to light a candle placed on the bedside table, and I was able to take in my new quarters for the first time.

There was a matching vanity and tall wardrobe with polished brass pulls and cut glass knobs that looked like diamonds. The wallpaper had a dark green background with bouquets of white blooms that looked so real I wondered if they had been painted by hand. Dominating the room was the largest bed I had ever seen. It even had a canopy. Unlike the foyer, this room evoked an elegant but welcoming comfort.

Mrs. Donovan put down the lamp and needlessly smoothed out the plush bedcover. I could tell it was more substantial than anything I'd ever slept in before. "Tomorrow the fog should let up enough," she said. "I'll have the room aired out in the daytime and make sure we properly set the fire to warm it for the evening."

The rain pelted against the glass behind long brocade curtains, trimmed with gold thread and tassels. Even the window covers were more exquisite than any lingerie worn at Miss Crane's. Considering I was supposed to be in a jail cell, I could handle a little staleness and cold air.

She opened the drawers of the vanity dresser. "I can help you unpack," she offered.

"That won't be necessary," I said, tightening my grip on the handle of my bag. I only had the clothes on my back—no need for the housekeeper to see my candles and ghost book. An image of my tiny room at Miss Crane's came to mind. I had nothing of any value there, but an extra change of petticoat would have been nice.

Mrs. Donovan's expression stayed solemn as she made her way to the wardrobe and opened its doors. I could not imagine having enough clothes to fill both it and the dresser. "Mr. Lockhart wrote that we should meet all your needs," she said. "I believe a few dresses will arrive tomorrow."

"For me?" I was genuinely surprised. Although Mr. Lockhart had never given me any reason to doubt his sincerity so far, this gesture evoked a sense of gratitude in my heart that was both touching and embarrassing. The tips of my ears warmed under my curls. "That's kind of him," I replied, smiling.

Mrs. Donovan's stern gaze skimmed over me, taking in my outfit. "You are a guest of Somerset Park. You should look like you belong."

My smile slid away. Still, I took comfort in the consistency of her cruelty.

Picking up the lamp, she motioned to the velvet pull attached to the wall. "Please ring the bell if you need anything."

"I wouldn't want to wake anyone," I said.

She stood by the open door, the darkness of the house behind her an audience of admiring shadows, eager to embrace her. "It would be better to ask for help than wander the manor in the middle of the night." Then she added, "Sleep well."

After she left, I pressed my ear up against the door and listened to her footsteps fade. Once I was certain she was gone, I turned and took in the plush bed. I was hardly under the covers before I dozed off, certain I could sleep for a thousand days.

WHEN I WOKE, the room was in absolute silence. I was already sitting up in bed, as if I'd been in that position for some time. The covers were kicked to the end of the mattress in a tangled pile. I pinched my arm to make sure I wasn't sleepwalking. Although it hadn't happened for a few months, more than once I had woken up at the top of the stairs, one of the girls holding my elbow and calling my name. That usually brought me out of my trance, but sometimes they had to pull my hair. They often whispered I was genuinely haunted, as if the spirits I'd contacted in my séances had followed me back to the boardinghouse.

This time though, I was wide awake, squinting at the darkness. Then I heard a faint scratching. I looked toward the window, wondering if a tree branch had grazed against the glass. I remembered a similar noise outside the carriage when we turned down the lane.

Scrape! Scrape! Scrape!

It sounded like fingernails. I reached for the candle, but I could feel only the bare surface of the bedside table. I could have sworn I'd left it there.

Another scratch pierced the quiet. It was coming from inside the wardrobe.

My shoulders eased away from my ears. I was no stranger to mice, and apparently even the grand Somerset wasn't either. Still, I grumbled at the thought of having to share this lovely room.

I tiptoed across the cold floor, feeling my way to the wardrobe. I gave it a hard knock, hoping to scare the wee thing. I waited and was rewarded with silence. Still, I thought I should probably check inside and be ready with my boot.

I went to the window and opened the curtains, hoping for enough moonlight to find the misplaced candle.

The clouds had cleared enough that I could discern the trim lawn below and a copse of trees in the distance. Eager for a bit of fresh air, I lifted the window and took a deep breath. The hair on the back of my neck stood at the soft, rhythmic whisper of waves and the unmistakable smell of salt air.

The ocean!

I had been told Somerset Park was by the coast, but I hadn't realized it was so close. I thought of Mr. Lockhart and Mr. Pemberton quarreling earlier. What if Mr. Pemberton remained unconvinced of my abilities? What if he had arranged for the police to collect me tomorrow? I remembered how Constable Rigby smiled as I left the police station.

I was as good as dead if I stayed. And if there was any doubt, the salty reminder of my ultimate demise blew through the window with an unexpected gust.

After getting dressed, I packed all my things in my bag and tucked it under my arm. I crept down the stairs, wincing at each creak underfoot. When I reached the main entrance, I froze at the sound of voices. There was a giggle, then something hit the floor with a thud and rolled in my direction from the shadows.

I stared at the wine bottle for a moment before I heard footsteps coming closer. Unable to go back up to my room without being seen, I turned and ran in the opposite direction. I'd been in enough stately homes with Maman to know where the servants' stairways were most likely hidden.

Camouflaged by the wainscoting, I found the door and descended to the kitchen. I paused by a wall of shelves, heavy with silver candelabras. Two of the smaller ones made their way into my bag. Purely for travel expenses, of course.

Someone cleared their throat.

I whipped around and saw the tall silhouette of a man standing in front of the fireplace. He was wearing muddy riding boots, and his overcoat was open. He reached for the lantern on the kitchen table and held it between us. My gaze shifted to the gold ring on the smallest finger of his right hand. Miss Crane once compared me to a crow, constantly distracted by anything shiny.

My eyes travelled up to his tousled blond hair, framing a tense jaw that could have been cut from stone. "Miss Timmons, I presume," he said.

I nearly dropped my bag to the floor. Even the stable groom knew who I was! I spied the darkened hallway behind him and guessed it led to a back door—my escape.

He stared pointedly at my bag. "I wonder why you feel the need to equip yourself with several candelabras. Are there not enough candles in your room to your particular liking?"

The fire sputtered and popped.

I lifted my chin. "I wonder why you're lurking in the shadows of the kitchen while the rest of the house is asleep. And in your muddy boots, I might add."

"I could wake the stable boy. He's an excellent rider, even in the dead of night. The police could be here by the morning." His blue eyes blazed at me. "Or perhaps I should throw you out now and let the elements have you."

The night held no punishment for me, only freedom. Still, his rudeness bristled me. I'd seen enough cruelty at Miss Crane's to recognize real danger from a man—this one was all talk. "Lay one hand on me and you'll have to answer to Mr. Lockhart," I threatened. "For it is he who has brought me here."

"He will most likely change his tune when he learns you tried to leave with a few extra pounds of silver. And I should have you know, Mr. Lockhart's approval is so eagerly given that it holds little worth to me."

"You're quite opinionated, aren't you?" I declared.

"It's my opinion you should be most concerned with, Miss Timmons, considering you're here to ease my grief."

I opened my mouth, then closed it. It was Mr. Pemberton, his lordship himself, in the flesh. I hadn't expected him to be so young—or arrogant, for that matter. Mr. Lockhart had painted the picture of a lover so brokenhearted he was ready to dig his own grave. No wonder I was fooled. The man in front of me had the air of someone who was ready to battle, and ready to win. Still, the gold pinkie ring should have been a clue. The silver in my bag suddenly weighed a ton.

He lowered the lamp somewhat, and a smoothness rested in his expression. "Mr. Lockhart told me you speak to the dead."

Despite the knot that was growing inside my stomach, I found my voice. "He wants me to help you to find peace," I said, hating how small I sounded.

"Mr. Lockhart means well, but he has underestimated my passion." There was a calm bitterness in his tone. "I don't believe in spiritualists, Miss Timmons. You have no more ability to conjure a specter than I do."

I imagined the stable boy, getting on his horse to summon the police. I couldn't produce a ghost for him at this moment, but I could give him enough to delay his decision. I said, "This house embodies many souls. They whisper to me even now."

He gave me a patronizing tilt of his head.

I considered why the lord of such a magnificent estate would be sitting alone in the kitchen, dishevelled from the outdoors and brooding in front of the fire. He was conflicted. "Somerset is full of secrets," I said.

He was unimpressed. "Every house has its secrets."

"Many serve you, but there are few whom you truly trust." Something in his expression shifted. My heart rate picked up, knowing I'd hit a nerve.

"You act out of duty," I continued, "but secretly despise the opulence that surrounds you."

The muscle in his jaw tightened, but he kept my gaze, daring me to continue.

Now for the final reveal, the unpleasant truth. There was an obvious connection to the stables. "If given the choice, you'd ride all night on horseback to escape yourself."

He stayed quiet, then lowered his chin in surrender.

It appeared I had earned my escape. "Please give my regards to Mr. Lockhart." I motioned to the door behind him, but he didn't step aside.

"You won't be leaving. At least not tonight." He stood taller, all his confidence reaffirmed. "The notion of this scheme upset me earlier, but after this clever parlour trick you just demonstrated, I believe you can be of use. Audra is dead, but not by her own hand. She was murdered."

Audra. This was the first time anyone had spoken her name.

The knot in my stomach moved up to my throat. "The police don't seem to agree," I said.

"There is no evidence to prove otherwise, so I must rely on the one thing that will hold up in court—a confession." He stepped closer, and it took all my nerve to keep my boots firmly planted on the spot. "A confession brought on by proof that Audra's spirit is in the room and pointing to her murderer. You see, what I need is your skill for illusion and persuasion."

I frowned as I considered his meaning. He was staring at me intently, as if trying to read my mind. I believed he was willing me to say the words that he would not. "You wish for me to perform a séance so convincing it will persuade a murderer to confess?" I guessed.

"Precisely."

CHAPTER FOUR

Lady Audra Linwood
Diary Entry
Somerset Park, February 15, 1845

My Dearest,

It is with a heavy heart I take ink to these pages. This journal is Mother's last gift to me, and I shall fill every page with all my heart's desires, for she wanted me to live the full life that she could not. She was so sickly and miserable for so long, she cried with relief when the diagnosis was confirmed.

Now Father and I are the ones who weep. But I must go on and be the epitome of a lady. Everyone at Somerset Park expects it of me.

I woke in the middle of the night, and for a moment I had completely forgotten Mother had died. Then it washed over me like a wave on the beach, drowning me in my sobs. All I wanted was to see her face one more time. I ran to the Gallery Hall with my blanket and pillow. Mrs. Donovan found me the next morning, asleep at the foot of Mother's portrait, the one that was commissioned as a wedding present for Father.

Mrs. Donovan rebuked me for being out of bed. How is it possible to feel so alone in a house full of servants?

However, later that day when I returned from the stables, my wardrobe had been moved to the other side of my room and Mother's portrait had taken its place, close to my bed. There was a note from Father, telling me that whenever I wake needing to see her face, she'll be there for me. Furthermore, he hinted at a secret that only a Linwood is allowed to know, and that my time had come.

It is the perfect distraction, Dearest. You watch me with your sad eyes, always seeing, never judging. When I write these words, I am writing to you. You are the guardian of all my thoughts and dreams. And now we share the Linwood secret! I know you will keep it well hidden.

It has been a month since Mother passed into heaven, but her spirit is close to me. I truly believe she is looking out for me. I never tell Father, though, as I know it will give him great heartache. His health wanes and waxes with the moon, and I would hate to cause him more pain.

Sometimes I lie awake at night and wonder what will become of me when Father dies. Surely, thirteen is too young to send me out on my own?

Orphaned. Homeless. That is exactly what I will be, Dearest. For when Father dies, Somerset Park and all its contents will go not to me. How cruel and unjust the world is for a young woman.

CHAPTER FIVE

Ghosts did not exist, and yet I had one.

I still heard Maman's voice, her French lilt so unlike my own East London accent. She came to England with my father, a Brit of no social standing, but a man of free spirit and a talent with words. When her family learned of the elopement, they disowned her immediately. She had previously been engaged to a wealthy acquaintance of the family, but he was too old, she had told me, shuddering with a cringe. He had thin lips and never smiled.

She and my father were young, but they were in love and thought they could survive anything so long as they were together. Whatever little money they had ran out quickly. They scrounged for work—he at the wharfs hauling goods off ships, and she cleaning houses.

One day, while working for one of the wealthier families, my mother was on her knees scrubbing the floor when word came that my father had been in an accident. He'd fallen off the plank under a heavy load and into the Thames between the wharf and the schooner.

Maman said the world changed forever that day. Penniless and pregnant, she knew her family would never take her back. She had nothing to offer her unborn child but a cruel life of despondent poverty. In a daze, she wandered through the city until the posh homes became row houses with slated roofs and narrow chimneys that puffed coal smoke. She found herself standing in the dock-yard, ready to fling herself into the harbour and join my father in watery eternity.

I shivered at this part of the story, imagining Maman sinking to the bottom of the Thames, unable to breathe. The weight of the river pushing her down until her feet disappeared in the oozing silt. What if she changed her mind then, but couldn't get back to the surface? Her hands clawing uselessly at the water as she stared at the hint of daylight far above.

Then she felt me kick inside her belly. A quick session of jabs that woke her from her morbid trance.

I was so unrelenting that she stopped in the street, hand on her belly, leaning over. A knocking sound made her look up. A wrin-kled face surrounded by white hair stared back at her from the other side of a dirty window. My mother thought she was seeing a ghost, but then the woman beckoned her inside.

The house was part of a bedraggled row of merchant establish-ments along the harbour. The space was sparsely furnished. There was a smell of cabbage, and dirt had gathered in the corners. The old woman invited Maman to sit down at the round table in the middle of the room. Then she lit the stub of a candle and took both of my mother's hands. Her bracelets tinkled, and Maman took note of how out of place the elegant jewelry seemed.

In a dreamy voice she told my mother that even though she was far from home and scared, there was a bright spirit keeping her safe. Maman nodded and squeezed the woman's hands. She was in awe, certain my father's presence was close by. Then the woman asked if she wanted to know the future for herself and her unborn daughter.

Daughter? Maman did not hesitate. The old woman's words had lifted the lure of death that had nearly convinced her to jump off the pier. She opened her purse and paid a sum to learn her future. Not a small decision when you have barely a penny to your name and a baby on the way.

"You are worried," the woman began. Maman nodded. "But you are strong," she said. "You work hard and are proud, but sometimes that pride is a curse."

Maman lowered her eyes. It was all true! She looked at her red and cracked hands cradled in the old woman's. She felt protected somehow.

"You will overcome your present hardships," the woman said with absolute certainty. "There is a great love in your future. A love that will change your world and make you stronger than you ever imagined. I see a beautiful baby and a happy mother."

When she was finished, Maman thanked the woman with tears running down her cheeks. The woman hugged her goodbye, also a little misty eyed.

Only when she had walked a few blocks from the shop did the euphoria wear off. Maman reconsidered everything the woman had told her. She felt so foolish! The old woman had noted her French accent, obviously pregnant belly, and drab cleaning uniform and had told her things that anyone would have been able to guess. And Maman had given her so many clues by nodding and squeezing her hand. She was only telling Maman things she wanted to hear.

So much of Maman's labour had gone into earning those coins, and yet she had willingly parted with them in exchange for a few pretty words.

At this moment Maman said I kicked her stomach again, harder this time. She told me it was my instinct that saved both of us that day. She marched back to the shop and called the old woman a thief and demanded her money back.

To prove it, Maman told the woman's fortune. It was all about noticing the little things, the truths, she called them. Most people weren't comfortable with their truths, so they tried to distract you with other qualities.

Maman could tell the woman had once been successful, as she had so many fine furnishings. But she had fallen on bad luck and had to sell many of her treasures, only keeping mementos that meant the most, like her bracelets—a gift from a lover long gone? And her health was suffering, but she was proud and presented herself as best she could. Maman sensed this woman was lonely. Hadn't she cried as well when Maman left? Then she added that she saw the old woman taking someone younger under her wing— like a daughter, perhaps? Maman was smart like that, a survivor.

The woman was impressed and asked Maman to work for her. She said Maman's accent and dark curling hair would bring in more customers. Soon, the little shop was cleaned, and instead of cabbage, the smell of fresh bread filled the air. Little by little, the business flourished.

I was born in that home, surrounded by talk of guardian spirits and the assurance that grief was always good for business. Happy people were never interested in their fortune; they already had what they wanted. Grief meant profit. Grief put meat in the stew and coal on the fire.

I remember little about old Mrs. Rinaldo. She died when I was four. Maman told me she loved me very much, though. She left me one of her most cherished possessions, a first printing of *The Hunchback of Notre Dame*. Little did Mrs. Rinaldo know I would spend days upon days absorbed in that story, imagining myself in Paris. I came to know the book by heart, but I would give it my own ending. One where Quasimodo and Esmeralda rose from the dead together and flew over Paris, haunting Phoebus and Frollo.

One day there came word that a spiritualist was working in Covent Garden, someone able to speak with the dead. This was considerably more profitable than a fortune-teller. Cholera had taken many a child from homes of the rich and poor. Grieving mothers who could afford it wished to know that their children were safe in heaven. And even though Maman and Mrs. Rinaldo had established a loyal roster of clients, many still considered it lowbrow entertainment.

But this spiritualist was different. Everyone was talking about it; theatres were filling up with nightly shows. Even nobility had requested private sessions. Maman sensed an opportunity. She put on Mrs. Rinaldo's bracelets and wore her best dress and took me along with her.

I was six years old, and my life was about to change forever.

CHAPTER SIX

The morning after my first meeting with Mr. Pemberton, I sat at the dining table opposite Mr. Lockhart, watching as he meticulously cut his breakfast sausage.

"You'll meet his lordship shortly," he said. "He always rides early, then settles in the study for business correspondence."

I nodded with my mouth full of egg, grateful Mr. Pemberton would not be at breakfast this morning. After our impromptu meeting in the kitchen, I had spent the rest of the night cradled in my luxurious bed going over my conundrum.

Mr. Lockhart had brought me to Somerset Park to help stage a fake séance to bring peace to his lordship. But Mr. Pemberton wanted me to stage a fake séance to scare a killer into confessing. I could only deceive one man for so long. It would be impossible to complete both tasks.

My instinct had always been to do whatever would fetch the most profit, but in this case the reward would be having my day in court to absolve the charges against me. A long shot, I had to admit. However, Mr. Pemberton was offering neither money nor help. Instead, he was holding the threat of having me arrested for my attempted theft of the candlesticks.

It was a perplexing conflict. Luckily, I had a delicious meal to keep me occupied while I figured it out.

"He is looking forward to meeting you," Mr. Lockhart said kindly.

I sincerely doubted that. Heat rose to my cheeks as I recalled our meeting last night.

"Did you tell him everything?" I asked. "Oh! Thank you," I added as a young footman placed another sausage on my plate. He offered me a shy smile, then went to stand in place by the buffet once more. There was a spray of freckles across his nose. If he ever showed up at Miss Crane's, they'd eat him alive.

Mr. Lockhart put down his knife and took great care to dab each side of his mouth, and then his mustache. "That will be all for now, Harry," he said. The footman gave a slight bow of his chin and exited the room.

Waiting a beat, Mr. Lockhart said, "He knows you are a successful spiritualist from London, but he does not know where I met you or our arrangement with the police."

Our arrangement. My unease about Constable Rigby resurfaced. "How exactly did you persuade the police to let me go with you?"

His eyebrows lifted in surprise. "I know I don't appear to be much, but I assure you my influence with the court reaches far. The fact that you're sitting here this morning proves it."

I took a bite of my sausage and chewed carefully. "Constable Rigby said there's more than enough evidence to convict me."

He chortled. "I've dealt with officers like him before. From what I heard at the police station yesterday, most of the evidence is circumstantial. You may not even have to go to court. Of course, I'll know more once I examine your file."

There was a sharp pain under my ribs. I pressed a hand to my side and wondered if he would still represent me once he read the file in its entirety. Still, not all the truth was there. I had kept one secret, cold and hard as the stone at the pit of my stomach.

I drained the last few drops of my coffee. There was a painted rose on the bottom of the fine china cup.

Mr. Lockhart cleared his throat and looked at me with a rather boyish grin. "I wonder," he started, "if I might ask you to explain a few details." A flush of color came to his cheeks. "How is it that you persuade people you can speak to the dead? The Hartfords don't sound like simpletons you can so easily dupe, and yet you had them thoroughly convinced."

I hesitated. Sharing Maman's techniques was almost blasphemous. But Mr. Lockhart was offering a substantial reward on the other side of the séance. I could afford to let a few secrets slip. "It's simple," I said. "You create an atmosphere of belief by reinforcing their desires." He frowned at me. I explained further: "Tell people what they want to hear, and their hope fills in the rest. The heart sees what the eyes cannot, Mr. Lockhart."

He nodded at this and leaned back in his chair. "After they had escorted you back to the cells, the officers were discussing your tricks, but they could not understand how you accomplished all of them in such a convincing fashion. For example, the ectoplasm young Mr. Hartford swears he saw you expel."

I must have thoroughly traumatized that shy young man. "The ectoplasm is proof that spirits have passed over into my dimension," I said.

He stared at me in disbelief.

I shrugged my shoulders. "A trip to the butcher afforded me a small piece of sausage casing. When mixed with water, the effect can be quite convincing." I did not tell him that I had to practise with cotton for months, just as Maman had shown me, keeping it hidden in my cheek while I spoke.

Mr. Lockhart's face twisted with displeasure. "Well, you won't need to showcase any ghoulish display for his lordship. I cannot stress enough how devoted he was to Lady Audra. Their bond was so strong, we worried for weeks afterward that he would follow her."

I had seen grief in different circles, from the rich to the poor, and there was one universal truth to death: it forever changed the people left behind. A heavy knowledge of pain filled their eyes. And just like the rose on the bottom of my teacup, you couldn't always see the pain, but it was there, underneath.

The man who caught me in the kitchen last night did not have eyes heavy with grief. They were bright and blue, like a summer sky with no clouds. Maybe it *was* the stable groom having a bit of fun at my expense?

". . . walk through the Gallery Hall," Mr. Lockhart said, catching me in the middle of my reverie. Using his cane, he pushed himself away from the table. I was tempted to sneak another sausage when I heard a substantial thump on the rug.

Mr. Lockhart winced with pain as he put one hand on the table to hold himself upright.

"Let me," I said, going to his side to pick up the cane, eager to guess its true value.

It was heavy, and if I wasn't mistaken, the snake's head was solid gold. I wondered how easy it might be to pluck out those ruby eyes. Mr. Lockhart cleared his throat. I must have been staring too long. "It's lovely," I said, handing it back.

"It's rather ostentatious as walking canes go," he said. "It was a gift from Lord Chadwick, Lady Audra's father." Then his eyes took on a mischievous glint. "Here, let me show you its secret." With a twist, he pulled the serpent head out of the cane, revealing a dagger. "I may be old and rather feeble, but I'm well-armed." He winked as part of the jest, and I was grateful he didn't laugh, as it would have likely only brought on another fit of coughing.

"And one should be well armed at Somerset?" I teased back, half-serious.

"Merely a prop, Miss Timmons. If I ever have occasion to require a dagger, I'd surely faint before I could use it."

THE GALLERY HALL was exactly that—a long hallway lined with many large portraits of dead people. It was Somerset's own personal museum. To be honest, I much preferred Madame Tussauds Chamber of Horrors.

Mr. Lockhart took it upon himself to educate me on the many ancestors who had resided in Somerset Park.

We made our way past dukes and great-uncles and such and such, until we stopped in front of a couple's portrait. The woman was fair and adorned with pearls, but the man had a harsh look about him.

"Lord and Lady Chadwick, Audra's parents," Mr. Lockhart said. There was an audible sense of pride to his voice. "She had a sickly life, poor woman. Spent most of her time in bed. Still, she lasted longer than any of us expected." He turned to me and lowered his voice. "She died seven years ago."

I studied their faces. The man had a cruel heat in his eyes that I'd seen before on the faces of the customers who frequented Miss Crane's. "And Audra's father?" I prompted.

Mr. Lockhart let out a sigh. "Alexander Linwood. He died a few months before Audra."

The air stilled around us. "Wait a moment," I said. "This is Audra's ancestral home? Not Mr. Pemberton's?"

"Indeed," he replied. "Somerset Park has been in Audra's family for generations. However, my lordship inherited the title of Earl of Chadwick, as he is the only male relation of legitimate birth in the Linwood family tree." He read my confused expression. "His father was a distant cousin to Alexander Linwood, Lady Audra's father."

A peculiar pressure pushed between my shoulder blades. We continued, then stopped at the base of the most impressive painting in the entire hall. I knew who I was staring at even before Mr. Lockhart introduced me.

He sighed. "And here she is."

Her flaxen hair seemed spun from gold, and her gown was adorned with enough pleats and embroidery that it must have taken the seamstress months to complete. However, that was not what struck me first about Audra. It wasn't so much that she was beautiful, or that her dress was exquisite, or that the tiara with the large blue stone made her look like a queen, but it was her expression of pure satisfaction. There was a luminosity about her. She knew she was lovely, and she knew she was loved. That kind of spark could not be imitated—no matter how many parlour tricks you knew.

"She sat for this on her nineteenth birthday," Mr. Lockhart said. "Look how the artist captured her eyes." He sighed again.

"Was she really that beautiful?" I asked, both of us still gazing up as if she might wink back.

"Oh yes." His took out his handkerchief and pressed it to his mouth. "It's hard to believe she'll never have another birthday. It's so unfair. I've lived to become a bag of wrinkles, and she, with all her youthful glow, is gone." He went to the long windows at the end of the hall that overlooked the grounds.

I joined him, peering out at the scenery. A road curved uphill and through the forest at the edge of the lawn. Somerset Park's land was vast.

Mr. Lockhart spoke again, but this time his voice was careful. "On the day of the wedding, Mrs. Donovan went with her breakfast tray, but Lady Audra's room was empty. We went through the entire house calling her name. For the first hour we thought it was a joke. She liked to play tricks on the staff, you see. But then, as the time for the ceremony approached, and she still hadn't appeared, we knew something was horribly wrong."

There was a rustling sound from the far end of the room. I saw a wine bottle lying on its side.

Still staring out the window, he continued the story. "Then someone saw footprints in the mud leading from the manor. They continued to the cliff overlooking the shore."

I peeked behind me at all the ancestors, half expecting them to be nodding along as Mr. Lockhart spoke. They stared back, unblinking, with their placid eyes and stiff, unsmiling lips.

"Her body was discovered two weeks later," Mr. Lockhart said. "She was still in her nightdress, but it was soaked through with blood. Her face had been . . . well, the fall to the rocks, you understand." The rest came out in broken sentences. "The tide can be violent . . . her body, rolling against the shore . . ." He ceased his desperate explanation to fumble with his handkerchief and press it against his eyes.

Any other time I would have put my hand on his shoulder and said that her spirit still lived on, but I thought he deserved a genuine reply. "I'm sorry her death hurts you," I offered.

"She was as dear to me as if she were my own daughter. I'm truly sorry for those who never had the pleasure of knowing her sweet soul. Even though they will never feel the sadness of her absence, they will never know the joy of her presence." He smiled, his eyes still bright with tears. "I confess, Miss Timmons, I find myself hoping that you really can contact our dearly departed angel. What a comfort that would give me."

There was a snort from the end of the hall. A dark head of unruly hair rose from the last settee. The man stood, wobbling in place. He raised a wine bottle as if toasting us. "Our dearly departed angel," he said. "How prettily you phrase it, Mr. Lockhart."

He closed the distance between us, not even bothering to tuck in his shirt. His clothes looked like they had gone off and had a few fights at the local pub and lost. His chin was also in need of a shave.

Mr. Lockhart's soft expression disappeared. "Miss Timmons, may I introduce William Sutterly. His late father was a valued labourer for Somerset, and after his tragic passing years ago, Lord Chadwick graciously took William as his ward."

"Which means I'm allowed to stay, but I will never be considered family." The man brushed a black wave of hair out of his bloodshot eyes. His features were handsome enough, and I guessed he was not yet twenty-five. But, although he was athletic in stature, his posture hinted at a more sedentary lifestyle of pleasures and selfish leisure.

"Upon my word, William," Mr. Lockhart reprimanded. "Show at least the effort of moral aptitude in the presence of this lady."

"I already know who our guest is." Then his eyes traced the length of my dress from collar to hem, just as Mrs. Donovan had done last night. I did my best to keep my back straight. "Miss Genevieve Timmons," he drawled. "Ghost mediator extraordinaire."

I gave a quick nod, keeping my hands folded in front of me. "Pleased to meet you, Mr. Sutterly," I said.

"I hope you are not too disinterested. Mr. Lockhart's favourite pastime is prattling on about the family and giving ghost tours." He stepped closer, regarding me. "I'm intrigued by your appearance," he said. "Such black and perfectly formed curls. I know ladies' maids who would kill for a chance to style such hair."

"Surely not, sir."

Mr. Lockhart stepped around William. "We are on our way to meet his lordship. We must not keep him waiting."

"His lordship." William rolled his eyes. "One day you'll realize how disastrous it was to ever let him in this house."

Under his white beard, Mr. Lockhart pressed his lips into a poorly disguised scowl. "You should change and have something to eat."

"Always the voice of reason," William replied. "What would the family do without you?" Then he gave an exaggerated bow as we passed. "Enjoy the rest of the tour," he told me. "I can only imagine what it must have been like for you last night, staying in a large house with no idea which staircase to take or which door to open."

I eyed the wine bottle on the floor and wondered if I had almost missed meeting him last night. He wasn't alone either, as I recalled. "I will pay attention, thank you."

"That would be wise," he said. "It's never too early to learn where the loose treads are. Sometimes bad things happen at Somerset when women roam unaccompanied."

CHAPTER SEVEN

Lady Audra Linwood
Diary Entry
Somerset Park, March 1, 1845

Dearest,

Another death has touched Somerset Park. Father was quite affected by Mr. Sutterly's passing; the blacksmith served our family's stables for decades. He remarked on what a loyal and skilled worker he was and how hard it will be to replace him. But then he said the real tragedy is that he leaves a son behind, only a few years older than I. And worse still, the only things the boy will inherit from his father are his bills.

The gossip among the staff is rampant! They say Mr. Sutterly had a ferocious gambling habit, and although the parish constable declared the death was a heart attack, it's the opinion of everyone (unqualified as they may be) that the blacksmith was murdered for the money he'd owed!

Terrified, I ran to Father. When I asked him if there was a murderer in our midst, he patted me on the head and told me not to worry. However, he did say he'd given Mr. Sutterly his assurance that if anything should happen to him, Father would take care of his son. And seeing as the boy is too young to be on his own, Father has declared the boy as his ward, and he will begin living with us next week.

I almost fell over! Father asked if I would mind, which I found quite flattering. Of course, I said we must do all we can to help the orphan. Secretly, I am charmed by the idea of a friend my own age.

I trust you, Dearest, but a flesh-and-blood playmate would help immensely. I have always longed for a sister or even a brother. It would make the Linwood secret that much more enjoyable. I have begun to pin my hopes on the orphan boy. Good heavens, I've only realized now that I don't know his name!

Even as a storm cancelled our riding plans, Father and I passed the afternoon in the library enjoying cake and hot tea as the rain and wind beat against the windows. Grandfather's portrait kept watch over us, with his usual stern expression. It used to scare me when I was smaller, certain the eyes followed me around the room.

I don't remember him well; I was very young when he died. Odd, though. When I look at his painted face, there's a strong notion of his personality. There's something at the back of my mind, something real. But whenever I linger in that place, trying to grasp for more, a heaviness wraps itself around my heart and I cannot take a breath.

The rain continues, even as I write this. What if this boy doesn't like me? What if he's mean and puts snakes in my bed? What if Father ends up loving him more than me? More than once I've overheard how different our prospects would be if I had been born a boy, how we wouldn't have to worry about Somerset.

And there it is, Dearest. The cruel truth of it all. I have comforts at my disposal except for my heavy heart. I love Father, but he is limited in his capacity to show affection. I've heard rumors that Grandfather was cold. I'm beginning to believe you need to teach children love just as much as sums and scales on the piano—even the ones who won't inherit. Especially the ones who won't inherit.

My apologies. I'm more misery than gratitude today. Such a tragic read already. But who will ever read this, I wonder? Certainly not someone hoping for a happy ending. How odd that I would write that? Have I given up hope already and not yet fourteen?

It will take a miracle to release me from this despair.

CHAPTER EIGHT

When we entered his study, Mr. Pemberton glanced up from the desk with an expression of annoyance. Then he stood and gave the bottom of his vest a slight tug.

I tried to reconcile this gentleman before me with the man I'd met the previous night. Gone were the muddy boots and tousled hair. Now he wore a tight necktie with a white shirt and fitted jacket. But the straight back and rigid set of his mouth were the same. However, his eyes were bluer than I remembered.

I noticed he was still wearing the gold ring on his smallest finger. Gold rings were easy to conceal, and they usually fetched a good price. It would likely be worth twice the amount of those silver candlesticks I tried to take last night. It must be of importance to him. But he'd have to remove it for the séance.

"May I present Miss Timmons," Mr. Lockhart said, coughing.

I stepped forward, partly to take the attention off sickly Mr. Lockhart. "Lord Chadwick, I presume," I said, holding his stare.

He gave a curt nod. "And you're the spiritualist brought into my house without my consent," he replied, the tone of self-importance as sharp as last night.

Heat prickled the back of my neck—I was already on the defensive from my encounter with William. I drew my shoulders back. "If my presence is too upsetting, I can leave at once. I'm sure you have a fine horse I may borrow." I failed to restrain myself from throwing his own threat back at him. Something unnecessarily risky, considering he could easily change his mind about the police.

Mr. Lockhart let out a nervous chuckle. "I'm sure Miss Timmons means she is hoping her stay at Somerset Park will evoke a sense of peace for all." He then snuck me a sideways look of confusion.

My wit hardly fazed Mr. Pemberton. He motioned to the chairs, and we all sat. "You may have been subjected to such treatment in London, Miss Timmons," he said. "But in the country, we are more hospitable to our company."

"Miss Timmons has a grand following in London," Mr. Lockhart started, hoping to repair whatever damage I may have done with my boldness. "As I told you last night, few have her credentials. Some of the finest families have benefited from her immeasurable talents."

Mr. Lockhart's lies were so blatant I could barely look at him.

Mr. Pemberton stayed quiet as he listened to my false list of accomplishments, all the while twirling the ring on his smallest finger. It was such a slight movement I wondered if he was aware. How many miles on the train could it buy? How many months' rent would it fetch? I imagined riding away in the middle of the night with my bag full of candlesticks, wearing that very ring. I most likely would only have an hour, at the most, before he noticed it missing.

He put up a hand, interrupting Mr. Lockhart. "Yes, you've already relayed to me her long list of satisfied customers." He said the last word with obvious distaste.

"Customers?" My voice went high. "My lord, Mr. Lockhart can list off all my prior successes; however, it does not take a seer to know that you have reservations about my abilities. I'm at a loss how to convince you. However, one thing is certain. If your bride's spirit wishes to contact you, she can only do so through me."

At this outburst, I was sure Mr. Lockhart would choke for good. Yet, both men remained silent for a moment. A minor victory for me.

There was a knock at the door.

"Come," Mr. Pemberton replied.

Bramwell, the head butler, appeared, polished and prim as ever. I wondered if the man slept standing up. "Pardon me, my lord, but Dr. Barnaby has arrived."

"Honestly?" Mr. Lockhart exhaled. He gave Mr. Pemberton a look of betrayal.

Mr. Pemberton stood. "I insist," he said. "You travelled by coach in the rain all day on my behalf, so the least I can do is repay you with much-needed medical assessment and care." He held out a hand for Mr. Lockhart to stand, but the elderly lawyer waved him off.

"Completely unnecessary," he said. His face remained in a pout.

"You know very well Dr. Barnaby has been a good friend of mine for many years. He can treat that nagging cough you've developed these last few months. There's no need for you to be stubborn. Besides, this gives Miss Timmons and me the opportunity to become better acquainted."

Mr. Lockhart sent me a regretful expression, as if to say he was sorry for leaving me alone with Mr. Pemberton. I replied with a small smile. There was a rare twist of guilt in my stomach as I feigned bravery.

Putting almost all his weight on the cane, he hobbled to the doorway, where Bramwell was still standing. "It's not obstinacy that makes me reluctant," he said defensively. "It's the uselessness of the exercise. I don't need a doctor to tell me what's wrong."

Mr. Pemberton said to Bramwell, "Ask Dr. Barnaby to dine with us this evening, please. I'm sure we can accommodate him easily."

"Certainly, my lord." He bowed, then closed the door, leaving us alone.

Was there no one Mr. Pemberton didn't give orders to? I wondered. What would he do if one of them said no? I could appreciate William's point of view of the man in front of me.

He returned to his desk, then dipped the quill in the inkwell and began to write. "I want to have the séance next week," he said, not looking up. "Tell me what you need," he commanded.

"A cooperative ghost."

He put down the quill and studied me. "We only have one chance," he said. "Every detail is important, from the size of the room to the wax in the candles. I want nothing to go amiss."

I crossed my arms in front of my chest. He continued to stare, and I wondered if he noticed I was wearing the same dress as last night. "I'll tell you everything I require," I promised. "But there is one question I need answered before we start this process—why do you think Lady Audra was murdered?"

He leaned back and rested his elbows on the arms of the chair. "She was in her bedroom. The door was locked from the outside."

"Locked from the outside?" I repeated, thinking I had heard incorrectly. "On the eve of your wedding? Why, so she wouldn't run away?" I couldn't help but laugh at my own joke.

"Tell me, Miss Timmons, is it your comfort with death or your lack of compassion that makes this humorous to you?"

I stared at his gold ring until my ears stopped burning.

He continued, "Mrs. Donovan had a strong inclination to be-lieve history was to repeat itself. She stayed outside Audra's room all night long. When she entered the next morning, the room was empty. The windows locked."

I raised my eyebrows at this.

"Her family has a history of unfortunate deaths." He cleared his throat. "Mrs. Donovan told me afterward that locking the door was for her own protection. I was irate. It was cruel, barbaric even. Although she was right, wasn't she?" The only answer was the wind rattling the pane. "Her body washed up on shore two weeks later."

"I'm sorry."

His blue eyes had a steely determination. "How did Audra get out of her room in the middle of the night?" he asked. "Only two people know the answer; one of them is dead and the other will be confessing at our séance."

I frowned. "And what if no one confesses?" I asked. "I can make it appear that Audra's ghost is singling out a certain person, but that doesn't guarantee they will admit their guilt."

He paused before answering, as if this hadn't even occurred to him. "Then together we must determine the most likely culprit. Otherwise, expect to be in the custody of the parish constable, charged with stealing my candelabras."

A tightness curled around my throat, stealing my voice and the last bit of confidence I had upon entering this study. Never mind the village law enforcement, Mr. Lockhart wouldn't hesitate to send me straight back to my cell in London if he found out about last night. I had to play along with Mr. Pemberton's plan, even if it meant framing an innocent person.

Then, as if a silent alarm had gone off, Mr. Pemberton started writing again. "I have it all planned out. I will host a party to celebrate Audra's life. There will be food and drink and dancing, and then the séance."

"Dancing?" I asked, still a bit overwhelmed at my new responsibility of detective. "I don't know how."

"Then you should hope no one asks you." Without missing a beat, he added, "For today I want you to become familiar with the main floor so you can choose a room best suited for the séance. Make a list of items you'll need." Then he nodded toward the door, dismissing me.

It was a relief to leave the study and his constant critiques. I was surprised that he didn't find offense with the way I breathed. He was handsome, that was certain, but his curt manner had tarnished his appearance, making it impossible to see him as anything more than a demanding person who felt entitled to order people at whim. He was less appealing than any other man I'd ever encountered. I couldn't imagine why Lady Audra would want to marry him.

I paused at the carved angel at the foot of the staircase—maybe she didn't.

My room was a pleasant escape. Someone had tidied the bed and opened the curtains. The window was open a sliver, enough to allow in the refreshing, crisp breeze. The fireplace was set with neatly arranged kindling, ready to be lit. I remembered how Mrs. Donovan mentioned it last night. The attention to my comfort was unexpected. I wasn't used to such thoughtfulness.

The doomed schooner over the fireplace was crooked. I went over and touched the bottom corner of the frame and was surprised to find how much pressure it took to right it again. I noticed small details I hadn't earlier. There were crewmen in the water;

the waves were about to take them over. One was still hanging on to the mast near the very top. I swallowed dryly and went to the window, needing fresh air.

I had an impressive view of the property, but as I looked to the ground far below, all I could think about was Audra locked inside her own room. What was her family history of unfortunate deaths? I would have to ask Mr. Lockhart for the full story. As for identifying the guilty party, I merely had to find the person most likely to be affected by my séance. A confession could be brought on by many factors. Fear being one of them.

I retrieved my bag and placed it on the bed. One by one I took out my props, until I found the ghost book at the bottom. As I lifted it, the card from Mrs. Hartford fell out from between the thin slates.

Did you love me?

I had labeled the family as being motivated by greed, but it seemed Mrs. Hartford, at least, had been grieving in earnest. Was she hoping to absolve regret, or an unyielding depression brought on by doubt in her marriage?

I reread the message and pictured her family sitting around the table, eager for the location of a special key, having no idea what she had secretly asked. I remember how she hesitated before slipping in her question. Maybe she was afraid it would be seen and read aloud.

Opening the ghost book to the trick panel, I saw the message I had written inside before the séance.

I am at peace now.

Not entirely the glowing profession of love she was hoping for. A dreariness settled in my gut. I slipped her note back in between the slates and closed it shut.

That matter was all done with, I told myself. I must concentrate on this new task. My very life depended upon it.

You can only depend on yourself, ma petite chérie.

Maman's warning echoed softly between my ears. At once an image of Notre Dame came to me. My mother rarely spoke of her home, but when I was little, I found a small portrait. I had been playing in her jewelry box, mere trinkets and Mrs. Rinaldo's bracelets, when I discovered the box had a false bottom.

Tucked inside the secret compartment was a beautiful sketch of Maman when she was a young woman, smiling in a lovely dress and holding a parasol. This version of her appeared to hardly have a care in the world. So different from the Maman that I knew. Behind her, the medieval cathedral filled the background, majestic and statuesque. For the next few nights, I would take it out and stare at it, wishing I could step into that time when Maman was happy and not so tired and worried.

On the fifth night, I worked up enough courage to ask her if we could ever go to Paris. I asked about her pretty clothes and if she lived in a big house with servants. And did she still have the parasol? And would she please take me to Notre Dame so I could imagine Esmeralda and Quasimodo walking beside me?

"*Jamais,*" she replied, her lips in a hard line. "Never. I can never return. My family have turned their backs on me. I'm dead to them."

"Do they know about me?" I asked, a spark of hope determined not to burn out.

She tucked her chin, almost shamefully. Then she ripped the sketch from my hands and threw it into the fireplace. Tears filled her eyes. I gasped and ran to our bed, where I hid my face in the pillow, horrified by her reaction and unnerved that I had upset her.

Moments later, her soft steps came close. "You cannot live if you are wishing for the past, *ma petite chérie*." Her hand made soothing circles on my back. "That girl in the picture was so silly and naive. She believed love would last forever. She had no idea of the pain that follows. Beware of what your heart tells you, Genevieve. It has the power to make you think you're invincible. Remember, the only guarantee love brings is heartache. You must lock away the most precious part of your heart, keep that power for yourself. Promise me."

"I promise," I said.

She nodded. "Good. That power will save you when you think you've lost everything. You are strong. You will depend on yourself, not others."

A gust of salt air pulled me from my daydream. Maman's words had never felt so relevant. I knew I was courting death being so close to the ocean, but the only way to earn my freedom was to perform this one last séance. Of course, that's what I'd thought I was doing at the Hartfords'.

I shut the window and decided my first task would be to find a suitable room.

CHAPTER NINE

Lady Audra Linwood
Diary Entry
Somerset Park, March 18, 1845

Dearest,

William Sutterly is the most impishly fun person I have ever met. He has only been with us a short time and already he's had Father and I laughing more than we can remember.

But while he's not a servant, he's not truly my equal either. His room is between our wing and the servants' quarters, but he always sneaks about, causing the most delightful mischief. He already knows the best hiding places. I may even share the Linwood secret with him, but not just yet.

The governess finds his constant fidgeting too distracting and allows him to leave when he's only done half of his geography. And during my piano lesson his black curls appeared at the window and his head popped up next. He winked at me before disappearing, just as the instructor turned around. I had to bite the inside of my cheek not to laugh and give him away.

However, I am terribly jealous at the freedom he has. If Mrs. Donovan ever caught me racing up the servants' stairs with a pocket full of freshly baked ginger biscuits, I would be punished with several rounds of recitation and an extra hour of lessons on the piano. But not William! Oh no, Mrs. Donovan merely held out her hand as he passed the biscuits back to her. Then she ruffled his hair and gave him back one. She treats him like a child even though he is sixteen, just two and a half years older than I.

I watched this exchange from behind the fern in the foyer. I was sure they didn't see me, but when Mrs. Donovan left, William placed the biscuit on the floor next to the fern. As if I need his handouts! I'm Lady Audra, and he is an orphan!

Still, I took the sweet, and am eating it now! I have discovered that a stolen biscuit tastes much better than cake served on a silver tea set.

CHAPTER TEN

I avoided the Gallery Hall, suspecting William to be lounging about, and instead found the library. Three long windows along the front wall faced the courtyard. Despite the curtains being pulled back and secured with tassels, there was little light. The smell of old leather lingered in the air. A grandfather clock ticked softly from the shadows like a quiet witness to my inspection.

Although I had been in several impressive homes in London, none of their libraries had a ladder on wheels that ran the length of the wall. I put my hand on the ladder and gave it a test push, but it only went a foot before getting stuck, squeaking in protest. The shrillness echoed.

Disappointed, I looked around the rest of the room. There were animal heads mounted at various heights. Stopping under the nose of a stag frozen in time, I pondered what kind of person would surround themselves with the heads of dead things.

The focal point of the library was a massive fireplace with an even larger portrait above it. The man had wild eyes framed by a thick fringe of hair that swept across his forehead. I instinctively took a step back. He was sitting in an ornate chair, leaning forward. One hand was curled into a fist and resting on his knee, the other gripping the hilt of a sabre. The knuckles of both hands were painted white, giving the impression he was posed to jump out of the frame, ready to kill. No wonder it wasn't in the Gallery Hall beside the other family members.

I turned away from his murderous glare.

There was a large round table in the middle of the room. I tested the weight by pushing down on one edge; it tilted, slightly off center. My fingers left marks in the dust. The staleness of the air and general neglect made me guess no one at Somerset was particularly interested in using this room.

It was a natural choice for the séance. The long, heavy curtains would keep out any natural light, and the eyes of all the dead animals staring down would create the perfect atmosphere—not to mention the ominous gentleman above the fireplace.

With that settled, my curiosity wandered back to the bookshelves. There was only one title I was interested in. Maman used to say there were signs all around us, and if we looked carefully, we would receive affirmation we were on the right path.

I desperately needed a sign. I looked for the name Hugo. It took a few minutes, but I finally found it. I climbed the ladder and stretched out my hand. Clouds of dust floated down from the higher shelves, making me sneeze. Trembling, I pulled out the spine, letting my fingers feather over the cover.

The Hunchback of Notre Dame.

Flipping through the pages, I found my favourite chapter, where Esmeralda is rescued by Captain Phoebus. It was like reuniting with an old friend. I could have wept. Then the cold memories surfaced, and I snapped the cover shut. The last time I saw that book, its pages were strewn on the floor, trampled and muddied by the coppers' boots.

A small squeak came from the doorway. A young girl in an apron and bonnet stared up at me. I tucked the book under my arm.

"Sorry, miss." She curtsied clumsily. "I only needs to wind the clock. I can come back if you're busy."

I made my way down the ladder. "I'm not busy," I said. "Come in."

She went directly to the grandfather clock that stood like a sentry in the dark corner. The middle of the clock's face was decorated with a star-shaped design. I watched her work, guessing that she was of similar age to me.

"I hates coming in here," she said. There was a light tremble to her voice, like she wanted to laugh but wasn't sure. "The others in the kitchen tease me, but you don't see any of them up here, do ya? Every time I turn me back on these animals I expect them to come to life and swallow me up."

She opened the glass door and fitted the end of a small winch in the star shape of the clock's face. "One, two, three," she counted softly as she turned the handle. Her hands were red and chafed, likely from years of washing laundry, I reasoned.

"You're very careful with this task," I said. "I'm sure it's for your skill and not just your bravery that you've been assigned this duty."

The girl smiled, touching her bonnet self-consciously.

"And you work in the kitchen too?" I probed, recalling the delicious breakfast I had enjoyed earlier.

"Aye," she said. "Mostly the baking and helping Mrs. Galloway." She closed the glass door of the clock and used a cloth to wipe her prints clean. She tucked the winch into her apron pocket. It was heavy enough to drag down that side of her uniform. "I do a bit of dusting too."

I looked at her incredulously. "You seem to have a lot of jobs."

"It's not that much, really. The housemaids do the rest of the basic upkeep. And we only cleans the part of the manor that's in use. No one goes to the third floor. It's been locked for years."

"What exactly does Mrs. Donovan do?"

"Judge others, mostly."

I laughed. We stood a few feet apart, the lull of our conversation hanging in the air.

"Don't you find it cold in here, miss?" she asked, rubbing her arms.

"No."

The girl regarded me for a moment, folding the dust cloth. "I guess you're used to this kind of thing, though, eh?" She nodded to the animals. "Death and all that."

"Not exactly." I frowned at the head of a black bear positioned beside the stag. "But yes, I suppose that's why I'm here. I'm considering making use of this room for the séance."

She went as still and wide-eyed as the deer on the wall.

In seven days, I would need to convince a room full of people that I was conjuring Audra's spirit. I reasoned that establishing some atmosphere with the staff would be wise.

I explained, "There's a certain frequency a ghost requires for a successful crossover. Only those sensitive to that quality, people like myself, can detect that difference. I'm seeking a room that doesn't contain too much lead or natural elements such as gold or silver. They can interfere with spiritual signs." The lie slipped calmly from my lips, the result of years of listening to Maman.

She let out a nervous giggle. "If I had any of those metals them spirits don't like, I'd be sewing them into all me dresses."

"Ghosts can't hurt you," I said. "It's the people on this side of the grass you should worry about."

"Tell that to him." She nodded to the portrait above the fireplace. "That there is Miss Audra's grandfather, Lord Chadwick the third. Me great-aunt worked here before me, and she swears the old man was pure evil. She believes he haunts the walls of this old castle, taking the place apart stone by stone until the whole lot tumbles into the sea."

I hugged the novel to my chest, suddenly aware of the chill in the air the girl had spoken of.

"He was mad," she continued. "That's what took him in the end. He ran off into the winter night, naked as the day he was born, screaming about a voice calling out to him!"

I looked at the portrait and made a face, imagining such a scene.

The girl read my mind. "Must've been a sight," she whispered. "Auntie Lil swears he was the devil himself and saw his wicked reflection in the mirror. That's what scared him so bad."

A heaviness settled in my throat. I tried to swallow it down. "When did he die?"

"When Lady Audra was just a young girl. But still, he lingers."

"That's quite a long time for a ghost to haunt a dwelling."

She nodded to the grandfather clock. "I'm no expert, miss, but this clock chooses when to stop keeping time. For months it'll work proper—then one day it just stops, all the weights inside tangled up or such. The others say it's the warped floors making it unbalanced. But a thing this heavy don't move by itself, can it?"

I stayed quiet, knowing anything was possible if someone knew enough tricks.

She rubbed her arms again. "So, you can really talk to ghosts?" She peered at me, equal parts fear and intrigue. I recognized that expression of curiosity and desire. I had seen it on the young constable too.

She had lost someone.

"That's why you're here, right?" she prompted. "To help Lady Audra?" She held the dust rag to her chest. "Oh, it was so tragic, miss. She died so young, before she could marry, before she really even had a life."

I sighed. "I'd say the real tragedy is the man who is in denial of his fiancée's suicide."

The girl gasped.

His voice came from the doorway, but it filled the room. "And does this perspective diminish your attention to the task at hand, Miss Timmons?"

The girl and I traded identical expressions of mortified shock.

Mr. Pemberton came into the room, stopping just short of where I was standing.

I forced myself to face him. "Of course not," I replied. "I'm sorry, my lord. It was not my intention to appear so insensitive."

"No, I'm sure you usually hide it better than that." His gaze did not flinch, those blue eyes settling on mine.

He turned to the girl. "Thank you, Flora. That will be all."

She rushed through a curtsy and practically sprinted out of the room, taking any distraction with her.

It was curious how much smaller the room seemed. I fought the urge to step back from him and held my ground.

"I have exhausted every means to bring justice to Audra," he said, his tone sharp and unforgiving. "I'm allowing you to stay because your unique gift may be of assistance capturing the person responsible for her death. But if you feel differently, I suggest you take your leave of Somerset Park at once. I can easily arrange for the parish constable to collect you."

Would he always end our conversations with a threat? Even though my blood boiled and a million retorts sat on my tongue, some in English, some in French, I stayed silent. The book was like a shield against my chest, reminding me of what had brought me here. Constable Rigby would not rest until he had a noose around my neck. Mr. Lockhart was offering me a chance at freedom, but Mr. Pemberton held another charge over my head. Neither could know of the conflict I faced; I had to come up with a solution that could somehow give both men what they wanted. I had no choice but to stay and see this through.

Leaving now would be as suicidal as Audra jumping off the cliff.

CHAPTER ELEVEN

Lady Audra Linwood
Diary Entry
Somerset Park, October 11, 1851

Dearest,

Father is lying to me. I can see through his charade. In truth, I have known for months. He is dying.

He tries to stand taller when I enter the room, but I see how he wilts over, his smile dropping, when he thinks I've turned away. His body is fighting every day, and it is losing.

Mr. Lockhart comes more often now. He is here at least three times a week, but Father usually retires early, leaving the two of us and William to dine together. William's good spirits are a great comfort to me these days, and I know he loves Father just as much as I. I would never dare say this out loud, but I am grateful for the tragedies in his own life that brought him to Somerset—to me especially.

Mr. Lockhart treats me like an adult, and his visits ease my heart. Tonight, I asked him outright about Father and what he is hiding from me.

Mr. Lockhart is a terrible liar. I can always tell; he will either take a sip of wine or touch the tip of his beard. But tonight, he confirmed my suspicions. He told me without breaking my gaze.

William was speechless. He could only stare at the fire. I thought he was in shock, but then he reached for my hand under the table. I squeezed back.

The inevitable weighs heavily on all our minds, Dearest. What is to become of my home? Of me?

CHAPTER TWELVE

rrange for the parish constable to collect you," I huffed under my breath as I walked up the stairs. It was hardly my fault the man was so blind and insolent that he couldn't accept his bride's suicide.

Mr. Pemberton was proving to be as enjoyable as a pebble in my shoe . . . on a long walk . . . in the rain . . . on a cold day.

I spent the rest of the morning and a better part of the afternoon pacing the room, too embarrassed to go down for lunch. I couldn't face Mr. Pemberton again so soon. Instead, I used that time to consider the information I had gathered since arriving in this house. Audra had somehow slipped out of a room in which the door was guarded, and the window was still locked from the inside. I was less concerned about what had happened to her afterward. That part was indisputable.

She could only have left through the door. I clicked my tongue at the obvious answer. Mrs. Donovan, the one guarding the door, was lying. There was already a deeply ingrained belief throughout the staff that the family was cursed. I knew how such a belief could warp sensibilities.

The fire crackled. Then something occurred to me that should have been my primary concern from the first time I met Mr. Pemberton. The very person who assisted Audra was someone close to this family—someone who may still be living under this roof. Even if their original intention had not been malicious, they would be desperate to keep their secrets. If I started asking questions, I could possibly make myself a target. I would need to be careful in the way I gained information.

From my window I studied the grounds. There was a fog bank in the distance, covering what I guessed was the cliff edge. I wondered how near the ocean was—certainly close enough to smell the salt air.

Maman's voice echoed. *Stay out of la mer, ma petite chérie.*

Stay out of the ocean.

The fire had warmed the room, but the air seemed too stifling now. It was foolish for me to be inside. The secrets of this house were heavy, and it felt like I was breathing them all in. I opened the top drawer of the dresser and took out my gloves and hat. The drawer looked so empty with only my few belongings.

I slipped on my bonnet, tying the ribbon under my chin, and made my way down the grand staircase. I heard Mr. Pemberton in the study. I immediately changed direction and took the servants' passageway to the lower floor.

The kitchen was busier than the last time I had visited. There were several staff at their own workstations. I spotted Flora rolling out a rectangle of dough. A pile of apple peels and cores filled a bowl. There was a sweetness in the air that made my mouth water. I regretted missing lunch.

Flora met my gaze. She bit her lower lip and exchanged a quick glance with an elderly lady who was lifting the lid off an enormous pot. A cloud of steam enveloped her, and I caught the heady aroma of beef and wine. Again, my stomach reacted. The woman came over to me, wiping her hands on her apron. "Is there something I can get you, Miss Timmons?"

"No, I just followed my nose, I'm afraid," I said, hoping to put them at ease with a compliment. She smiled, then looked down at my gloves. I'd forgotten to hide the one with the rip in the seam.

"Actually," I said, "I wonder if I might borrow some needle and thread for mending. In London we don't get the cold fresh wind like the country."

Mrs. Donovan stepped into the kitchen with hardly a sound, but the temperature of the room seemed to drop. She gave the cook a stony stare. "Mrs. Galloway, your soup needs tending." She held out her hand to me. "I shall do the mending. It's my duty to make sure your needs are met." Her expression was flat as her eyes raked over my outfit. "I will see if I can find you more appropriate attire for the weather."

"Thank you," I said, struck by her capacity to offer assistance and be insulting at the same time. "I was hoping to walk the gardens." Then I added, "As soon as possible."

She smiled stiffly. The cook, Mrs. Galloway, went back to her pot, watching coyly over her shoulder.

"I'll do this at once," Mrs. Donovan said. She slid away like a snake down the hall, disappearing into one of the many doors off the corridor.

The entire kitchen seemed to let out a breath, and the easy bustle resumed. I had a notion the staff wouldn't mind seeing Mrs. Donovan accused by Audra's ghost.

I went to Flora, hoping I could amend whatever unease still lingered between us. She appeared as awkward as I felt. I'm sure she was also replaying Mr. Pemberton's criticizing words. She abandoned her dough and pulled a tray of pastries out of the oven.

"That smells scrumptious," I told her. The look of desire must have been apparent on my face, because she beamed back at me.

"Hand apple pies, I calls 'um. It's a recipe of my own."

Mrs. Galloway cleared her throat from across the room.

Flora sighed. "With a bit of Mrs. Galloway's help."

"Someone will be lucky to enjoy those," I said.

Smiling, she tucked one into a cloth and passed it to me. "A walk outside will be more enjoyable with this."

"It will," I said, fighting the urge to eat it all at once. "Thank you."

She leaned closer and said, "I'm sorry 'bout what happened in the library with his lordship. It was me fault."

"I was the one who spoke out of turn. Pay no mind."

The others moved about, discussing meal preparation and making an order for the village market in Wrendale.

A door closed roughly from down the hallway. Moments later a boy appeared, red-faced and smiling. He took off his cap and slipped it under his arm, then blew into his cupped hands a few times. "Good day, ladies," he said. "One o' the mares is soon to have her foal. We're making a list of names. Know any good ones, Flora? You're smart like that."

"Doesn't take a genius to name a horse, fool." She tossed him one of her apple pies.

He juggled it between his hands a few times. "Are you trying to burn me to death, woman?" He had half of it gone in two bites. Finally, he noticed me. "Oy, hello, miss."

"Never mind flirting, Joseph," Mrs. Galloway said. She pointed down the hall. "Be a dear and fetch some peach preserves from the cellar pantry, would you? That door sticks something awful this time of year."

His face lost all color.

"It'll be worth two more pastries," Flora tempted him.

He gave her a weak smile, then finished the apple pie by pushing the rest into his mouth. I watched as he walked down the corridor and disappeared through a doorway.

"Why doesn't Joseph like the pantry?" I asked.

"It's so old," Flora said. "And too close to the cliff. They say the ocean's crumblin' away at it."

I put my hand on the counter, feeling the floor pitch as I imagined the castle toppling into the salty water.

Joseph returned with an armload of jars, which Mrs. Galloway took to the sideboard.

"I see you survived," Flora joked.

"Aye," he said. "I think you lot stick that door on purpose so you won't have to go down there yerselves. I can hear the ocean, I tell ya! The waves lapping right up to the wall, I bet. One of these days Mrs. Galloway will go down there looking for her preserves and get eaten by a shark."

Flora laughed and tossed a handful of flour at him. The easy teasing continued. The boy was the same height as her, but he took great effort to stand taller. His eyes followed her as she moved about the kitchen. The attention was genuine.

The only guarantee love brings is heartache.

When he left, I watched him from the kitchen window as Flora returned to her baking. He paused before he reached the lane and glanced back, but it was only my face he saw in the window.

"How far are the stables from here?" I asked her, thinking of last night when I had planned on escaping by stealing a horse, regardless of the fact I had no riding experience.

Flora's steady hands worked the pastry. "'Bout half a mile. It's an easy trail that curves through the woods."

"He had no scarf or gloves," I said. "He must have been eager to know your suggested name for the horse."

She smiled at the pastry instead of looking me in the eye. "Joseph never complains," she replied. The tenderness in her voice transformed her simple reply into sweet praise.

The air stilled in the kitchen as Mrs. Donovan arrived with my freshly mended gloves. She also handed me a scarf. "It would be insensible to go outdoors without one," she said.

Regardless of my feelings toward her, the scarf was a welcome addition. I took the same hallway as Joseph and was soon outside, walking alongside the kitchen gardens. Fir branches covered the various vegetable plots while bushels of turnips and carrots lined the brick wall. The cold air was sharp, stinging the inside of my nose.

I purposely turned my back on the direction of the ocean and took the walkway that circled around the perimeter of the manor. Leaves crunched underfoot as I unwrapped Flora's treat and took small tastes, letting the spicy apple filling warm me, forcing myself to make it last. I could have eaten the entire tray, I'm sure.

An easy path led to the ornamental garden. The shrubs were neatly pruned, and the flower beds had gone to seed and were covered for the winter. Not a vegetable plant or fruit tree in sight. Beautiful, but useless.

I glanced back at the house, observing the long veranda that ran partway across the first floor. Had Audra hosted parties there, donning her tiara with the blue stone?

I smoothed the borrowed scarf against my cheek, noting the softness. Audra must have always enjoyed the finest clothes. I doubted her stomach ever grumbled, knowing that the next meal wouldn't come until the following day. She certainly never went to bed with the covers pulled over her head, attempting to stifle the sounds of what happened on the other side of the thin walls of Miss Crane's boardinghouse.

But then I hesitated.

If life at Somerset Park was so wonderful, why did she kill herself?

A figure exiting the house caught my eye. Even from this distance I recognized the thick hair and surly gait. I cursed and ran deeper into the garden. The footpath curved through a tangle of rosebushes. The thorns caught my hem the last few steps. At last, I came to a greenhouse.

I slipped inside, immediately thankful for the warmth, and slunk between the large potted plants, hoping William would pass by unaware. I followed a gurgling noise and found a large fountain. In the middle was a statue of a weeping angel. Even here I couldn't escape death.

The door opened with a violent commotion. I crouched down and scurried to the far end of the room where there was a large mound of dirt and a potting table. I was trapped.

Voices echoed faintly—he wasn't alone.

"It's the only way," a man's voice said. "He'll never leave Somerset Park as long as he thinks her death could have been prevented. He's determined to see someone pay, William."

My heart raced. It was the voice of Mr. Lockhart. I squinted at them through the foliage.

"And we all know who he's most likely to blame, don't we? The unworthy ward." William's tone was full of bitterness.

"This will work," Mr. Lockhart replied. "I have been travelling to London all these months making enquiries to find the perfect spiritualist. She can do this."

I was stunned. Mr. Lockhart had told me our meeting was a coincidence. What else had he lied to me about?

"Do you trust her?"

Mr. Lockhart replied, "She desperately needs my services. Even if she does come to suspect that something is amiss, what can she do? Stop fretting; it will all work out." Their footsteps shuffled closer, accompanied by the unmistakable tapping of the cane.

I tried to interpret his ambiguous answer, hoping my growing apprehension about him was wrong, and that this kind man was still an ally.

William laughed, but it sounded distressed, on the verge of tears. "I trusted you once before, and look what happened. She'd still be alive if it wasn't for you."

I held my breath. They were only a few yards away. Mr. Lockhart stabbed the floor with his cane. He let out a soft stream of curses at William.

Taking advantage of their confrontation, I got on my belly and slipped under the potting table, praying there was enough shadow to conceal me.

Mr. Lockhart's voice was like gravel. "Don't you dare point that accusing finger at me. Your foolish impatience brought all of this into being."

"She had a right to know the truth."

"You had only one reason for attempting to prevent the wedding," Mr. Lockhart said, "and it had nothing to do with Somerset. No, stop! I don't want to hear your explanation. Ever since you arrived as an orphan, you've tainted everything you've touched."

There was a strength behind his words that surprised me. It was unnerving to hear him angry.

I heard a sniff. Two pairs of shoes made their way closer. I could practically count the buttons on Mr. Lockhart's boots. A dangerous tickle in my nose threatened to turn into a sneeze.

When Mr. Lockhart spoke again his tone was gentler, apologetic even. "This is our only option. I've searched her room several times and found nothing."

"What if one of the servants stole it?" William asked tentatively.

"No one goes in that room."

There was a pause. "It could have changed everything."

Mr. Lockhart sighed heavily. "No point in lamenting your poor choice, William. You'll have to trust me—really trust me this time. After the séance, everything will fall into place and you won't have to worry about his lordship any longer."

CHAPTER THIRTEEN

Lady Audra Linwood
Diary Entry
Somerset Park, October 28, 1851

Dearest,

My world is caving in. I had such a fright last night! Father was found roaming the cliffside in nothing but his bedclothes. He was inconsolable for hours, insisting that he had heard a voice crying for help. Thinking it was me, he had gone out to find her.

Dr. Mayhew was summoned at once, and he spent the whole afternoon observing Father. I hovered in the hallway, fearing the worst. When he finally emerged, he proclaimed that infection was the most likely cause. He left us with instructions to bring down the fever—time spent in front of an open window and a diet consisting of nothing but fruit. If we see no improvement after one week, he will return to bleed him and release the poisons in his system.

I truly want to believe in Dr. Mayhew's diagnosis, but I am unable to find comfort in it. Could he be lying to me? I am always being treated like a delicate child, incapable of coping with the truth.

But the truth will come for me no matter what Dr. Mayhew says. Every day my worry grows, for Father's health and for my own future. The two are intertwined.

William, at least, understands my broken heart. In a moment of tearful sorrow, I confessed that I fear losing both him and my home. He pulled me into his arms and vowed he will let nothing happen to me. I'm well aware that he does not possess the means to keep such a promise, but still, I was grateful to be held in his embrace.

I hear what the staff whisper. They call this a curse passed down from Grandfather, destined to kill us off one by one until there is no longer a Linwood living at Somerset Park.

I want to scream at them for being so cruel. But how can I? What shall I do? Somerset Park has always been my home. It is here I was born, and it is here I should die.

CHAPTER FOURTEEN

I waited for what seemed like an eternity as the numbness settled into my cramped body. I was too afraid to move, certain William and Mr. Lockhart were waiting for me outside the greenhouse. My muscles had turned to stone, as if I had become one of the fountain statues.

Once I was certain it was safe to leave, I slunk back to the house, my mind racing.

Any trust I'd begun to build with Mr. Lockhart had been severed. I was nothing but a cog in whatever sinister plan he and William had concocted. And what did they suspect Audra had hidden in her room? Something that would force Mr. Pemberton from Somerset, apparently. Regardless, whatever happened the eve of the wedding, they both had information they were purposely keeping from Mr. Pemberton, and probably the police.

On shaking legs, I stood outside his study. It was quiet, but I could see a sliver of light under the door. I paused, hand about to knock. If Mr. Lockhart and William had secrets, conceivably Mr. Pemberton had some as well?

I needed the safety of my room to put my thoughts in order. I rounded the top of the stairs and made my way down the hallway. Flora was there, dusting an otherwise perfectly clean hall table. She looked up as I approached, and the expression of surprise was so exaggerated it was clearly fake. She'd been waiting for me.

I smiled at her, welcoming the opportunity. I had performed enough séances in large manors to understand the staff know most of the secrets of the house.

"Which room is Audra's?" I asked outright.

She blanched and fumbled with the duster. "It's the one at the far end, beside the alcove with the statue of the tiny cherub." She looked at me cautiously. "Why, miss?"

"I wonder if you might let me inside," I asked. She flinched, apparently appalled at my brazen request. I quickly added, "It's helpful in a séance to have a personal item of the dearly departed."

Flora shook her head vehemently. "No one is allowed in Lady Audra's room. Mrs. Donovan forbids it."

"Why?"

"Out of respect for the dead."

"No one has more respect for the dead than me," I said. "And wouldn't Audra want me to do whatever I could to help her communicate with those she loves on this earth?" I smiled, hoping it looked genuine. "I'm sure you'd be able to let me in for a quick moment. No one would be the wiser."

She shook her head again. "I couldn't even if I wanted to. I don't have the key."

Her reluctance called for a different tactic. I was determined to get into Audra's room, and Flora was my best chance. Luckily, she had sought me out, and I had a notion why.

Maman said no matter how alone someone seemed, they could always think of a person they hoped was on the other side, missing them just as much.

I tilted my head and studied her. "There is a particular glow about you, Flora," I said. "I noticed it earlier in the library. I don't see it often, but when I do, I know that person has a special guardian angel close to them."

Flora's brows lifted and her mouth formed the smallest O.

"I wonder if you might let me do a conjuring with you?" I dropped my voice to a whisper. "A private séance."

Her eyes went wide, taking over her innocent expression. Still, I could sense her eager hope, and would use it to my advantage. Questions were piling up, and no one was giving me the right answers. Flora could be a valuable ally, and I was in desperate need of one. In the greenhouse, Mr. Lockhart had spoken of my future as an afterthought, so flippantly cool. I put my hand to my throat, imagining the rough edge of the noose starting to tighten.

"I suppose so," Flora said hesitantly, but I could tell this was exactly what she'd come looking for. "If you think it's safe, miss."

"My name is Genevieve, but you can call me Jenny if you like. All my friends do." Although I'd never liked the pet name Miss Crane had given me, I suspected Flora would be more likely to consider me a confidant if I insisted we drop the formalities between us.

She nodded. A soft rose bloomed in her cheeks. "What do the ghosts say?" she asked. "What do they think about?"

I smiled. Flora wanted something I could give her. "Ghosts usually stay with those they were closest to in life," I said.

"And do ghosts know things . . . like people's secrets?"

"I believe they tell me what they perceive to be true." I found Flora's particular question interesting.

But as Maman used to say, grief never leaves the soul.

Footsteps came from the open area below, followed by the soft jingle of keys. Mrs. Donovan crossed the foyer with her usual straight posture and soldier-like gait. She glided in her black dress like an omen. "Come," I said to Flora, letting her into my room and quickly shutting the door.

I removed my gloves and untied the ribbon of my bonnet. "Let me gather my items," I said. The ghost book was still on my bed. Opening my bag, I took out one candle and one chimney and placed them on the vanity in front of the mirror.

Flora went directly to the fireplace and tidied.

I casually asked, "How long have you worked here?"

"Three years now," she said. "They needed an extra laundress, but then Mrs. Galloway was kind enough to take me on to help in the kitchen."

"So you worked here when Lady Audra was alive."

Her face lit up. "She was lovely and so kind too."

"I see," I said, recalling my earlier assumption of the spoiled girl. "Lord Chadwick told me the family has a history of unfortunate deaths."

She stayed quiet, but I suspected she knew something.

"What do you think happened that night?" I asked.

Flora frowned like a battle was waging inside her. She tucked the duster into her apron pocket. When she spoke, her voice was hardly above a sigh. "Just like her father, and his father before him. The doctor said it was an illness, but it was more like a curse."

"What makes you say the family is cursed?"

"Not just the family—Somerset itself! Me aunt says Audra's great-grandfather built it with stolen money. I don't know much about him, but I can tells ya it all started with his son, Audra's grandfather."

"The one whose portrait is in the library," I confirmed.

She nodded and marked herself with the sign of the cross. "Ever since he leapt off the cliff all those years ago, nothin' but misery has fallen on this family."

I heard a faint scratching from the wardrobe. *Evening, Mr. Mouse*, I thought. Flora didn't seem to hear, or perhaps she was used to the sounds the mice make in the walls at Somerset.

She moved about, lighting the candles on the bedside table, then the sconces on the mantel.

"What's London like?" she asked. The change of subject caught me off guard. "It must be a frolic goin' to all them shows and fancy restaurants."

"I don't know that side of London," I answered truthfully. "What about Somerset Park? I imagine there have been some lovely parties."

Her expression changed completely. "There was a ball planned, in celebration of Lady Audra's upcoming wedding. They practically invited everyone in Wrendale. Maisie, me best friend, and I, we were so excited, we even had special dresses for the occasion." Sadness lingered in her voice.

The scratching sound came again. I was getting tired of the interruption. I slipped off my boot and went to the wardrobe. I opened the door, ready to pounce. "Goodness," I breathed.

No longer empty, the wardrobe contained at least half a dozen dresses, a pair of black shoes, and even a smart black cape with gold piping. They were simple and elegant, a perfect disguise for someone like me to appear she belonged here. My eyes found a black gown with lace on the cuffs and red satin underneath. It would make even the most stylish of Miss Crane's girls look like oyster mongers in comparison.

I lifted a sleeve and rubbed the fine material between my fingers. It was lovelier than anything I had ever worn. But there must have been more buttons on this garment than stars in the sky. How was a young woman supposed to get herself into such a frock? I let out an embarrassed laugh, knowing I'd never be able to convince anyone I was a proper lady simply by putting on a new dress.

"What's that, then?" Flora asked.

I closed the doors of the wardrobe and turned to her. "Mr. Lockhart was kind enough to have a few dresses delivered," I said.

An expression of whimsy lit Flora's rounded features. "Lady Audra was kind like that too. She lent Maisie and me two of her old dresses to wear at the ball." She smiled weakly, the happy memory tinged with loss and grief, my constant companions.

She continued, "Mine had to be shortened and let out a bit at the waist. Maisie's fit perfect, though—she was the same size as Lady Audra, same hair too. They could almost be sisters." Flora's smile slipped away. "Maisie looked perfect in her dress."

I let the silence linger, sensing Flora needed to be coaxed carefully. I didn't want to scare her away. "I'm sure you both looked as pretty as a painting at the ball," I prompted.

"No." Flora sniffed. "Although Maisie got to wear the dress one last time. They buried her in it."

I nodded and put a hand on her shoulder. She moved her gaze, and it settled on my bed, where the ghost book lay closed.

"It allows the spirits to write a message to this world," I told her softly.

She went to the edge of the bed and reached out to touch the cover. "Maisie loved to dance," she said. "And she had the most beautiful blond hair. She could do any kind of braid." Flora dabbed her eyes with her sleeve.

"If you could talk to Maisie again, would you like that?" I asked. I could feel Flora putting more and more trust in me.

The room continued to darken. The few candles Flora had lit brought a new atmosphere to the room. I wouldn't have to do very much to convince her Maisie was in the room with us. All she needed was a small token, a sign from the other side. I lit the candle on the dresser and put the protective chimney back in place.

"Maisie was afraid of the dark," Flora whispered.

"It's not dark for her," I answered. "Spirits are drawn to the flame of a candle."

What people don't see with their eyes, they fill in with their hearts. The heart sees.

I picked up the ghost book and remembered Mrs. Hartford's card was still inside. I took another approach. "Normally I ask someone to write a message on a card and then slip it into these pages, and when I open it again, there is the answer from the other side."

Flora's bottom lip stuck out a bit. "I don't write too well."

"Not to worry." I smiled. "Remember how I told you the spirit was strong with you? It's very rare. In your case, all you need is to put your hand on the cover and think about your question. Would you like to see if Maisie has an answer for you?" I held the book closer to her.

With a shaking hand, Flora laid her palm on the cover. Then she closed her eyes tight. Her lips moved in an indistinguishable whisper.

There was no need to write a new message in the ghost book. The one from Mr. Hartford's séance was still there. And knowing Maisie was at peace might help bring Flora into my confidence. I envisioned the two of us breaking into Audra's room that very night.

Flora opened her eyes and briefly nodded.

I then placed my hand over hers. I was purely making the mannerisms up on the spot. "Is there anyone who wishes to speak with us?" I asked. I let the wind outside fill in the silence. "Is Maisie here? Maisie, do you wish to speak to Flora?"

The candle on top of the vanity went out.

Flora gasped. As if nature were in on my plan, the wind picked up, rattling the panes fiercely. "Maisie's mad," she said.

"She's not mad," I soothed. "She's just excited. Sometimes ghosts don't know how to control the energy around them."

Flora screamed and pulled her hand away from the book. "It burned me!" The ghost book fell to the rug with a thud. I watched as her silhouette stumbled toward my door. "Sorry, miss—I mean Jenny—but I can't face Maisie!"

Her running footsteps faded down the hallway. I slouched in failure. Flora was probably too spooked to ever come within spitting distance of me again. The wind suddenly calmed. The ghost book had fallen open to the secret page.

I had to blink a few times, unsure of what I was seeing. The pit of my stomach dropped. Instead of Mr. Hartford's message of peace in my handwriting, there was an elegant new script. It was only two words, but they were written repeatedly, the small penmanship filling both pages. It started out legible, then became severely messy, as if the writer had grown increasingly panicked by the end.

Only two words, over and over.

Help me.

CHAPTER FIFTEEN

Lady Audra Linwood
Diary Entry
Somerset Park, November 25, 1851

Dearest,

Even after two bloodletting treatments, Father's health is rapidly declining. Several times now he has left his room in the night, only to be discovered roaming the cliffs. We've had no choice but to lock his door and keep someone posted by his bedside. I try to stay with him as much as I can, but witnessing his achingly frail state erodes my heart like saltwater pounding against a bluff. I could drown in this sorrow.

Dr. Mayhew paid us a visit this afternoon. After examining Father, he pulled me aside and told me that he has done everything he can. All we can do now is wait.

The servants' whispers of a curse have grown bolder. They fear it so much, I think they are eager for Father to die. Mrs. Donovan oversaw the conversation between the doctor and me without an ounce of sympathy. I find myself wondering about the soothing teas she brings Father.

William has offered to stay with Father when the need to rest my eyes becomes too great. He has been a dear, so different from that reckless, troublemaking boy I once knew. I overheard Mr. Lockhart saying to Dr. Mayhew that sometimes moments of great stress can bring out the best in a man. I hope this means William is becoming a gentleman, someone whom I can truly rely on. Someone I can trust with my heart.

CHAPTER SIXTEEN

I rushed down the grand staircase. The chill was long gone from my bones and replaced with fury. I made my way to Mr. Pemberton's study and lifted my hand to knock. There was a shift from the other side; I imagined him working at his desk.

"May I be of service?" Mrs. Donovan asked. She slunk out of the shadows as if she was made from the very darkness.

"I believe someone has been in my room and tampering with my belongings," I said.

Her face remained stoic. "I was in your room earlier, Miss Timmons, and I can assure you I have not tampered with any of your belongings. I placed several gowns in your wardrobe and items in the dresser. Did you find them? I hope they're to your liking." She looked down her nose at my dress. "It was my impression that you would be quite eager for a change of clothes."

An unexpected blush burned my cheeks. Even though a servant, I sensed Mrs. Donovan had the entire household under her control. I worked to keep my voice level. "I would like a key to my room, so I may safeguard my belongings."

"I'm the person responsible for all the keys of the house," she replied coolly. "It's unnecessary for you to have your own. Is there something of value you would like to put in the safe? I'll ask the lord myself." Then she stepped in front of me and rapped three quick knocks on the door.

"I have nothing worth stealing," I told her. "But I would like my belongings to remain untouched. And I would like to lock my door."

Her unflinching gaze held mine. It was like having a staring contest with a statue.

"Mr. Lockhart promised I would have all my needs met. I shall have a key to lock my room or I will leave tonight." The last bit was much louder than I intended, but my nerves were raw, and I was close to tears.

The lines in Mrs. Donovan's face smoothed out. There was a hint of a cruel smile under the veil of servitude, something I had no doubt she had perfected over her many years of running Somerset Park.

The door opened. Mr. Pemberton stood there, glancing back and forth between me and Mrs. Donovan. I automatically dropped my gaze, remembering how awkward I had been the last time we'd spoken. He was wearing riding boots. "Is there a problem?" he asked. The impatient tone was hard to miss.

Mrs. Donovan showed no sign of docile submission. Instead, she raised her chin. "Your guest is demanding a key, my lord," she said.

I finally looked at him, ready to plead my case. His hair was windblown, and there was a hint of fresh air on him. He fixed his stare on me and waited, but the words seemed to flee from my head. I imagined explaining finding the "help me" message in the ghost book—but he would only accuse me of more parlour tricks. To him, I was simply a fake whom he was blackmailing to service his own goals. What would he care if someone was snooping around my room? I decided to stay quiet.

He looked back at Mrs. Donovan, some exasperation draining from his expression. "Anyone in this house can have their own key if they desire," he said. "I would think the past has taught us that much. If Miss Timmons wants a key to her room, she shall have one. Kindly fetch it from your office downstairs."

"Of course, my lord." Her head did the slightest nod as she reached for the large key ring on her belt. "I, in fact, have it on my person." Meticulously, she chose a key and unfastened it from the ring. She held it an inch from her nose, inspecting it before passing it to me.

There was the vaguest of tugs from her as I took the key. "Thank you," I replied.

Ignoring me, she turned to Mr. Pemberton. "Drinks will be served in an hour's time. I believe Mr. Lockhart is resting. As per Dr. Barnaby's suggestion, he'll be having his evening meal in his room."

"Thank you," he replied. "Has Bramwell told Mrs. Galloway that Dr. Barnaby is staying for dinner as well?"

She nodded dutifully. "All taken care of."

"That's fine," he said, but he had already looked away from her, his attention shifting to me.

Either Mrs. Donovan was used to being treated so abruptly by Mr. Pemberton or she was eager to leave. She soundlessly slipped away like the half snake she was, making her disappearance through the servants' door that led downstairs to the kitchen.

His eyes quickly glanced over my dress. "When you come down for drinks, Dr. Barnaby will be there. He's under the same assumption as the rest of the manor, that you're here to contact Audra and ease my suffering."

"Have no reservations, my lord, easing your suffering is my paramount goal."

He gave me a patronizing look, nearly rolling his eyes. Then he lowered his voice and said, "Be aware your every action and choice of word are being examined by those in this house, most of all the servants. I understand you were in the kitchen today. You would do well to keep a more appropriate distance with the staff. I suspect you're not accustomed to the importance of such etiquette."

I gripped the key in my palm, feeling the edge dig into my flesh. I had never met a man whose personality was so vexing it overshadowed any handsomeness. "You're quite right," I said. "I'm not familiar with the etiquette of being less respectful to people whose status society perceives to be lower than my own."

He only stared back at me, with his lips opened slightly. Before he could reply, I made my way up the grand staircase, silently cursing with each squeak of the steps. Only when I had closed the door behind me, pressing my back against it, did I realize what a risk I was taking each time I opened my mouth around him.

I had probably given him more than enough reason to cast off the whole scheme and follow through with his original threat of summoning the parish constable. There was a shaking at the base of my spine. I may not even last my first full day here. I needed to hold my tongue and keep my focus on preparing for the séance.

Placing the key on the vanity, I opened the top drawer. True to Mrs. Donovan's word, there were stockings, several petticoats, and nightgowns. I smoothed my hand over the perfectly folded clothes.

The mirror on the wardrobe reflected a sullen creature. One of my hairpins was sticking out, and the other three were barely enough to contain my natural curls. I thought of Flora and wondered if she could help me. I hoped I hadn't spooked her too much. She might never want to come in this room again. Not everyone was accustomed to death as I was.

I studied the beautiful dresses now at my disposal. The options were staggering. I had never seen so many lovely clothes in one place. Then something struck me as odd. I pushed the dresses to the side and inspected the bottom of the wardrobe. There were no marks or any other signs that a mouse had been there. I couldn't even find a small hole. The scratches must be coming from the wall behind the wardrobe. That made more sense, and I was thankful for that, at least. I would hate for the dresses to be ruined.

My eyes went to the black-and-red gown. I held it up in front of me before the mirror and was pleased to see the length seemed about right. I stepped out of my frock and pulled the dress over my head. The fabric cascaded over me like water. I slipped on the black shoes and tilted, unbalanced.

When I turned to the mirror, the truth was so cruel it was almost comical. The waist was too big, emphasizing how gaunt I was beneath it, and my barely contained hair looked like a madwoman's. "I could be the ghost," I said to my reflection.

I carefully returned the dress to the wardrobe. This time I chose the plainest of the collection. The grey lace and pleated fabric were high around the neck, and even though simple, it made me feel less of a fraud. I was grateful that all the buttons were in the front and the hem was long enough to hide the scuffed toes of my boots.

A strange sense of unfairness washed over me. I went over the misery-filled timeline of my life and all the occurrences and choices that had brought me to this crumbling castle by the ocean.

Maman's voice resurfaced from a memory. *We have the skills to survive, you and I. Whenever it seems most bleak, remember, you will always find a way. You can only depend on yourself,* ma petite chérie.

"Trust your skills," I whispered. "Depend on yourself."

I counted on my fingers what I knew was true. Mr. Lockhart

and William had a secret about the night Audra went missing. Ghosts were not real. Someone was sneaking into my room and going through my things. But how would they know about the ghost book? Were they trying to scare me into leaving? A rather pathetic attempt by my standards.

All the staff knew I was performing a séance to conjure Audra's ghost. Whoever wanted me gone must be afraid of what the séance would reveal. Was it possible there was some nugget of truth in Mr. Pemberton's theory?

I had to get into Audra's room and search for what William was so desperate to find. It might even help me decide who to target.

Once I'd organized my thoughts, the message from the ghost book no longer looked so threatening. I wiped away the "help me" messages with my palm and returned to my bag.

I WAS MAKING a final attempt to pin up the last strand of curls when a knock at the door interrupted me. "Miss Timmons, I've come to accompany you downstairs."

I groaned, hating how everything Mr. Pemberton said sounded like an order.

When I opened the door he leaned back, startled. The oil lamp he held was the only light in the hallway. He took in my poor attempt at dressing for dinner. By contrast, the glow from the lamp played off his polished buttons and fair hair. The square jaw and blue eyes were a striking combination. He looked as elegant as royalty in his dinner finery. If I didn't know his distasteful personality, I would say he was rather fine. I imagined the jealousy he would stir up at Miss Crane's.

"Follow me," he said, already turning away.

I locked the door behind me, pocketing my key. I snuck a long-

ing glance down the hallway toward Audra's room. I would have to
wait until the entire house was asleep.

The manor was oddly dark, with candles placed at far intervals.
I carefully made my way down the grand staircase, making sure to
hold on to the railing as Mr. Pemberton held the lamp between us.

When we walked through the Gallery Hall, I noticed the portraits loomed taller in the evening. I slowed in front of Audra's
frame, watching the shadows flicker across her face. She was smiling, but it seemed there was a secret only the painter knew.

Mr. Pemberton paused, but he was looking at me instead of
his bride. Oddly, he said nothing, content to let this moment pass
without critiquing me.

We continued walking, and the silence grew more pronounced.
The lamp between us created a shared circle of light, making the
hallway seem like it was growing longer with each step. Would we
ever get there?

"You've had the day to explore," he started. I jumped at the sound
of his voice. "Have you found a suitable room for the séance?"

The image of Mr. Lockhart and William were fresh in my mind,
but again I hesitated to share that information. I had no reason to
trust him. And would he even believe me? Until I had a more definite idea of who were my allies, I decided to keep the secret a little
longer—just like Audra in her portrait.

"The library seems suitable," I answered.

Relief took over his expression, improving his demeanour. "Tomorrow, we can discuss plans to prepare the room," he said. "It's
important for us to be seen cooperating."

"It's also important for me to be able to approach anyone I feel
has information about Lady Audra's last night," I said. "Even if
some consider it a breach of etiquette."

He sighed. "Your point is taken, Miss Timmons. You may speak to whomever you wish."

Surprised, I turned to study his expression, but he was looking straight ahead, hardly giving me more than a profile to consider.

There was a glow from the room up ahead. He slowed our pace and said, "However, in order for our scheme to be successful, no one should be aware of the true intention of your enquiries."

"Conversation isn't the only way to learn about someone," I said, recalling how I'd read him correctly last night. "My mother taught me that people reveal more about themselves by what they don't say. The trick is knowing how to listen."

He held my gaze. "I'm counting on all of your tricks and persuasive talents."

I wished I felt as confident as he seemed. "And so is Mr. Lockhart," I reminded him. "When he realizes I'm not doing the séance I promised him, he'll be quite upset with me." I wanted to gauge his reaction, to see if he understood I had more to lose. He needed my skills to pull this off. Perhaps he'd be willing to offer me something, or at least remove the threat of sending me back to jail.

"I suspect your reputation will be glorified in his eyes if Audra's killer is found, Miss Timmons. But by all means, continue to make this about yourself."

I frowned at his useless answer and said, "It's a habit one develops when you're the only one you can count on, my lord."

CHAPTER SEVENTEEN

Lady Audra Linwood
Diary Entry
Somerset Park, December 12, 1851

Dearest,

My tears have soaked this page so thoroughly I fear the ink will never dry. I woke from a horrible dream, unable to recall the robust image of Father's face before it was thinned and paled by illness. Distraught, I went to the Gallery Hall in search of his portrait.

William was there when I arrived, staring up at my own painting, the one I sat for recently. He has grown into a broad young man, and I know half the maids are smitten with him, but he is as unfortunate as myself in this world. How cruel it is to be born into a station in life that determines your worth, no matter all your good intentions.

But at least he was born a man. William can work to earn a living; he will always have the autonomy to go where he pleases and start again. When I told him as much, he gave me the strangest look. He said he will never leave Somerset Park, and that he will never leave me.

He took my hand and kissed it, holding it against his lips a moment longer than necessary. I felt a force wrapping its arms around us, urging us closer. I was unsure of my own body. Part of me wanted to give in to that heat, to let myself be embraced. But somewhere in my mind a distant alarm was ringing out, rooting me to the spot. Only when he took a step toward me did I move. I quickly curtsied and ran straight to my room.

But as I write this, I think I must have imagined those feelings. William is as dear to me as a brother. It was sincere gratitude I was feeling, nothing more. I would not allow myself such a disastrous attachment.

There, I have settled the matter in my head. No more of it; I am completely content to fall asleep now.

CHAPTER EIGHTEEN

Mr. Pemberton and I entered the drawing room, pausing under an enormous chandelier. Walls covered in golden damask reflected the candlelight, giving everything an opulent sparkle, except for myself. The scuffs on my boots seemed to burn through the hem of my skirt.

Heavy brocade drapes dressed each window, their pleats perfectly spaced. I imagined Flora on a stepladder with her duster, trying to reach the very top. On the other side of the room a bar cart was laden with various crystal bottles and glasses.

In front of the fireplace, a red chaise lounge and accompanying chairs created an elegant seating arrangement. A gentleman rose from his chair. He was slight in build, with a gentle expression. His light brown hair was trimmed, and his dinner jacket was clean but plain. He seemed out of place among all the shiny objects, just like me. However, whereas I stuck out like a piece of coal among diamonds, he faded unremarkably into the backdrop.

"May I present Miss Timmons," Mr. Pemberton said. Then he turned to me. "This is Dr. Barnaby, a good friend of mine whose skills medical and otherwise I am indebted to more than once."

"Oh, come now," the man said. "You make it sound as if you lead a dangerous life and I'm arriving in time to save you."

"Just that one time." Mr. Pemberton smiled as the men shared a hearty handshake.

"I'm very pleased to make your acquaintance," I said.

Dr. Barnaby was all smiles and bright-eyed interest—a strong contrast to Mr. Pemberton's critical reaction when he came to collect me. If he was conscious of the fact I was drably put together, his welcoming demeanour hid it well.

I sat with him on the settee, feeling more at ease.

Harry, the young footman I recognized from breakfast, delivered drinks to us on a silver tray. Bubbles sparkled on the surface. It tasted like drinking stars. I had another sip.

Mr. Pemberton stayed beside the fireplace with an amber drink in his hand. "How is Lockhart?" he asked Dr. Barnaby.

The young man's smile faltered. "The cough worries me," he said. "I gave him some tonic. I want him to visit a specialist in London, but he is so stubborn."

"And devoted to this family," Mr. Pemberton added. There was a solemn tone to his voice.

I took another sip from my glass with a silent mix of guilt and curiosity.

"Is William not joining us?" Dr. Barnaby asked.

Mr. Pemberton sighed. "William's schedule is not quite in time with a regular manor. He prefers to acquaint himself with a bottle of brandy before every meal." Then he lifted his own drink and said into the glass, "Or instead of a meal."

"He looked well-fed the last time I saw him," I said. I went to take another sip, but my glass was already empty.

Clearing his throat, Dr. Barnaby said, "I believe there was some discussion of him going into town to look at a property." His voice lifted at the end. I suspected he was lying, or at least stabbing at conversation. I envied Mr. Lockhart having dinner in his room.

"He's considering alternate accommodation?" I asked. I watched Mr. Pemberton over the rim of the glass as I pretended to take another sip.

"William enjoys relaying the grave injustice of his situation for anyone who will give him a willing ear," he replied.

Harry caught my eye. I raised my glass in his direction and was promptly served another. I could see Mr. Pemberton's reflection in the mirror over the fireplace. He was staring at me with an odd expression. Was it confusion or disappointment?

Tension crept up my neck. It was foolish to think I could pass in this company. The toe of my boot peeked from under the skirts.

Dr. Barnaby looked back and forth between me and Mr. Pemberton. He cleared his throat, then said, "This is such fine gin. And you are right to satisfy your thirst, Miss Timmons." And although his glass still had a mouthful, he held it up to Harry. "It would be a disservice to the fine craftsman who prepared it." He smiled at me encouragingly. "It's such an interesting process, how patient and particular the distillers have to be. Think of all the care that went into the very drinks we now hold. We are fortunate to enjoy them while we can." He took a sip. "Don't you agree, Pemberton?"

His chivalrous rescue did not go unnoticed by me. The awkwardness eased from my stiff posture.

Mr. Pemberton regarded us with a cautious expression, then said, "I wouldn't deny anyone the pleasure of a fine cocktail, least of all Miss Timmons." He stayed by the fireplace with one hand on the mantel and the other holding his drink, which was still half-full.

From the hall, rushed voices made all of us, Harry included, turn to the door. Bramwell arrived with a breathless young man dressed in a long riding coat. There was a satchel over his shoulder.

"I'm sorry, my lord," Bramwell said. "But the lad had special instructions."

The young man took off his hat and tucked it under his arm as he stepped forward. "My orders were to hand deliver this," he said. He passed over a wrapped parcel, roughly the size of my ghost book.

Mr. Pemberton took the package and frowned. "There's no name, only Somerset Park's address." He lifted his gaze and looked at the messenger. "You came all the way from London? On horseback?"

"Aye, m'lord."

Mr. Pemberton nodded to Bramwell and said, "Pay him appropriately and arrange for lodging at the stable for the horse and a bed at the guest cottage."

A relieved smile graced the young man's features. "Thank you, m'lord." He left the room.

Mr. Pemberton placed his drink on the mantel and held my gaze. "I should take this to my study. Anything hand delivered at night can't be ignored. Forgive my absence."

Bramwell nodded. "Of course, my lord. I'll have dinner held."

"No need. Please don't let my business delay the meal for my friends." And with that, Mr. Pemberton disappeared from the room, leaving me with Dr. Barnaby and Harry.

CHAPTER NINETEEN

Lady Audra Linwood
Diary Entry
Somerset Park, January 3, 1852

Dearest,

I can barely get the words down, my hand is shaking so badly. A miracle has happened. Mr. Lockhart has found an heir to Somerset Park!

He is a distant cousin, only a few years older than I. Mr. Lockhart told me that he hails from the north, and is a well-educated man who has taken over his late father's business of horses and such. I did not get all the details, but the principal reason for my lightness of heart is that he has agreed to come to Somerset Park and meet us.

William has voiced his suspicions about bringing a complete stranger into our midst. My cheeks burned when he spoke ill of Mr. Lockhart, accusing him of using me as a lure. I know William is only being protective; he has always cared deeply for my well-being.

We have not been alone together since the night in the Gallery Hall. I wonder if he has wrestled with the same thoughts as I. But no, I must not let myself enter that way of thinking. Somerset is what matters, and that is what I must focus on.

This good news has filled Father's body with a new vigor I haven't seen for many months. He has finally left his room, shaven and in fine clothes, ready to make a favourable impression on the young man.

I already feel a kinship with him, as he has suffered losing his mother as well. I wanted to ask Mr. Lockhart what he looked like, not that I'm so particular to his physical attributes, but this man could be my husband! And although I am wholeheartedly my own person, marrying this man will grant me the means to stay in my home and keep those I care about in the manor, including William.

There is an immense pressure building inside my chest. I must do my best to make myself as amiable as possible to this man if we are to be successful. But surely Somerset Park and all its splendor will be enough to woo him over?

I invited some maids to my room to help me decide what to wear to entice this mystery man. They're so excited about this possible match. Even the kitchen maid, sweet Flora, and her dear friend Maisie were here. We spent an entire afternoon trying on dresses and deciding how I shall wear my hair and which shoes to show off.

I do not think I could be any happier. Actually, I do. If this man accepts the manor and decides to marry me, then I will be the happiest.

I'm lying, Dearest. I will be the happiest if he is handsome.

CHAPTER TWENTY

In the evening, the dark red walls of the dining room reminded me of Miss Crane's lipstick. I shuddered at the thought. It was like being inside the mouth of a giant. But the fireplace was roaring with plenty of wood, and the comfortable warmth put me at ease.

The long dining table seemed overly adequate for myself and the doctor. The selection of silverware alone for one person was laughable. The most I knew about forks and knives was how much silver was in them based on their weight.

Bramwell stood at attention at the sideboard between serving the courses. I watched Dr. Barnaby choose the large spoon beside the knife and mimicked the selection for myself. The creamed soup was followed by roasted pheasant and tender carrots that had been drenched with a sweet buttery sauce. My taste buds had never experienced such richness. And with each serving, Bramwell would fill my wineglass.

It was easy to stay in conversation with Dr. Barnaby, which I found astonishingly enjoyable. The wine most likely helped. I was equally surprised to learn he and Mr. Pemberton had known each other since they were young boys.

"Oh yes," he said, spearing a piece of carrot. "We grew up in the same northern part of the country. Our fathers were first acquainted through the hunts. Then my father took over as their head stable groom. Pemberton and I spent many enjoyable days riding. And as you can see, we're still close friends."

"But you hardly have anything in common. You seem perfectly affable, and he's . . ." I paused. From the corner of my eye I saw Bramwell stiffen. He was staring straight ahead, but I knew he was watching me. "He's, well . . . he's mentioned you had saved his life once?"

Dr. Barnaby blushed and looked at his plate. "I was hardly the hero, I assure you. We were at his father's stables, preparing for our usual ride, when Pemberton took out a horse that had a reputation for being wild. The animal became violent and tried to buck him off. I came alongside with my horse and got his under control." He shrugged and picked up his fork again. "We were fifteen, more brass than brains, I'm afraid."

I tried to hide my smile behind my wineglass. "Was he punished for his recklessness?" I asked, my voice rising with anticipation.

He frowned. "No, they put down the horse. A tragedy, really. It was a fine animal, and Pemberton's father had planned on grooming him to be a stud."

"That's so unfair!" I exclaimed. "It wasn't the animal's fault. I know little about horses, but I know the nature of man, and it was Mr. Pemberton who should have been put down."

There was a quick gasp from Bramwell. I wasn't sure if my callous opinion or not addressing him as Lord Chadwick had shocked him more.

Dr. Barnaby hesitated a moment, then he said, "The intense guilt he felt was punishment enough. Pemberton's father was strict. He believed anything worth learning was best learned through the most extreme means."

"I see." My toes curled inside my boots as my wine-addled

mind began to realize how foolish I had been to blurt out such careless words.

He met my eyes with a thoughtful expression, void of ridicule or judgment. "I've had the benefit of knowing Pemberton before he was burdened with all this responsibility," Dr. Barnaby said. "When I began my studies at medical school, he came into possession of his father's estate and all that entailed." He let out a sigh. There was a heaviness in it I couldn't quite fathom.

"And why does he live here now?" I asked, thinking about William. If someone who had two estates were trying to push me out of the only home I had, I would be upset too. No wonder William wanted him gone.

Dr. Barnaby used his napkin. "He's needed here more, obviously." He leaned in and lowered his voice. "Many people rely on Somerset Park to stay operational, and there is no one else trustworthy to run this estate."

There was the smallest movement from Bramwell's eye. A twitch, perhaps.

"Are you employed by Somerset Park as well?" I asked Dr. Barnaby. I had never been to a doctor in my entire life. Maman believed in home remedies.

"No, at least not in the way you imply. I'm the doctor in Wrendale, but it's close enough to Somerset that I'm able to come here whenever needed." A flicker of something like remorse flashed across his eyes.

"Did you follow Mr. Pem—I mean, Lord Chadwick here from the north?" I asked, wondering how they could be such good friends when they seemed so opposite.

"Not exactly." He took a sip of wine. "I came to visit when he and Audra were officially engaged." His faced seemed fixed in a sad smile. "I toured Somerset Park and Wrendale, and I fell in love. I knew this was where my future lay."

He put a small piece of pheasant on his fork and added a dollop of cream sauce with the tip of his knife. "It's such a tragedy," he said. "I don't know how Pemberton copes. He hides it so well." There was an interesting hitch in his tone. "They were a perfect match, even in their looks, so similar."

There was a distant vagueness in his expression, as if he were watching a memory played on the wall behind me. "All of Wrendale felt the loss," he said. "Especially since it was so close to the other girl's death. It was such a miserable time. It still clings to everything in this house." He studied me, then asked, "Can't you feel it? You're much more sensitive than the rest of us, so you'd have more of a connection, I suppose."

I felt a curious sense of caution, unsure how to reply. "I feel nothing unexpected," I said. "Every house has its own energy, and Somerset Park is no different."

Bramwell came around with dessert, but my appetite had disappeared. There was something different in the air, something that left me in a state of unease. I wondered if Dr. Barnaby would be at the séance. It might be hard to fool a man of science.

We left the room together, both declining the offer of a nightcap in the drawing room. My stomach was full, and my body was groggy with the satisfaction of a decadent meal. Was this what it was like for the rich? To go to bed every night drowsy with the indulgence of food and drink?

Dr. Barnaby held the lamp in one hand while offering me his other arm. Again, I was struck by how opposite his company was to Mr. Pemberton's, remembering how he kept the lamp between us like a shield.

Bramwell followed behind, snuffing out the sconces along the wall, one by one. We were in a slow race as the darkness clipped at our heels.

A faint light came from under the door of the study. Dr. Barnaby whispered, "If he doesn't take a rest, I'll have two patients to contend with. And one stubborn patient is enough."

I wondered about the package from London.

We climbed the staircase together. "I hope Mr. Lockhart's health improves soon," I said. It was not lost on me that he'd been in the greenhouse that very afternoon, cussing at William. I didn't remember him coughing either. "How long have you known him?"

We reached the landing and walked down the hallway. "I met him the same time I met Audra, so for almost a year now. He's been the family lawyer for decades." His expression caved visibly in the same way as when he'd spoken of her at supper, and I was reminded of something.

"Earlier, you mentioned there was another death close to Lady Audra's," I said.

He nodded. "A young girl from the village. The sickness took hold of her quickly."

From over the railing, I could see a single lamp move through the foyer. "Was no one else afflicted?" I asked, putting my attention back on Dr. Barnaby.

"A few elderly people—one especially frail woman who was determined to cure herself with herbal tea." He paused. "There's something so unnatural about the death of a young person, isn't there?"

"That's an interesting point of view from someone who must come in contact with death regularly."

"Perhaps that's why I'm working so hard to prevent it, Miss Timmons."

When we came to my room, Dr. Barnaby kept the lamp in place while I unlocked my door. After I lit one candle from his light, he nodded good night and continued down the hall to Mr. Lockhart's room. I noted with relief that it was the opposite direction from where Audra's room was located. And yet there was something itching at the back of my mind that made me watch him until he vanished around the corner.

I shut the door behind me and placed the candle on the mantel. My attention was drawn to the painting of the schooner. This time I was able to make out a shark fin in the waves, inches from a drowning sailor. I shook off an annoying shiver, then changed into my borrowed nightdress and pulled the covers up to my chin and waited. The house creaked and groaned outside my door as it settled for the night.

ECHOING UP FROM the library, I heard the gong of the grandfather clock toll twelve times, surely a safe time to prowl the dark corridors. I pulled on a dressing gown, tied the sash tightly around my waist, then took a single candle and locked the door behind me. Padding down the hallway, I turned the corner and found the alcove with the cherub, just as Flora had told me.

I took my own room's key and slid it into the lock. There was resistance. I pulled it out and tried once more, but it would not fit. Deflated, I returned to my room.

I shouldn't have been surprised. Why would my key open the door to Audra's bedroom? And that was when I realized what had stood out at dinner. When Dr. Barnaby was speaking about the engagement, he had said "Audra," like Mr. Pemberton did, not "Lady Audra," as did everyone else.

I blew out the candle and tucked into bed, falling asleep almost immediately.

When I next woke, my heart was smashing against my ribs, and I was covered in a clammy sweat. Someone gripped my shoulders. I opened my eyes and saw Mr. Pemberton looking down at me, his face contorted in terror.

CHAPTER TWENTY-ONE

There was never a time when I didn't realize what my mother did for a living. My earliest memories were of cutting candle wicks and playing with the ghost book. While other children did sums on their slates at school, I practised cursive messages from the dead at home. I spent hours copying text from *The Hunchback of Notre Dame*.

I was seven years old and skinny as a lamppost. My black curls were kept under control with thick braids Maman's fingers nimbly weaved. We arrived at a beautiful house so huge our little home could fit several times over. I carried her bag, holding it high in front of my chest.

The servant nodded and took us to a room with heavy drapes and ornate furniture that looked uncomfortable. Even though the fireplace was lit, I felt a draft on the back of my neck. I moved one step to the side, but the coldness followed me.

Maman set her table, placing the candles at each chair, and then laid the ghost book in the middle. She spoke in simple sentences, instructing the family.

I remained off to the side. I was the mysterious element in Maman's séance. The women, especially, snuck glances my way while playing with their necklaces or twirling their rings. They regarded me with equal parts unbridled curiosity and tempered voyeurism. A child at a séance? How ghoulishly unexpected and thrilling.

I knew exactly what would happen next. Maman would summon the ghost of the house! The very one whose absence had left holes in their hearts. At first, the family would be afraid, squeezing their eyes shut and whimpering. But magically, Maman's skill and rapport with the spirit would make speaking with the dead seem like the most natural thing in the world.

"Of course they miss you," she said to the ceiling.

Then she closed her eyes and said, "I can feel so much love from this spirit." Next, she addressed the family. "He watches over you from above."

I held my breath as she took the ghost book and slowly opened it, showing them a message where there was only a blank page before.

My love surrounds you every day.

I bit the inside of my cheek to stay quiet. Maman made me work on the letters over and over until it was to her satisfaction.

An airy celebration replaced the heaviness in the room. Maman comforted those who were grieving. I saw it every time we came to these houses that smelled of flowers and clean floors. When Maman and Mrs. Rinaldo had worked as fortune-tellers, they only attracted those who were burdened financially, desperate for a hint of encouragement or hope. The idle rich lived in the present and had no interest in someone confirming the fate of their future.

But being a spiritualist gave me access to the world of affluence. Death, unlike poverty, visited every family. And when the rich confronted death, they did so with Maman easing their conscience.

She came into the fold of pain and left the room the recipient of gratitude. It ended with tears and hugs, and an envelope of money pressed into her palm.

No one hugged me, but I didn't mind. It was Maman's arm around my shoulders I needed to feel. That was the sign that everything had gone well, that we'd done a good job.

Maman said, "Grief is heavy; it pulls the soul down. That's why the house feels like it can breathe again after we've done a séance." Her French accent blended her words unlike any other adult I'd ever heard. She was magical to me, like a queen of spirits.

Afterward, she praised me for doing my part so well. "You're my lucky charm," she said, kissing the top of my head. "The ghosts all like you."

I spun around with the heavy bag, but lost my footing and tripped onto the cobblestones, twisting my ankle. There was a scream of horses. My foot felt like it had blown up. My mother's face was over mine in an instant, pulling me to her chest. The bag lay open on the cobblestones. I worried the ghost book was ruined.

Maman held me close, murmuring into my braids. When it was obvious I wasn't dead, but had only suffered a broken ankle, I joked that if the horse had run me over, I'd be her little ghost. I would haunt her forever and write silly messages in her ghost book, making the people at her séances laugh too.

"You know it's all fake, *oui, ma petite chérie*? Once you die, that's it; you're never again."

It was the first time my mother ever spoke of death with a sombre face and such a definite ending. And even though I knew of the tricks my mother did at her séances, a part of me believed we were shining the light on something that was already there, but too shy to show itself.

But now the truth was in front of me. I saw the cruelty of how we pretended for those people. We played off their fear—like the fear etched in my mother's face when the horse trampled toward me.

A seed of doubt was planted in me that day. It would continue to grow and spread its roots through my heart and consciousness for years. One day it would burst with an anger so vile and unforgiving another accident would prove how definitive death was, giving Maman the last and fatal word.

And making me a murderer.

CHAPTER TWENTY-TWO

iss Timmons!" Mr. Pemberton gave my shoulders a quick squeeze. "Can you hear me?" His tone was urgent.

"Yes," I said weakly. I blinked a few times, trying to focus. I was sitting at the top of a small flight of stairs that led down to an archway. It was a part of Somerset I hadn't explored yet. A chamber candle placed nearby, flickered its light on the scene.

He released his grip but stayed crouched beside me. He was still dressed in his dinner shirt from earlier, but a few of the top buttons were open and the jacket was gone.

"I was on my way to my room when I saw you standing at the top of the stairs," he said. "You didn't respond when I called your name. You stepped out and would have fallen down the entire flight, I'm sure."

"What stopped me?" I asked, putting a hand to my head, feeling the remnants of a headache. I most definitely had been sleep-walking.

"I did."

There were papers strewn across the floor behind us, as if dropped in haste.

"Can you stand?" he asked.

I nodded. His hand cupped my elbow and we rose together. "I should fetch Barnaby," he said.

"No, I'm fine. I sometimes sleepwalk." I realized I was only in my nightdress, but my head was spinning too much to muster a blush. "I'll make my way back to my room. Kindly point me in the right direction."

Mr. Pemberton shook his head and said, "You should sit and have something to drink. My room is closer. Here, hold on to the railing." He left me and then gathered the papers into a bundle and tucked them under his arm. Returning to my side, he held out his elbow.

"This isn't necessary," I said, sounding rather feeble as I reached for his arm.

"I beg to differ, Miss Timmons. I'd hate to cancel the séance because you tumbled to your doom."

I let out a dry chuckle, even though I could tell he was completely serious. We made our way through the archway and down a dark hall. He opened the door at the end and led me into a room that looked more like an elegant apartment.

The walls were covered in blue silk with a silver design. We padded across thick carpet to a substantially cushioned chair in front of the fireplace. A pile of glowing embers in the grate still emitted a bit of heat. I stretched my bare frozen feet closer. How long had I been wandering Somerset? Through a gap in the tasseled curtains, I saw the sky was still dark.

Mr. Pemberton went to a desk in front of the largest window. He pushed aside a stack of books and placed the bundle of papers there. "Is that the package from London?" I asked. "Have you been studying it all night?" What would have occupied him all this time? Information about Audra?

Wordlessly, he moved across the room to a small table and chairs. He lit more candles, and I saw a covered tray and small pitcher sitting there. I wondered how often he dined here by himself. "Yes," he said. "But I wouldn't call it studying. The contents require deciphering rather than memorization."

He filled a crystal glass and brought it to me. A green blanket was draped over the footstool, and I took it to pull around my shoulders, now more conscious of the fact that I was without my dressing gown. I took the wine and mumbled a thank-you, suspecting that he was being vague intentionally. I took a small sip, noting the bitterness.

He returned with a plate of what I recognized as the supper I'd enjoyed with Dr. Barnaby and set it on his lap. As he cut into his meat, the clinking of cutlery was the only sound that filled the room. I squirmed in the chair, feeling self-conscious to be in such an intimate setting with him. I tipped back the glass for a second sampling.

"The servants have access to your room?" I asked, nodding to the tray. I thought of Mrs. Donovan's large key ring. "You don't lock your door?"

He pressed his lips together. "The appearance of trust is just as important as trust itself. That's why the staff must see us together each day leading up to the séance. I'll pretend to be reluctant, of course, but you'll eventually earn my confidence. Therefore, when Audra's spirit points to the target, no one will ever imagine we orchestrated it from the beginning."

"Least of all Mr. Lockhart," I prompted. "How much do you trust him?"

The fork and knife paused. Mr. Pemberton's expression grew thoughtful. "I have no reason not to trust him. For his part, he has every confidence that your séance will be a success. He's also expressed a protectiveness for you. He's been staying at Somerset regularly for the last six months, but he made it clear he'd be available to you this week and will be staying here until the séance is completed. It's rather endearing, I think."

"Quite," I replied, thinking Mr. Lockhart probably wanted to keep a close watch on me considering he'd freed me on bail. Still, the information was useful. Mr. Pemberton considered the elderly solicitor an honest and compassionate man. I waited, but he didn't mention the state of his health, which reaffirmed my suspicions that he was unaware of Mr. Lockhart's fatal diagnosis. Could there have been a reasonable explanation for what Mr. Lockhart had said in the greenhouse earlier?

"And Mr. Sutterly?" I asked.

Mr. Pemberton's eyes darkened. "I have no reason not to trust him either. However, more important, I have no reason *to* trust him."

"It sounds like you already know who I should target."

"I understand you have gimmicks and methods for reading people, or rather by listening to what they don't say—but don't let my bias cloud your instinct."

I was momentarily surprised that he remembered what I'd said earlier.

"Still," he continued. "It would be best to update me if you discover any news you think might be helpful in laying our trap. You have the skills and unclouded judgment, and I have the knowledge of the household."

"Agreed," I said. "Success is more likely if we collaborate."

Together we'd make quick work of this. But the more I thought about William as the target, the more concerned I became. I was relying on fear as much as guilt to motivate someone into confessing. And William did not strike me as the kind of person who scared easily.

As Mr. Pemberton continued with his meal, I took in the rest of the suite. A canopy bed sat on the other side of the room, flanked by two walnut armoires. Several tall shelves were filled with books. Above the fireplace hung a gilded mirror. A clock was placed exactly in the middle of the mantel, its soft ticking soothing the silence. The time was two thirty. I wondered how long I had been wandering.

The room was refined, but with a definite masculine quality. Every painting on the walls was of either pastures or horses. One smaller frame caught my attention. It was a portrait of a beautiful young woman on horseback. A beautiful woman who was not Audra.

My attention slid back to Mr. Pemberton. "Thank you for allowing me to have a key to my room," I said. "I don't have anything of value, but I want to ensure no one but myself has access to my props."

"It was a reasonable request," he said, not looking up from his plate.

"Do you think it might be possible for me to see Lady Audra's room? It would contribute to the atmosphere if I had something personal of hers to place on the table, something small."

He chewed slowly, like he was considering how to answer. "Yes," he finally said. "I'll ask Mrs. Donovan for the key. It might be beneficial for us to go through her room together."

I examined the design on the rug, worried the excitement would show on my face. I wasn't bothered about having Mr. Pemberton with me when I unlocked her door; I'd deal with that when the time came.

After taking the last bite, Mr. Pemberton placed the empty plate on the floor. "Sleepwalking," he said, leaning back in his chair. "Is this affliction a regular occurrence?"

I took a generous swallow of wine, purposely delaying my answer. The tartness on my tongue was followed by a smooth warmth in my stomach. "It hasn't happened for a number of months," I replied, trying to keep my voice steady.

"What brings it on?"

Guilt. "Stress," I said. "And perhaps sleeping in a new place."

He tilted his head. "Do you think the séance will be too stressful for you?"

"No more than being sent to jail."

He made a sound at the back of his throat, then retrieved the pitcher and refilled my glass. I realized I was drinking the wine that was intended for his supper. It seemed an unlikely gesture of kindness. He settled back into the chair and stared at the last few coals in the fireplace. "How long will it take you to prepare the library?" he asked. There was a curious tenor to his voice.

"A day," I answered, relieved for the change of topic. "I'd like to replace the painting of the grandfather with Lady Audra's portrait from the Gallery Hall. That way, her image can watch over us during the séance." I sipped my wine. "No? You look like you don't approve."

"It's a fair idea," he said, continuing to stare into the fire.

I sneaked another glance at the picture of the unknown woman on the horse. Perhaps someone he had to leave behind? "Lady Audra's portrait is very beautiful," I prodded. "Mr. Lockhart said she was even more so in life."

Mr. Pemberton turned and studied me with his unwavering blue eyes. There was a weight to his stare, a warning. I waited to see if he'd agree with me. I remembered what Dr. Barnaby had said about the pair making such a handsome couple.

"Yes, she was," he answered.

It was the first notion of regret I'd sensed from him. "I'm sorry," I said. I finished the last of my wine. "I'm quite recovered now. Thank you for the assistance." Still wearing the green blanket like a shawl, I began to take my leave.

He stood and followed me to the door. The lamp he held accented the tired darkness under his eyes. I wondered again about the paperwork on the desk and what could have demanded so much of his attention this evening. "I'll escort you back to your room," he said. "After midnight, Somerset takes on a life of its own."

"I assure you, I'll be safe." I rolled my eyes to the corniced ceiling. "As a seasoned spiritualist, I'm familiar with the unseen pulse of a household, especially one that has seen such tragedy over the years."

He paused at the doorway, partially blocking my way. I noticed a key poking out from the inside of the lock. "Perhaps I want to make sure you don't return to the kitchen to steal more silver."

As usual, Mr. Pemberton kept the lamp between us as we journeyed back to my room, which I was soon to discover was in the opposite wing of Somerset. I found it curious. Was there a reason he chose to be so far from Audra's chambers?

We finally reached a familiar hallway. I peeked over the railing into the blackness below, unable to see the beautiful Persian rugs.

My door was open. Not surprising considering I'd left in a trance. Mr. Pemberton stood at the threshold while I lit one of my candles from his lamp. A quick inspection showed everything was still in its place. I made a mental note to check my props in the morning, especially the ghost book.

"Thank you for seeing me back," I said, too tired to disguise the sarcasm in my voice. "Your silver candlesticks are safe for another day."

He frowned. "I'm afraid my wit wasn't as apparent as I intended. I only wanted to ensure your safe return. Sleepwalking is a dangerous affliction, it seems."

"No need to explain, my lord. I should be grateful for the escort, and the earlier rescue. If I'd been injured, I'd be useless to you."

A glimpse of disappointment graced his features. "Do you think I would only be concerned for myself if you were hurt?" He studied my face so intently I was taken aback by his interest.

Why would he even be concerned about my thoughts of him? Finally, I said, "What other opinion should I have?"

His posture caved. "Mr. Lockhart isn't exactly misguided in his quest to offer me peace through your assistance," he said tiredly. "I should have shown Audra more attention. If I hadn't been so preoccupied with the grounds and the title, I would have seen what she was going through."

I could hear the heavy burden of regret in his words.

"I feel responsible for her death, Miss Timmons, and the only way I can atone for this neglect is to find out what happened that night. I'm not so much looking for someone to arrest, but someone who knows the truth of her last hours on earth. She deserves more than the story we've all assumed."

The heartfelt confession gave him a softer edge, making him seem more honorable.

"I'll do my best," I answered. I had no choice, of course; he was blackmailing me, after all.

He tapped the doorknob. "I suggest you use your room key to secure the door from the inside to prevent any more nocturnal adventures. I know I sleep better when I do." He nodded good night, then turned to leave.

"I thought you didn't lock your door."

He looked over his shoulder at me. "Only once I've settled for the night. Somerset has a way of putting people at unease—even seasoned spiritualists."

I WOKE TO sunlight streaming through the window. The blanket from Mr. Pemberton's room was still tucked around me. I was more than grateful for the change in weather. Dr. Barnaby was right. Grief clung to this house, as penetrating as the cold outside.

There was a knock, followed by Flora's voice, pleasant but drowsy.

I kept the blanket over my shoulders as I unlocked the door.

Flora came in, laden with a pitcher of steaming water in one hand, and an armload of kindling in the other. "Sorry, Jenny, I meant to leave the extra wood to stoke the fire last night, but I couldn't unlock the door while you were at dinner."

She paused, probably hoping for an explanation, but I stayed quiet. I wasn't ready to tell her my suspicions. I reasoned a little mystery would only add to my persona.

As Flora busied with the fire, I poured some water from the pitcher into the basin and washed my face. "You must know most of the rooms at Somerset well," I said.

"Aye, most of 'em. Have ya decided where to do the séance?"

"Not quite," I lied. "But I have been exploring the house. There is a portrait of a beautiful woman with a horse in Mr. Pemberton's sitting room. Do you know who she is?"

Flora almost tipped the bucket of soot. "No." She kept her chin dipped down. "I don't go into his room so much."

Flora's discomfort was obvious, but I didn't press her on the subject. She was a sensitive creature, and I had to ensure she felt comfortable with me. People tell their secrets more easily when they trust you.

I went to the wardrobe full of dresses, once again confronted with the challenge of trying to disguise myself as a lady.

"Breakfast is waiting for you downstairs," she said, still on her knees. "I believe Mr. Lockhart is already there."

"Alone?"

"Aye."

I pulled out a light blue sleeve, mesmerized by the detailed embroidery. It was difficult to reconcile the kind and generous man who bought these dresses to the lying lawyer now tucking into his eggs one floor below.

Flora wiped her hands on her apron, leaving sooty fingerprints. She groaned tiredly. "Mrs. Donovan will have a fit if she sees me like this in the halls, but I'll just have to tell her I couldn't have Miss Timmons gettin' dressed in a cold room." She brightened when she saw the blue dress in my hands.

"That was one of my favourites," she said adoringly.

"Your favourites?" I asked. "I thought they only delivered these yesterday. Did you help Mrs. Donovan unpack them?"

An expression of woeful regret pulled down the edges of her mouth. Flora looked like she wanted to swallow her words. "I suppose you're right, Jenny, it only *looks* very similar to one that hung in Lady Audra's closet."

The blood rose to my cheeks. I turned back to the armoire, partly to hide my embarrassment. But it made complete sense since they appeared so quickly after my arrival. How could I have believed otherwise? What else was I missing? I stepped aside to allow Flora a closer inspection of the garments. "Are these her dresses?" I asked. "Please tell me the truth."

"I know they were in her collection, but I don't remember her wearing any of these," she said, pointing out several dresses, the black-and-red one among them. "No matter, Jenny. You'll look nice in any of 'em."

I put a hand to my stomach, replaying how foolish I must have appeared wearing Audra's dress last night. No wonder Mr. Pemberton backed away from me when I opened my door. I had thought it was my lack of style, but I'd shocked him by wearing his dead bride's clothing.

"Here," Flora said, taking the blue dress and laying it down on the bed. "We can change it up a bit, make it simple, see? These long sleeves come off like so, leaving the puff at the shoulder. And you can pull on this shawl. Trust me, men don't notice dresses; they only want to see them on the floor."

I gave her a playful look. "And you know a lot about men?" I poked her.

She blushed and busied herself reworking the dress. When I put it on and faced the long mirror on the wardrobe, I saw that she was right. It looked different enough, and more important, it suited me. "Thank you, Flora," I said. "I'd be hopeless without you."

She rolled her eyes, but I could see the smile she was fighting. She then sat me in front of the vanity and began to gather my hair. "Mrs. Donovan was going to take care of you, but I told her I'm just as good as any of those trained lady's maids." I watched her reflection in the mirror as she worked. A lump rose in my throat. No one had touched my hair since Maman.

Flora gave me a perfectly acceptable hairdo with the few pins I had. "I must fetch some more pins for your dinner tonight, Jenny," she said. "But I have to say your curls are doing half the work themselves. I wish I had curls like this, or at least just one. Will you give me just one? I'll tuck it under my bonnet and let it drop right in the middle of my forehead."

She went to the fireplace and picked up the bucket of soot. "Enjoy breakfast. If you need anything, I'll be in the kitchen." Then her face fell. "Are you okay? Jenny? You look like you've seen a ghost." Her eyes grew wide. "Is it Maisie?"

"No," I replied, except I wasn't looking at Flora. I was looking at the perfectly straight picture above the mantel—the perfectly straight picture that was upside down.

CHAPTER TWENTY-THREE

Lady Audra Linwood
Diary Entry
Somerset Park, January 19, 1852

Dearest,

I finally met him.

I wore the yellow gown with the pearl buttons. Mrs. Donovan styled my hair in a series of loose waves to accent my heart-shaped face, then pinned the chignon at the nape of my neck. She suggested I wear the tiara, so I would twinkle in the candlelight.

He is handsome, very much so. Eyes like the sky and a wave of blond hair that seems spun of gold. I'm jealous of his natural beauty. And he has all the manners and grace one would expect, but there is a distance to him I find unnerving. He is cordial but cold. I can barely get a smile out of him.

Father is enamored. And I will give Mr. Pemberton accolades for slowing his pace to match Father's as we made our way through the Gallery Hall. Soon, though, Father tired and Bramwell had to come with his wheelchair. He gave us permission to walk to the *greenhouse without a chaperone. The look on Mrs. Donovan's face almost made me burst!*

We continued along the garden path. I'm ashamed to say I was jittery and dull-sounding all at once. I hardly recognized myself. I, who have been in society for two years, was tongued-tied like a kitchen maid in front of this young man from the north. I am surprised by how proud he seems. I know for certain that although Mr. Pemberton is a distant cousin, he is hardly in our rank of society.

He was mostly silent while I rattled off every topic I could think of. It relieved me when we reached the greenhouse, as it is one of my favourite places. I told him so and gave him a tour, stopping to mention certain plants along the walkway. His gaze lacked the earnest attention I was hoping for.

It is difficult not to compare him with William. I've never had to work for his attention. I confess, I wonder what an unchaperoned trip to the greenhouse would be like for William and me.

We came to the statue in the fountain, and perhaps I was distracted by thoughts of forbidden passion, but before I could stop, I told him the story behind the crying angel. My cheeks burned as I mentioned her lost love and how she threw herself into the sea to be with him. I dared myself to look him in the eye, to gauge what he was feeling. Surely, being in a warm room surrounded by lush plants with the woman you may possibly marry—surely I should have seen a spark of something.

But he turned away from the statue and peered out the window toward the forest, quite disinterested. I coughed but still could not rouse his attention. I even considered fainting, if only so he would acknowledge my presence.

Finally, I told Mr. Pemberton that if he wished to see the rest of the grounds, the stable would be the best option, as touring the property on horseback is most satisfying. In an instant, his face lit up like the sun itself.

I insisted he go to the stables at once, as I could see myself back to the house. With another one of his curt nods, he was off.

It pleases me that I could give him something he is fond of. I hope it will be enough to secure the match. I can put my own happiness aside if it means keeping my home. As unromantic as it seems, I cannot lose my head in fanciful daydreams of love. I must think of the future of Somerset.

CHAPTER TWENTY-FOUR

I made my way to breakfast on shaking legs. I was going to confront Mr. Lockhart about the greenhouse, but my attention was partly back in my room. Even though I'd left the door open, the thought of someone going into my room and flipping the picture upside down was bizarre enough to bother me more than any outright threat.

It was heavy to be sure. Even with Flora's help, I couldn't move it back into place. When I had brought her attention to it, she'd grown pale and trembled. I tried to soothe her fear by saying the spirits of the house like to let me know they're close by, and that the flipped picture was a favourable sign for the séance. She couldn't get out of the room fast enough, promising to have the footmen fix it later. At least the stunt added to the mystique Mr. Pemberton and I were hoping to achieve.

Mr. Pemberton.

He was also occupying my thoughts. There was more to him than the man I'd met in the kitchen that first night. He seemed more devoted to Audra's memory than the bride herself. And who was the young woman in the portrait in his room? Curious, indeed.

I pulled the shawl tighter as I walked into the dining room. The fireplace was radiating a lovely heat, and the sideboard was laden with delectable-smelling food. Mr. Lockhart was partially hidden behind his newspaper. Harry was serving again and held out my chair. I steeled myself, trying to drum up courage.

"Good morning," Mr. Lockhart said, putting down his paper. The darkness under his eyes was apparent, and his sunken cheeks seemed more pronounced today. "I'm sorry I missed dining with you last evening. Though Dr. Barnaby said he was delighted to make your acquaintance."

"He was an agreeable dinner companion," I said. Harry poured my coffee. I helped myself to a plate of eggs and toast, but purely for show. My stomach was jittery with nerves. A silver tray with an array of preserves sparkled in the sunlight. I noticed Mr. Lockhart's plate was almost empty.

"Have you been eating alone?" I asked, putting a dollop of raspberry jam on my plate.

Harry arrived with a platter of sausage, and I nodded. I added cream and two sugar lumps to my coffee and stirred it with the tiny silver spoon.

"Mr. Pemberton was here earlier," Mr. Lockhart answered. "He rises with the sun. I suppose that's a difficult habit to break." He kept the newspaper flat but continued to read, one wrinkled finger moving along the words.

I took a small bite of sausage and organized my thoughts. If I threatened to tell Mr. Pemberton what I'd overheard, perhaps I could gain some leverage. Mr. Lockhart and I could strike a deal, one that would allow me to leave Somerset with enough money to settle far out of the reach of Constable Rigby's noose. I swallowed a mouthful of coffee, ready to confront him.

"I explored some of the grounds yesterday," I said.

"How lovely," Mr. Lockhart replied. "I believe fresh air is the cure for almost everything." As if on cue, he started coughing and put a white handkerchief to his mouth. "My apologies," he said, patting his lips. He tucked away the handkerchief in the breast pocket of his jacket. Harry poured more steaming coffee into his cup. "According to Dr. Barnaby, this is supposedly helpful to open up the lungs." He gave a half-hearted smile as he took a sip. "I appreciate a treatment so easily added to my daily routine."

I found it odd that he hadn't coughed in the greenhouse. Still, I had to be wary. Impending death can make even the most sensible man desperate. And sometimes desperation leads to danger.

"Tell me," he said, "have you enjoyed touring the property? Somerset's land is vast. To see it all, you'd need to travel on horseback. Do you ride?"

I ignored his question. "I went to the greenhouse," I said, observing him. The only shift in his expression was a slight twitch of his eye. "Such a warm and lovely place. No wonder I ended up sharing it unexpectedly."

Harry began to clear away the dishes. I grew impatient for him to leave, but I was also curious to see how Mr. Lockhart might react in front of the footman.

I continued, "You and Mr. Sutterly seemed to be having the most interesting discussion." My heart was in my throat, but I kept staring at him.

He was still as stone. For a moment I thought he'd died in front of my eyes, but then he excused Harry.

He most definitely had something to hide.

As soon as Harry was gone, Mr. Lockhart's eyebrows came together. "How much did you overhear?" he asked.

I told him every word. There was no point in holding back.

"I'm sorry you had to hear that," he replied.

Stunned at his easy admittance of the truth, I said, "You knew who I was before we met."

Mr. Lockhart pushed the paper aside. "I'd been considering hiring a spiritualist for Mr. Pemberton for some time and made discreet enquiries. Naturally, I heard of you, but you went by so many different names that you were impossible to track down." His words were calm, but heavy with concentration. "Our paths crossing at the police station was purely circumstantial. When I realized who you were, I saw an opportunity I could not ignore." He put a hand to his chest. "Please, you must believe me."

"That's not what it sounded like when you spoke with Mr. Sutterly. And what were you searching Audra's room for?"

Mr. Lockhart sighed. "Mr. Sutterly's situation is unique. A stipulation in Lord Chadwick's will allows him to remain at Somerset, and he was granted a small living. However, he has told me that he discovered the present Lord Chadwick, Mr. Pemberton, is not the actual heir to the estate. He provided proof to Lady Audra on the eve of her wedding, thinking, well, rather hoping that she'd call off the nuptials." His face clouded over. "But, of course, none of us know what happened."

"And what is this proof?"

"He won't say, but there can't be any truth to his story. I've been this family's solicitor for decades, well before Lady Audra was born, and my father before me. If there were any secret regarding Somerset's rightful heir, I would know."

"Is Mr. Pemberton aware?"

"If there was even the slightest chance it could be true, I wouldn't have hesitated to bring it to his attention. However, he and Mr. Sutterly have always been at odds, and since Lady Audra's death, my lord has been consumed with revenge. I feel this information wouldn't serve any purpose but to create further hate in this house. He'd have Mr. Sutterly locked behind bars, or worse, seek justice himself." Then he pinned me with an uncharacteristically fierce stare. "I brought you here to help this family heal, not rip it apart."

It appeared Mr. Lockhart was not a candidate for blackmail. But I wasn't finished yet. "Why did Mr. Sutterly say she'd still be alive if not for you?" I asked.

"He blames me for locating Mr. Pemberton. I suspect he even believes I'm part of a grand scheme to hide the true heir. He never accepted Mr. Pemberton as Lord Chadwick—especially now that he's considering selling off parts of the estate."

As I sat there listening to him, something struck me as peculiar, but I couldn't put my finger on it. "And nothing was ever found," I said, "even though Lady Audra's room was searched?"

"It was turned upside down when she went missing. And still they do not understand how she left without being noticed." He took a sip of coffee.

I let that sink in. The window was locked, and Mrs. Donovan claimed to be outside her door all night long. "How did Mr. Sutterly enter her room that night?"

"Mrs. Donovan must have let him in. She would have kept it secret, especially after Lady Audra's body washed onto shore." He paled considerably and his eyes glistened. The handkerchief came out again to pat his tears.

I waited, listening to the sound of logs crumbling in the fire. Still, there was one last item that didn't make sense. "You told him he wouldn't have to worry about Mr. Pemberton once the séance was over. Why?"

"To keep him calm by saying what he needs to hear, of course. There is no proof to disclaim Mr. Pemberton as Lord Chadwick,

Miss Timmons," he said, tired and dismissive. "And I'd be lying if I didn't say I sensed Mr. Sutterly has an unhealthy preoccupation with Lady Audra's death. I'm only hoping to distract him until you perform the séance. In fact, your attempt to bring peace will be as much for him as it is for my lord."

I did my best to ignore the usual jab of guilt each time Mr. Lockhart mentioned my séance of reassurance.

We left the room together, walking in silence until we entered the Gallery Hall.

"Are you still going to represent me in court?" I asked, straightforward.

He gasped. "My dear girl, of course I will." He touched the tip of his beard and regarded me with an intense expression. "I'm aging exponentially at the moment, but I assure you, I have decades of experience, and I promise you justice."

His tone was steeped in conviction, and I finally felt reassured that he was an ally in this house. Mr. Lockhart had never treated me like a charity case. But that momentary relief was quickly snuffed out. I still needed to pinpoint a target in less than a week, or Mr. Pemberton would reveal my attempt at petty thievery and turn me over to the parish constable.

"Do you not suspect that Mr. Sutterly is responsible for Audra's disappearance?" I asked. "He admits he entered her room that night."

"It is plausible," he replied. "I admit the thought occurred to me in those first horrific weeks following her disappearance." He slowed his pace, leaning against his cane. "But as the shock of the ordeal diminished, I had to accept that Lady Audra saw to her own fate that night. Mr. Sutterly is not talented enough an actor to keep the charade going this long."

We made our way to the long windows to take in the expansive view. I spotted the pathway to the stables in the glade, disappearing into the woods. "Let me assure you," he continued. "I would not bring you here if I had the slightest inclination that I was putting you in a precarious situation."

"You plucked me from jail and hired me to fool your lord that his fiancée's spirit is at peace. This is precarious indeed, Mr. Lockhart."

He chuckled softly. "I promise you will have your defense for the police. Won't it be nice to earn your freedom?"

Living without Constable Rigby breathing down my neck would be pleasant. But I would never be free from my guilt.

We entered the foyer and stopped dead in our tracks. Mr. Pemberton was coming in through the main door in his riding attire. He handed his hat and gloves off to Bramwell. "Perfect timing, Miss Timmons," he said. "I believe you promised me a list of items you require for the upcoming session."

His cheeks were rosy from the recent exercise, and his tall, straight posture was in opposition to my exhausted stance after last night's escapades.

Mr. Lockhart gave me an encouraging smile, probably pleased by the notion that his lord was warming up to the idea of the séance. "Good luck," he whispered to me.

Full of conflicting notions, I followed Mr. Pemberton to his study. I had been certain that I'd have my answers after confronting Mr. Lockhart, but now I was more confused than ever. I also noted, most grievously, that it was becoming increasingly difficult to deny Mr. Lockhart his dying request. He was so kind to me. I began to consider if I could somehow satisfy both him and Mr. Pemberton at my séance, thereby keeping my end of the deal to both men.

Despite the long curtains being pulled open, looking out over a cloudless sky, the study remained dark and gloomy. Mr. Pemberton closed the door behind me.

"I haven't made a list yet," I started. "I've brought most of my props with me."

He put up a hand. "That was a lie for the benefit of Mr. Lockhart. Early this morning, I went to Mrs. Donovan for the key to Audra's room, but after searching the key ring twice and the cupboard in Bramwell's office, she declared it was missing. She's quite upset and assured me she had it in her possession the day before you arrived."

I pictured her lurking about in the darkness, spying on me last night as I tried my key in Audra's door. Perhaps Flora had mentioned to the other staff that I had requested access. I had a strong notion that she knew exactly where the key was, but was lying to Mr. Pemberton. "Is she implying that I stole it? How convenient."

He ran a hand through his golden hair and sat down behind his desk. He opened a drawer, grumbled under his breath, then slammed it quickly. "It's extremely maddening, to be honest. I have to rely on Mrs. Donovan to keep the rest of the staff in place, but her loyalty is to Somerset and those already established within its walls—not me."

It appeared Mr. Pemberton felt like an outsider, even in his own home. I offered, "I believe this is encouraging for the séance. If someone has stolen the key to Lady Audra's room, that means someone is afraid the truth will be exposed. Fear is an accurate indicator of guilt."

He lifted his gaze to meet mine with surprised gratitude. "Thank you for saying that," he said.

I was struck by his affable temper. There was a curious sense of understanding about him that was completely lacking the first few times we spoke. What had changed?

"I hope you're right," he continued. "Even so, what's the purpose of being Earl of Chadwick if a simple key is beyond my reach?" It was a complaint, but he sounded almost helpless.

"Mr. Lockhart mentioned that you are considering selling some of the land."

"I've been making enquiries, yes." He took out a paper and dipped his quill. "How many guests do you intend to have for the séance?" he asked, swiftly changing the topic. "Do we have any ideas whom to target yet?"

"It's unclear at this time," I answered. Although Mrs. Donovan may have just earned herself a chair. "Is that a difficult decision?" I pressed. "To break up Somerset? It's your home, now, isn't it?" I couldn't imagine anyone giving up such a place, where there was always plenty to eat and a soft bed to sleep in.

He looked up from the paper. "This will never be my home."

"Oh." I had nothing to relate; the notion of a home had never been a reality for me. The only constant in my life had been Maman. "Still, you have the means to go wherever you please. You can choose where to call home. That's rarer than you realize."

There was the hint of annoyance behind his words. "Because I'm wealthy?"

"Because you're a man."

He blinked, surprised, and then his expression grew thoughtful. He put down the quill and said, "I don't pretend to be blind to my advantages. I'm simply saying that Somerset, even in all its grandeur, can never be a place where I feel at ease."

I pictured the key, always on the inside of his door.

His voice took on a careful tone. "I do find it intriguing that you've chosen the library for the séance," he said. "The staff avoid that room primarily because of the portrait of Audra's grandfather. They're convinced that he haunts this estate. I believe they're correct. Maybe not in a spiritual way, but certainly through a legacy of fear."

The hair on my arms stood at attention. Why had he not mentioned this last night? "What do you know about him?"

"When I received the letter from Mr. Lockhart explaining that I was next in line for the title of Lord Chadwick, I was completely taken aback. I had never heard of Somerset Park. I was curious as to why my own father had never spoken of it, so I searched his office and found a trunk of his old correspondence. There were letters from Audra's father, from when they were younger, not yet twenty. And it was clear after reading them that my own father had visited this manor several times throughout his youth, but something happened on the last visit, and he never returned." He tapped his fingers against the desk in thought. "Somerset Park was built by Audra's great-grandfather. I've heard rumors of a fortune made in smuggling. Apparently, the caves along the shoreline are ideal for such activities."

"Like pirates?" I breathed. I couldn't deny my interest. It sounded like the sort of adventure I would read about in books. "What would they smuggle?"

"Rum, gold . . . people, even. Imagine Audra's grandfather, Lord Chadwick the third, as a young boy, growing up here. I wonder what he may have seen if his father was involved in that trade. He has a lasting reputation for being cruel. Perhaps there's a reason."

"This is very interesting." However, I knew men needed no reason to be cruel.

He rested his elbows on the arms of the chair and began to twirl the gold ring. "During that last visit, my father had been exploring and found something incriminating. I don't know the particulars, only what I can glean from their correspondence, but my father was so affected by the elder Lord Chadwick's reaction that he was too scared to return. Ever."

"What do you think he saw?"

"I can't imagine. My father, at least when I knew him, feared nothing. I don't believe in ghosts, Miss Timmons, but I believe cruel fathers can bear cruel sons."

I let that thought settle in my brain. "There is a difference between cruelty and evil, don't you think?"

"Evil is cruelty unchecked, when it's allowed to flourish."

I thought of Miss Crane and the men she allowed inside. "I agree," I said. I silently wondered what old horrible Lord Chadwick had hidden at Somerset. What could so unnerve a young man that he would never return here, or even mention the property to his own son? Mr. Pemberton was looking at me with a similar quizzical expression. For the smallest moment, it felt like we were on the same team, but I had to be careful. I applauded myself on accurately reading people, but this man was still such a mystery to me.

With a promise to do a mock séance for him in the next few days, I returned to my room.

A small package was in front of my door. True to her word, Flora had left a generous sample of hairpins. Most were plain and meant to be invisible in the hair, but some were jeweled and decorated with pearls.

Using my key, I opened the door and found the room as I had left it. I sat at the vanity with the package of pins, wondering if Flora might put the nicer ones in my hair tonight. Then I practically slapped myself!

If I could pick a handcuff, I could open a locked door. And now I had a box full of pins to use.

FOR LUNCH I ate nearly my weight in a selection of Mrs. Galloway's sandwiches and creamy potato leek soup. I had to make up for the breakfast I'd hardly touched. I intended to take a quick nap, but instead slept through the rest of the afternoon and woke with a raging headache. Flora was kind enough to give my regrets to Bramwell for dinner. As a result, the evening meal was brought to my room, where I dined on second and third helpings without having to dress up. Although I purposely limited myself to one glass of wine, needing to be sharp later. Even though Mr. Lockhart said Audra's room had been searched, there was an intangible pull I could not resist. And since the key had suddenly gone missing, I was motivated more than ever.

Again, I waited until late in the evening, making sure all were asleep. With a box of pins in my grip, I knelt in front of Audra's lock and gently coaxed one into the opening. I turned my head to the side, with my ear close to the lock, and concentrated on envisioning the inside of the mechanism in my mind. The hairpin advanced bit by bit. At once there was a pressure under my touch. Then the pin twisted on its own. I let go and watched, dumbstruck, as the doorknob turned by itself. There was a resounding click, and the door opened inward.

CHAPTER TWENTY-FIVE

Lady Audra Linwood
Diary Entry
Somerset Park, January 21, 1852

Dearest,

The tiara did not win him over.

I smiled and twinkled and laughed with all the pretend gaiety I
could muster, and yet Mr. Pemberton merely nodded across the
dining table in response to my efforts. I suppose he realizes that
he does not need to earn my favour in order to inherit Somerset
Park. It will be his as soon as Father . . . oh, I cannot even write
the words; it makes me ill to think of it.

He is lovely to look at, and I've found no hint of malice in his
manners or expression, but his apathy is worrisome. He knows
my situation. A smile or word of assurance would go far in easing
my fretful state.

Strange, isn't it? How someone like Mr. Pemberton can be closer
to the common folk and yet have rightful claim to Somerset Park.

And it is I, a full-blooded Linwood descendent, who must coax and win over this man.

Forgive me, Dearest. I suppose this is only my bruised pride talking. Mr. Pemberton can be forgiven for not dropping to his knee and proposing on the spot during our very first meeting. But unquestionably, the second time together, it would have been very much acceptable to speak of marriage.

William was absent during dinner. Part of me finds it admirable that he refuses to fawn over Mr. Pemberton as the rest of us do. Still, our marriage will secure William's future as well. I wish he would see that. I wish he wasn't hurting as much as I suspect.

After dinner, someone called out my name as I walked through the halls. I entered the library, but no one was there. I stared up at Grandfather's portrait above the fireplace. The staff say he haunts this room. Even in death they still fear him. Something admirable about that, actually.

I wonder what Grandfather would have done if he'd had a daughter instead of a son. I can't imagine him giving up Somerset. He may have been cruel, but he wouldn't have pinned his hopes on a stranger to save him. Of that I am certain.

The library grew cold. I turned to leave, but then I found William standing in the doorway, staring at me with a wounded look in his eyes. He asked me what I thought of Mr. Pemberton—if I still wanted to marry him, and if I was ready to be his wife, in all aspects.

My face burned with anger. I marched up to him and demanded to know why he had not joined us for dinner. Didn't he know

I was giving up any genuine happiness to save Somerset? How could he ask me something so intimate with such barbarity? Didn't he know how helpless I felt? I pounded my fist against his chest as tears ran down my cheeks.

He caught my hand and brought it to his lips. I did not pull away. He leaned close and whispered into my ear that we cannot fight fate.

The clock began to chime the hour. A reminder that we were running out of time. Wordlessly, I left and ran straight up the stairs to my room. As I write this, my heart is still racing. So much confusion, Dearest! But none of it matters, not really, especially when I'm so unsure of my own desires. I might as well wish for the moon. True love is not my destiny.

I thought Mr. Pemberton would be my destiny. But it seems he wants neither Somerset Park nor me.

CHAPTER TWENTY-SIX

I walked into the darkened room and was aware of two things at once: how cold it was and the powerful smell of liquor. The door slammed behind me. The only light was from the candle he held in his hand.

My heart eased back down my throat, and I found my voice. "Mr. Sutterly," I said. "What are you doing here?"

He let out an exasperated half laugh. "I could ask you the same question."

"I was hoping to borrow something of Lady Audra's to help connect me to her spirit," I said, knowing I should keep my lies consistent.

"You're in a place where you are not welcome and do not deserve to be." He backed away and then lit the candelabra on the bedside table. The bed was elaborately made up with decorative frills and pillows; it looked more like a dessert than a place to rest your head. One side of the bed had the vague imprint of a body.

"Is this your room now?" I asked, wondering what William was going to do now that he'd caught me trying to break the lock.

"It should be." He swayed on the spot. His tie was undone, and his jacket and vest were crumpled on the floor. "But no, I'm as much a trespasser tonight as you are, Miss Timmons." He let the "s" sound elongate like a hiss.

"It was you who stole the key from Mrs. Donovan," I said.

"Merely borrowed." He steadied himself, then went about the room, lighting the other candelabras.

I should have been prepared for the grandeur, but even knowing the scale of opulence at Somerset Park, my eyes grew large in amazement as Audra's bedroom emerged from the shadows. The elegant furniture was upholstered in fabric bursting with pastel floral patterns. The brightness and gaiety evoked the very essence of a summer garden. I was almost convinced I could smell roses.

The stately fireplace was three times the size of the one in my room and had a massive mirror over the mantel, reflecting the superfluity of the suite.

The room was large enough to have its own tiny library and sitting area. There was a table, perfect for serving tea and sweets. I imagined the many leisurely afternoons she must have spent here, reading and enjoying her soft lifestyle.

All of this for one person? I thought about the purse I'd kept hidden inside my thin mattress and how achingly long it had taken to amass enough to finally escape Miss Crane. And still, that pile of coins wouldn't have been enough to afford even one of the throw pillows on the settee.

She had so much, and I so little! But I was the one who was alive, at least for now.

Don't be foolish to envy the dead, Maman used to say. *If ghosts existed, they would say only one thing: let me live again.*

Even for the sad parts? I had asked.

Bien sûr, especially the sad parts. That's what the dead would crave, ma petite chérie, to feel again. But we know better.

William placed the candelabra on the small table beside a bottle and an empty glass. He poured himself a drink and turned to me. With his shirt unbuttoned, I could make out a faint red mark across his throat. "I see what you try to hide from everyone," he said. "What you really want."

A waft of stale wine hit me, but I kept his gaze. I detected his enjoyment at trying to scare me. "I only want to contact Lady Audra so I can share her message with her husband," I said.

William's face twisted into disgust. "He's not her husband. They were never married." He regarded me over the rim of his glass and asked, "Are you an orphan? There's an unloved look about you."

"I had a mother," I told him.

"Your overly appreciative attitude reeks of a simple upbringing. You wish you had this privileged life."

"To be alive is the only privilege I strive for," I said.

He ignored my answer as he poured himself another drink. What was he doing here at this hour? If he was hoping to search Audra's room again, then why did it look perfectly kept?

With a grunt, William slumped into the nearest chair, stretching his legs out straight and crossing his ankles. "I would not have expected such gumption from someone who raises the dead."

"I don't raise the dead," I said, watching him finish his drink. "I'm simply a conduit for something that already exists."

He refilled the glass, emptying the bottle this time. He was laborious in making sure he decanted each drop. I looked at the white-and-pink carpet and marvelled that it wasn't peppered with drops of red wine.

For an unexplainable moment, I imagined Audra lying here in a pool of blood. Her blond hair out of its pins and splayed around her head. Her tiara askew, her lifeless eyes staring up, wide open and accusing. The vision was sharp and took me by surprise. I moved closer to the mantel, putting more space between myself and William.

I picked up one of the candelabras and went to the bookshelves, searching for a heavy enough novel to throw at William if necessary. I was in a locked room with a man who, from every meeting I'd had with him, was full of bitter resentment. Mr. Lockhart had even admitted to believing William could have been responsible for Audra's disappearance.

There was a large portrait on the wall that must have been Audra's mother, Lady Chadwick. She was much younger here than in her picture in the Gallery Hall, closer to my age, I suspected. There was a definite family resemblance, especially the blond hair. However, instead of Audra's confident radiance, her mother had an unyielding hardness behind her soft features. I grew uncomfortable under her stare, as if she were ridiculing my poor posture. She posed grandly in a rose garden with a dog on her lap. Her lips were full but unsmiling. The artist had captured more empathy and life in the dog's deep brown eyes than in hers.

"You believe she still exists, then?" William asked. There was a slight slur to his words. But the collapse of his countenance led me to believe the grief was affecting his articulation as much as the wine. He leaned forward, elbows resting on his knees as the empty glass dangled from his fingertips.

"In spirit," I answered.

"Spirit," he whispered. A mournful grimace pulled at his young features, aging him before my eyes.

I needed to tread carefully. I wanted to bring up the eve of the wedding and ask him how he'd gotten into her room, but that would mean admitting my eavesdropping. I needed to be clever with my questions. "Why are you here?" I asked him again, sensing that if I kept him talking, he might divulge some of his secrets.

William put down the empty glass and went to the window. He pulled back the thick curtain, letting the moonlight spill in. "I ask myself that question every morning I wake and remember the love of my life is dead and I am not."

I nearly dropped the candelabra. Of all the things he could have told me, that was the least expected. It took a few heartbeats to find my voice. "Lady Audra?" I asked carefully.

He nodded.

I tried to make sense of what he'd just revealed. How was it possible? He was a ward of the family, and she was the lady of the estate. I studied him, trying to visualize Audra on his arm. There was too much desperation about his situation for him to be considered a suitable match for her. Even in appearance they were opposites. She was elegant and prim, where he was unmannered and rough around the edges. As much as I concentrated, I could not muster a believable image of them as a couple.

His breath made foggy shapes against the pane. "I grew up in the orphanage in Wrendale, until I was thirteen and began an apprenticeship with the blacksmith, Mr. Sutterly. He adopted me, but I was more of a worker than a son."

He faced me again, but this time there was a gentleness in his features. "Every night for the next two years I went to bed with muscles aching, my hands full of blisters from the hot irons. And then one day Mr. Sutterly left and never returned. He was headed here, to the stables at Somerset. The parish constable told me he was found beaten to death and left on the side of the road. Mrs. Donovan arrived shortly after, saying I was to be taken in by Lord Chadwick himself. I certainly had no grief over the blacksmith.

And who was I to turn down this chance at a better life. I thought I'd found heaven, Miss Timmons." His wistful expression melted. "Little did I know I was destined for hell."

Destined for hell? I glanced at the dog in the picture and raised my brows. "What happened?" My tongue was heavy with a thousand questions, but I thought it best to keep leading him with vague prompts.

He pushed himself off the windowsill. "Taking me on as a ward was not motivated out of kindness. Lord Chadwick had a plan, one that would take years to fulfill. And by the time he brought the entire scheme to its disastrous conclusion, both he and Audra were dead."

The flames of all the candles flickered in unison. "What was his plan?" I whispered.

"Audra could not inherit Somerset Park. He needed a son. He groomed me for years, preparing me for a lifestyle that becomes a Linwood. He planned to claim me as his rightful heir once he found the proof he needed."

All the air left the room at once. I struggled to take a breath, nearly dropping to my knees. The candelabra hit the floor, extinguishing the tiny flames. "Lord Chadwick was your father?" I choked out.

William walked toward me. "I had no idea until he confessed on his deathbed. And by that time Audra and I had been secretly in love for two years."

"And the proof?"

He shook his head, the epitome of a tragic figure. "Gone forever, it seems. Audra was the only other person who knew the truth."

I stood and put a hand on the mantel. As I absorbed these new facts, a theory began to piece itself together. All this time I imagined Audra had been in love with Mr. Pemberton. He was handsome and rich enough, and most important, he would inherit the title to Somerset. Rumors of a family curse aside, what could consume Audra with enough torturous misery that the only solution was to jump to her death to the rocks below?

But if she was secretly in love with William, the marriage may have seemed like a death sentence. And if that wasn't enough, discovering your true love was in fact your half sibling might have been too much to bear.

William's eyes became glassy. "Tell me, Miss Timmons, who would be happier now—a young blacksmith apprentice planning to one day run his own shop, maybe catch the eye of a pretty girl over the hymnal in church? Hmm? Or the broken man you see before you." He reached up and pulled down the open collar of his shirt so I could see the mark across his neck more clearly.

"Even after three months you can still see where the rope broke," he said. The darkness under his eyes and hollowed cheeks made him look old beyond his years. "I lost my birthright and my love all at once."

Maman would have called him the walking dead.

I swallowed, knowing my own close relationship with the noose. A sliver of pity prompted me to tell him the truth. "I'm sorry I disturbed you," I said. "I only came because I wanted to see her things."

He put a heavy hand on my shoulder. "I'll leave you to it, then. Please touch nothing." And with that, he nodded and closed the door behind him, leaving me alone in Audra's room.

CHAPTER TWENTY-SEVEN

O nce I recovered from William's revelation, I went over the entire room at my leisure to study all the small details. Unlike the library, there was not a speck of dust to be found. From the bookcases to the mantel, everything had been kept clean. However, personal items were still in place like an untouched display.

A pair of satin slippers were tucked under a chair. There was a handprint on the throw pillow that might have been hers. An embroidery loop lay on one of the settees. The floral design was half-finished, with the needle and thread still secured on the edge as if Audra had just stepped away and would return at any moment.

This wasn't a bedchamber; it was a tomb. A museum of treasures its owner would never enjoy again.

I put my attention on the bookcase. The titles were neatly arranged in alphabetical order—except for one on the bottom shelf whose spine jutted out. When I looked closer, I noticed the cover wouldn't close flatly. I opened it up and found a flower with cream-colored petals had been pressed in between the pages.

A peculiar feeling pushed at the edges of my heart. I moved next to Audra's vanity, spying a silver hairbrush. Several strands of blond hair were caught in the bristles.

The top drawer was surprisingly shallow and contained only an array of perfectly folded handkerchiefs and a thin red box. I opened it and immediately recognized the tiara with the blue stone. Even in the candlelight it sparkled like a million stars. She must have felt like royalty wearing this. It didn't seem proper that something so beautiful should be stored away, never to be worn again.

I looked at my dull reflection in the mirror. Then I looked back at the open box.

After arranging my curls, I placed the tiara on my head as if crowning myself. I leaned closer to the mirror. Yes, it was an improvement.

I moved next to the chest of drawers; inside, I found a folded list of wedding tasks. Audra's elegant handwriting filled the single page. One particular item had been underlined twice with a heart drawn around it: *Helleborus orientalis. Bridal bouquet.*

I wrinkled my nose at the oddly named flowers. What's wrong with roses?

Next, I examined the immense armoire. It was mahogany and twice the size of the one in my room. Light cedar planks lined the back. I only had to gaze upon a few frocks to know that the style and size were comparable to the ones that had appeared in my cabinet. But I didn't get to linger on that fact very long before something caught my attention. The clothes were mostly pushed to the side, giving one garment enough space to ensure the fabric wouldn't be crushed. The white satin was as luminous as starlight, with delicate pearl buttons running down the front bodice. The skirt was full and trimmed with intricate lace that matched the white bonnet and veil carefully stored beside it. Like everything else in this room, the dress had been preserved, as if waiting for the rightful owner to return from the grave and give these things a renewed purpose.

I pictured my own small room back at Miss Crane's. My meagre belongings would have been thrown out by now. No one would worry if I stayed in jail or went to the gallows.

A chill sliced across my throat like an unseen knife.

I pictured Mrs. Hartford writing the small note to her late husband.

Did you love me?

No one will pay for a séance for me. No one will write to me, desperate to find my message in the ghost book. There will be no mourners. The irony was unexpectedly cruel and heavy.

One of the candles sputtered and went out. I took that as my cue.

I blew out the rest of the lights and made my way back down the hall. After unlocking my door, I sat on the bed and went over the details of Audra's room. There was something about her wedding list that lurked annoyingly in my mind. It had settled between my ears, refusing to budge. I could see the words in her perfect script: *Helleborus orientalis.*

Then I remembered! I had seen that handwriting before, especially the capital "H" followed by the "e." The "help me" message! I pulled the ghost book from my bag, but when I opened to the secret page, the message had been erased. I groaned. I had erased the message myself.

Or had I?

The weight of the evening's activities and revelations pulled on my tired memory. Maybe I was only imagining the handwriting was the same. I put the bag back under my bed and began to take off the dress robe.

Something glinted in the mirror's reflection above the vanity. I hissed a trail of curses. I was still wearing the tiara! I didn't dare pick the lock again to return it; it was too risky. Mrs. Donovan was already setting me up as the person who'd stolen the key. Being found with the tiara would be disastrous. I paced, trying to come up with a plan. There was no way I could ask William to let me back in, especially after he'd asked me not to touch anything.

The only reasonable action was to keep the tiara, at least for tonight. I wrapped it in a petticoat and shoved it to the very back of the top drawer.

Once in bed, William's story played over in my mind. If what he told me was true, it was no wonder he loathed Mr. Pemberton. And it was obvious that neither Mr. Lockhart nor anyone else at Somerset was aware.

But none of this new information would help me get closer to finding a target for the séance. And what did that mean for me?

I flopped an arm over my eyes and groaned, unable to come up with a solution. "Stop thinking and go to sleep," I told myself.

The mouse scratched on the other side of the wall. "You too," I mumbled.

I woke to the sound of running footsteps. I sat up in bed, my ears straining in the darkness. Someone was crying. I grabbed my dress robe and went out to the hallway. There was a lingering smell of decay. The silence was as thick as the darkness, and I began to suspect I had dreamt the noise, but then something large tumbled down the stairs.

After locking my door, I took a candle and went down the grand staircase, making sure to keep my hand on the railing. The small shadows from my lone flame played against the wall, making it seem like I was being followed by my own dark twin. The staircase curved as the newel post came into view. My fingers brushed the face of the carved angel. I snapped my hand back in surprise. My fingers were wet. There appeared to be tears on her face. I caught one on the tip of my finger and tasted it. Salty, like tears—like the ocean.

The decaying odor was stronger on the main floor. I followed the scent, squinting against the dark as I held the candle out. It led me to the foyer. The only sign of life was the soft, flickering light from Mr. Pemberton's study.

I found him hunched over the desk, several candles providing a soft light for him to work by. Stacks of paper formed a wall in front of him. He squinted at the clock on the shelf. "What in heaven's name are you doing up, Miss Timmons?"

"I thought I heard something," I said. "Was it you?"

He shook his head. "I've only been catching up on correspondence."

I took a step closer, nodding to his overflowing desk. "What is this?"

"It's what running an estate looks like." He pinched the bridge of his nose and blinked a few times. "The noise, what do you think it was?"

It seemed foolish to bring up the possibility of someone running about with a pail of water, considering the amount of people he was responsible for employing. I had a vague notion William would not be as conscientious.

"It's not important," I said. "But I have to tell you something Mr. Sutterly revealed to me. He believes he is the rightful heir to Somerset. He said Lord Chadwick confessed this to him on his deathbed." I excluded the fact he and Audra were secretly in love, deciding to keep that information to myself until I was more certain of how he would react. I worried that jealousy would only cloud his judgment.

His eyes immediately sharpened, all sign of exhaustion erased from his expression. "And when was this conversation?"

"Earlier this evening," I said. "I was able to confront him after he'd been drinking for some time." I purposely avoided mentioning her bedroom, and of course, the tiara I accidentally stole.

He stood and came around to my side of the desk. His shirt was untucked. It reminded me of William the first time I saw him, except Mr. Pemberton was very much sober and smelled only of soap. "And what does your instinct tell you?" He folded his arms in front of his chest and regarded me with a stare that left no place for me to hide. "In other words, what did Mr. Sutterly not tell you?"

I remembered the red mark across his neck. "He didn't tell me what he wanted," I said. "Only what he had lost. He seemed nothing more than tragically desperate."

He nodded. "An accurate assessment. I've known Mr. Sutterly for nearly a year. He has never struck me as anything other than vulgar and useless. I'm more than happy to sign Somerset over to him if he wants to buy it. I'd gladly give up the title as well if it was within my means."

I was surprised by his candor. "You're not threatened by his allegation?"

"It's no secret he has hated me since I set foot on this property. No, I'm not concerned by his claim. By his own admission, the only other person who can corroborate this story, Audra's father, is dead. He's trying to control the narrative in his favour."

"True," I replied. William's claim had also been rejected by Mr. Lockhart. "But I would be remiss if I did not mention it to you."

"I'm glad you did. This is exactly what we need to do to ensure the séance produces the desired result. Thank you for coming to me, although it didn't have to be at this hour. You should get your sleep."

His comment felt like praise. And oddly enough, his easy dismissal of William's story had put me at ease.

I returned to my room, unaware that I was smiling until I unlocked my door and was hit at once with the same staunch odor from earlier. I froze, my muscles going taut.

There was a long, odd-shaped lump under the bedcovers. A large mass lay near the pillow like a head, and thin limbs stretched out below it.

The stench was putrid. I edged closer to the mattress, waiting for the figure to move, but it was still as a corpse. Dark wisps peeked out from the edge of the blanket like tangled hair.

Finally, I was standing before the bed. With a shaking hand I grabbed the bottom corner of the blanket and pulled. The dark bundle lay there, unmoving. I brought the candle closer.

It was a thick mass of seaweed. The sheet beneath it was stained dark from its slimy wet tendrils.

CHAPTER TWENTY-EIGHT

Lady Audra Linwood
Diary Entry
Somerset Park, January 23, 1852

Dearest,

I am engaged. I cannot believe I am writing these words with
such little enthusiasm.

Mr. Pemberton hardly looked my way during dinner tonight.
I sat opposite of him, with my hair bedecked with flowers and
gems. I twinkled away unnoticed. I could have sat there naked
and received the same amount of attention.

William was absent once again. I truly miss his support, as does
Father. But I admit I think it is best that he and I share little time
together, especially in the presence of Mr. Pemberton.

Oh! Listen to me! Speaking such things. How I wish you were
a real friend; I would hug you and cry on your shoulder. How I
wish William were still the good friend I knew years ago.

But as I mentioned, I am now engaged.

After dinner I retired to the drawing room while the men enjoyed their brandy and cigars. When I heard the door creak open, I jumped to my feet, thinking it was William. But Mr. Pemberton stood there—looking lovely in the candlelight, I begrudgingly admit. If only he would smile at me even once, he would be much more amiable.

He entered the room and stopped at a respectable distance. Then he said, "I wonder if I might enquire as to your opinion about my inheriting the manor, Lady Audra."

Well, Dearest, you could have knocked me over with a feather! He was asking for my opinion. Something I realized at that moment was quite rare indeed.

I told him, "If you are happy with the manor, Mr. Pemberton, it is my father's hope that you and I will marry. Therefore keeping Somerset Park in our family and myself off the streets begging for a living."

If this were a novel of tragic romance, he would have been charmed by my plucky response. We would have laughed until we fell into each other's arms. And then he would have told me how beautiful I was, and we would have kissed, sealing our promise of love. Hooray! A happy ending for all!

But that did not happen, as you have probably guessed by my lackluster announcement at the beginning of this entry. He only replied that the prudent choice would be for us to wed. He'd already asked and secured Father's blessing, but he wanted to be sure that I was agreeable to the match.

Oh, how gallant! Asking me if I'm agreeable to marrying him! I dare say, I've had more passionate conversations with Mrs. Galloway over pie filling. I said yes, I'd be a fool not to. Then he took my hand and bowed over it, not even leaving a kiss.

I curtsied, then numbly returned to my room. Only when I shut the door behind me did I throw myself on the bed and cry.

It is selfish of me, I know. I should be happy that Somerset Park will stay my home. Although Mr. Pemberton is distant and dispassionate, at least he is not cruel.

Some men seem to have a direct link to the devil himself, I think.

CHAPTER TWENTY-NINE

I stared at the tomato bisque soup. The steam had long gone from its surface. Every time I lifted the spoon to my mouth, my stomach protested. A cheese biscuit lay on the side plate, only one nibble missing from its otherwise perfect roundness.

I had locked the door to my room, but still I found myself barraged by images of Mrs. Donovan sneaking in and prowling through my things. It was like hearing a mosquito in the dark and having to wait for the bite. Obviously, she had a duplicate key to my room. How else could the seaweed have gotten in my bed? It would only be a matter of time before she discovered the tiara. Several times already I had jumped when Bramwell arrived, first with the post, and second with the tureen of soup.

"The invitations for the party will go out today," Mr. Pemberton said. He sat at the head of the table. Bramwell served him a second ladle of soup. "Thank you." He nodded.

"Party?" Mr. Lockhart asked. He looked across the table at me for more information. I picked a small crumb from the biscuit.

"A celebration for Audra." Mr. Pemberton blew on his spoon. "It's been six months since her death. It's time we should acknowledge her in a way that honors her life."

"Well, yes," Mr. Lockhart said timidly. "I think a party is a lovely tribute."

"And less emphasis on the way she died," he finished.

Mr. Lockhart smiled, but it looked forced. Although his posture was stooped, the color of his cheeks was rosier than the last time I had seen him. Dr. Barnaby's attention must have done some good. He moved his spoon around his bowl a few times. I sensed he was trying to summon some courage. "And will you have this tribute before or after Miss Timmons's séance?"

Mr. Pemberton glanced at me for the briefest of moments. "The séance will happen directly after the party," he answered. He began to meticulously butter a biscuit. "With only a few select guests."

I watched the stress evaporate from Mr. Lockhart's face, then he gave me a quick nod.

He was so oblivious to the facts. An alarm sounded in my brain. If he was this obtuse about the goings-on at Somerset, was he clever enough to earn my freedom in court? Even if he still agreed to represent me after the séance, that was not a guarantee that he would win. My pulse began to hammer in my throat. I needed another plan. The tiara came to mind. It was already in my possession, and it was valuable enough to pay for travel far away—far enough that Constable Rigby would never find me.

The more I thought about it, the more I reasoned the tiara was my best solution. No matter how the séance went, I'd sneak it away with me. Until then, I'd have to hide it somewhere that wasn't my room.

"Mrs. Galloway has begun to make preparations," Mr. Pemberton continued. "And Bramwell has booked the musicians, if anyone wishes to dance." There was a playfulness to his voice that was unexpected. I swore there was a grin beneath the surface.

"Are you unwell?" Mr. Lockhart asked me. He nodded to my hardly touched meal. "Perhaps Dr. Barnaby should make another visit?" Then he looked at Mr. Pemberton as if waiting for his permission.

Being under the scrutiny of both men made me feel like I was about to ruin my cover and spill all my lies at once. "The meal is lovely," I said. "But I am eager to start preparing for the séance. I prefer to spend time in solitude, to become more sensitive to the house."

Mr. Lockhart nodded approvingly, thinking I was adding the right amount of mysticism to our little ruse.

"Have you finally decided on the library?" Mr. Pemberton asked, knowing full well I had. He placed his spoon diagonally in the bowl and leaned back in his chair. Bramwell took the dish away at once. Next, he came around with a carafe of hot tea.

Both men waited for my answer, and I was all too aware we were part of a con in which only I knew the full truth. It was a deception on many levels. "Yes," I answered.

"Good," Mr. Pemberton replied. "I'm most interested to assist you. We can discuss it further this afternoon. I'll make sure no one disturbs us."

A rare smile of hope enhanced Mr. Lockhart's expression. "I'm glad to hear you're open to the talents Miss Timmons possesses."

"I'm sure Miss Timmons's talents will rival anything I've seen before." Mr. Pemberton ignored the freshly poured tea. "But since she has come all the way from London, it would be a shame not to allow her to exhibit her skill. As well, I cannot deprive the servants of their share of the fun. I understand there's a wager among them."

Bramwell stood by the sideboard, staring straight ahead.

"Not that I blame them," he continued. "It must be quite intriguing, watching from the sidelines."

Mr. Lockhart's lips pressed into a hard line. He put down his spoon and placed both palms into the table. "You have tried every route with the police," he said. His voice was on the verge of scolding. "Somerset Park needs a master who is present and attentive. You have become obsessed with Lady Audra's death, and it must be dealt with. She is gone, and you must accept that. The welfare of this manor, even the village of Wrendale, depend on you getting a grip on this morbid devotion. You are not the only living soul on this earth with a broken heart, my lord."

"This has nothing to do with my heart," Mr. Pemberton replied calmly, but there was a steely-eyed gaze that added a hardness to his words. "This is about justice. I'd rather see Somerset Park fall into ruin than go on pretending nothing heinous happened within its walls."

Mr. Lockhart curled his fingers under his hands and gently rested both fists on the table. "Remember," he said, "that you are speaking in the house where she was born and raised, and to a person who knew her since she was a child. To turn your back on Somerset is to turn your back on Lady Audra herself."

"And you repay her memory by bringing in this charade and making me the center of everyone's attention," Mr. Pemberton said.

The tips of my ears burned, but I pushed aside my discomfort. I thought about Audra's room and all the things she would never again touch or enjoy. "I may be many things, my lord," I said, working to keep my voice above the level of a mouse. "But I assure you, the one thing I am not is a charade. No one can ever say they have been unaffected by one of my séances."

The only sound in the room was the floor creaking under Bramwell's shoes as he adjusted his weight. Mr. Pemberton stared back at me challengingly. Then he gave the smallest lift of an eyebrow.

I took a breath and said, "I have only been at Somerset a few days, but it is obvious everyone loved and misses Lady Audra very much. If there is the smallest chance I can contact her, isn't that better than nothing at all?"

Mr. Pemberton didn't reply, but I got a nod of approval across the table from Mr. Lockhart.

LATER THAT AFTERNOON, I met with Mr. Pemberton in the library. He had his back to me, touching the spines of the books, one by one. The fireplace gave off a pleasant heat and one of the side tables had been set for tea with a plate of scones and sandwiches. I wondered how anyone at Somerset Park wasn't too wide for the doorways. I already found Audra's dresses were fitting better after only a few days of Mrs. Galloway's cooking. Even the times I ate in my room, the helpings were generous and never-ending—almost as if they knew I needed every last bite.

I placed my bag on the large circular table in the middle of the room. "The charade has arrived," I announced.

He turned around and gave me a confused glance. "Were you affronted by my choice of words? You know it's imperative for me to keep up the appearance of being reluctant to participate."

"Yes, my lord," I said, taking out my candles and laying them one by one on the table. "The effect will be all that much greater."

He picked up a candle and inspected it. "The title is unnecessary. You may call me Gareth."

I wasn't aware of anyone calling him by his first name, even Dr. Barnaby. I stayed quiet, even when he looked at me expectantly. Then I finally said, "And you may call me Miss Timmons." I waited to see his reaction.

To my surprise, he chuckled dryly.

I smiled. "And was that remark about dancing a veiled jest for my benefit?"

He handed me back the candle. The tips of his fingers brushed against mine. "You can hardly expect me to be as accomplished a liar as yourself, Miss Timmons. I was merely stating a fact. If you read anything more into it, I would suggest the desire was on your part."

"Desire?" I huffed, hating how warm my neck felt. I turned my back and pretended to fuss with my bag. I took out the ghost book and placed it gently on the table. "You were teasing me; don't deny it," I said over my shoulder. "I saw you grinning into your soup as you said it."

"With all these questions about dancing, one might suspect you're asking for a lesson."

I froze. Surely, this was a jest. I tucked a loose curl behind my ear. "You enjoy teasing spiritualists on their lack of social graces, don't you?" Despite enormous effort and concentration, my voice quivered. I turned around, expecting to find him helping himself to a cup of tea and sandwich. Instead, he stood tall and inviting, one hand stretched out to me.

"I never joke about dancing, Miss Timmons." There was barely the hint of a smile, but his blue eyes had the softest expression. A million heartbeats elapsed between us. Then he said, "All you have to do is take a step forward."

It was true. One step and I'd be in his arms. I had the feeling of falling, like my chest was leaning toward him, but my legs would not work. Maybe it was guilt keeping me in place.

The door to the library opened unexpectedly. "Forgive me, my lord, but there's a . . ." Mrs. Donovan halted midsentence, taking us in. She was as still and judgmental as a lurking crow. Confusion and anger fought for purchase across her expression before her usual glare slipped into place.

"I gave instructions we were not to be disturbed," Mr. Pemberton said, his hand now by his side.

She gave a curt nod. "Mrs. Galloway has a question for you regarding the completed menu for Lady Audra's celebration-of-life party. In addition, the head groomsman requests your presence at the stables at your earliest convenience." Then she trained her eyes on me. "Everything to your liking, Miss Timmons?"

"I require nothing at the moment, thank you," I answered, hoping she would have no excuse to linger. I was certain snakes would pour out of her mouth if she said another word.

With a bow to the room, she turned in place and closed the door behind her. I whispered a sigh of relief under my breath. But the interruption had changed the air of the room. Without realizing it, I had stepped away from him.

The unscripted delight of possibility had been replaced with caution and doubt. How foolish was I for even entertaining the notion of being a proper dance partner? He was only seeing how far the joke would go, I'm certain. There was only one reason I was at Somerset.

Mr. Pemberton picked up the ghost book, flipping it over in his hands, inspecting it.

"Please be careful," I said, taking it from him. "The pages are slate. I'll show you how it works, but you must be patient."

"My apologies." He put up his hands as if surrendering. "May I ask a question instead?"

"Of course."

"Timmons is an interesting name for someone who has a French accent."

"That's not a question. And no, I don't."

"Yes, you do. It's not always there, but it surfaces with certain phrases." He needlessly touched the candles lying in a row on the table, making minute adjustments. "Usually when you talk of death."

"My mother was French," I replied. "If there is anything about me that reminds you of France, it is from her. I've never been there." I tried to answer succinctly, hoping he couldn't hear the secret sadness in my voice. I snuck a glance at the tray of sandwiches, the aroma of roast chicken reaching my nose. My stomach had settled enough to realize it had missed lunch. My body was growing used to the regular meals.

"Would you like to go one day?"

I thought of the picture of Maman, posing in front of Notre Dame. "Yes," I replied. He waited, as if expecting me to elaborate. "Why are you asking me this?" I asked.

"I understand that Spain is renowned for their magnificent stallions. I've sometimes considered if I might make a life there." He absentmindedly twirled the gold ring. I had the notion he wanted to tell me more.

Instead, his gaze settled above the mantel, on the portrait of Audra's grandfather, Lord Chadwick the third. His voice became cautious. "Sometimes I think this place is alive and everyone inside is dead." He turned back to me. "Does that sound very morbid?"

"Not to me." We both regarded the image of Audra's grandfather. There was no denying an essence of evil about the man's features. "I know you believe that his childhood may have contributed to his cruel temper, but the staff are convinced he was possessed by the devil."

He scoffed. "People are more capable of believing the devil is some external force we have no resistance against, instead of accepting their own capacity to be cruel. Do you believe in the devil, Miss Timmons?"

I thought about my police file. There was only one reason I'd been hiding at Miss Crane's and using false names. I answered truthfully, "I think the devil is already inside us. It's there, behind the wrong choices we make, ensuring we sabotage any chance at happiness." The words came out with a weight I wasn't expecting, making it feel like a confession. But there was no relief.

The fire crackled, the only sound breaking the silence. The grandfather clock ticked away, measuring each beat before his reply. Finally, he said, "It sounds like you speak from experience."

"It's better to be miserable than to be nothing at all." At once I felt too exposed. How had he coaxed those words from my soul? I reached for my bag and spoke quickly. "If you're finished discussing the devil, we should get started. I can show you how I do a séance from start to finish."

"Then I'll know all your secrets." A suspicious glint flashed in his eye.

At that moment I was unsure if his question was more salacious than I had imagined, but maybe I was looking for a reason to explain why my heart was whispering a warning.

CHAPTER THIRTY

I explained the ghost book to Mr. Pemberton, showing him the blank slates. "You'll write a message for Audra on a small card, which I will place between these pages." I closed the book, then opened it again, showing him the secret page. "It will appear that the card has disappeared and in its place is a message left by her spirit. I will have already written her reply beforehand," I explained.

"Ingenious," he said, picking up the book, this time very carefully. His arm brushed against mine. He squinted at the thin slates. "I wonder if I should read the message out loud before I hand it to you?"

"What will your message be?" I asked. I took off my shawl and laid it over a chair. I glanced at the fireplace, wondering how I could feel its heat in such a sizeable room.

"Something that will help steer everyone's thoughts toward her murder." He was still inspecting the book. "What if I wrote, 'tell us who killed you'?"

I made a face. "If you're trying to draw out a confession, that would most certainly put the guilty person on guard. You need to handle it gently. Write something ambiguous, but morbidly suggestive at the same time."

Placing the book back down, he went over to the table that had been set for tea and poured a cup. Then he added two sugars and a dollop of cream. "Let's enjoy this before it gets cold," he said, passing me the cup and saucer.

The surprise must have shown on my face. "Yes," he said. "I know how you take your tea. One doesn't require supernatural powers to be observant. We've shared the same table several times."

"Thank you," I said, taking a grateful sip. I chose a sandwich, and then another. I found the roast chicken and cucumber selections easily digestible.

"I'm glad your appetite has returned," he said. "You hardly touched your soup earlier."

My hand hovered, unsure. Was my chronic hunger that obvious? Bramwell must have said something. My face burned with embarrassment. Not being able to afford proper dresses was one matter, but living day to day on porridge was another. Instead of taking another sandwich, I sipped my tea. As ridiculous as it seemed, I wanted to keep that part of my life secret from him. I didn't want him to picture me as such.

"It was your mention of dancing," I said. "It turned my stomach."

"Seems that will be a lingering issue for us. Please," he said, taking two sandwiches for himself. "We cannot send a full plate back to the kitchen. Mrs. Galloway will be insulted. Have you tasted the butter and pickle? They're my favourite."

I nodded and took two more as he refilled my cup. The silence lingered, but this time it was comfortable.

When we finished, I smoothed the front of my dress and returned to the larger table. "I've wasted too much of your afternoon already. I promised you a séance, so you shall get one." I took out one of the glass chimneys and placed it over a candle.

"I will set a candle in front of each person at the table," I explained. "That way I can make it seem like her ghost is picking someone specifically—their candle will blow out first."

"How?" He took off his jacket and placed it over one of the chairs.

I continued to set the table with my props. "In order for this to be authentic you shouldn't know all the techniques. I don't get the impression you have a wide range of emotions to play off."

There was a sigh. "Are you implying that I am a poor actor?"

"The most successful course of action is to have you as shocked as the rest of the room." I looked up at him. My attention went to a scar on his jaw. Maman said scars were the true witnesses to battles. I wondered what Mr. Pemberton's battle was. I realized I had lost my train of thought. "We . . . we must compromise expectations to have the greatest effect."

"I will endeavour to appear surprised," he said.

I continued, "I chose this table because the pedestal has four clawed feet. A large enough tablecloth will hang to the floor, hiding the underside." I turned two of the chairs to face each other and sat in one.

"And why is that?"

"Because there will be a shimmy under one of the claws, one long enough for me to press down with my foot. It will make it seem like the table is rocking on its own."

He stayed quiet, but there was an expression of surprised approval. Then he sat in the chair opposite mine. With our knees practically touching, I reached out, palms up, and said, "We should hold hands."

Without breaking his stare, Mr. Pemberton lightly placed his hands over mine. I imagined a blush moving up my neck. "I rarely make this request," I said. "But for this time, we'll close our eyes."

He did as I instructed. I was aware of every incremental movement of his fingertips. My thumb smoothed over his pinkie ring, and I could feel the hollow where a stone might have been.

I began, "Lady Audra, we bring you gifts of love from our hearts to reach you in death. Commune with us and move among us."

I heard him swallow.

"Commune with us and move . . ." Then I gasped. "She is here!"

A sticky heat grew between our palms.

"Will you speak with us?" I continued.

Three distinct knocks were the answer.

His chair creaked, and I sensed him leaning closer. I opened my eyes a slit to find him staring at me with a daring expression that bordered on wolfish. "You're supposed to have your eyes closed," I said. "You're ruining the ambience."

"But I want to know what you're doing."

"Once you deprive one sense, the others become more acute," I explained. "I want to test you. Now close your eyes."

He seemed satisfied with that and shut his eyes again. Impulsively, I took this opportunity to inspect him. The scar that ran along his lower jaw was faint, but there was almost a puncture-like mark under his right ear where it started. I wondered what could have made such an injury. His eyelashes flickered, bringing me back to the moment.

"Lady Audra," I began. "Will you speak with us?"

Again, we heard the three knocking sounds.

"How are you doing that?" he asked.

The room had become a cocoon, making any noise or sensation immensely exaggerated.

"Stop interrupting," I whispered.

"Do it again," he said. "I want to see if I can guess." There was an intense curiosity about him.

I made the three knocks again.

He opened his eyes, and then leaned to the side, ducking his head under the table. "Aha!" he said. "Your boot is off."

My foot squirmed away, already slipping back into the boot. There was something unusually embarrassing about him seeing my stocking.

Sitting upright again, he looked rather delighted with himself. "You're cracking a toe, I believe."

"An ankle," I corrected, unable to hide my sourness.

"Tell me, were you born with such a talented joint or was this the result of a chill that settled in your bones?" Now I was certain he was teasing me, but I could sense a deliberate attempt to his question.

"No," I told him truthfully. "There was an accident with a coach and a horse—I was seven."

His face paled. "Seven? You must have been quite scared."

The thoughtful consideration did not go unnoticed by me. "I don't remember it that well," I lied.

"Regardless, you're very good. I wouldn't have noticed if I hadn't been listening so carefully. Even though I know you're trying to fool me, I'm sitting here, believing you." He hit me with his sky-blue eyes. "I underestimated your talents. If I'm not careful, you'll have me convinced ghosts exist. I feel like I'm already under your spell."

His playful praise washed over me, warm and light as a summer breeze. I began to calculate how I could stretch out this afternoon so that we'd have to supper here as well. Just the two of us. I'd never been so comfortable. How could I have ever thought this room was cold and musty?

The grandfather clock chimed. My attention went to Lord

Chadwick's portrait. He glared down at me as if he could read my mind. In a few days it would be replaced by Audra's. The reality slammed into my chest.

Maman's voice chastised me. *Beware of what your heart tells you, ma petite chérie. It has the power to make you think you're invincible.*

The conflict must have shown on my face, because his amused expression faded. "Has my lucky guess resulted in wounding your pride? I apologize."

"I care not for your ability to detect my methods. I merely forgot my purpose, so the apology should be mine. We are planning to catch the person you believe to be your bride's murderer, but we're treating this venture with no more dignity than a game of cards."

His lips parted in shock. "The art of illusion and conning others isn't my forte. You're the one with all the power. I'm merely your prop."

He was right, of course. I stood on shaking legs. I was angry at Mr. Pemberton for deciding to be charming, I was angry with the unfairness of the world, but most of all, I was angry at myself for forgetting Maman's most fundamental rules. "I'm supposed to comfort those who are desperate for peace," I said. "Not this sinister scheme you've forced me into."

He rose to his full height, a head above me. "You have a short memory, Miss Timmons. You're the one who came to Somerset, committed to deceiving me." His eyes took on a fiery intensity. "As with all your other clients, you were going to fool my broken heart with all your grand trickery, weren't you? Seduce my bereaved soul, while secretly thrilled at the dreadful splendor of it all."

His words stuck in my ears, echoing cruelly. "You have no idea who I am."

"Actually, I do. The package that arrived from London the other night was your file from the London police."

I could have crumpled to the rug. The images came fast and without warning: the screams that filled the house, the crunch of a skull on wood, the pages of *The Hunchback of Notre Dame* torn free and fluttering down. "You've known all along?"

"Tell me what really happened," he said. I was taken off guard by the undisguised plea in his voice.

I started grabbing candles and tossing them into the bag. I tucked the glass chimney under my arm. "Why should my version matter to you?" I dropped a candle, and it rolled off the table.

"It's obvious the police are biased." He picked up the candle and held it out to me. "All I need is the truth from you, and I'll consider the matter closed."

The truth was impossible to tell him. "It will never be closed for me." I took the ghost book and held it against my chest. I hated how the moment had turned to this battle of wills. There was no version that could absolve me completely. "I am here to perform a séance," I choked out. "That does not entitle you to any part of my life. I hope that is clear."

Mr. Pemberton wiped a hand down his face and took a step back. I tried to read his expression, but all I saw was a man who had never had to face the gallows.

The memory I had pushed down so many times rushed to the surface. Maman's face was frozen in a deathly expression, her mouth opened in an unending scream.

With a waterfall's worth of tears building behind my eyes, I tore out of the library. When I reached my room, my hands were shaking so badly I fumbled with the key several times. I collapsed on the bed, burying my face into the pillow, letting the tears spill out.

After I finished and my breath had returned to normal, I recognized the bitter reality: I couldn't escape, no matter how far I ran or how many keys I had to lock away secrets. The truth would always wait for me.

I lied for a living, but in all those private gatherings, one thing remained the same—my truth. I craved to belong to a family.

During a séance, when I was the conduit for a loved one, the family would look at me like I was the most important person in their lives. I felt loved. Among all that death was the only time I was truly alive—that was my dreadful splendor.

And that's what I should have told Mr. Pemberton, but fear kept my mouth shut. I couldn't reveal too much of myself.

The smile on Constable Rigby's face lurked under the surface of all my unease.

You can only depend on yourself, ma petite chérie.

I went to the window and looked toward the direction of the cliff. It seemed closer than yesterday. I imagined the next wave sweeping onto the land, creeping closer, and not stopping until it reached my door. Even though the window was closed, the air tasted like salt.

CHAPTER THIRTY-ONE

Lady Audra
Diary Entry
Somerset Park, January 25, 1852

I am at a loss, Dearest.

I know I should be grateful for Mr. Pemberton's proposal—and I am, truly. But there is a barrier between us I cannot name, a wall he keeps around himself that I cannot pierce.

More and more I'm aware of subtle changes in the staff. They whisper all the time, their words cutting off abruptly whenever I enter the room. Father tells me I read too many Gothic novels and that my imagination has taken over my senses.

But what of this voice that calls out to him at night? Why does he wander through Somerset, testing the locked doors, determined to go outside? His hollers are enough to wake the dead. It frightens me so.

I worry Mr. Pemberton will call off the engagement if he discovers the true extent of Father's condition. But for now, wedding preparations have begun. This will be the event of the year, and

Father wants everything to be perfect. However, I fear the excitement has taken a toll on his frail health.

Dr. Mayhew wants to send him to an institution, but I refuse. He has been the family physician for decades, but he's too old now to properly manage Father's care. When Mr. Pemberton heard of my concerns, he took it upon himself to hire another physician, a friend of his apparently. I was so grateful I burst into tears.

But, even in my state of complete gratitude, Mr. Pemberton only nodded and handed me a handkerchief. How can someone be so unromantic? The only thing he seems to find pleasing is taking a horse to explore the grounds—soon to be his grounds—in solitude.

The other day, he disappeared for hours and returned drenched in mud! He told me he had slipped on his way to the stables. But there was a rip on his sleeve and a stain that looked like blood. I wanted to press him further, but I did not dare! I smiled and watched him from the corner of my eye, noting all his mannerisms.

There is only one reason people lie, and that's to hide an ugly truth.

What if everything Mr. Pemberton has said has been a lie? I know we are not in love, Dearest, but how can I marry a man who lies to me? I must have Mr. Lockhart investigate his history more thoroughly. Surely, he wouldn't have invited a man to Somerset—a man whom I will marry—if there was the slightest hint of malice in his past.

And William? Since the engagement he has become sullen and prone to fits of temper. Even the kitchen staff, who are usually so enamored by his charm, have become leery of him. This is all due to Mr. Pemberton. I know William is hurting, but we all must be brave, mustn't we, Dearest? We had such fun together as children. Now that old companion is gone, and I can no longer trust him.

I am grateful, at least, that I never told him the Linwood secret. I can only imagine the unease he would have unleashed on Somerset.

CHAPTER THIRTY-TWO

I was fifteen when a caravan of entertainers came to our part of the city. The sides of their wagons advertised the various performers, painted with large swirling letters, and faces that were both scary and comical.

Maman was taking me to see them. It was a rare event for us to be the ones watching a performance rather than playing the parts ourselves.

The entertainers transformed their wagons into booths, the side doors opening wide. The air smelled of roasted nuts and a thick sweetness. Flute music was playing, but I couldn't see the musician through the growing audience. The sun was low in the sky, and when the performers lit the numerous candles and lanterns it transformed the space into a fairy garden. The buzzing anticipation of the crowd mingled with my own excitement as we walked along, basking in the magical glow of it all.

Maman kept reaching for me, but I was too old now to hold her hand. I was a few steps ahead of her when I spotted the side of a wagon advertising a fortune-teller. Magnificent owl eyes stared back at me from the painting. There was no line to enter.

Maman's fingers rested on my shoulder. "Genevieve," she warned. "Are you sure you want to spend all your money on frivolous entertainment?" She pointed to the other attractions that were free, and then motioned to the doughnuts and ginger beer wagon. When I didn't move, she whispered, "A fortune-teller reads us, not the cards—like I do at séances."

I was stubborn and did not heed her words. It had been two months since our last séance, and she was particular about saving money, which meant we'd been eating porridge for every meal. The spiritualist business had become more dangerous. The chief inspector was rumored to be especially hard. He said what Maman and I did was criminal activity. "Worse than robbing a bank!" he exclaimed to the *London Times*. "They prey on the vulnerable emotions of grieving souls. No worse vermin than that lot."

Having his words in print set flame to a general sense of unjustness among the public. Work came less and less. The money stopped, and our home slowly lost its comforts one by one as it forced Maman to sell anything that would fetch a price—even Mrs. Rinaldo's bracelets.

I dreamt of a day when I wouldn't have to deal with death so much. But what else was I going to do? What skills did I have other than speaking a bit of French and being able to recite *The Hunchback of Notre Dame* by heart?

I envied the women of the stately homes we visited. They knew how to do needlework, painting, dancing, and all the other skills that accomplished ladies possessed. I had nothing to look forward to but following Maman around as I grew taller, wearing dresses with a hem that was already let down to the longest length.

However, my height was not all that had changed. Men treated me differently. Their eyes lingered on my face longer. There was a power about it, a power I did not yet know how to harness.

I was determined to go to the fortune-teller. I was not in the mood to be told I didn't deserve at least one small pleasure.

Her eyes were as dark as the Thames at night. She had brightly painted lips and rouged cheeks. Her black braids were thick and decorated her head like a crown. But even with all the makeup, I sensed she might only be a few years older than me.

My heart raced, urging me forward. I no longer felt the touch of my mother on my shoulder, trying to pull me back.

I put down two pence, all the money I had to spend.

She kept her eyes on me as she covered the coins with her hand and slid them toward her. Then she fanned out the deck. I had never seen cards like those. There were fanciful creatures painted on each one. Some were beautiful, with jewels for eyes and flowing hair; some were hideous demons with two heads and covered in fur. My eyes traced the intricate details of each image, mesmerized.

Her voice was musical, an accent I had never heard before. She flicked her finger, and the whole fan of cards flipped over to the other side, showing the same solid red background with a gold star. She shuffled with well-practised hands. I wanted to ask her how long she'd been giving fortunes. There was a curious pull under my ribs, and I wondered if there might be room for Maman and me in their caravan. Surely, a spiritualist would only enhance the show.

I felt grown-up for thinking this, but not so grown-up that I wouldn't appreciate having a friend, someone my age who might understand what my life was like. I already had a connection with this girl, and I was certain she would come to the same conclusion.

The fortune-teller stopped moving the cards. Her hand froze as she looked over my shoulder. Her finely lined eyebrows came together. I didn't have to turn around to know Maman was there.

She asked me to separate the deck into two halves and to choose a pile. I repeated this task until there were only a handful of cards left.

She flipped them over one by one. "There will be a significant change in your life," she said. "I see you taking an alternative path, but one that is chosen for you, not forced." My future was before her eyes. Would Maman and I join the caravan? When she turned over the last card, every part of my body was rigid, waiting to exhale.

"You will be an orphan soon," she said. She tapped the card depicting a beast with horns and a tail like a fish. "And I see you underwater, as a young maiden."

A bark of nervous laughter came out of me.

Maman was by my side at once, spitting out a sharp retort in French.

The fortune-teller kept her gaze on me. "You will die a young girl. I see the number nineteen."

A chill crept over my skin. I forced a smile. I couldn't appear affected in front of Maman, not after ignoring her advice. "I will die when I'm nineteen?" I asked, still trying to make sense of her words.

She shook her head. "No. You will never reach your nineteenth year."

Later that evening, as Maman brushed out my braids, we watched the flame of the candle sputter.

"I'll be around forever, *ma petite chérie.*" She tried to soothe. "That girl was only trying to make an impression. Even so, she could have sweetened it a bit. Most people only want good news. She has not learned that yet."

"But we lie to make people feel better, so they'll pay us well at the end of the séance. She already had my money, so there was no reason for her to lie."

Maman continued to work my hair. "That fortune-teller looked young to me. She might not have a nice mother like you do, and seeing us together made her sad. When people do something mean, it's because they are secretly hurting."

I considered this bit of wisdom. She put down the brush and kissed the top of my head. "So you won't die?" I asked.

"Someday, Genevieve. But with a pile of white hair. And I'll be spoiling all your *enfants*."

I smiled, wishing the fortune-teller had told me that version. Maybe people only believe in the things that scare them.

Maman blew out the candle and we tucked in for the night. For the first time in a long while, I was grateful that we shared a bed. Her soft breath against my neck lulled me to sleep.

Then her voice broke the silence of our small room. There was a careful edge to her tone. "Promise me one thing, though," she said. "Stay out of *la mer*." *The ocean.*

I told her I would. She sighed and rolled over, and was soon snoring softly.

Not long after our encounter with the fortune-teller, a woman with a hat that looked like a stuffed parrot came to our apartment, asking if Maman would do a ghost cleansing of her boardinghouse.

Maman informed the woman that she could contact the dead, but she could not make a spirit do anything against its will.

The woman laid a hand on her hip. "I'm losing customers because of that damn ghost," she said. "My girls are too afraid. I don't care what you do, just make it go away." She opened her embroidered reticule and handed my mother enough pounds to buy us meat and cream for two weeks.

Then the woman took notice of me. Like some men, her gaze lingered on my face before sweeping down to my toes and back. "She yours?" she asked Maman.

Maman's back straightened. "Genevieve is well versed in the art of spiritualism," she said. "That is where her future lies."

The woman smirked as if Maman had told a jest, and a tightness squeezed my chest. Then she introduced herself as Miss Crane.

That night, Maman and I arrived at the address Miss Crane had provided. Imagine my surprise when I saw a parlour full of women, some only a few years older than I. They all wore rouge and silken dressing gowns trimmed with lace that swayed when they walked, accentuating the full curves of their hips.

The air was heavily perfumed, but not enough that I couldn't detect a sourness beneath it. A settee was covered in a gaudy fabric with mismatched patches sewn on the armrests. A stack of books propped up one corner where it was missing a leg. Miss Crane stood with a hand on one hip and a cigarette between her red lips. A comb with tiny blue stones pinned back her hair. When I looked closer, I saw the gems were painted on.

She accompanied Maman and me to the second floor. The stairs creaked with each step as we walked up. Down below I could see the chandelier that hung over the foyer was home to several spiderwebs.

The haunted room in question had a double bed with a lovely pink cover. There were flowers on the wallpaper and a tall chest of drawers with a mirror. The small coal grate was full, and lace curtains framed the room's one window. How could a space this lovely be haunted?

Maman set out her candles as Miss Crane watched us from the doorway. She spoke with the cigarette still in her mouth. "He died in that bed," she told us. "Drusilla damn near suffocated under the weight of him, fat bastard." The cigarette bobbed with each word.

"They refuse to come in here anymore—all the girls. They say

they can hear him moaning at night and the window keeps opening on its own." She pointed a long fingernail at the window. "They
think it's his spirit trying to get out."

The soft bed lost its appeal.

"Moaning at night?" Maman repeated. I could hear a tinge of
sarcasm.

Miss Crane snorted. "This isn't an all-night operation. These
noises happen after I lock the front door. I treat my girls good, give
them a warm, safe place. If they didn't have me, they'd be out on
the streets freezing and starving, or worse, doing the same thing
they are now but with a rougher crowd. They pulled a girl out of
the Thames yesterday, throat cut."

Maman's eyes hardened, and she announced that she was ready.
Then she asked if she could meet the girl who was last with the
departed.

Miss Crane hollered down the hall. "Drusilla!"

When the girl appeared, she stayed behind Miss Crane. I could
make out a thin shoulder and the side of her angular face.

Maman smiled gently and beckoned her into the room, holding out her hand. Hesitant, Drusilla took it, and together they
stepped into the middle of the circle of candles. "Don't let go,"
Maman whispered to her, but it was loud enough for Miss
Crane and the other girls who had begun to gather in the hall
behind her.

Maman outdid herself. It was undoubtedly one of her best per-
formances. She made the ectoplasm purge seem so real, even I
gaped in awe. "He is here!" she said.

Startled whimpers echoed through the hallway.

"This spirit will not rest if ever another man enters this room,"
Maman said. "He considers it very much his own now."

Drusilla hesitantly mumbled, "No one has been in the room since—"

Maman shook her head. "He will not leave."

Miss Crane's mouth opened so wide her cigarette fell out. "That's what I paid you for!"

"I told you. I cannot make demands of ghosts, only hear their will."

"So no man can come in here?" Miss Crane squinted up toward the ceiling. I imagined she was doing sums in her mind.

"Where's my room gonna be?" Drusilla asked. "How am I supposed to earn me rent now?"

Maman finally let go of Drusilla's hand and lifted her shoulders. "Ghosts are incapable of lying. He will haunt this room forever. His spirit is bound here."

Drusilla crossed her arms in front of her chest. I overheard murmurs in the hallway as each girl declared she would not, under any circumstances, take Drusilla's old room.

"Then this room is useless," Miss Crane said with thinly veiled anger. The girls in the hallway scattered.

I began to collect Maman's things, but she stayed still and regarded Miss Crane. "You need someone to pay rent?" Maman asked. "How much?"

Miss Crane stared back, locked in a battle of wills. I sensed she knew exactly what Maman had just done and was torn between avoiding being conned and having another paying tenant.

They struck a deal, and Maman and I had new accommodations. She told me it would only be temporary, and that we could save a bit more this way if we continued to work hard.

That night I dreamt that I ran away and met up with the caravan.

THE FORTUNE-TELLER MAY have been nothing more than a con. Perhaps she was bitter, as Maman suggested, and purposely wanted to hurt me. Or perhaps she had told the truth, hoping it might somehow spare Maman and me—a warning for us to heed. Whatever her intentions, it set me on the path of a self-fulfilling prophecy.

I hadn't told anyone at Somerset Park, but my nineteenth birthday was in five days.

CHAPTER THIRTY-THREE

Lady Audra Linwood
Diary Entry
Somerset Park, February 10, 1852

Dearest,

There are no words to describe how I feel today. In this never-ending graveyard of dread, a ray of sunshine has transfixed me with its glare.

Love has finally made itself clear to me, and most unexpectedly. I was unsure before, but now that I have felt it, really and truly, I will never mistake it again. Is it possible to look into a pair of eyes and immediately know? Yes! It is true!

I can hardly explain it—how one day there is nothing and the next, everything. His smile is the sun, and all I want is to bathe in its warmth forever.

Love is glorious and miserable all at once. He meets my gazes, returns my smiles, but he is always aware of Mr. Pemberton's presence and turns away first. Ours is an affair of secret glances. But how can we proceed? I must speak with him alone. I must! For if he feels the same, and declares it for certain, we will find a way.

Mr. Pemberton does not want me; that is obvious. And as much as I have tried to make him happy, I know our marriage would only end in misery. What kind of home would we give our children?

My fiancé takes no notice of my emotions, but nonetheless, I must at least try to be discreet. So rather than gaze at my love's face, I stare at his hands. I observe his careful manners, his easy gait as he moves throughout the house. It's fascinating how watching a man complete simple tasks can be so enthralling.

How I crave to know what women before me have experienced. I can hardly contain my feelings, my own body, and I fear that if I don't confront him, I will burst. But it is impossible to speak with him privately; Bramwell or Mrs. Donovan are always close by. It's absurd that I should feel so guarded in my own home.

But today I did something devious! After he had visited with Father and sat for tea with Mr. Pemberton, I suggested we take a short stroll to the greenhouse. Imagine my surprise that Mr. Pemberton agreed to join as well. I positioned myself between them, walking with my fiancé on one side and my love on the other. I matched my steps to his, secretly hoping he would understand my message. I snuck a peek around the edge of my bonnet and saw that he was watching me as well, paying no attention at all to Mr. Pemberton's dull remarks about the weather. I smiled at him, and this time he held my gaze, almost daring me to not look away.

We entered the greenhouse, and he began to ask me about each plant as if he'd never seen one before. He seemed so calm, but my *voice shook when I replied. I found it impossible to look him in the eyes as I spoke. It was almost too much to be that close to him, with Mr. Pemberton just behind us.*

We paused before the winter roses, and I told him that while it wasn't a particularly beautiful bloom, it was a hardy plant that only flowered in the coldest months. He proclaimed that it was the most beautiful flower he had ever seen. Then he shifted his stance and our hands brushed against each other, almost as if by accident—but his fingers curled and briefly caught mine before letting go.

There can be no surer sign that he loves me. When I returned to the manor, my feet did not touch the pathway for I was gliding on air. I shall always remember falling in love over the Helleborus orientalis.

CHAPTER THIRTY-FOUR

After the disastrous moment in the library, I sought asylum and requested to have supper brought to my room. When Flora arrived with the tray, I was grateful for the distraction of her company. The dregs of my conversation with Mr. Pemberton, and the memories of Maman it had brought to the surface, were horrible and exhausting. My only grace was that he hadn't dismissed me from the house. Yet.

I sat at the small table and tucked into my meat and gravy. Oddly enough, my appetite was unaffected.

Flora kept herself busy. "I heard the invitations for Lady Audra's party were sent out today," she said. "The kitchen is right busy with all the prep and such."

"I can imagine," I said, using my bread to sop up the extra sauce.

"Do you need to do any exercises to prepare for the séance? Or maybe practise on someone?"

Flora was as subtle as a thunder shower at a picnic. She wanted another conjuring, and I was glad to appease her. There was something comfortable about routine, about doing the one thing I was good at.

I dabbed my mouth with the soft napkin and laid it over my empty plate. "There's a peculiar quality in the air tonight," I said. "When there is a lot of activity in the other dimension, I can feel it. It's subtle, almost like butterfly wings."

Flora stared at my forehead, eyebrows together in concentration.

"I see a potent presence around you," I told her. "It's not always there, but tonight you are being shadowed."

"Shadowed? That sounds bad." She looked over her shoulder. Flora was what Maman would call "the perfect customer."

"No," I assured her. "It's lovely, actually. Shadowing means the spirit is close because you have called them to your side."

"What? You mean, like you do?"

"Not quite." I motioned to the other chair, inviting her to sit with me. "When we think of a loved one, it calls through the fabric between our worlds and they're able to pass through—if only for a moment."

Flora smiled. "Someone I've been thinking about is with me now?"

"Yes," I said, wiggling my foot out of my boot. "Close your eyes and concentrate on their name. It will help keep them here." She did as I asked. Taking advantage of the distraction, I moved my dishes to the floor and slipped the dinner knife under one table leg.

"I'm confused," she said, clutching her apron, now looking at me again. "The person I've been thinking about most of today is still alive. At least he was this morning when I gave him an apple pie."

Joseph's kind smile came to mind.

"The shadowing doesn't lie," I told her. "Someone is with you now. Would you like to know who?" She nodded. I reached across the table and asked for her to hold my hands. "I want you to relax and remember that nothing can hurt you."

She nodded again.

"Is there anyone here who wishes to speak to us?" I asked. Three knocks sounded under the table.

Flora gasped. Her eyes were wider than the supper plate. I waited, then brought my knee up, making the small table wobble.

I said, "I'm seeing the letter 'M.'"

"Maisie," Flora whispered.

I nodded. "She is telling me something." I paused for two breaths. "She knows your love is close by."

Gripping my hand tighter, Flora said, "Ask her if he's tellin' me the truth. I needs to know if I can trust him or not."

I wondered what Joseph could be telling her.

"She said he is telling you mostly the truth," I answered carefully. Her expression was hard to read with her eyes so intently searching mine, but I was certain I detected a pout. "However," I added, "I don't always get direct words. Sometimes the message comes as a feeling. I believe she is trying to say that the thing you are wondering about is the thing he might be lying to you about."

"Oh." The crushed tone in her voice was enough proof I had disappointed her.

Maman would not approve. *We do not lecture, ma petite chérie. We tell them what they want to hear. We tell them enough so that their heart fills in the rest.*

The heart sees.

I tried again. "But she says he's lying for a good reason and he wants to make you happy."

Flora's grip loosened. I sensed I had satisfied her.

"She's fading," I said.

A faint blush bloomed on her cheeks. "If you don't mind me saying," Flora began, "it's been nice having someone close to me own age to talk with again. I don't mean you should have servants as friends. I miss Maisie something awful, but when I'm with you, I don't miss her as much." She shook her head. "I'm sorry, I can't use my words as fancy as you."

Me, fancy? That was a new one.

"Thank you, Flora," I said. I could tell that at last she was comfortable with me—trusting. "I'm glad you're here too."

She made to stand up, but then hesitated, chewing her bottom lip. "I heard you and the lord were in the library this afternoon," she said.

"Mm-hmm." I kept my answer short. Had the staff overhead us? Did they all know the truth? I practically held my breath while I waited for her to continue.

She shoved her hands in her apron's pocket. "I'll never forget when he first came to the manor," she said. "I thought he was the most handsome man I'd ever seen. You should have seen him and Lady Audra together. They were like two angels or somethin'."

Supper lay heavily in my stomach. I remembered how I had blushed when our hands touched. "I can tell you admired her," I said.

Flora sniffed. "I have to tells you, Jenny." Her voice quivered. "A few nights before the wedding, I saw somethin'. Somethin' I ain't never mentioned. I wonders now if I may have imagined it, but then sometimes I think it may have been real. I've told no one, except Maisie when I visit her grave."

My ears perked up. "It's all right if you share it with me," I said. "The only people I talk to are ghosts." I reached across the table and touched her arm. "What did you see that night?"

She adjusted her white cap, then took in a few breaths. "I was workin' late in the kitchen, gettin' everything ready for the wedding feast. I had pies to cool, but I didn't want to go into the cold cellar." She leaned closer and lowered her voice. "I hates it there."

I remembered how Joseph had been so reluctant to get the preserves for Mrs. Galloway.

"Instead, I took 'em out to the back garden to cool. It was dark,
so I didn't see him until he stumbled into view, walking like he'd
been drinkin'."

A quick knock interrupted her. Flora clamped her mouth shut
and shook her head as if scolding herself. I feared the intimacy
between us had been broken. The knock came again, making Flora
rush to answer the door.

With her back turned, I easily slipped the knife out from under
the table and placed it back on the plate.

"Evenin', m'lord," Flora said, head bowed.

Mr. Pemberton was dressed in his dinner finery. His style was
impeccable, as always, and his golden hair seemed to steal all the
light in the room. However, there was a weariness to his posture
that did not fit his usual demeanour. He saw the empty plate, then
nodded to me. "I'm glad to see you've eaten. I was worried you'd
fallen ill."

"Mrs. Galloway's stew is hard to resist," I said timidly. Our last
conversation ended with me running out of the library, barely able
to hold back my guilty tears. I couldn't imagine what he thought
of me.

"Oy, forgive me, Jenny," Flora said, running to retrieve the
dishes from the floor.

Mr. Pemberton gave her a quizzical look, then he put his attention back on me. "The night air is particularly refreshing," he
said. "The greenhouse was a favourite of Audra's, and I thought
you might want to see it."

There was nothing in his tone to hint at the confrontation of
our earlier conversation. He was a better actor than I'd given him

credit for. Still, I could not turn down his invitation, and certainly not in front of Flora. I had to be mindful of the staff gossip.

"Yes," I said, forcing a smile.

"I'll wait in the foyer." And with that he turned and disappeared.

Flora blew the air out of her cheeks. She nodded to the armoire. "Wear a scarf; the wind is biting tonight."

WHEN I REACHED the main entrance, Mr. Pemberton was waiting, top hat in place, an umbrella tucked under his arm, and a lantern in his other hand.

"After you, Miss Timmons," he said, opening the door for me.

I nodded. "Lord Chadwick."

The night air scratched at my throat with every breath. A strong gust blew against my hair, rustling my bonnet. I lifted a hand to hold it down. Before meeting Mr. Pemberton in the foyer, I knew I couldn't leave the tiara in my room unguarded and risk Mrs. Donovan discovering it. Instead, I took it with me, wearing it beneath my hat, carefully tucked close against my curls.

"I should ask Flora how to earn your favour," he said. "She must be a confidant to feel comfortable calling you Jenny."

"She calls me Jenny because I invited her to do so," I replied. I was grateful again for the wide brim of the bonnet. Our last conversation rang in my ears with a tired shame, turning them red.

We paused at the top of the steps. "It's raining," I said unnecessarily.

He put up the umbrella, holding it in the hand that was closest to me. Once again, he preferred a barrier between us.

With the dim light of the lantern, we made our way past the stone lions, then to the side of the house, following the footpath to the back gardens. I moved to the side to avoid a large puddle.

The umbrella moved with me, keeping me dry. I had no time to appreciate the gallant gesture; my mind was tumbling over possible scenarios of what Mr. Pemberton really had planned. Was he leading me to the parish constable? Was he going to send me off into the night with only the clothes on my back? Was he going to push me off the cliff? I shivered against the chill.

The wind picked up, lashing at us. I clutched my bonnet as he struggled to keep the umbrella over our heads. The lantern created deep shadows under his eyes. "Come, we're getting close," he said, leading me to the greenhouse. "It's the only part of Somerset where we can truly be alone."

Alone for what, though? I wondered. I walked into the glass building first. He handed me the lantern, then shook out the umbrella and propped it against the door. Water dripped down, making a pool on the stone floor.

The quiet of the room surrounded us. It was warm in here, a stark contrast to the icy rain. He took off his top hat and ran a hand through his thick blond hair a few times.

"This way," he said. We started to make our way through a path of potted ferns. I held the lantern out, craning my neck around the curve of greenery, expecting to see a copper hidden among the leaves. If I had to, I would make a run for it.

He cleared his throat. "I want to apologize for what I said in the library this afternoon. It was an unwarranted reaction on my part with no consideration to your feelings. I'm afraid I treated you unfairly."

An apology was the last thing I'd been expecting. I timidly replied, "I've been speaking liberally since I've arrived."

He turned to me, holding the top hat with both hands. "I owe you an explanation for my motivation. When I realized the package from London was a copy of your police file, I had to read through it in its entirety. On my way back to my room that night, I had made up my mind to confront Mr. Lockhart the next morning, but then I saw you standing at the top of the stairs. You were about to throw yourself down." Mr. Pemberton looked pained, then shook his head. "I didn't hesitate to lunge for you. It was a great fright, I confess. And once I realized you were sleepwalking, I became intrigued. I felt there was more to understand about you."

My heart was racing. I didn't dare reply. A small part of me was eager to hear more about his interpretation of our meetings, even though I knew it would end badly. I touched the edge of my bonnet, making sure the tiara was still completely tucked out of sight.

He continued, "After our first few meetings, it became clear to me that you are not at all the person those reports suggest. I decided to trust my instincts and let you stay."

I recalled what Mr. Lockhart had told me in the carriage—that I was the only one capable of giving him what money could never buy. Peace.

Mr. Pemberton frowned, the lines on his forehead deeper than usual. "This afternoon, when you accused me of not taking Audra's death seriously, I retaliated most viciously. And I would like to make it clear that my anger was not with you, but with myself. I should have been more attentive to her, regardless of the nature of our arrangement. It pains me that she will never know my regret."

I had a repertoire of replies that would have been appropriate, but he knew too much about my profession, and I worried anything I said would sound inauthentic. So I simply replied, "Thank you for your apology." Then I could not help but ask, "Does this mean you still want to continue with the séance?"

His voice was steady. "Yes, of course. Our original plan hasn't changed."

We resumed walking. The path narrowed, and our arms brushed lightly.

I noticed that he had made no mention of the parish constable. "Where is the file now?" I asked.

There was the smallest notion of a sheepish expression across his face. "I repackaged it and had it delivered to Mr. Lockhart this evening. He is unaware I saw it and is probably looking it over himself as we speak."

Relief washed over me. All this time I had been worried what his reaction would be when he discovered the extent of my criminal past. But he hadn't summoned the police—instead he was requesting that I stay. Since he had been truthful with me, I justified that it was time I shared the nature of my bargain with Mr. Lockhart. "He promised to help clear my name."

He nodded, hardly surprised. "I reasoned that was why the file had been sent. No wonder you were worried about disappointing him."

The quiet of the greenhouse flowed between us like an unwanted chaperone. My boots squelched with each step, but I didn't mind. It seemed disaster had been avoided. And not only was I still a guest at Somerset Park, but it appeared Mr. Pemberton and I would continue as allies. The notion was comforting.

We came upon several rows of the same stocky plant. The nameplate made me stop in my tracks: HELLEBORUS ORIENTALIS. It was the same word written on Audra's wedding list. Why would she insist on having this unextraordinary flower as part of her bridal bouquet?

"The winter rose," Mr. Pemberton said, leaning over my shoulder.

"It looks unremarkable."

"Not striking as roses go, but they thrive under the harshest of circumstances." He paused and looked at me over the glow of the lantern. "There's something admirable about that."

A warmth swept down to my toes. It felt like a secret compliment. But how much had he been able to garner from the police file? Did he have a clear image of my life? Maybe he had only been talking about the flowers after all. "Were they a favourite flower of Lady Audra's?" I asked.

The emotion slipped from his face as his expression grew blank. "I have no idea. From what I know of her, she was fond of bold and colorful blooms. Nothing as unassuming as this."

The lack of affection in his voice did not go unnoticed, but the remark itself fit well with what I had gathered about Audra. Her room was decorated with patterns of flamboyant flowers. Maybe this winter rose meant nothing.

Picturing her list reminded me she that would never wear her beautiful wedding dress. It would hang in the back of her wardrobe, waiting for her eternally. I was beginning to understand the justice that Mr. Pemberton was trying to give her. And in a way, she was the very reason that Mr. Lockhart had saved me that night. I was in her debt, and yet I would never be able to thank her.

A windy gust rattled the large panes. Resigned to stay inside longer, we continued our walk until we came upon the fountain with the weeping angel. I sat on the edge and noticed a few coins at the bottom of the pool. Instinctively, my fingers started to reach forward. Only when I touched the water did I come to my senses and pull my hand back. Old habits.

Mr. Pemberton eased in beside me. "Have you seen the rest of the grounds beyond the gardens?" he asked.

I shook my head. I had no desire to explore the cliffs.

"I confess," he started, "the stables are the only part of Somerset Park I've ever found attractive. I have little use for the sea."

I couldn't agree more. And it wasn't lost on me that he hadn't mentioned Audra among Somerset's attractive qualities. I tried to ignore the tiny flame of hope igniting in my chest. It was reckless of me. And there was also, for the first time, a sense that I was being disloyal to Audra herself.

"You know, Miss Timmons," he said. "We may be here for a while, so I would appreciate any attempt at conversation."

"Yes, my lord," I replied.

A rare burst of laughter escaped him. "Are you doing this on purpose? I already invited you to call me by my Christian name. And even some of the staff call you by your first name."

I took in his smug expression. Here was my chance to learn a bit more about him. "Your scar is more noticeable when you laugh, Lord Chadwick."

"Ha," he said stiffly. Reaching up, he touched the spot under his jaw.

At once I felt foolish. "I hope it has a good story," I said, disguising the reason for my interest. "I'll be disappointed if there aren't pirates involved."

Looking down, he turned the gold ring. "Barnaby mentioned he'd told you the story of when he saved my life."

"You lost control of the horse you were riding," I confirmed. My cheeks burned with shame, hoping his friend hadn't also told him about how I'd declared he should have been shot instead of the horse.

Mr. Pemberton nodded. "When my father ordered for the horse be put down, I felt a part of myself die as well. The innocence of childhood, possibly." He was speaking to his shoes. I watched the muscles of his jaw tighten. "I declared I would never go near a horse again. But my father insisted and forced me to ride again that very next day. Afterward, I realized he was right. He said if I make my decisions based on fear, I will never live life as I was meant to. Fear leads us down the wrong paths, only to be met with misery."

He took in a sharp breath. "To be sure I'd learned this lesson, he struck me. He was wearing this ring and the stone caught on my flesh."

I could only imagine the force that would be required to leave such a mark.

"When he died, I inherited this ring, just like his father before him and many generations back. I did not wish to break tradition and refuse to wear it. But I had the stone removed." There was something different in his voice, almost a quiet embarrassment. "You see, I already have a daily reminder of that legacy." He smiled, and although it was weak, it was the first one I'd seen on him. It took me aback. "I'm afraid I possess no talent for inventing stories, Miss Timmons. I can only tell you the truth."

I peered down at the ring again.

"I've never told anyone. Except, I suppose, now you."

It felt like an unearned honor to be considered a confidant. I relished the compliment, until it occurred to me that he might have only shared this to earn my trust, so that I would be more likely to share my secrets in return. It was a technique I had often employed myself.

He must have been able to detect the conflict warring within me. When he spoke next, his tone was hesitant, uncharacteristically so. "I should be completely honest. Once I was aware of your police record, I gave your name to a well-trusted solicitor friend in London. He's been sending additional information. After our unfortunate encounter in the library, I received a small envelope from him. Inside were various statements from families who employed your services years ago. There was no mention of robbery, only how you were able to ease their sorrows. They even described you as an angel."

I worked to keep my bottom lip from quivering. I'd forgotten what pride could feel like.

"I deeply regret my insult to your skills," he said. "The testimonials also afforded me another chance to consider your capabilities— how you can reach out to people from all different levels of society and comfort them in their most crippling time." A strand of blond hair fell across his eye, but he ignored it.

A strange energy rolled across my skin. I could feel my body absorbing the humidity of the greenhouse.

He continued, "I'm envious of the intimate connections you make so quickly. I've never been naturally at ease where strangers are concerned."

"Nothing comes easily for me. Maman was the talented one," I said, tucking my chin. "I am nothing compared to what she could do." My throat dried up, catching on the last word. The ache was always there, as was the guilt.

Another gust of wind lashed at the walls. I was grateful for the noise it made.

"I'm sorry you lost her," he said.

"All those years dealing with death, and the thing I fear most is living without her." I paused. The story of that horrible night was too close to the surface.

He let the silence hang between us. Then he said, "I was thinking about how you said people sometimes make decisions they know will sabotage their own happiness. But, I wonder, if those people delved into why they felt so unworthy, perhaps they'd discover they deserved more."

It was a sweet sentiment. His hopeful tone had touched something deep inside me. But no matter how pretty his words, the truth remained. I knew exactly what I deserved, and it was the furthest thing from happiness.

CHAPTER THIRTY-FIVE

Lady Audra Linwood
Diary Entry
Somerset Park, February 27, 1852

Dearest,

My heart is broken, and yet it still beats. Father is dead. I was not there with him. I am too ashamed to write what I was doing and with whom.

In all my time at Somerset, just this one stolen moment of pure and beautiful passion cannot erase all that I've done for Father, can it? I pray that his soul will recognize my devotion and grant me forgiveness from heaven.

We buried him in the family crypt next to Mother. I ran my hand over her name and felt as if someone were walking on my grave. Somerset Park will be my home forever, but it might as well be that tomb.

I fear everyone knows my shameful secret. Mr. Pemberton has been more inquisitive than usual, and now it is I who is lying to him. My love has left the manor and my life. I am racked with savage sobs that the staff assume are for Father.

I am in mourning, Dearest—for the loss of my true love. He attended the funeral, and all he could give me was a stiff bow over my hand. Still, the touch between us, even through my glove, was enough to kindle the fire inside me.

I must find a way to go on with only the memory of our stolen night together. It is a curse to have loved so fiercely, and so passionately. Everything else pales in comparison; my life will be a cruel void of emptiness. I must be vigilant, though, for Mr. Pemberton watches me like a hawk.

He has chosen to become interested in the preparations for our wedding. He is always arriving when I least expect him, and he asks such probing questions: how I spent my day, where I went, who I was with. There can only be one reason for his increased curiosity. He suspects I have given my heart to someone else!

I try to answer politely, but his gaze is like steel, hard and unyielding. I used to think his eyes were beautiful, but now they only remind me of the coldest ocean storm. A storm I will be forced to sail the rest of my life. I have an unwavering fear that I will drown in those eyes someday.

I wish he'd never come to Somerset.

CHAPTER THIRTY-SIX

I returned to my room in a state of confliction. I was relieved Mr. Pemberton still wanted me for the séance, but there was a nervous energy as well that made me pace the floor. So much so that my boots were practically dry. There were still too many scenarios where I could end up back in a London jail cell. Even if my séance was successful in producing a confession, there was no guarantee Mr. Lockhart would still want to represent me in court. And if he did, I would be putting my very life in his hands. His feeble, gnarled, and dying hands. I shivered at how weakened he'd be . . . or if he'd even still be alive by the time of my trial.

I took off my bonnet and held the tiara up to the candlelight. That was my only guarantee. I opened the top drawer of the vanity and pulled out a petticoat.

A quick rapping at the door interrupted me. "Yes?" I said, wondering if Flora had returned.

There was a click, then the knob turned, and the door began to open. I had been so distracted by my latest conversation with Mr. Pemberton, I'd forgotten to lock it behind me.

"Nightcap, Miss Timmons," Mrs. Donovan announced, her tone cold and formal as ever.

In a flurry of nerves, I messily wrapped the tiara up and rammed it to the back of the drawer. I whirled around in time to see Mrs.

Donovan stepping into the room, carrying a small tray in one hand and a lamp in the other.

I shoved my hips back, closing the drawer.

Mrs. Donovan stood like a grim sentry as she gave the room a critical scan. Her attention paused on the bed. The green blanket from Mr. Pemberton's room was neatly folded at the bottom.

"Thank you for the tea," I said. "Although the supper was more than substantial. You didn't need to tax yourself bringing this to me."

"A nightcap is not tea," she corrected, taking the tray to the table where I'd eaten supper earlier. She carefully placed down a steaming teapot and a crystal glass. "Mr. Lockhart is still ill," she said. "But his nightly hot toddy seems to improve his health. I was worried when Bramwell confirmed you'd missed dinner. We cannot risk you becoming sick."

She focused on me, then slid her gaze to the top drawer of the vanity. I was certain she could smell the guilt on me.

I kept my stance. "An earlier headache kept me in bed. I am fine now, I assure you."

Making no move to leave, Mrs. Donovan said, "Is everything to your satisfaction? I hope you are enjoying your stay here." Except her expression looked like she was getting ready to use the chamber pot. She took a step closer. The lamp filled in the space between us, throwing shadows over her face. The effect was not an improvement.

"I know you like being waited on," she said. "I see how you look at the lord too. I suppose you fancy this for yourself. But it will take more than dance lessons in the library and dark strolls in the greenhouse to become the next Lady Chadwick."

The words wrestled so fast to get out, I practically choked. "I don't want any part of Somerset Park," I declared. "Or Lord Chadwick. And I don't want you coming in here writing messages in my ghost book or moving the paintings on my wall." I pointed to the picture of the schooner, now upright and perfectly straight.

The corner of her mouth curled into a sinister smile. "You sound positively mad. Perhaps I should call for Dr. Barnaby."

I'd reached my limit for her interference and snide remarks. And knowing that Mr. Pemberton trusted me made me bold. "Perhaps you should stop spreading falsehoods and giving your opinion on a matter in which you are most grievously misinformed. Lord Chadwick and I only meet to discuss the séance. His sole purpose is to contact Lady Audra so he may tell her how much she is loved and missed." A lie, of course, but one that needed to be reinforced.

Her face turned red. "Generations of Linwoods are rolling in their graves at the injustice of his taking the title." She made a disgusted sound at the back of her throat. "He never cared for Lady Audra's well-being."

"And you did?"

"Of course!"

I'd never heard such passion from Mrs. Donovan. She was close to losing control, vulnerable even. I crossed my arms in front of my chest. "Then why did you let Mr. Sutterly visit her room the night before the wedding? You were aware he opposed the marriage. Why did you willingly put Lady Audra in that precarious position?"

Her eyes flashed accusingly at me. "I was the only one to see her that night."

"Mr. Sutterly admitted it himself. Why would he lie?"

She shook her head. "You're the one who is lying."

"Only one of you can be telling the truth, Mrs. Donovan. And I find it interesting that of everyone at Somerset Park, only you and Mr. Sutterly have ever mentioned Lord Chadwick not being the rightful heir."

The lamp in her grip started to shake. Her eyes lost their sharp intensity. There was no doubt that I had found Mrs. Donovan's weak spot. I had to take advantage.

I softened my tone. "You were outside her door all night, carefully keeping watch, but something happened that was beyond your control."

Her gaze wavered downward.

"You know what happened and now you're scared." I let a moment pass, then I added, "I can help you not be afraid."

Lifting her chin, Mrs. Donovan gave a tired sigh. "Fear does not tax me; it fades . . . unlike guilt. I owe you no explanation, but I swear on Lady Audra's grave I do not know what happened to her. She was safe and very much alive when I delivered her nightcap."

Despite my strong dislike of Mrs. Donovan, my bones knew she was telling the truth. Particularly about the guilt. It never fades.

She straightened her posture, reclaiming her usual serious manner, and made her way to the door. She turned and looked pointedly at the green blanket again. "Asking for a key to your room was wise. Make sure you use it. We want all good girls tucked away safely for the night."

After she left, I locked the door and tried to shake off the chill. Her comment about Mr. Pemberton hung in the air, confusing and irritating. My romantic notions were few and far between. The only men I knew were customers at Miss Crane's and greasy coppers. Regardless of Mrs. Donovan's preposterous notions, my heart would not be given away so easily.

Maman told me, *Love brings pain*, ma chérie, *we see it every sé-*

ance. It's my job to heal their grief. I tell them what they want to hear, and their hope fills in the rest because they are looking with their hearts, not their eyes—the heart sees. Even weeks later, they will not remember the vague promises I made or the things I guessed incorrectly. They only remember what they want to believe.

If it's so easily fooled, how can anyone trust their heart? I had asked, absorbing everything she said.

Exactly, she praised. *The only guarantee love brings is heartache.*

I knew she was talking about my father and the tragedy that happened. But I couldn't help but feel a sting because I was the result of their love. I often imagined what my life would be like if my father hadn't fallen into the harbour that day.

I went directly to the vanity and opened the top drawer. I took the tiara and rewrapped it in several petticoats and shoved it to the back. It needed a new hiding place, one where no one else would come across it, but one I could easily access without being seen. I'd do it as soon as everyone was asleep—or, in Mrs. Donovan's case, when she hung upside down in her cave.

I frowned at the drawer. The sparse contents contrasted to Audra's vanity drawer, giving me a peculiar sense of déjà vu.

Despite my full stomach, I poured myself the hot toddy and prepared for bed. I wondered who had helped Mrs. Donovan turn the painting upside down. There was no way she could have done it herself. And even more so, I was eager to learn who Flora had seen stumbling out of the woods that night.

"You can't trick me," I said to the darkened room. Still, Mrs. Donovan's warning about locking my door had put me on edge. I wedged a chair under the doorknob, a trick I learned at Miss Crane's. "Let's see you get by that, you scowling cow."

Satisfied, I finished my toddy and slipped into my bedclothes.

Just before dozing off, a vision of Audra's top drawer entered my mind once more. I had the answer, but it slipped away like water through my fingers.

It seemed I had only just closed my eyes before there was a knocking at the door. The cobwebs of a troubling dream clung to my sleepiness. I had been on the cliff with the wind blowing my hair.

The knocking came again, harder this time. Flora's urgent voice was on the other side. "Jenny?"

"Coming," I said drowsily. I winced as I made my way to the door. My body felt stiff.

I removed the chair and unlocked the door.

Flora came into the room holding a tray, but instead of her usual rosy cheeks she was pale and harried-looking. "I have your morning tea. You have to get dressed quickly and meet the others downstairs." She filled the basin on the nightstand with fresh hot water.

"Mm-hmm," I said sleepily, dunking the cloth into the steaming water and washing my face.

"His lordship is some upset." She continued buzzing around my room. "The parish constable had to be summoned."

All my blood whooshed to my feet. I dropped the cloth into the basin. I had slept all night instead of hiding the tiara. I cursed Mrs. Donovan and her nightcap. She must have found out about the tiara and told Mr. Pemberton. I had to leave at once! "Can you sneak me down to the kitchen without being seen?" I asked Flora.

She snorted. "The kitchen? That's the last place you want to be, what with all the panic going on down there." Dishes clinked as she continued to set up my breakfast. "Mrs. Donovan was found this morning in the back garden, lying still on the ground and drenched in mud. Joseph thought she was dead. He nearly died himself when her eyes snapped open after he'd been patting her cheeks and hollering her name. They're saying she's been attacked!" Flora paused and added thoughtfully, "I wonder what I would've done if I were the one who found her."

My mouth hung open. "Attacked?" I asked. Even though she'd shown a glimpse of vulnerability last night, Mrs. Donovan was hardly the sort to play victim.

"She was hysterical at first, but since then she's been coming in and out of consciousness. Dr. Barnaby is with her now."

I couldn't imagine her in that state. "And that's why the police are coming?" I asked.

She handed me a cup of tea with a strange look. "Why else? But don't you worry, Jenny. I'm sure whoever it was will be caught soon. Probably a drunken vagrant who got kicked out of the Plough and Bell and wandered along the road until they ended up here. It's happened before."

"The Plough and Bell?"

"The village pub."

"Oh." Picking a slice of toast off the tray, I ignored the butter and preserves and took a bite. I turned so Flora couldn't see the immense relief on my face. "How awful for her," I said. In honesty, I was glad it was Mrs. Donovan and not Flora who had been accosted.

"Hurry, now. I'm under strict orders to get you downstairs."

Taking the last sip of tea, I passed her my cup and fixed my attention on the wardrobe. I chose a light brown dress with a high neck and a simple lace trim on the cuffs. It needed to be taken in at the waist, but there was no time to worry about a proper fit.

Flora helped me as I stepped into the skirt. I could feel her hands working the back buttons. With an attacker on the loose, my thoughts turned again to the story she had started to tell me previously. Was it possible the two were related? "Remember what we were talking about before Mrs. Donovan interrupted us last night?" I started, half turning to glimpse her expression. "You were telling me about a man you'd seen coming from the woods."

She grimaced. "I wish I hadn't said anythin'. Please, too many horrible things are goin' on, I can't bear to talk about it now. I might have the hysterics if I think about it too much." She patted my back. "There now, all buttoned up. Hurry, get yer shoes on."

"Please, Flora," I pleaded. "I'll tell no one." I knelt down, reaching for my boots, and froze. They were covered in dried mud. A lump of toast threatened to come up. I knew for a fact my boots were clean and dry when I took them off last night.

"Mrs. Galloway is beside herself," Flora continued. She reached around me and took out the white shawl. "She said there's been a fairy ring around the moon, and the ghosts in the pantry have been howlin' more than usual. She claims an entire wall of preserves was smashed the other night."

With my heart in my throat, I pushed my boots back into the closet and instead chose the polished black shoes. The girls at Miss Crane's said they were scared to wake me when I was sleepwalking. I could be very strong and combative. They only touched me when I came too close to the top of the stairs.

Flora sat me at the vanity and quickly pinned my curls in place. She chattered on as my gaze took in the room. On the rug were dried footprints going from the door to the wardrobe. How could someone get in without disrupting the chair? There was one answer, but I didn't want to acknowledge it.

I wobbled in the tight shoes. Flora noticed and offered up a weak grin of encouragement. "Your hair is so lovely no one will notice," she said.

When I entered the sitting room, Mr. Pemberton and William were in opposite chairs, neither paying attention to the other. They both stood when I entered. I wasn't sure how I made it to the nearest chair as my legs had gone numb.

"Nice to see you at last," William said, though his unpleasant tone conveyed otherwise. Although his gaze was focused over my shoulder. I turned to see Flora in midcurtsy. She handed me the white shawl, gave another curtsy, and then left the room.

Sitting back down, William said, "Tragic news has befallen Somerset Park this morning. I fear we may be unable to guarantee your safety while you stay here." He was cleanly shaven, and his clothes were pressed, but the hardness of his eyes hinted at a darker meaning. I wasn't sure if he meant safe from the police or whomever had attacked Mrs. Donovan.

It seemed whatever comradery we may have shared in Audra's room was forgotten. I wondered if the drink had dulled the memory of our exchange.

Mr. Pemberton scoffed under his breath. "No one is leaving," he said. "Least of all Miss Timmons." He twirled the small gold ring.

I recognized his anxious gesture. And this, in turn, made me more nervous.

The muted light of the grey morning gave an ashen hue to everything in the room; even the golden wallpaper seemed pale and washed out. The moldings that adorned the ceiling and cornices looked cracked and ready to drop on our heads at any moment.

Dr. Barnaby arrived with a weary hello. He sank into the chair next to mine. His light brown hair was practically standing on end, and there were shadows under his eyes.

"How is she?" William asked. "When can I see her?" There was an impatience to his tone.

Shaking his head, Dr. Barnaby said, "I gave her a sedative to help her rest. She was hysterical earlier."

William grimaced. "Did she say why she was outside in the middle of the night?"

"She received an anonymous letter to meet someone outside with the promise of secret information about Audra. You know how devoted she was to her. Foolish as it was, she went on her own." He let out a sigh and ran a hand through his hair. "They must have come up behind her. She doesn't remember seeing anyone before the attack. There's a terrible lump on the back of her head to substantiate this. It's a curious-looking injury too; I'm not sure what kind of tool would have left such a uniquely shaped wound."

"An anonymous letter?" Mr. Pemberton repeated. "That's impossible. All the mail goes through Bramwell. If there was no return address on the envelope, it would have alerted him."

"Are you saying Mrs. Donovan is lying?" William's tone was fierce.

Dr. Barnaby put up a hand. "The note was pushed under her bedroom door after midnight. She said a knock woke her."

"Then it was someone who has access to the house," William said. His chin inclined toward me.

I stayed quiet and preferred to study the design on my cuffs. My toes throbbed in the small shoes.

"Even you, Doctor," William said. A snide expression settled on his features. "You still have your own private key, if I'm not mistaken."

"Honestly." Dr. Barnaby sighed. "You'd make a terrible police detective. I was delivering a baby in the village until five this morning.

I had only gotten home when the stable boy rapped on my door."

Mr. Pemberton gave his friend a sympathetic glance. "Even so," he told him. "The parish constable will want to speak with all of us when he's finished with the staff."

I put a hand on my throat, imagining the noose. Parish constable or not, coppers always made me uneasy. Especially when I had a pair of muddy boots hidden in my room.

William put his attention back on me. "I heard from a reliable source that you and Mrs. Donovan had an angry exchange last night. Perhaps you wanted to give her a proper warning. Is that how they handle things in your part of London?" He leaned forward in his chair, glaring at me.

"I beg your pardon?" I asked. It was more maddening to have William skirt around the accusation than coming right out to say it. Coward.

"You don't deny you were arguing with Mrs. Donovan last night?"

I didn't reply. I had no desire to share any information that might incriminate me.

"Your silence practically admits your guilt," William said, almost triumphant.

Mr. Pemberton's voice was strong but controlled, a jarring contrast to William's emotional accusations. "If you're insinuating that Miss Timmons had anything to do with Mrs. Donovan's attack, you can provide sufficient evidence or leave at once. And if you're thinking of relaying this inane theory to the constable, you should know that I've made him aware of your nightly drinking rituals. Alcohol disorients the mind; a drunkard's testimony alone can hardly be considered reliable."

His defense resulted in an unexpected boost of courage. I dared to hope it was genuine.

William's lips pressed into an angry line.

Dr. Barnaby leaned forward, resting his elbows on his knees. "I wouldn't mind a bit of breakfast while we wait for the constable," he said. "Or at the very least some strong coffee."

Mr. Pemberton pulled the velvet rope in the corner. Moments later, Bramwell entered.

"The dining room is set, my lord." He bowed. "The constable has finished with the staff. Where would you like him to wait? The library?"

"No, the Gallery Hall. Take him there first, please. I'll follow shortly once the others have had something to eat."

We all stood. Mr. Pemberton said, "A word, please, Miss Timmons."

I had no other option but to stay behind. And even though I was grateful to watch William leave, I couldn't ignore the truth.

Only one person had the ability to get out of my locked room and then back—me. But I had no memory of it! I only had the dream. A new terror paralyzed me. My muscles felt sore this morning. What if it wasn't a dream? What if I was sleepwalking again? Mrs. Donovan had threatened me, that was certain. And my final thought last night was to wish her harm.

Was I capable of such a thing?

Yes.

I locked eyes with Mr. Pemberton. He knew I was capable of this, and much worse.

CHAPTER THIRTY-SEVEN

Lady Audra Linwood
Diary Entry
Somerset Park, March 10, 1852

Mr. Lockhart read Father's will today in the library.

I am numb as I write these words. According to my father's last wishes, William has been bequeathed a substantial living. He will be allowed to stay at Somerset, officially, as one of the family.

Even though Father had allowed William to cavort and be at ease at Somerset while neglecting his studies, this incredibly generous inheritance is still shocking. I expected he would receive a modest living and perhaps a parsonage in the village, but Father has all but bestowed upon him the title of Earl of Chadwick. Mr. Lockhart seemed as mystified as I.

The manor is full of staff gossip, some of it unnecessarily cruel. They think I'm unaware of the things they whisper.

However, one person was not at all surprised by this turn of events: William. He has been all smugness and vengeance. Gone is the hurt man who fled Somerset after my engagement. He has now returned and appears ready to stake his claim. He said Father told him of this plan on his deathbed, but made William promise not to speak of it until the will was read.

I felt it like a stab to my heart, Dearest. For we both know where I was while Father was dying. I had no defense but to stay silent. I wonder if William knows.

His open glares toward Mr. Pemberton during the reading of the will were ridiculous. As if he had any right! What has William ever done to improve Somerset Park? Nothing. He only indulges in its comforts. I am the one who should be enraged. Such a scandal to be presented in front of my future husband.

I considered every man in the room as Mr. Lockhart read Father's will. William has developed into a spoiled man, convinced he is owed whatever he desires. Mr. Pemberton, now Earl of Chadwick, is fully aware that Somerset Park and all its contents are now his. Mr. Lockhart was of no use as he stared at the document.

But it wasn't the living that bothered me so. It was that my own father could not tell me himself. I deeply resent the thought of he and William sharing a secret. I feel as though he stole my father from me.

They all consider me beneath them, something to be dealt with as an afterthought. I looked up at Grandfather's portrait during the reading for support. He is a mystery to me, but one thing I am sure of: he would never let himself be treated the way I have had to endure.

William took no time in assuming a place in the family and has moved all of his things from his old room to one just down the hall from me. I will make sure to lock my door every night. He is like a shadow I cannot abolish, no matter how many candles I light.

I privately took Mr. Lockhart aside and expressed my worry, but he was no help. He shares my concern, Dearest, but he said the will was quite clear: William may stay at Somerset. I can't even trust my own father to do the right thing for me.

It is impossible to trust any of them.

CHAPTER THIRTY-EIGHT

Once we were alone, Mr. Pemberton crossed the room to me, his eyes fiery and intense. "Fetch your coat and bonnet," he ordered. "Then wait out of sight at the bottom of the staircase. Bramwell will be bringing the constable up from the kitchen via the servants' passage. Once they've passed into the Gallery Hall, come to my study."

"Are you trying to keep me out of sight?"

"Simply avoiding an unwanted complication. Please hurry."

I quickly returned to my room, jittery and unsure. I was relieved that Mr. Pemberton had thought of a plan to help me avoid being questioned, yet it only proved he was aware of the threat I represented. I hardly felt myself as I retrieved my coat. I slipped on my muddy boots, hiding them under the long hem of the dress.

Watching from the grand staircase, I saw the constable follow Bramwell into the Gallery Hall. He was stout and walked with a limp. There was a noticeable accent as he commented on the number of large portraits.

Mr. Pemberton appeared around the corner at the newel post, ushering me with a crooked finger. "I'll take you as far as the lane that leads to the stables," he said, walking toward the main door. "You'll be fine to spend a few hours there. Joseph can take care of anything you might need."

Practically running to keep up, I clumsily tied a bow under my chin.

The rains from yesterday still rendered the ground soggy, and I was grateful for every step that added more mud to my boots. Wordlessly, Mr. Pemberton led me around the side of the house, away from the windows of the Gallery Hall. Both of us walked briskly, our breaths coming out as puffs of steam.

I jogged to keep up with his quick pace. "What about the constable?" I asked.

He spoke over his shoulder. "As far as I'm concerned, once he leaves today, everyone will have been questioned and there will be no need for him to return. I understand the word of an earl holds merit with the magistrate."

I wanted to be grateful for his assistance, but I didn't want to bring attention to the real reason he had to do this in the first place. "Thank you," I murmured to his back. Without warning, he stopped, and then turned to me. The wind blew his hair back. He was only in his suit jacket, and his ears were red from the cold.

He was about to say something when Flora came bustling from the direction of the kitchen garden. Her coat was buttoned up to her chin, and her bonnet was pulled down low. An empty basket hung from the crook of her elbow. She jumped when Mr. Pemberton called out to her, staring at us with wide eyes. He beckoned her over.

"Good day, m'lord," she said, chin bowed.

Mr. Pemberton nodded. "I know the staff are concerned about Mrs. Donovan, but I want to assure you the police will be thorough. I'm sure Mrs. Galloway is relieved to have him out of her way. Is the kitchen busy with preparations for tomorrow night?"

"Aye, m'lord," Flora replied. "She's set the menu. I'm on me way to the village to pick up the last ingredients." She then awkwardly motioned to the path.

"Our meeting is lucky coincidence," Mr. Pemberton said. "As Miss Timmons was just mentioning she longed for a walk, and she hasn't had the chance to tour Wrendale."

I couldn't help but admire the smooth lie. I began to anticipate his performance for the séance. He looked at me, then nudged me with his elbow when I did not reply.

"Yes, Flora," I said. "I'd truly appreciate your company as well."

She mumbled assent, barely lifting her eyes.

Mr. Pemberton stepped back. "I hope you find Wrendale to your liking," he said.

FLORA WAS QUIET until we reached the edge of Somerset Park and turned onto the road. The ruts of the path were filled with puddles, so we stuck to the raised ridge in the middle. Now that I was clear from having to face the constable, my attention returned to Flora and what she'd seen the night before the wedding. However, I sensed her reluctance to tell me hadn't changed since this morning.

When she finally spoke, it was about Mrs. Donovan. "Everyone thinks she might have staged the whole thing. She's so bitter, I bet she's tryin' to stir up trouble. You know, she warned us before you showed up that night. She said nothin' good would come from havin' you in the house."

"She did? Why?" I nearly tripped.

Flora grabbed my elbow, pulling me back. She linked her arm through mine. We continued to walk that way, giving each other more balance.

She shrugged. "Don't matter, she's lyin', I bet." The basket swung off her other arm.

As much as I wanted to believe Flora, I knew someone couldn't fake a bump on the back of their head. I tried to change the subject. "What's so important about tomorrow?" I asked, thinking of the errand I was accompanying her on. "It sounds like an elaborate meal is planned."

"A special guest will be attendin' for dinner. Miss Gibbons has connections and a rather rich American cousin who's developed an interest in English estates. Joseph said that Mr. Pemberton is hoping to do business with some developers she has influence with." Then she scrunched up her face. "Can't say I'm too excited about it, though. I hates the idea of Somerset Park being cut up and sold off in bits and pieces."

"I'm sure the new owner will keep Somerset intact. Even so, I can't imagine someone with your skills will be in want of employment. There must be many manors in need of staff."

She laughed so hard she lost her footing, almost taking me with her into a puddle. "Yes, I want to be a scullery girl the rest of my life."

"I didn't mean it like that."

"Oh no, I imagine you didn't." She snorted again, and I knew she was being lighthearted. The clouds thinned above us. Soon, the sun warmed our chilled faces. Although most of the trees had lost their leaves, the walk was pleasant, and the fresh late-autumn air was the perfect respite to the heavy suspicion of the manor.

"I'm glad we have this time, Jenny." Flora sighed, content.

We travelled along the road as the village came into view. I was curious which shops Flora would take me to, but we turned up a lane and came to a sweet cottage. Its stone walls were covered in vines, and there was an impressive garden that took up much of the property.

"This is my auntie Lil's," Flora explained as she opened the gate for me. "She used to work at Somerset back when Lord Chadwick the third was alive." She lowered her voice. "Her mind's been slippin' a bit these last few years, so take everything she says with a grain of salt."

"Ta, Auntie Lil," Flora said as the elderly woman placed a serving of sliced cake on the table between us. White spirals of hair peeked out from under her plain headscarf that tied under her chin. Her thick skirt reached the wooden floor, making a sweeping motion as she hobbled about, serving us. A pot of tea came next. Flora's aunt then dropped herself into a rocking chair by the stove and lit a small pipe. She wore several sweaters but was small enough to still appear slight.

The home was humble, but cozy and clean. Tiny paintings of village scenes were hung in homemade frames. Across from the table where Flora and I sat were a hutch and buffet of simple design with blue-and-white dishes displayed neatly. Everything was in its place, and everything was practical. Not unlike my first home with Maman and Mrs. Rinaldo.

"Auntie Lil knows everything about gardening," Flora explained. Bundles of herbs dried from an exposed wooden beam above us. The aroma was intense.

"She even makes her own pipe mixture," Flora continued. There was a sense of pride to her tone.

"I gots bad hips," Auntie Lil explained. "I find me pipe takes care of the aches better than anything that young doctor could give me." She squinted as she spoke, creating a starburst of wrinkles on either side of her eyes.

I took a bite of cake, letting it melt on my tongue. Flora must come by her cooking skills honestly. The basket had been filled with jars of mint jelly, made especially for the pork that would be served tomorrow night. "The cake is perfection," I told her.

She smiled, deepening the wrinkles.

"I understand you used to work at Somerset Park," I said, eager to hear her version of its history.

Leaning forward in her rocking chair, Auntie Lil said, "Be careful up there. Flora doesn't heed my warnings, but that place is cursed."

Flora reached for another piece of cake. "Auntie, please. Jenny is our guest."

"I don't like you workin' there," she said, pointing her pipe at Flora.

"But there's good people at Somerset Park now." A blush came to her cheeks. "And who knows," she added, "maybe I won't be a kitchen maid much longer."

Auntie Lil chuckled. "Is that why you asked for the love bundle from my pantry? Oh, don't be red in the face now, you can have it." Then she winked at me. "Don't know why she needs it—Flora's a mighty lovely girl. Any boy who's worth marryin' will know it without my herbal interference."

Huffing, Flora added more hot tea to both our cups. I thought about Joseph and what specifically she was worried about him lying to her about. "What do you think of Mrs. Donovan's attack?" she asked her aunt. I presumed it was to take the attention off her love life.

"Pfft," she answered. "Doesn't take a genius to recognize the curse is at work. That grandfather was a cruel bastard, and now his family and all who were loyal to him are payin' the price. Mark me word, girls, Somerset Park will crumble into the ocean before another heir is born."

Flora grumbled something into her teacup.

I, however, was intrigued by her theory about Mrs. Donovan, especially since I still couldn't explain my muddy boots the next morning. Maybe it was easier to believe in a curse when the alternative was admitting my own guilt in the matter. "Are you saying Mrs. Donovan was a victim of the curse as well?" I asked.

"I sees her come into the village now and then, thinking she's one of them, all right." Then her expression softened. "Not like that lawyer, Mr. Lockhart. He treats me with respect and always pays a little extra for me herbs and such."

I wondered if he used her pipe mixture for his own ailments. A dying man will leave no remedy untried, I suspected.

"He's not one to put on airs," she continued. "He even made a generous donation to the church. Wouldn't be no roof if he hadn't helped pay for repairs."

"Yes." Flora sighed tiredly. "He's humble."

"Mr. Lockhart is a saint, I tells ya. What he's still doin' around Somerset is beyond me."

"He's the estate trustee, Auntie," Flora said, reaching for another piece of cake. "And with Lady Audra's death, he has a lot of paperwork to sort through. It's not as simple as handin' over the keys to the new Lord Chadwick. And who knows? There might be another legitimate Linwood out there."

"Really?" I asked, surprised by Flora's knowledge of estate planning.

Auntie Lil rocked herself a few times, gently pushing the toe of her shoe against the floor. The creaking was a gentle backdrop to our conversation.

"What about Mr. Sutterly?" I asked, wondering what other tidbits she knew.

Flora choked on a piece of cake. She took a quick sip of tea. Maybe I was being too intrusive, but her wealth of knowledge was too tempting to ignore.

"Ah," Auntie Lil said, letting the one word linger in the air. "There's plenty o' rumors about the blacksmith's demise. Curious how a man finds death on the road to Somerset, then lickety-split, the lord of the manor takes his adopted son as his ward." She raised her white eyebrows. "Another finger of the curse, I'd reckon."

I wondered if Auntie Lil had heard rumors about William's secret lineage. "How did the curse start?" I asked, ignoring Flora nudging me under the table.

Her eyes got bigger. "Servants would go missin', usually the young, pretty ones. A few times their bodies were found, washed up on shore weeks later, beaten by the rocks and bloated from the sea. But I'll tell ya one thing, ain't no mystery who'd done it." She lifted her chin and focused on the door. "Lord Chadwick the third."

"Audra's grandfather?" I clarified, thinking of his leering portrait in the library, the blaze of his eyes, his white-knuckled grip.

"Aye." She nodded. "One night I heard it me'self. I was doing the final cleanup in the kitchen. Everyone else had retired to their rooms. I put the last bundle of logs on the fire, and then I heard someone hollerin'. It was comin' from under the pantry floorboards, I tell ya."

"Could have been the wind, Auntie," Flora said. There was no conviction in her voice. I reasoned she'd heard this story many times.

"Does the wind call out for help?" she snapped back. Then she turned back to me, eyes bright. "It was soft at first, real weak-like." Then she imitated the voice. *"Help me. Help me."*

A million shivers skittered across my skin. My hand flinched, hitting my teacup, almost spilling it. I mumbled an apology and crouched in my chair.

Auntie Lil continued, "I ran as fast as me boots could carry me. I woke the head maid, but by the time I dragged her down to the kitchen, the voice had stopped." She leaned back in her chair and took another inhale from her pipe. "She says I imagined it, but I'll tells ya this, whatever was calling out for help probably died that night. 'Twas my cowardice that sealed her fate."

"When was this?" I asked, feeling goose bumps pepper my arms.

"Fifty years ago, miss. I left Somerset Park soon after, and I ain't never been back."

I took the last sip of tea, but I couldn't taste anything. All I could think of were those two words: *Help me.*

Auntie Lil reached for her cane and stood, wincing as she rose. Still, she had enough strength to stare down Flora. "You ignore my warnin', but I'll tell ya, Lady Audra paid for her grandfather's sins. The ghosts of those dead servants lured her out to that cliff. And they won't be satisfied until the whole place ends up in a watery grave."

BEFORE WE LEFT, she gave Flora a kiss on the cheek and slipped her a lovely autumnal posy. I supposed the gesture was meant to end the visit on a pleasant note, but I could see a weariness in Flora's expression. I remembered what she'd told me about her aunt's mind, and I worried I had enabled the embellishment of a false memory.

But as each step took me farther from the cottage, her words clung to me like an impending sickness.

Help me.

A coincidence, surely.

CHAPTER THIRTY-NINE

Lady Audra Linwood
Diary Entry
Somerset Park, April 13, 1852

Dearest,

Something is wrong with me. For the last few weeks I haven't been able to eat, and I am always tired. But that's not the worst part.

I started hearing her voice. It was so strong it woke me from a dead sleep. She called out to me, begging for help. Although her pleas chilled me to the bone, a powerful pull inside my soul made me leave the comfort of my room to find her.

Mrs. Donovan discovered me, huddled in the doorway to the wine cellar. My feet were caked in mud, and my hands were covered in rust.

I have no memory of how I got there.

It was William who carried me back to my bedroom. He and Mrs. Donovan stayed with me all night, although I have only the vaguest memory of what they said. They told me I must have been sleepwalking. They exchanged a look of knowing. I am certain they are plotting a scheme. I trust neither of them.

Mr. Pemberton was summoned. When he arrived, he voiced his concern that a doctor had not been sent for. Mrs. Donovan merely told him that I had only a slight chill, nothing she couldn't take care of with some tea and rest.

I dared not mention hearing the voice to Mr. Pemberton. There was enough suspicion surrounding Father's death. I cannot risk him breaking off the engagement for fear of acquiring an unstable wife. He asked me if he could call upon his friend to assess me, just to be sure. I could hardly look him in the face. My guilt must have shown. Perhaps he is waiting for an opportunity to see us together, so he can accuse us of having an affair.

As soon as he took his leave, I turned my head and cried into the pillow. How can I ever face my love again? My heart will break, and I am so frail, I fear it may stop the very moment I see him.

Mrs. Donovan brought me a cup of tea, and although my stomach will not tolerate food, I found her bitter brew surprisingly calming. She stayed and watched me take each sip, making idle comments about how it will be good to have the wedding soon, something to rally everyone's spirits. But there was a wickedness to her grin. It reminded me of William when he used to steal treats from the kitchen, knowing he wouldn't get in trouble.

They've stationed someone to sit outside my door. They do not trust me to be alone. I can still smell the rust on my palms. And as I lie here alone, it unearths a memory long forgotten.

I only knew Grandfather as an old man, stooped over his cane. He never looked at me, always through me. One night he appeared at the foot of my bed, nightshirt on and wiry hair standing on end. I screamed, thinking he was a ghost.

He put a hand over my mouth and pushed his face up against mine. His breath was rancid as he told me he needed my help. Terrified, I just nodded and got out of bed and followed him. The house was in total darkness, and we were the only ones moving about.

With a single candle in his shaking grip we made our way down to the kitchen. My bare feet were so cold. I noticed his were covered in mud. This made no sense, as it was winter. When I started to cry, he tugged on my arm fiercely and told me to be quiet. He said we had to stop her. Then he asked if I could hear her, calling out.

I shook my head. The only thing I could hear was my own heartbeat in my ears.

He dragged me down to the wine cellar, a part of Somerset I had never visited before. He showed me a wooden door with rusted hinges and said we had to stop her from crying out or else she would get out and kill us all.

I began to cry louder, asking for Mother. He dropped the candle and put his hands up to his ears, yelling for her to stop.

Leaving him there, I ran back to my room and pulled the covers over my head. I lay awake all night, convinced each creak outside my door was Grandfather coming back. Finally, at dawn, I fell asleep.

Later that day, the low tide revealed Grandfather's body at the bottom of the cliff.

I never told anyone what happened. I wanted to pretend it was a nightmare. Sometimes I think it might have been his ghost that fetched me that night. Regardless, the memory faded. Over the years, I pushed it far down so I wouldn't have to relive it again. But now I feel as if I'm that little girl again, and more memories of Grandfather are coming back. More secrets about Somerset.

I am so sleepy, Dearest. I can hardly keep my eyes open.

CHAPTER FORTY

I was more determined than ever to get back to my room and check on the tiara. I had the perfect hiding place in mind.

". . . for years," Flora said. "Even people in the surrounding villages visit for her herbs and such."

I blinked a few times and realized I had been daydreaming while Flora had been talking.

"She wants me to take over for her, says she's gettin' too old, but I'd rather go somewhere else. I can't stand the thought of stayin' in the same place I was born. Maisie used to say I was like a dandelion: bright and cheery but would scatter on the wind when I got older." She looked up at the sky. "Letting destiny decide where I'll land and take root."

Flora's perspective on life struck me as naive, but there was something comforting in her romantic notions. That kind of optimism was rare in my world. "Does that mean you have no connection to Somerset Park?" I asked.

Her smile became secretive. "Well, maybe one thing."

The questions built up in my mind, but I held myself back. Unlike her aunt, Flora wasn't ready to divulge all her stories.

"Thank you for letting me accompany you to your aunt's," I said, thinking of Mrs. Rinaldo. "She's very kind."

Flora switched the basket to her other hand. Then her face took on a curious expression. "Where was you and the lord coming from this morning?"

"Just taking a stroll through the garden," I lied.

She chewed on her lower lip. "I can't tell you what to do, Jenny, but I wouldn't be caught alone with him for all the silverware in Somerset Park."

I laughed. "He's been a perfect gentleman, Flora."

Stopping in the middle of the road, she gripped my arm. "That's not what I'm talkin' about. He's the one I saw coming out of the woods that night." She leaned closer, even though we were the only ones on the road. "I was in the shadows as he staggered into view. He had this fierce expression on his face, but he looked exhausted, as if he'd been fightin' someone. I held my breath, praying he wouldn't see me."

A coolness crept up my back. "And did he?"

She nodded. "He handed his shirt to me, telling me to clean it for him. I asked if he was hurt and if I should get the doctor. He seemed really upset. His nostrils were flaring like a horse's. I'd never seen anythin' like it, Jenny! Then he told me not to mention it to anyone."

I felt like I couldn't take a breath. "Why the secrecy?" I asked.

Flora set her mouth in a grim line. "I knows blood when I sees it, and his shirt was covered. There was no way that stain would come out. I ended up tossin' it in the fireplace. When Lady Audra went missin', I was too scared to say anythin', sure he would do the same to me. I can't even look at him now without shakin' in me boots."

My mind was trying to take in her words. "Has he said anything to you since?" I asked.

"Only the usual greetin's."

What I had taken as Flora's shyness around her employer was fear. The ground no longer felt solid under my feet. A huge part of my understanding had been erased. I had begun to trust Mr. Pemberton, or at least feel secure in our alliance. Now my reasoning was in turmoil. The image of him soaked in blood ran rampant in my mind.

Flora was watching me, waiting for a reply. It took all my concentration to push that vision away for later. "I see," I said. It was all I could muster.

We passed a graveyard encircled by a low stone wall. Flora put down the basket and picked out the posy her aunt had given her. "I'll be right back," she said. Beyond a few rows of grave markers, she knelt in front of a polished headstone and carefully placed the bundle of flowers.

I stayed a respectful distance away, but I could still read Maisie's name. Dr. Barnaby mentioned a sickness in the village had taken the life of a young girl around the time of Audra's disappearance. I wondered if it was Maisie he'd been speaking of.

When we continued back to Somerset Park, a particular melancholy had settled around both of us. I wanted to help her feel better, but being a friend was something foreign to me. Miss Crane's girls only saw me as an anomaly—more of a ghost herself than a spiritualist.

Flora switched the basket to her other hand.

"I can carry that for you," I offered.

She hesitated. "It wouldn't be proper, Jenny."

"It's no bother; besides, I feel useless. When we get closer, I'll hand it back to you and no one will be the wiser."

A frown took over her face as she thought it over, then her characteristic smile slipped into place, and she handed me the basket.

Grunting, I altered my gait to accommodate the basket, which was much heavier than I'd suspected. Flora was stronger than she looked.

"So," I began. "There's a love potion in here? I hope we don't mix it up with the mint jelly. I bet that would liven up a dull dinner party. Although, from what I've seen, I don't think you need a love potion to capture the attention of your heart's desire."

I was a few steps ahead before I realized Flora had stopped in her tracks. She stared back at me, eyes enormous with surprise.

"Is it plain for everyone to see?" she gasped, touching her fingers to her lips.

"A man shows his genuine feelings by his actions, not his words," I said, thinking of all the false whispers of devotion overheard at Miss Crane's.

"He'll be upset. I promised I would keep it a secret."

"Why? He's the one who walks through the cold purposely to see you. Or maybe it's the lure of your apple pies," I teased.

Flora fretted with the ribbon of her bonnet, wrapping the end around one finger. "I suppose," she said, sounding unconvinced. "But he's promised me a ring, so that's somethin', isn't it?"

"A ring? I had no idea your relationship was that serious."

She scoffed at this. "He's promised to make me his wife." She lifted her chin. "I will not be a scullery maid much longer. Soon, I will have the last name of Sutterly."

I choked out a laugh, certain she was teasing me. "You mean William?" I asked. We stopped on the road, both of us staring at each other.

She giggled behind her hand. "Your face is so red! I knew you'd be surprised! It feels so nice to finally tell someone, though." She touched my arm. "We're keepin' it a secret for now. What's wrong? Ain't you happy for me?"

I grabbed her elbow. "You can't be serious." I pictured him drunk and lying in Audra's bed. "This makes no sense."

A flash of hurt crossed her face. "Why's it so hard to believe? He's not uppity like the rest of 'em."

"You cannot trust him with your heart. He's obsessed with Audra. He was in love with her!"

She tugged her arm away roughly and threw an angry pout at me.

I needed to make her see reason. "He's even cavorting with one of the other maids," I said. "I saw him the very first night I stayed at Somerset."

"That was me!" Her eyes filled with tears. "I'm the only one who's been able to heal his grief. I'm the only one that can make him forget all about her. He told me so."

My heart broke for her. If I hadn't seen him the other evening in Audra's room, I might have accepted her announcement with more understanding. I said, "He's only telling you what you want to hear."

"You don't know anythin'!" Flora grabbed the basket from me and raced ahead.

A sense of dread lay heavy as I realized I may have lost perhaps the only person I completely trusted at Somerset Park.

CHAPTER FORTY-ONE

Lady Audra Linwood
Diary Entry
Somerset Park, April 16, 1852

Dearest,

I can scarcely believe how my world has turned upside down in one small afternoon.

He arrived earlier today with his doctor's bag in hand. I could hardly raise my face to his. But oh! His hands were so gentle and his voice so achingly sincere and warm. He remained professional throughout his examination—something I found both endearing and disappointing.

However, we were both astonished when he determined that my sickness was in fact not a disease at all.

I am pregnant.

It was as if a spell were broken. His mask of medical competence slipped away, revealing an expression of exquisite joy. We collapsed into each other's embrace, both of us crying. Tears of *immense happiness, but also anguish. For how can we ever be together?*

He told me it is enough to know that I will be taken care of and that our child will be much loved. He truly believes Mr. Pemberton is an honorable man who will be a good husband and father.

He confessed his agony at not having been able to see me since Father's death. He was willing to accept this pain as penance for seducing his best friend's fiancée.

I laughed, Dearest, for my heart was full again! I told him we had all the right in the world, for we are true loves. Now that I am certain of his feelings, I am determined to have him as the family doctor. Mr. Pemberton will not question my reasoning, as he deemed old Dr. Mayhew insufficient. Just knowing he will be back in my life has electrified my spirits.

My smile is impossible to hide. He will deliver our child; he will be the first to see its face, and the one to place the babe in my arms. How is it possible to be this happy?

CHAPTER FORTY-TWO

I could barely look at Mr. Pemberton during dinner. Flora's description of him stumbling out of the woods with a shirt soaked in blood kept overlaying the fine evening jacket he wore. He asked about the village, but all I could give him were brief answers. I didn't dare bring up Auntie Lil's story.

Even Harry and Bramwell exchanged curious glances at our lackluster conversation. The sound of cutlery punctuated the uncomfortable silence. Finally, I excused myself, claiming the rainy weather had given me a slight chill.

Mr. Pemberton stood. "I'll have Joseph ride into the village for Barnaby."

"I only need rest," I told him. "I'm sure I'll feel much improved in the morning."

He looked unconvinced. "Is there a problem about the séance?" he asked, and I was surprised by his boldness in front of the others.

"Not at all. Good night, my lord." I was sure they could hear my hurriedly retreating footsteps all the way to my room.

I LAY IN bed, wide awake, until I was certain every soul had retired for the night. The very house seemed to breathe. There were mysteries within these walls, but I was more worried about my own secret being found out.

With my dressing gown tightened, I slipped out of my room. Tucked under my arm was the tiara, along with the copy of *The Hunchback of Notre Dame*. Sneaking around Somerset in the middle of the night with stolen jewelry wasn't my finest hour, but I had no choice. The séance was only days away—as was my nineteenth birthday. The sooner I completed the conjuring and left Somerset and the ocean, the better.

The small lamp I carried was the only speck of light in the entire house. The shadows took on the shapes of all my uncertainties. I saw Mr. Pemberton ready to jump out at me from behind the heavy drapes, awash in blood and asking to dance. William was there too, smelling of wine and pointing an accusing finger. Finally, Mrs. Donovan slinked into the light, her head caved in and calling me a murderer.

I would have welcomed a specter, a voice, anything to break this sense of foreboding. I took the stairs as quietly as I could.

The library door moaned on its hinges as I closed it behind me. It was like entering a cave. The air was still and heavy. The only noise came from the steady ticks of the grandfather clock.

The ladder was in the same place where I'd left it, stuck on its rusted track. I carefully climbed until I could reach the top shelf. I slipped the tiara into *The Hunchback of Notre Dame*'s empty slot, then returned the novel to its original place, pushing it back until it touched the tiara. The spines did not quite align, so I pulled out a few of the other books in that row a few hairs until they were mostly flush.

When I reached the bottom of the ladder, I looked up at my work and smiled. It was completely undiscernible. I would be able to retrieve the tiara the night of the séance and slip it into my bag. No one would be the wiser.

I turned to leave and nearly bumped into the table I'd chosen for the séance. A memory played against the darkness of Mr. Pemberton and me sitting in these chairs, facing each other. My cheeks warmed as I recalled the feeling of his palms against mine, and how I studied his face while his eyes were closed.

My whole body slumped. The pull of regret was stronger than I'd expected. How disappointed he would be to see me now. Then I pictured his bloody shirt once more; I had to focus.

The lamp pulsed for a few beats, and then the flame lowered. I frowned; something in the room had changed, an intangible shift in the dark. Holding up the lamp, I inspected the corners of the room, but nothing seemed out of the ordinary. All the animals were still dead. My attention wandered to the fireplace. Only the mantel was within view.

I moved closer, wondering if Lord Chadwick had finally come to life, climbing out of the painting with one hand clutching the gold frame, and the other brandishing the sabre, ready to slice off my head.

A floorboard creaked just behind me. I held my breath, building my courage to turn around, fully aware there would be no one to come to my aid, just as with Mrs. Donovan. The person who had lured her outside had access to the servants' private quarters. Dr. Barnaby said the weapon had left a curious wound. I waited stiffly, with each muscle aching, afraid to move.

An icy breath brushed against the back of my neck. I pictured the weapon being raised over my head. It was now or never. I whipped around, ready to kick or throw a punch, whatever was needed to save myself.

The library was empty.

Once I swallowed my heart back down, I noticed the room had

become uncommonly quiet. Even the wind outside had eased up. And that's when I realized what had changed.

The clock had stopped.

A shiver rolled along my spine. "Time for all good girls to be locked in for the night," I said, sounding like Mrs. Donovan. I made to leave, but when I reached the other side of the room, the chill became electrified, prickles shooting through the tips of my fingers. The door was wide open. I was certain I had closed it.

A sob echoed from the grand staircase. It sounded like Flora.

Had she confronted William about Audra? Was she hurt? My unease was pushed to the side as I rushed to find her. I followed the echoes of heaving cries to the servants' door and then down the narrow staircase.

The kitchen was abandoned, but the crying was louder now. "Flora?" I whispered, squinting at the shadowy corners.

"Help me."

I froze. That was not Flora's voice.

"Help me."

I pinpointed the source of the sound. Auntie Lil's voice narrated the scene inside my head as I entered the pantry and went to the far end. A set of steps descended to the wine cellar. Ignoring the shaking of my lamp, I took the stairs down into the cold room. Racks of dusty bottles created several rows reaching for the low ceiling. At the back wall, behind a pile of crates, a narrow door grinned back at me.

I tried the rusted knob. It resisted at first, then gave way as the hinges protested loudly. I was hit with the pungent scent of seawater, but there was something else—death. An actual rotting, as if I was walking into a fresh grave.

With the lamp in one hand, and my other palm splayed flat on the outer wall, I tentatively took the curving stairs, feeling like I was entering the bowels of hell itself.

The lapping of waves echoed up to me, matching the thumping of my heart. I could only see a few feet in front of me. The stairs grew more slippery with each step downward. The ocean was claiming Somerset from the bottom up. After generations of smashing against the stones, the sea had finally sunk its teeth and begun to consume. Any moment, the icy water would reach up with a seaweed fist and grab my ankles, pulling me down under the surface, claiming me.

The waves crashed again, much louder than before. A plume of mist rose, soaking the bottom of my nightgown. Each time I took a breath, I felt the sea air slip into my lungs, eager to drown me inside out.

Stay out of la mer, ma petite chérie.

Every part of my soul urged me to turn around and leave, but I had to know. I had to understand who was behind all of this.

Bit by bit, the inner wall gave way, and I gained a sense that I was edging along the outside of a deep pit. My fingers skimmed the slimy surface. The methodical ebb and crash of waves was hypnotic.

Was I going to walk into the ocean? Was this what happened to Audra?

Without warning, a hand pushed between my shoulder blades, and I stumbled forward, pitching headfirst into blackness.

My ribs smashed into the steps, taking my breath away. I slid against the wet, salt-crusted steps for what seemed like an eternity. Then my hand finally found purchase and I came to a stop. Miraculously, the lamp had remained in my other hand, unbroken.

Catching my breath, I gathered my bearings and moved to stand upright. "Who's here?" I called, holding the lamp out.

Nothing.

I could faintly discern the bottom of the chasm, made up of uneven rocks carpeted with seaweed. Again, there was the sound of spray, then water gushing and slipping away. There must be a small opening in the outer foundation. I sensed movement far below.

Then she screamed in my ear, so close I could smell her sour breath.

"Help me! Help me! Help me!"

I dropped the lamp. Its small point of light fell to the bottom of the pit, where it smashed on the rocks and extinguished completely.

I scrambled upward, with both hands clawing the steps above me, and did not stop running until I was back in my room. I would never forget what the lamp illuminated before it shattered and went out: rusted chains with cuffs, splayed across the rocks, and what looked like a gleaming white bone.

CHAPTER FORTY-THREE

Lady Audra Linwood
Diary Entry
Somerset Park, April 20, 1852

Dearest,

They found me near the cliff last night. I have no memory of getting there. Is it the family sickness? The pregnancy? Mr. Pemberton suggests we retreat to his home in the north, but I cannot leave Somerset. And I will certainly not leave with Mr. Pemberton to a place that is entirely his own, with his own staff, so that he might unleash his sinister nature.

I am safest here, with my love keeping close watch. I do not wish to be surrounded by strangers. My love is certain the pregnancy has aggravated my sleep patterns. He told Mr. Pemberton that I have the same illness that is inflicting the village, and that journeying north would only further risk my condition. Still, I worry. We must be so obvious; our love outshines everything and everyone around us.

We have moved the wedding date up.

Flora was crying today. Her dear friend Maisie has taken ill. She is worried that it is the same sickness that took the souls of a few elderly villagers in Wrendale already this month. She said she was concerned for me as well. I used to think Flora an amiable and perfectly harmless girl, but something in her tone put me on guard. I believe she suspected the pregnancy and was waiting for me to tell her. I've heard her gossip enough about the other staff to know she could never keep this secret. If Flora ever understood my true situation, it would be the downfall of Somerset Park, and I would be as good as dead.

Flora is not so innocent as she appears. I've seen how her gaze lingers on my jewelry and dresses. I wouldn't be surprised if she comes in and tries them on occasionally. Should I lock my door? What if someone is poisoning me and carrying me out to the cliffs? William is certainly strong enough. Mrs. Donovan's tea always makes me sleepy. I will only pretend to drink it henceforth.

My love attempted to ease my suspicions when I told him this. He told me that fear is warping my good judgment. Then his smile took on a peculiar angle, and he whispered that we should consider an alternative to my marrying Mr. Pemberton.

It was an odd way to see my love. There was almost a devious quality about him that frightened me. Does he know something nefarious about Mr. Pemberton? Is my love keeping secrets from me out of loyalty to his old friend? He was more than happy to let him raise our child. What has changed?

He told me that the only way we can be together as a family is to leave Somerset Park. He might as well have asked me to rip out my heart. But it is the only way we will be free to love. And then, as if to guarantee my silence on the matter, he kissed me, and I was at once lost in his arms.

As I write this, I am beginning to understand his reasoning. What use is living at Somerset if my heart is with him? Wasn't I only saying a few pages ago that this place felt like a tomb? What kind of life would that be?

We stayed in each other's arms for most of the afternoon. Being the family doctor affords time without need of a chaperone. It was William who interrupted us with an impatient knock on my door.

He is always lurking these days. If I leave, I will not miss him one jot. I swear, I wish he would walk off the cliff.

CHAPTER FORTY-FOUR

The following morning, I ate my eggs and sausage without noticing their taste. I was in a fog. I'm sure I could have poured a scalding pot of coffee down my throat and it wouldn't have even registered. My mind was too preoccupied with trying to make sense of what I'd experienced last night. Perhaps Flora's aunt had somehow filled my head with an imaginary voice. Or Mrs. Donovan had faked her own attack like Flora suggested, and she was using that cover to terrorize me. It would be a conniving plan of immense trickery, which, I reasoned, was within her villainous ability. Both were long stretches, but neither explained the chains secured to the rocks, or the piece of bone.

I was dining alone as Mr. Pemberton was at the stables and Mr. Lockhart was taking breakfast in his room again. I pictured him hunched over his tray, coughing between sips of coffee. He'd been working for the Linwoods all his life, and I didn't remember him mentioning having his own family. Mr. Pemberton said he'd been staying at Somerset off and on for the last year. I wondered if Dr. Barnaby knew his true diagnosis. If he was only getting a nightly hot toddy as a treatment, perhaps I should intervene. At the very least I should pay him a visit.

Relieved to push the dungeon to the back of my mind I made my way to Mr. Lockhart's room after receiving directions from

Harry. The hallway was empty. I was about to knock on his door when I heard the muffled sound of an argument. I leaned closer, pressing my ear to the wood.

Mr. Lockhart's hushed words were undistinguishable, but the urgency hinted at anger. There was a pause, then he spoke again, this time more in control. He let out a sigh, then something slammed shut. I jumped back, feeling the vibration against my ear.

I knocked, then said, "Mr. Lockhart? It's Miss Timmons."

To my surprise, he opened the door without hesitating. He was cleanly shaven and dressed in his shirt and tie. "Lovely to see you." He smiled. He stepped to the side and motioned for me to enter.

"I was concerned when you weren't at breakfast," I said, taking in his room. It was larger than mine, with a palette of gold and dark blue. Instead of a vanity, he had an extra chest of drawers and a writing desk. An oval table held the breakfast tray with remnants of dried yolk and a bread crust. A large portrait of a long-dead relative took most of the wall space opposite the canopy bed. I wondered how he slept knowing those eyes were watching him in the dark.

The room was grand, but it only had Mr. Lockhart.

"I'm sorry to have worried you, my dear. I'm feeling quite well today, but I wanted to stay in my room so I could build your case." He cleared his throat and motioned to the desk. I saw the stack of papers that had been in Mr. Pemberton's room—my police file. "I've been through it twice now, and I have to be honest, I'm eager to take this on." He brought out his handkerchief and coughed into it lightly.

I noticed a cut on his hand. "Did you hurt yourself?" I asked.

He looked confused, then examined the cut across his knuckles. "I have no idea. When you get to be my age, you can bump against the bedpost and break a hip. But do not fret, Miss Timmons. I have a clear strategy in mind to clear your name. I don't even anticipate it taking longer than a few days." He pocketed the handkerchief and clapped his hands together in glee. "I have to thank you, actually. I feel like this has given me new life."

I glanced again at the file. He sounded confident, but there was a lingering sense of disquiet about the room.

"Before I knocked, I heard you arguing," I said.

A blush colored his pale cheeks. "Just practising. Giving the argument out loud to an invisible jury helps me prepare."

His grey eyes smiled back at me with hope and promise. In that moment I wished I could give Mr. Lockhart the séance he wanted. I wished he would forgive my lies. But most of all I wished for him to be proud of me.

I took his injured hand in mine. "Thank you," I said.

FLORA HAD BEEN avoiding me since our argument, which unfortunately left me to my own devices to prepare for the special dinner that evening. Darkness fell quickly. I lit every candle in my room, which was odd for someone who was never afraid of the shadows.

I begrudgingly chose the dark green dress with the low neckline as it was big enough for me to do up the buttons on the back and slip it over my head. With the extra hairpins, I could make sure all my curls were flattened at the sides and neatly held in the back. The result wasn't outstanding, but it was passable.

I considered faking another headache to avoid the company, but when I learned William would be in attendance a part of me relished the thought of glaring at him from across the table for his despicable treatment of Flora. Besides, as uninterested as I was in dining with this stranger, the thought of spending time alone after the sun went down bothered me more than I wanted to admit.

I hoped the candlelight and a warm meal would lift my spirits.

Spirits.

Ghosts did not exist. It wouldn't do to have a spiritualist scared of shadows and voices in the dark.

A burst of fierce scratching noises made me jump. This time I was certain the mouse was inside the wardrobe. I gave a growl and grabbed the chamber pot, ready to trap the little nuisance. I flung open the door so quickly a few of the dresses swayed back and forth. But instead of a scampering creature, there was only silence.

I pushed the dresses to the side and scanned the bottom. There was a pile of shavings. No mouse, though. And no mouse hole. I straightened up and stared at the back of the wardrobe, now visible with the clothes pushed to the side. No critter was capable of what I saw.

Thin, jagged letters had been scratched in place: *Help me.*

The chamber pot dropped to the floor and clattered loudly. I stared at the words, almost feeling splinters in my own fingertips.

With shaking hands, I lit a candle and stared at the tiny flame. What I was considering made no sense, and yet, I had no idea what else to do in that moment.

"Is there anyone who wishes to speak to me?" I whispered. I waited, hearing only the wind outside. I asked the question again, my heart sputtering, for there was only one ghost I desperately wanted to hear from. However, as the next minutes passed in silence, it was painfully obvious my experiment had simply proven what I already knew.

I blew out the candle and cleared the foolish melancholy from my mind. I knew there must be a plausible explanation, but at that moment I wanted nothing more than to leave the room and never return. I slammed the wardrobe shut, then made my way to the drawing room for cocktails.

Miss Gibbons was all brilliance and sparkle in her blue dress and black diamonds. With her shiny hair and porcelain skin, she looked like a life-size version of a doll. I guessed she was not yet thirty, but a soft lifestyle had made it difficult to tell for certain. She was beautiful and wealthy, but the strongest of her talents was shrewd initiative. I had a notion that if she wanted to purchase Somerset, it would be hers before the second course was served. Everything about her caught the glow from the candles, as if she absorbed their very light. The men surrounded her like moths to a flame, listening intently.

Standing at his usual spot by the fireplace, Mr. Pemberton looked very fine in his dinner jacket and white tie. Every time I happened to glance in his direction, he was looking at my corner of the room. He would reply with a questioning frown as if asking if I was all right. I responded with a slight nod and took a sip of my drink. Anything we had to discuss was impossible in the present company. It was better to give him a temporary assurance.

I put my attention on the other men in the room. Mr. Lockhart sat in the chair to Miss Gibbons's right with the cane at his side. One ruby eye winked. I had the feeling that snake and I could share some secrets.

William was surprisingly dapper and sober. He complimented Miss Gibbons from head to toe. I seethed from across the room, knowing he was breaking Flora's heart. I wished I knew how to win back her trust.

I sat alone, nursing the cocktail Bramwell had served me almost an hour ago. I couldn't stop thinking about the message in the wardrobe. It was possible it had been there for a few days, as I hadn't checked the back since the night I arrived. Then an idea struck me. Mrs. Donovan could have made those marks the day she hung the dresses. There, it was settled. A plausible explanation after all. I just wished the goose bumps on my arms would smooth away.

I looked up, only to catch Mr. Pemberton's eye again. He must have thought I'd been staring at him the whole time. I turned and asked Bramwell for a refill, hoping I didn't appear as distressed as I felt.

The only other person who looked more uncomfortable than me was Dr. Barnaby. He'd been regularly checking in on Mrs. Donovan. Mr. Pemberton had made him stay for supper, unwilling to send him back to the village without a proper meal. I could tell from his heavy lids that he would have gladly fallen asleep on the kitchen table, never mind a candlelit dinner.

We traded weary glances as he joined me on the settee.

"How is Mrs. Donovan today?" I asked him. "Is she able to walk yet?" I hoped my face remained neutral, or at least something close to sincerity.

He took a sip of his drink. "She'll heal from her physical injuries, but the emotional strain will take much longer. Her fear will stay with her for some time, I imagine."

"Has she spoken any more about the attack?" Not having Flora around had deprived me of the house gossip.

"No." He shook his head. "She has nothing new to add."

"But she's content to stay at Somerset Park?" He frowned at my insistence, and I made a note to ease my manner. I added, "I wonder how she can feel any kind of safety here."

"Because it's her home," he said.

I knew home didn't always guarantee safety. I pictured myself at Miss Crane's, feeling the threat of having to join her girls if my séances didn't bring in enough money. I attempted to deflect the topic. "I meant to ask you about the young girl who had died in the village. Was that Flora's friend Maisie?"

He finished the last of his drink. "Such a sad case. Despite her youth, the sickness hit her worse. There was a history of poor hearts in her family, I believe. It happened so fast. One moment we were talking, and the next she closed her eyes and died." He stared at his empty glass. "I suppose it's the most comfortable way to die: no pain, no fear—just slipping away."

"You were with her all night?"

"Yes, that's what doctors do, Miss Timmons." His voice was weary, but he smiled warmly at me.

I smiled back. "Whomever you marry will have to be a remarkably understanding woman."

His face reddened.

Worried that he suspected I was flirting with him, I stammered something ridiculous about the recent rain. I was saved when Bramwell announced dinner was served.

THROUGH THE BEET salad and vegetable consommé courses, the talk varied between business and travel. Mr. Pemberton sat at the head of the table with Miss Gibbons on his right and Mr. Lockhart to his left. I mostly stared past William's shoulder at the window behind him. The darkness was more interesting than Miss Gibbons's opinions on everything I never cared about.

"You didn't lie," she said to Mr. Pemberton. "Somerset and its surrounding grounds are quite spectacular. I can think of several acquaintances who would very much appreciate the opportunity to tempt you with an offer."

"I'm glad you find it appealing," he replied.

Mr. Lockhart chuckled into his napkin. "Anyone would be tempted, but that doesn't necessarily mean they deserve it. A house of this standing needs the consistency of an esteemed linage. It's been home to the Earl of Chadwick for generations."

"Are you saying Somerset would be less grand if it belonged to someone without a title?" Miss Gibbons asked. She smiled, but I could hear the sharpness behind her words.

Mr. Lockhart put a hand to his chest apologetically. "I didn't mean offense. I have a deep fondness for this house, of course. Somerset requires the passionate consistency and devotion only a family line can provide."

Miss Gibbons turned to Mr. Pemberton. "Are you looking for a buyer or a wife?" She grinned, but there was a calculating quality to her stare.

"Neither, at the moment," he said over the rim of his wineglass.

From the corner of my eye, I saw Dr. Barnaby wince.

I wished I had faked a headache.

By the time Bramwell and Harry served the stuffed pork loin on a bed of apricots soaked in brandy, most of the topics had been exhausted, and so conversation turned to gossip. I noticed the side servings of Auntie Lil's mint jelly in crystal dishes.

"What news have you brought us from London?" Mr. Lockhart asked Miss Gibbons. I noticed he hadn't coughed once this evening. I wondered if wanting to impress a beautiful woman could suppress that reflex.

"Have you heard the recent calamity of the Hartfords' estate?" she said, reaching for her wine.

The knife slipped from my hand, rattling against the plate.

Mr. Lockhart glanced at me for the briefest of moments. As far as he knew, we were the only ones at the table who were aware of my history with the family. I didn't dare look Mr. Pemberton's way. The daughter had called me a common swindler. I thought of Mrs. Hartford's note she'd slipped into the ghost book.

Did you love me?

I couldn't imagine spending a lifetime with someone and doubting if they loved me.

We tell them what they want to hear. We tell them enough so that their heart fills in the rest. The heart sees.

Maman would have been upset with how I'd treated them.

"—tore the front room apart." Miss Gibbons ended the sentence with a laugh.

I took a sip of wine, letting it warm my throat the whole way down. It was a terrible coincidence Miss Gibbons was familiar with the family who'd seen me off to jail.

"And it was all because of that dreadful séance. Imagine! All of them spellbound by the seer. She was discovered to be a fake, but before they took her away, she whispered to my friend that her father's ghost told them to look in the fireplace."

My heart grew larger, making it hard to breathe. I imagined it bursting out of my chest, splattering blood all over the finely set table.

"A séance?" William lifted an eyebrow. "How ridiculous they are in London." The jab was purely for Mr. Pemberton. I tried to crouch lower in my chair.

"Grief can make people vulnerable," Mr. Pemberton said. His glance alighted in my direction. I dropped my chin at once. Too strong were my insecurities to afford a fake smile his way.

Dr. Barnaby sighed under his breath. His plate was already empty.

"But that is not the end of the tale," Miss Gibbons continued. "Once my friend told the rest of the family, they started looking. Can you imagine all the soot? Mrs. Hartford almost had a heart attack when Mr. Hartford's portrait fell off the wall and into all that mess." She raised her glass. Bramwell was at her side, pouring the last of another bottle.

She smiled at Mr. Pemberton and fluttered her eyelashes with a confidence surely cultivated from a life of privilege. I suspected she didn't know her teeth were purple from the wine.

After cutting the most insignificant bite of apricot, she said, "Would you believe young Robert was the one who found it?" She paused again, painfully. Waiting for the obvious question.

"Found what?" Dr. Barnaby asked. I wondered if he was interested or trying to hasten the storytelling along. Bramwell slipped in and removed his plate.

Mr. Lockhart smiled at the head butler. "Please let Mrs. Galloway know the meal has been exemplary."

Miss Gibbons chewed thoughtfully. Then she said, "While everyone else was arguing, Robert took the lamp and stood inside the flue. He's so skinny he was the only one who could fit. He found a tin box stuck between the bricks. Inside was a key to Mr. Hartford's safety deposit box at the bank."

A strange flutter filled my stomach. The key had really been in the fireplace! I told myself it was only a lucky guess. There was no way I was a conduit for the other side.

"You'll never guess what he'd put there." She looked around, waiting.

"A new will disowning his ridiculous family," William said.

"Deed to an unknown property?" Dr. Barnaby guessed.

She shook her head. "You're terrible at this game. I'll give you a hint. It's smaller than a dinner plate."

"A love letter," Mr. Pemberton said. His answer surprised me so much I didn't look away when our eyes locked for the hundredth time that evening. I couldn't tell if he was hoping to build suspense for his own séance. I tried to ignore how hard my heart was pounding.

"Miss Timmons?" he prompted. "We're waiting for your guess."

My cheeks were burning. "It must have been important, but only to him," I said. "Something he wanted to keep secret, even from his own family."

"Family secrets," William murmured. "How unoriginal." He turned his attention to the lovely guest. "Tell me, Miss Gibbons, do you always take such joy in retelling a grieving family's misfortune?"

Mr. Lockhart smoothed his mustache with the napkin. "Miss Gibbons is merely constructing a game for us to play. I'm sure the details have been embellished by her lovely friend. No harm if the mystery is playfully revealed." He coughed. Finally.

Miss Gibbons lifted her glass for another refill. She impressed me with her ability to put away the drink. She looked at me. "Inside the box was a school medal."

"That's rather sad," I replied. "The medal must have been important to him. Why would he lock it away instead of sharing it with his family?"

"So true," Dr. Barnaby added quietly. "But if the seer knew about the fireplace, then why have her arrested? Seems rather unkind to the poor girl."

Good ole Dr. Barnaby! He was defending me without even knowing it.

"Poor girl!" Miss Gibbons rolled her eyes. "The sentimental value of the medal was nothing compared to the jewels she was stealing. Regardless, I hear she's set for the gallows. I told my friend she should wear her father's medal to the hanging."

CHAPTER FORTY-FIVE

Lady Audra Linwood
Diary Entry
Somerset Park, May 4, 1852

Dearest,

It is the night before the wedding. My hand is shaking from ex-citement and fear. Everything is falling into place. My true life starts tomorrow. I am sad to leave you behind, though, Dearest. You've been my constant companion all these years. However, I must say goodbye to everything that reminds me of Somerset, including you. You have served me well and kept my greatest secret. No one knows, not even my love. At first it was a fun way to snoop on the staff. Now it is my salvation!

I have packed my bag and stowed it away in a secret location.

I know it is foolish to put all of this down here, but I will hide this book well. I wonder if anyone will ever find it. Maybe I'll even return one day and retrieve it!

At dinner, I said I was fearful tomorrow would never come. Mr. Pemberton raised his glass at me from the other end of the table as if congratulating himself on a successful business deal. I might have felt guilty for abandoning him if not for the fact that Somerset is already his.

William, though, stared at me throughout the meal. I can still feel the burn from his glare. I am wondering if he has snuck into my room and found this diary. Does he know? I shudder at the thought. Father's death rattled something deep inside him, and now it has finally surfaced.

When I look at William now, I am reminded of Grandfather's eyes. Can you inherit cruelty like hair color? And if so, am I capable of what Grandfather did? Perhaps leaving Somerset is the best thing for me and my baby.

Midnight cannot come soon enough.

CHAPTER FORTY-SIX

I sat at the vanity taking out the hairpins one by one. Although my stomach was satisfied, my mind was amok with visions of the gallows. A sliver of panic wedged itself like a splinter under my skin, impossible to ignore. No matter how confident Mr. Lockhart professed to be, I couldn't rid myself of the image of him standing in front of the jury, covered in cuts and bruises, losing track of his argument.

And what of Mr. Pemberton? I had begun to trust him, only to find out he had his own secrets. Was he using me to cover his own crime? I rubbed my arms, suddenly chilled. Did he know about the dungeon?

Cruel fathers bear cruel sons.

He had admitted his own father struck him so hard it left him with a scar.

The wind howled outside as the last embers in the fireplace crackled. A strange weight settled over the room. I glanced at the door to make sure the key was in the lock. I had the oddest notion of—

"Help me."

The pin froze in my hand. It was only a whisper, but it was most assuredly a female voice, and it was in the room with me. Something creaked. In the mirror I watched the wardrobe door open slowly. I was still as a rock until it finally stopped moving, halfway open, like a mouth caught midyawn, showing nothing but black within.

My emotions came to a boil. Frustration and fear had combined and exploded with a fury. No more! I rushed to the wardrobe and flung open the door the whole way.

Only the rack of dresses greeted me. I let out a long breath, my pulse easing.

Then the garments quivered. I heard something shift at the back of the wardrobe. I squinted between a gap in the dresses. Through the shadows, a huddled form took shape. Instinctively, I leaned closer, trying to focus.

An eye blinked back at me.

Clawed fingers darted out from between the clothing, reaching for me. I screamed and fell backward, crashing to the floor. The weight of my attacker crushed my chest. Her face was stretched in a grimace with veins bulging and purple. "Help me," she cried out, grabbing at my collar.

I coughed out another scream, slapping at her wrists. Mrs. Donovan was unexpectedly strong. Her unkempt hair was covered in twists of cobwebs. A string of drool dripped from her mouth, almost reaching my own as I struggled underneath her.

"Help me," she repeated. "Help me save her. It's my fault she's still here! Can't you hear her at night?"

As I tried to push her face away my fingers found the chain of a necklace and pulled. There was a snap as it came loose in my hand. Something flew off the chain and clinked under the bed.

There was a pounding at the door.

I twisted my hips and managed to throw her off. She flung herself at my legs, pulling me back.

Mrs. Donovan pressed her face close to mine. She sobbed between words. "She won't let me have peace. You must help me! Please, I'm begging you, make her stop."

"Lady Audra?" I asked carefully, hoping to calm her down. It was obvious Mrs. Donovan was violently unstable.

She dropped her chin and continued to cry. I saw the shaved patch of her scalp and the oddly shaped wound. The stitches had let go, and it was bleeding freely. "I took the baby, but I should have taken her too. But now she's angry with me. She wants me to suffer like she did."

"You don't have to be afraid," I said. "Just tell me what happened." Mrs. Donovan started to sob again. I took advantage and scrambled to the door to unlock it.

William rushed in, pushing me to the side as he crouched beside her. She looked at him with imploring adoration as he wrapped his arms around, cradling her. They began to rock back and forth on the floor.

"I saved the baby," she murmured.

"Shh," he soothed, tucking her head under his chin. He was oblivious to the blood seeping onto his hands.

"Of course you did," I said, eager for her to keep talking. "It was very brave of you."

William threw me a warning look. He then reached into his pocket and produced a flask. He was able to persuade Mrs. Donovan to take a few sips. Soon, her eyes closed, and she fell asleep.

I stayed crouched on the floor with them. Even though I had been upset with William, this tender version was diluting my ire. "I had no idea she was this ill," I said.

"The attack has brought her guilt to the surface," he replied. His voice lacked the usual spite. "Despite the obvious culprit, she feels responsible for Audra's death."

"Obvious culprit?" I pried.

"People didn't start dying until he came to Somerset."

"What did Mr. Pemberton do?" I asked.

He tiredly shook his head at me. "Flora told me you were asking about the portrait in his bedroom. Just like Audra, she is no longer alive. I find it interesting how all the beautiful women in his life die young."

I swallowed.

"Does anyone know you're here?" he asked. "If you don't return home, will anyone know where to look for your bones?"

Sadly, I could only think of Constable Rigby.

Mrs. Donovan squirmed in his arms. Her eyes fluttered open. She looked at William and smiled, then a frown of confusion took its place. "The baby?" She raised a hand to the back of her head and winced.

"All is well," he said calmly. "Let's get you back to your room." He helped her stand, keeping an arm around her waist. In her nightgown, she looked rather frail and not at all like her grimly staunch self.

I took the green blanket from my bed and laid it over her shoulders, then picked up the lamp, prepared to go with them.

"No need," he said. "I know my way in the dark."

I opened the door for them. William leaned down and said, "I know it's hard to deny those blue eyes, but I warned you when we first met. Remember? Nothing has changed, Miss Timmons. In fact, I would say your peril has increased. You're taking a dangerous risk staying here."

I watched as they inched down the hallway before being swallowed by the darkness. Mrs. Donovan may have had a head injury, but her fear was real, and so was her request to contact the spirit world.

Exhausted, but still rattled, I tidied up the closet, picking up a few of the dresses she must have pulled down. My eye caught a glimmer on the rug.

I bent down and found the chain that broke in my hand during our struggle. I checked under the bed, remembering how something had fallen off. Halfway under the bed a key lay innocently in the dust. I knew she had a double key to my room! But when I compared it to the one in my lock, it was different. Then something pieced together in my mind. If this wasn't the key to my room, it must be the missing key to Audra's. However, now that I had the tiara tucked away in the library, I had no need to go back there.

I went to the window, tapping the sill with the key, trying to process William's warning. The full moon illuminated the grounds. A lone figure cut across the lawn to the forest at a frantic pace. The posture was unmistakable—Mr. Pemberton.

A surge of adrenaline pushed my weariness away. I was tired of secrets, and I was not about to let another get away from me.

I made a dash for the front door, too impatient to put on my coat.

My boots pounded on the frozen ground of the forest path. Every intake of cold air was a knife to my lungs.

Soon, the stables came into view. All the windows glowed. What could be happening in the middle of the night? I paused to catch my breath, bending over with a hand on one knee.

Rasping screams shook the air, followed by a man swearing a stream of curses. I could have swallowed my own teeth.

Light shone through the slates of the stable, outlining the main door. I moved closer. Details emerged from the shadows. There was a neat woodpile to the side with a hatchet sticking out of the cutting stump. The moonlight glinted off the corner of the sharp blade.

Pressing my palms against the main door, I leaned forward, my nose almost touching the wood. There was barely enough of a crack to see inside. Mr. Pemberton was moving about and yelling. His shirt was covered in blood.

The ground disappeared under my feet; I was in a death fall. Before my very eyes was the exact story Flora had relayed. I gasped, then put a hand over my mouth, certain he'd heard me.

The screams came again.

I fought every instinct that urged me to turn around and run. I did not want to see the rest of this scene. Flora's earlier description came to me.

. . . I knows blood when I sees it, and his shirt was covered.

Perhaps Audra was dead before she went over the cliff. My entire body started to shake. He could have killed her and thrown her body into the ocean.

And now he was using me to help him frame someone innocent!

Joseph came into view. His young face was etched with fear. He too was smeared with dirt and crimson.

"Hold her now, steady!" Mr. Pemberton ordered. "Get the ropes!"

Her. Fear and anger mixed creating a tidal wave of instinctive rage. Auntie Lil's voice retold the cruelty of Audra's grandfather as

I replayed the horrid images of the bone still in the iron shackles. I grabbed the hatchet, pulling it free from the stump.

Something I could only explain as passionate insanity made me burst into the stable with the small axe raised above my head. I hollered, "Stop!"

Mr. Pemberton stared back at me quizzically. A bizarre quiet filled the room as I took in the entire scene.

CHAPTER FORTY-SEVEN

There were four men all together, including young Joseph and Mr. Pemberton. All had their sleeves rolled up to the elbows. One of them sat off by himself, his arm at an awkward angle. The straw floor was soaked.

The mare screamed and thrust violently to the side. Joseph and the man holding the ends of the reins gave out a surprised holler as they tried to keep from being trampled.

"Pray! What are you doing here, Miss Timmons?" Mr. Pemberton was at the back end of the horse with the tail draped over his shoulder. His forearms were slick with blood.

I could not peel my eyes away. "Me? What are you—" I began.

He let out an exasperated sigh. "We're helping this mare foal, and unless you know how to ease this poor animal's stress, sit in the corner and be quiet. And for pity's sake, put down that hatchet."

The horse gave another violent shudder, and I was promptly forgotten as they returned to the task at hand.

I stood still, transfixed. The hatchet dropped unnoticed.

The horse backed up, almost crushing Mr. Pemberton under its weight. "Hold her up," he hollered. Her eyes rolled back, showing only the whites.

"We're going to lose her like the last one," Joseph whimpered.

"Aye," one of the other men said. "Been goin' on almost an hour, m'lord. Might be best to put the poor thing out of her misery." He nodded toward the wall, and I saw he was looking at a long rifle hung on a rack.

"If you'd fetched me earlier, we wouldn't be considering that," Mr. Pemberton snapped. He reached forward, his hands disappearing into the beast. "I've got the hind legs," he grunted. "Damn, one slipped back."

"Breach?" Joseph went pale. "This will kill her."

A splash of fluid soaked his boots, but Mr. Pemberton ignored the mess. "Come on, girl," he said through gritted teeth. "One more push."

The mare swayed on her legs. Then she collapsed, making the men scatter, except for Mr. Pemberton, who knelt at her hind, shouting instructions. Joseph came with fresh hay, padding her sides.

The only sound was the mare's heaving gasps.

"Now, m'lord?" one of the men quietly suggested.

"No," he panted. "We can't give up yet." He looked at the stable hand. "Come here, Marchand, I need you."

The man stepped back and shook his head. "She's having a fit! I don't need *my* arm broken too." The other man sitting in the corner winced.

"Now is not the time to lose your nerve!" Mr. Pemberton looked at them one by one. They all dropped their chins. Then he looked at me. "Miss Timmons?"

"I beg your pardon?" I said.

"Grab that strip of cloth and come over here." His voice was hard, but there was a desperate plea to his tone. When I didn't move, he added, "Look at the mare. If we stop now, Mr. Marchand will have to put her down. We can still give this foal and her mother a chance."

Something strange stirred in my chest. I had a vision of my mother, pregnant with me, and walking toward the Thames that fateful day.

"Miss Timmons, please." His eyes implored me. "We will lose both lives."

I grabbed the cloth and joined him at the rear of the horse, squatting shoulder to shoulder. He adjusted his grip and leaned back. Slowly, the hind legs appeared, encased in a silvery membrane.

"Wrap the cloth around both hooves," he said. My hands shook as I did what he instructed. "Good, now take the ends and don't let go. I'm going to reach in farther and pull again. You must keep the cloth taut, but don't pull, and don't let go until I say." He stared at me with those blue eyes, willing me to be brave.

My mouth had gone dry. I wouldn't have been able to choke out a word. I nodded and tightened my grip.

"All right, then." A trail of sweat rolled down the side of his face. With a curse, he leaned back, the tendons in his arms straining as he pulled. There was a pause, and more of the legs emerged, then a hint of the back. There was a great gush, and the rest of the foal slipped out. We backed up together. The mare lifted her head.

Mr. Pemberton pulled the sac away, exposing the foal's muzzle. Taking a cloth, he wiped its face vigorously. The newborn finally gave a gentle snort, and we all cheered. The charged air had given way to euphoria.

"Congratulations." Mr. Pemberton smiled at me. "It's a girl."

It didn't take long for the men to clean the area and bring in fresh straw. Mr. Pemberton moved about the two animals, gently coaxing the mare toward the newborn. I was content to stay at the edge of the activity. My hands were still shaking. Under the soft light of the stable lanterns, the pair nestled together.

Mr. Pemberton washed up at the pump in the corner, stripping to his waist to scrub his arms and shoulders. I watched as the water droplets trailed down his back, contouring around each muscle. I admit, seeing him shirtless was a powerful distraction. I sat on the top of a barrel, indulging myself in the view.

Joseph came over, his amiable smile in place. "Well done," he said.

"I've seen nothing like it," I said, still under the spell of the moment. "How many times have you done this?"

He blushed and pushed some straw around with the toe of his boot. "Only the second time, miss, but this was much better. The first time the mare didn't live. Tragic thing, it was. M'lord was here then too."

Mr. Pemberton slipped on a clean shirt one of the stable hands had lent him. It was intriguing to see him don such a simple garment. "You did well tonight, Joseph," he said. "You'll make a fine head groomsman one day."

Joseph answered the compliment with a quiet nod, attempting to appear unaffected, but I could tell the praise was appreciated. He rejoined the other men.

Mr. Pemberton sat down on the rim of the barrel beside me. "The men are surprised you didn't faint at all the blood," he said. "I've had a few stable hands lose their dinners at just the smell."

"I should think not," I replied. I had mastered the art of hiding a mouthful of ectoplasm, after all. "Besides, with all the orders you were giving out, I could hardly spare a moment to think of my stomach."

He considered that, and then his face took on an earnest expression. "I imagine this is a novel experience for you."

"This may surprise you, but delivering horses is probably a novel experience for most people." I laughed.

"I meant birth instead of death."

His words carried a thoughtfulness that took me by surprise. I had no smart reply. After a moment, I asked, "When was the last time you helped a mare give birth? Was it before the wedding?"

"Yes," he said, a cautious edge to his voice. "A few nights before the wedding, actually. I remember how terrible it all was."

I thought of Flora's story. "Was it a long struggle for the horse? Did you have to spend the whole night in the stables?" He frowned at my questions, so I quickly added, "I can't imagine how horrible that must have been for all involved."

"It was," he said. "But at least the animal didn't suffer for very long. It was over by midnight. I remember when I returned to the manor, I tried to sneak back without being seen. I didn't want to appear as though I was already claiming ownership of Somerset and the stables."

He ran a hand through his hair. His voice was softer, more solemn. "I may not be proficient in most things involving status and titles, but I know horses, and I couldn't help but try to prevent the tragedy. I scared one of the maids to death, I believe. I know my actions were not expected of someone who was to oversee the running of Somerset Park."

Relief flooded over me, releasing the grip on my heart. I was certain Flora would not be afraid if she knew the truth. Still, there was one lingering concern I needed clarity on. I began, "The night you found me on the stairs and took me to your room, I saw a portrait of a woman and a horse." I purposely let the sentence hang.

"My mother," he answered. There was a new sense of admiration in his tone. "She taught me how to ride. My father was all business, but she was the one who instilled the importance of connecting with the soul of the animal." His expression grew wistful. "She died when I was ten, and consequently so did a part of my father. He was very much changed afterward." His shoulders curved inward, as if burdened by the recollection of all that he had lost.

The mare gently neighed toward her foal, alleviating the solemnness of the moment. Mr. Pemberton's face brightened. "That's why I love the stables," he said. "Riding reminds me of being with her."

"But doesn't that memory bring you grief?" I asked.

"Yes, but it also brings comfort. Whenever I need to feel her close, I go to the thing she loved the most: riding. I always find her there."

I stayed quiet. This was so different from Maman's words about love only guaranteeing heartbreak. Love after death was an intriguing concept. I reasoned that was how grief felt in the absence of guilt.

There was a gentle laugh from Joseph. "She's standing, now. Aw, ain't she perfect."

I had to agree. The foal was nothing short of spectacular.

"She needs a name," Joseph said.

A few suggestions went around, but nothing seemed to grab the group.

Mr. Pemberton nudged me with his elbow. "You should do the honors, Miss Timmons. You're the reason she's here, safe and sound."

With her sleek body and thick black mane, there was only one name that would suit her. "Esmeralda," I said.

He smiled. "Esmeralda it is."

I almost didn't recognize him.

It was on the tip of my tongue to tell him about the dungeon, but the prospect of saying the words aloud brought a trickle of doubt. Had I really seen a human bone? It had been so dark.

Maybe the better choice was to dismiss that horrible memory as nothing more than a nightmare.

After another hour of staring at the mother and her newborn while they slept, Mr. Pemberton took his long coat from a hook and motioned for me to stand. "I'm afraid we'll have to return on foot. Once the mare's labour started, the other horses were released to the pasture, and you're not dressed for a walk in the cold."

I was about to remind him I had, in fact, come from the manor in only my dress, but then he placed his coat over my shoulders. I tolerated the gesture silently.

The first rays of dawn brightened the sky. I slipped my arms into the long coat and buttoned it up to my chin. I tucked my nose under the collar and detected the scent of soap and fresh air.

Joseph pulled at the front of his cap. "Come back anytime to see Esmeralda, miss."

Mr. Pemberton and I stayed quiet as we made our way through the forest path, but it wasn't uncomfortable. The birds serenaded us as our easy gait continued in unison. I was very much aware of how many times our hands almost brushed. The mystery of Mr. Pemberton was being peeled back, one small revelation at a time. The more I discovered, the more I liked about him. However, there was one more pressing matter I needed to ask about. It would require tact, and near-perfect ambiguity on my part.

We emerged from the shelter of the trees to watch the sun rise higher. We paused, taking in the view. As light touched the frosted glade, the land sparkled as if dotted with jewels. I had a faint inclination of what it might feel like to be a queen, or at least someone of consequence. Somerset Park was perfect in the morning.

As if reading my mind, Mr. Pemberton said, "It's a shame you don't ride. It really is the best way to see the grounds."

"What makes you think I don't ride?"

I was expecting a laugh in reply. Instead, he stared in the road's direction that led to the village.

"I look forward to the day when I can travel down this road for good," he said.

"You can leave anytime you want."

He shook his head. "Death may have severed any future Audra and I were to share, but it doesn't erase the obligation I owe her memory."

An intangible weight settled over me. The time we spent in the stables after Esmeralda's birth and the walk back through the forest had seemed like a dream. I was beginning to care for him. And even though someone of his social standing would never consider me, my heart still needed to know. Tact be damned, I had to ask him before we spent any further time together. "Do you still love her?" I asked.

His brow knit together. "I'm unsure how to answer," he said.

I held my breath, wishing I hadn't mentioned it at all.

"There was hardly time," he said. "But I was committed to the arrangement. Once I received the letter from Mr. Lockhart about Somerset Park and my connection, I understood it was my duty to become its sole caretaker. And then Audra accepted my proposal; she had her part to play as well. I cannot speak for her, but I don't think it would be a grave injustice to assume she saw the arrangement the same as I."

I kept his stare, realizing he hadn't yet denied his affection for her.

His tone became softer, and yet more determined. "So it's impossible to answer your question, Miss Timmons, as I was never in love with her to begin with."

There was a quickening in my chest. Although it hardly changed our relationship, my relief was immediate and true. I looked down at my boots, afraid my pleasure would be obvious. "You asked for her hand out of duty?" I asked.

"I would have been a fool not to accept Somerset. And as the title of earl was to be passed down to me, I certainly needed to think about heirs. The arrangement suited both of us." Then he shrugged. "It simply made sense."

"That's a very practical answer," I said. "Someone more romantic might have called it fate."

When he didn't reply immediately, I glanced up. He was biting his lip, fighting the shape of a grin. "Fate isn't independent, Miss Timmons. It's shaped by our reaction to the world. I could have eluded my responsibility and refused the title of Earl of Chadwick. And take your own situation for example. Here you are, wearing my coat after helping a mare foal. Was it your choices that made this moment possible or events beyond your control?"

The wind whistled around us, rustling a golden wave of hair across his temple. I thought of the fortune-teller's prophecy.

"My choices are made only with regard to my own self-preservation," I replied. "Besides, isn't it tiresome to imagine all our desires and efforts are meaningless in the face of some greater plan?"

"Or perhaps you set yourself on fate's course through the choices you make."

"Even if you have the worst luck in the world?" I replied.

"Especially then."

Now I was the one concealing a smile. "Worrying about fate seems like a luxury meant only for people with too much time on their hands."

His blue eyes glinted. "A fair point to end this discussion," he said. "I concede this argument in your favour." He gave the road to the village one last look before we continued toward the grand house.

"Thank you," I said. "For letting me experience the foaling. You were right. I've been surrounded by death and grief my entire life. It can be isolating—and exhausting. For all the energy that was expended in the stables, the birth brought a lightness. Sometimes I think all that death weakens the spirit. I know it weakens mine."

I wasn't sure where that confession came from, and I wished I had stayed quiet. The moment felt spoiled.

Then Mr. Pemberton said, "'Weak' is the last word I would use to describe you, Miss Timmons. Death makes people feel powerless, but not you. If you feel any weakness, it's because you're carrying the grief of others. It's that very burden that makes you strong."

The compliment resonated within me, sinking into my bones. I had forgotten how proud Maman's work used to make me.

He stopped walking, his hand reaching out to touch my elbow. We were stepping onto a path I had never considered before.

"Thank you," I said. "I don't believe anyone has ever phrased it so eloquently."

"Do not praise me for my choice of words," he said. "I am only commenting on what I see as the truth."

I had no word for this place that only we occupied, where the air turned thick and my heartbeat was in my throat. How easy it was to imagine the two of us taking the road to Wrendale. How easy it was to forget whose place I was taking—the reason I was at Somerset Park at all.

When I didn't reply, he finally said, "Come. I've kept you out long enough." He turned toward the kitchen's entrance.

My heart and head were a jumble. The security I felt with him seemed so real, but I knew it was only a fleeting illusion. Maman's voice reached out to me.

The only guarantee love brings is heartache.

CHAPTER FORTY-EIGHT

I woke in my room later that afternoon, wonderfully rested and motivated. The séance was to take place in two days, and even though it still was not clear who I should target, I wasn't desperate yet. Even though she wouldn't be there in person, Mrs. Donovan might be the best scapegoat for my purpose. Her bellowed confession about saving a baby rattled in my mind. Whose baby? I shook the memory away. Knowing the complete truth wasn't essential for a successful séance.

Yawning, I began to prepare myself for the day. After dressing, I settled in front of the vanity to fix my hair. The drawer looked absurdly empty with only the box of pins, a few garments, and my mended gloves. I ran a hand along Mrs. Donovan's expert stitching. Her wound was such an odd shape. What weapon could have made such a mark?

Familiarity washed over me. I stared down into the drawer again. When I'd hidden the tiara here, it was deep enough that I'd been able to roll it up in a petticoat. But Audra's drawer had been so shallow that the thin red box had barely fit inside. In every other regard the two pieces seemed identical.

The sketch of my mother in Paris came to mind—the one I discovered hidden in the secret bottom of her jewelry box. The truth slammed into me like running into the chest of the copper. My eyes slid to the key I'd left on the windowsill last night. I would be paying another visit to Audra's room.

I ventured down the hallway with the key tucked under my sleeve. There was no one about. When I reached her door, I fished out the key and slipped it in the lock as smooth as a practised dance step. The knob turned easily, without protest, and I was inside Audra's room with the door closed behind me faster than Joseph eating an entire pastry.

I went directly to the vanity and opened the top drawer all the way. I knew it was much too shallow for a reason. My fingertips reached in and skimmed the sides until I felt a tab near the back. When I pulled it, it lifted, revealing a compartment underneath.

"Aha!" I whispered, victorious. There was nothing but a small leather-bound book. My pulse raced. As with Mr. Hartford's school medal, no one hides an object of no significance—even if it is only of personal value. I dared to hope as I read the first page.

My Dearest,

It is with a heavy heart I take ink to these pages. This journal is Mother's last gift to me, and I shall fill every page with all my heart's desires, for she wanted me to live the full life that she could not.

My entire body shook. It was not a letter proving William's claim to Somerset as he'd wished.

It was a diary. Audra's diary.

ALTHOUGH IT WAS midafternoon, the room was much too dark for reading hidden books and the secrets they may contain. I gathered all the candelabras and settled into one of the armchairs. I glanced up at the large portrait of Audra's mother. The dog stared back at me sympathetically. "You knew all along, didn't you?" I whispered to him.

On the next page, the same delicate script described a new day. Her words surrounded me with the images and sounds of a manor not in mourning, but full of her laughter and optimism. Even with the future of Somerset Park unsure, Audra leapt off the page in girlish exuberance.

I had a notion of who Audra was based on the stories of those who knew her. But this diary afforded me an intimate insight to her character, perhaps the truest version of herself. There was a sense of sharing a special secret with her. A closeness beyond the grave.

I read through the many entries, mostly about daily life at Somerset and her growing curiosity with William, and her early questioning at his special treatment from her father. I remembered Auntie Lil's remarks about how the blacksmith died on his way to Somerset. Was Audra's father responsible for that? A chill rolled down my back.

It was also apparent that Audra wrote sporadically every few months. I read through several years in a few pages. My pulse quickened as I came to an entry dated just over a year ago. I was not prepared for what I was about to discover. Mrs. Donovan could have exploded into the room on fire and I wouldn't have looked up. I hungrily turned the pages, pausing only to replace the burned-out candles one by one.

A curious sense of mourning settled over me. I had imagined her life as one of spoiled opulence when compared to mine—but her words proved me wrong. For all her wealth, Audra had very little autonomy, even less than I, and she was just as susceptible to the cruelty of a man's world.

I was sorry to have never met her. An echo of thunder rattled the windowpane, pulling me from my forlorn thoughts.

I returned my attention to Audra's writing. The last entry was from the eve of her wedding. The book shook in my hands so badly I almost dropped it. Finally! I would learn what truly happened to Audra that night.

Lady Audra Linwood
Somerset Park, May 4, 1852

Dearest,

This is the last and most difficult entry I will write before I leave Somerset.

William has just left my room, and I am a trembling mess. Nothing is what I thought it was. He came with a tray of Mrs. Donavan's tea. Even though my door was locked, he used a key and gained access, catching me in a state of half dress. I grabbed my dressing gown and yelled at him to leave.

He ignored my plea and set down the tray, then made himself comfortable in the chair. I smelled wine on him. He handed me an envelope and told me I would no longer need to marry Mr. Pemberton to secure the estate. He said it was something Father had been working to acquire for several years. After his death, William took up the task himself.

This was the reason for all his trips away. He wasn't disappearing into Wrendale to frequent the pubs; he was visiting various churches throughout the north. And today he finally received what he and Father had been searching for.

Despite my anger with William for barging into my room, I agreed to hear him out. If there was a way to marry my love and still have Somerset, I was willing to look.

My hands shook as I read the yellowed document. It was a ledger entry from a small church in the northern region. The certificate stated that Father had married another woman the year before he and Mother! William had written to every parish in the surrounding counties before he found the right church.

I told him this couldn't possibly be true. How could this give me Somerset?

He then told me a horrible story.

Father fell in love with one of the servants and she became pregnant. They ran off and wed secretly. When they returned to Somerset, Grandfather was irate and declared the marriage invalid. My mother's hand had long been promised to Father; their wedding was set for the following summer.

Grandfather paid the servant well in exchange for her silence and ordered her away. But she never had a chance. Another servant found her hiding in the wine cellar that very afternoon, howling in agony as she went into labour. And that child, William told me, was himself.

This document proves he was born in wedlock. He is a legitimate Linwood and the rightful heir to Somerset!

I was so astounded I could hardly breathe. But then I realized what this meant for us. With William reinstated as the rightful Earl of Chadwick, Mr. Pemberton would have no claim to Somerset. I wouldn't have to leave! I could even marry my true love.

I began to cry tears of utter relief as I fell into William's open arms.

He kissed the crown of my head and whispered that he'd always take care of me. I was so happy, Dearest. I felt nothing could ruin that perfect moment.

Then William kissed me again, on my cheek. His lips lingered there. At once, everything felt wrong and dangerous. I pulled away, trying to make sense of his expression. There was a fierce determination in his eyes that frightened me. He told me Somerset would be ours, and we could finally be together, secretly able to express our love for each other within its walls.

It was impossible to share his dream of us.

At one time I may have believed I felt romantic inclinations toward William. But now I know what it is to truly love. And—he is my half brother! How can he even entertain the thought of such a union? What matter if we could keep it a secret? I would know the truth. I was almost sick at the notion.

I fell to my knees, my legs giving out. William carried me to the bed. He gently swept the hair away from my face, and I stayed very still. He said it had pained him, all this time, to keep secrets, to witness my distress as I prepared to marry Mr. Pemberton. But he'd wanted to protect my future so that I could remain head of Somerset if proof could not be found.

He then told me one last secret. William said my mother had learned of his existence and forbidden Father from rescuing him from the orphanage. It was only after Mother died that Father allowed Mrs. Donovan to fetch him from the blacksmith. However, Mr. Sutterly refused to give up William so easily, demand-

ing to be paid. William said Father never confessed to it, but Mr. Sutterly's unfortunate end came the very day he was meant to go to Somerset and collect payment.

As horrendous as it seems, my bones sense he is telling the truth. And I have always detected a special secret between Mrs. Donovan and William. I asked him if she knew who he was.

He nodded and revealed Mrs. Donovan was the servant who'd delivered him! To secure his safety from Grandfather's wrath, she'd brought him to the village church. When she returned to Somerset, his mother was gone. No one heard from her again.

Then William asked when I would tell Mr. Pemberton there would be no wedding. The backs of his fingers brushed across my cheek as he said this. His meaning could not have been clearer, Dearest.

I told him I would never be with him.

He began to cry. He lowered his head against my lap and begged for me to understand. He knows it is wrong, but cannot ignore the stirrings in his heart that have loved me all these years. It is impossible, he said. He will always love me more than anything. It has been pure torture for him to hold himself back, and then to watch Mr. Pemberton walk in and take everything that is rightfully his . . . including me.

A rage I did not know I possessed flared without warning. I scratched at his face and wrangled myself from his arms, but he caught the hem of my dressing gown, and I fell hard on the floor. At once there was a cramping in my stomach. I cried out.

William crouched beside me, but I pushed him away again. I screamed that I hated him and wished he'd never come to Somerset.

In that moment he looked so much like the young boy I knew when he first arrived, thin-faced and uncertain of his place here. He touched the red marks my fingernails had left on his cheek as he said I would regret marrying Mr. Pemberton. Then he promised me two things: First, that he will leave Somerset directly after the wedding and never return. And second, the last word from his dying lips will be my name. Then he made his retreat, quietly closing the door behind him.

I sat on the floor as I waited for my stomach to ease. Then I saw a shadow of movement beneath the door. I threw it open, prepared to scream, but it was Mrs. Donovan. Seeing my distress, she promised to stay outside my room all night under the guise of protecting me from wandering off again. But I don't trust her words. She knew all along about William! She must have been the one who gave him the key to my room tonight.

That yellowed sheet of paper was sitting discarded on my rug. I picked it up and read it again. It appeared legitimate. I may leave Somerset, but this will forever be my home. I'd rather have dull Mr. Pemberton looking over its welfare than William.

I tore the paper into pieces, then held each one over the flame of a candle, watching as every scrap burned to ash. I have no remorse for what I've taken from William. Let this be my last act of love for Somerset Park.

CHAPTER FORTY-NINE

I stared bleakly at her last sentence.

What happened to Audra was still a mystery. However, it was obvious she was in love with Dr. Barnaby and they had planned to leave together. And how shocking to discover William was telling the truth about his inheritance!

My mind was a mess of half-formed theories. She may have loved William when they were younger, but that all changed when she met Dr. Barnaby. William, though, was still in love with Audra, despite their blood connection. He sounded obsessed. And if he couldn't marry her, maybe he'd made it so no one else could.

Next, I tried to reconcile the affable doctor with the man who would carry on an affair with his best friend's betrothed. I couldn't summon a passionate figure of him. How had he convinced her to leave Somerset behind? I replayed every encounter we'd had together with fresh eyes. Men had an unfathomable capability for romantic manipulation. Although love was never my strong suit.

An image of Mr. Pemberton entered my mind, bringing with it another flutter of confused emotions. Audra had found him impersonal enough to dull his handsome looks. And like Flora, she had harboured suspicions about him.

Audra didn't love Mr. Pemberton, but she accepted his proposal to save Somerset. I knew now that he also considered their marriage a sensible arrangement, but I'd glimpsed beneath the veil of his cold demeanour and could attest to his hidden depths and passionate heart.

What if Mr. Pemberton had found out about Dr. Barnaby? A double-sided betrayal from his best friend and his fiancée could make a man act irrationally, and I had witnessed firsthand his desire for justice.

I groaned in frustration. He was still adamant about hosting the séance to expose her killer. He had told me she deserved more than the story everyone had given her death.

I pushed him from my mind; he made it impossible to think clearly.

I needed to understand what happened that night, after Audra tucked her diary away for the last time. She was as real as ever. The shell of my ear still burned, as if she had pressed her lips there and read her diary to me. Her yearnings for her mother, her desire for a friend, kindled a spark within me that made me feel less alone.

I flipped through the first few pages again. Who was "Dearest" with the sad eyes? And what secret did they share to help Audra escape?

Someone in this house knew more.

I considered everyone on the property, even Joseph the affable stable hand, but I couldn't imagine a likely match. It had to be someone who knew all the secrets of Somerset Park, someone Audra trusted implicitly. The beginnings of an idea rippled just beneath the surface, but then a clap of thunder sounded outside. I looked out the window at the churning clouds and the thought slipped away.

Audra wrote about hearing a voice call for help—just like I had. But I no more believed in family curses than I did ghosts. The same person who had haunted Audra was now turning their trickery on me. Most likely to lure me to my own death, or at the very least make me leave Somerset. Did they know about Mr. Pemberton's plan to evoke a confession? Or was the guilty party convinced Audra's ghost would be summoned for revenge?

Some men are the devil himself, Audra wrote. I agreed. Ghosts had nothing on the cruelty of real men. Thunder rumbled again, this time closer.

I left her room, making sure that no one saw me slip down the hallway. I had the diary tucked under my arm; it was simply too precious to leave behind. I wasn't stealing it like the tiara, I reasoned, but it was priceless nonetheless. And I knew exactly who I had to tell first.

I ran down the stairs, jumping the last two steps. Bramwell came around the corner carrying a stack of letters. His bushy eyebrows rose in surprise.

"Beg your pardon, Miss Timmons," he said. "Are you in need of assistance?"

I nodded. "Is Mr. Pemberton in his study? I need to speak with him directly."

Bramwell straightened. "His lordship is at the stables."

"When do you expect him back?"

He frowned. "I believe they left an hour ago. Dr. Barnaby arrived in time for lunch and accompanied him to see the new foal."

My rushed excitement turned to anxious worry. Dr. Barnaby was a cheater and a liar. And now he was with Mr. Pemberton, who was wholly unaware of the conniving nature of his best friend. I had to go there at once.

I stowed the diary in my room before grabbing my coat and bonnet. In addition to keeping it away from Dr. Barnaby, I didn't want to risk it becoming wet and smearing the ink. Then I took the forest path toward the stables as fast as I could.

I emerged into a fine mist. Fog had crept in from the sea. I ran into the stables, feeling my heart keep time with the running footfalls of my boots.

Esmeralda was in a large pen with her mother, looking well. Mr. Pemberton had his back to me and was speaking with one of the stable hands. He was dressed in his riding attire and high boots. His blond hair was mussed by the wind, the honey color like a jewel in contrast to the greyness of the day. There was an ease to his stance that was so unlike his usual rigid posture. He laughed, and it struck me how at home he seemed among the horses.

I craned my neck, but I could not see Dr. Barnaby.

"This is a pleasant surprise," Mr. Pemberton said as he saw me approach. His smile was as natural as his stance. "I was going to call on you before I left the main house, but I didn't want to disturb you." His manners were genuine, and the relaxed charm suited him much more than the harsh lord I'd met the first night. "I'm glad you came of your own volition," he added, almost sheepishly.

Looking at him in his riding attire, all fresh and full of vigor, I would hardly have guessed he'd been up all night birthing a foal. There was an infectious energy about him I'd never sensed before.

"Bramwell told me Dr. Barnaby would be here," I said.

"Oh?" There was a pause, and I suspected he was willing me to tell him the reason for seeking him out.

I stayed quiet.

"He just left," he finally answered. "He has a full roster of patients to visit. Besides, he didn't want to get caught in the rain."

Esmeralda nudged his hand. He bent on one knee and patted her nose.

"How is she?" I asked, taking a step closer.

"Esmeralda is perfect," he said. The adoration was hard to miss. "Here, come. You can pet her if you like."

Hearing him say the name of my favourite character, a name I had used as an alias myself, gave me a small thrill. I took off my glove and tentatively held out my palm. The foal leaned into my touch. Her coat was warm and velvet soft.

I wanted to keep this moment for ourselves, with no thought of Audra. I wanted to keep Esmeralda our story alone. So I held my tongue for a moment longer, indulging in the strange pocket of escape we had created, knowing it would burst as soon as I revealed my reason for coming here.

"Your ride is ready, m'lord," Joseph said, standing with a coat draped over his arm.

Mr. Pemberton stood and slipped his arms through the coat sleeves. A fine chestnut horse was saddled and off to the side. "May I offer you a ride back to the manor?" he asked me. "We could have Joseph bring around the step. I don't suspect you've had much experience riding in London." His tone was serious, but a grin pulled at the corner of his mouth, and I wondered if he knew how disarming it was. I believed this was the most smiles I'd seen from him since arriving here.

Audra's diary would shatter his claim to Somerset. He seemed too honorable of a man to ignore its contents. William was the legitimate heir, and everything would be his—including the stables, and even Esmeralda. Once I showed him the truth, everything would change.

So I endeavoured to stretch out these last moments for a little longer. "Actually," I said, "I was wondering if you could give me a riding lesson."

His surprise flowed into another smile. He looked at Joseph and said, "Best get Sadie saddled."

Joseph retreated to another stall. I walked outside with Mr. Pemberton as he led his steed. "When we return to the house," I said, "I will need to speak with you privately."

He raised his eyebrows quizzically. "Is this not private enough?"

Before I could answer, Joseph brought out a feeble-looking white horse.

"Here you are, miss," Joseph said.

I swallowed dryly, examining the mare with a combination of curiosity and dread.

"She's not the fastest," Joseph said. "But old Sadie always obeys her rider." Then he made a foothold with his hands for me to use.

With a hard push off my boot, I landed most ungracefully, with my legs jutting out behind me. After some minor adjustments, I sat upright in the sidesaddle, but I still felt off-kilter. The ground looked much farther away than I'd expected. I determined that I did not enjoy riding.

"You're a natural," Mr. Pemberton said.

I cleared my throat as I righted my bonnet. Sadie snorted, startling me. "Whoa!" I clutched her mane.

Joseph squinted up at me, uncertain. He handed me the reins. "Don't worry," he said. "Sadie knows the grounds better than anyone. She was Lady Audra's favourite."

Mr. Pemberton mounted his own horse with an ease that set off a series of trembles all the way to my toes. He brought his horse alongside mine. "You're sure about riding, Miss Timmons?" he asked with a teasing curl at his lips.

"Of course," I huffed. I may have looked silly, but I wanted this last memory of him, of seeing him at his happiest. A moment that I could catalogue away and revisit when I felt most alone.

"Very well," he said. "All you have to do is hold her reins." And sure enough, the dear nag was slowly walking toward the forest. I sat stiff as a board, holding the reins for dear life, but with each rhythmic hoofbeat against the ground I found my muscles loosening.

The wind wafted across my face, bringing the taste of salt with it. The rim of my bonnet fell over my eyes.

Mr. Pemberton slowed his horse to match my pace. "How are you enjoying riding Sadie?"

"I wouldn't exactly call this 'riding.' But I haven't fallen off yet, so I will consider it a success." I attempted to straighten my bonnet with one hand while the other kept its white-knuckled grip on the reins.

He tipped his head back and laughed—not at my expense, but in appreciation of my attempt at humor. I wanted to make him laugh again. "You confuse me," I admitted. "I cannot reconcile this jovial version with the man I met in the kitchen that first night. I honestly thought you were the groomsman, covered in mud as you were and surly as could be. You're all smiles and laughter today."

As if to prove me wrong, the smile vanished. His blue eyes became twin flames, their glow as warm as any hearth. It was desire—more intensely romantic than any salacious grin. "I was taken off guard," he began. "When I was informed that Mr. Lockhart was bringing a spiritualist to me, I imagined someone old and grim. I hadn't expected that she would be beautiful."

Heat rose in my chest, so intense it made me light-headed. I stared at him dumbly.

Then he clicked his tongue and was off, racing ahead. Rider and horse were both virile specimens, much the opposite of my sweet nag. I was grateful for her slow gait, though, as it allowed me a moment to catch my breath.

The fog bank crawled over the lawn as Mr. Pemberton disappeared into the mist. I believed he was purposely showing off how fine a rider he was. And I'll admit I was purposely watching.

Sadie stopped on her own. I squirmed and clucked my tongue, but she ignored me. I turned in the saddle to see if Joseph might be around to help, but we'd journeyed farther from the stables than I'd realized. I could barely make out the peak of its roof. I settled forward again, hoping for Mr. Pemberton to return. The mist swirled around me and grew heavier, slowly enveloping the landscape and transforming the world into a white sheet of silence.

Sadie remained perfectly still, only occasionally rotating her ears. What was she listening to? My eyes squinted against the fog, but nothing was discernible. I paused; I could smell roses. Impossible, though, since all the bushes had gone to seed.

Sadie turned her head sharply to one side, nostrils flared.

A faint voice carried on the wind. "*Help me.*"

"Who's there?" I turned my body as much as I dared, but could make out no recognizable shapes.

Sadie grunted and pawed at the ground.

"*Help me.*"

At this, Sadie exploded into a full gallop. I let out a shriek, clutching the reins.

We were moving so fast that my eyes watered. She took us straight into the heart of the fog, plunging us both into the clouds. I pulled on the reins and screamed in her ear, but nothing would stop her. I couldn't see where we were headed. My body braced, expecting to smash into the forest growth any second.

With the wind pulling at my curls, the mist lifted, revealing an impossible image ahead. Time seemed to stop completely. She stood at the cliff's edge like she had been waiting for us. Long blond hair swirled around an angelic face as her arms reached out in a pleading gesture. Her mouth was open in a silent scream. I couldn't speak, for death had me by the sternum, pulling me forward.

There was a ramming to Sadie's side, making me lose my grip. Mr. Pemberton raced beside me. In one quick motion, he grabbed Sadie's reins, grinding us to a halt at the cliff's edge. The mare threw her head back and screamed, rearing up on her hind legs. Pebbles kicked out from under her hoofs, soaring down toward the jutting rocks below, lost to the violent surf.

Mr. Pemberton took hold of my waist and pulled me onto his horse in front of him. I turned toward his chest and clutched his coat's lapels as Sadie continued to snort and kick in a temper tantrum. I couldn't stand to watch; I pressed my face into his shoulder. A black vignette crept into the corners of my vision, and I let it swallow me.

CHAPTER FIFTY

I was in a state of shock as I was carried up the grand staircase and placed atop my bed. Whoever carried me must have had a key to my room. Everything was numb, and yet I realized that I was shaking. The incident played again and again in my mind. The salt in my lungs. The mare's cries. The voice calling out to me.

Seeing *her*.

Was it possible that everything Maman had taught me was wrong? Despite the warm duvet that was laid over me, goose bumps crept across my arms.

They had called Dr. Barnaby. The irony was not lost on me that Sadie's stunt had resulted in a private meeting with him.

After a quick exam and a few questions, he administered a tonic to ease my nerves. It helped immensely, and I was able to get my mind in order. Then he settled into the chair beside my bed. There was a tray with tea and a plate of sliced bread and preserves on the small table, but I had no appetite. The rain ran down in thick rivulets against the windows.

"You've given Pemberton quite a fright," Dr. Barnaby said. "He'll never forgive himself for letting you ride Sadie. She may be old, but she can still be unpredictable."

"It wasn't anyone's fault," I said, too tired to explain my reasoning. "Something spooked the horse. I couldn't stop it." I kept the rest of the story to myself. It wasn't unnatural for a spiritualist to see ghosts—except when it was.

"Yes, and if he hadn't been there, you both may have ended up at the bottom of the cliff."

True. I would never forget the sound Sadie made as she came up short of the edge, like she had realized at the last second what was about to happen. It was a thousand times more horrific than a mare foaling.

"Luckily, the tide was high, though," he said. "If you had gone over, you would have at least stood a chance." He shook his head. "But sometimes luck isn't enough."

There was a hitch to his voice. Once, I might have assumed he was expressing sympathy for my own situation; now I recognized that he was reminiscing about his secret lover. The tonic was starting to blur my mind. I had to make the most of this private encounter before I fell asleep.

"Yes," I said, letting myself sound feeble, hoping my weakness would disguise any threat in my next words. "I hope Sadie will recover. Joseph told me she was Audra's favourite." He only nodded, saying nothing. I tried again. "It must have been such an awful time. Were you with Mr. Pemberton the day he discovered her missing? The morning of the wedding?"

"As his best man, I stayed with him all night in the cottage at the edge of the property."

His answer only further proved that he was a skilled liar. I chanced pushing again. "You were with him all night? You didn't leave for any reason?"

He tilted his chin at me, suspicion flaring across his face. "Despite his cool demeanour, Pemberton can be rather anxious. You can imagine how it must have been for him, suddenly coming into possession of an estate the scale of Somerset. His world was about to change forever."

I lay back against my pillow, considering his words. Dr. Barnaby poured himself a cup of tea. There were dark circles under his eyes. "The tonic is making you groggy," he said. "Just close your eyes, Miss Timmons. Rest is the best medicine."

"Perhaps you could use some tonic yourself," I said, fighting against the exhaustion. "I understand you had a full day's work ahead of you in the village, and here you are, back again to Somerset. You must be tired, keeping a watch on Mrs. Donovan, and now myself."

Dr. Barnaby ignored my comment; he was probably hoping I'd soon be asleep. Either way, I was growing weary of his façade. I may not know much about passion and romance, but lovers who pined for their dearly departed were my specialty.

"This house has many spirits, Dr. Barnaby, and they've been speaking to me."

The teacup paused halfway to his lips. His gaze met my own, unreadable. "Pardon?"

I had looked into the eyes of many skeptics, but he was listening to me. "Ghosts only haunt when they need a message delivered," I began. "The only way to clear a house of a spirit is to make their desires known."

His Adam's apple moved up and down. The teacup was still frozen in his grip.

"Audra told me about you," I finally said.

There was a pause; I counted each thump of my heartbeat. Then he leaned forward, delicately placing the cup back on its saucer. "What do you mean?" he whispered.

"She told me of your love. That you planned to run away together the night before the wedding."

He was stone, unmoving. Then his eyes shifted to his black medical bag.

"The dead speak to me," I said again, wanting to reclaim his attention. "They have no reason to lie." I pushed as much strength into my voice as I could, but my muscles were heavy. How much tonic had he given me?

His voice was quiet, controlled. "So you're the only one who knows? Or rather, the only living person?"

My throat tightened. "She left her room that night to meet you," I continued. "But you weren't there. Why? What happened?"

His jaw hardened, the veins in his neck becoming visible.

I sensed peril, but I didn't care. "Or maybe you were," I said. A vision flashed before my eyes: Dr. Barnaby with his arms outstretched, Audra's cries disappearing beneath him as she plunged into the rocks below. He was a convincing liar; perhaps he never loved her at all. "How could you, knowing she was carrying your child?"

His veneer finally broke. His body shuddered, and he pressed a fist against his lips as he closed his eyes. A quick succession of deep gasps broke the silence. I watched his chest quiver with each sob.

The torment was authentic.

He took several breaths to calm himself, wiping the corners of his eyes with a handkerchief. "My apologies," he said, voice thick. "You are the first person I have been able to grieve Audra, and our child, in front of." His brown eyes pleaded with me. "You don't understand what it's been like to stand alongside her family and her fiancé as they mourn, all the while hiding my own unfathomable heartache. Some days the promise of the cliff's edge is too sweet to ignore. Just one step and I'd never have to feel this insufferable agony anymore."

I was in awe of his profound pain. How had he managed to hide it for so long? "Why didn't you meet her that night?" I asked.

"I tried! I waited in the stable for hours. She'd specifically asked me to saddle Sadie, but she never arrived. I assumed she had changed her mind. I confess, I completely understood why she would. She was leaving the only family and the only home she'd ever known. A doctor's salary could hardly afford her the lifestyle she was used to."

He stood abruptly and went to the window. The light illuminated the deep frown lines etched across his face. "I lied to you just now. I wasn't with Pemberton all night, obviously. I slipped a tonic in his nightcap to make sure he wouldn't wake until we were long gone. He was still sound asleep when I returned to the cottage at sunrise."

"You went nowhere near the cliff?"

He turned to me, the anguish so apparent I could see it pressing down on him, threatening to send him to his knees. "It is the second-greatest regret of my life that I didn't take Sadie and wait for her directly outside the kitchen door."

Now I could see it; he'd adored her. I imagined them living together in a quaint cottage, far away, their sweet little baby playing at their feet. It was an incomprehensible loss. This was his torture—to be in this house, to pass by her portrait in the hall, to stroll the greenhouse and think of a future that would never be. It was cruelty beyond measure.

"I'm sorry," I said, watching him behind drooping eyelids. The tonic was taking effect.

Regaining his composure, he reached for his bag. "I know they brought you here to bring peace to Pemberton. But I wonder if I may join your séance. I am a man of science, but I've witnessed events that defy explanation. You must have a connection to the other side if you know about Audra and me. No one was aware. We were very careful. She needs to know I will never forgive myself for not being there when she needed me most."

My answer came quickly, a result of so many years of practise. "It will be a benefit to have you at the séance," I said. "Her connection to you is strong."

"Thank you. I beg you to not divulge this secret to anyone, especially Pemberton. He's the only one left in my life that matters. If I lose his friendship now, I'm not sure I'll ever recover."

"He has a right to know," I said. I felt my bones sink deeper into the bed.

"I will tell him when the time is appropriate. I promise," he answered.

The air felt different, the earlier tension having dissipated, or maybe the medicine was taking effect on my senses. Still, I had one more question before he left.

"You said not meeting Audra at the kitchen door was your second-biggest regret," I asked. "What's the first?"

His posture caved. "Audra told me she was sleepwalking," he replied. "She was worried she was going mad like her father and her grandfather before him. I told her it was only the pregnancy."

"But now you're uncertain?"

"We all wonder what happened to Audra, but I believe the most plausible explanation is that she went off the cliff of her own volition." The lines in his face seemed more prominent. "Rest now," he said. "Pemberton is waiting for me to give my report."

I was already partly asleep. The rain continued to batter against the panes. Audra's words appeared behind my eyelids.

Dearest. You watch me with your sad eyes

. . . we share the Linwood secret

. . . it is my salvation

I envisioned Audra in her room, sitting on the overstuffed chair, writing under the portrait of her mother. A portrait so large it belonged in the gallery—not a bedroom.

. . . a fun way to snoop on the staff

The answer came to me so perfectly, I felt stupid for not seeing it from the beginning. Every house has its secrets. Somerset Park was no different.

I bolted upright in bed, gasping. The rain had stopped, and the room was considerably darker. I did not remember Dr. Barnaby leaving.

I lit a candle and slipped on my dressing gown, tying it around my waist. I grabbed the key to Audra's room and raced out the door.

"Oh!" I dropped the candle, almost setting myself on fire. It sputtered and went out as it hit the floor. Mr. Pemberton was sitting in a chair beside the door frame. He jumped to stand when I nearly fell into his lap. "What are you doing?" I asked, untangling myself from his arms.

"I've been here since Barnaby left," he said, pulling at the bottom of his vest. His jacket hung over the back of the chair. There were a set of dirty dishes and an empty wineglass on the floor. "I should be asking your intentions, Miss Timmons. You're supposed to be resting." His tone was stern, but it didn't match his relieved expression.

"I'm fine," I said, forcing my eyes not to skim past him toward the hall that led to Audra's room.

"Fine? Do you not have any memory of what happened?" His eyes were so intense—the deepest blue of the ocean.

"Someone carried me back," I recalled. "Was it you?"

He lowered his voice. "We should speak," he said. "In private."

I stepped back into my room and waited for him to follow. He hesitated before crossing the threshold. "Close the door," I told him, lighting the candles on the mantel.

He stood across from me, arms at his sides. "How are you really feeling?" he asked.

"Improved," I said.

"Good. I want you to leave first thing in the morning."

Betrayal shot through me. I turned sharply to look at him, trying to decipher his expression. Was he upset with me because of Sadie? Had he lost all confidence in my abilities? Had he given up on the séance? "What? Why?"

"I will pay you generously," he said. "Anywhere you want to go. You'll have enough money to bribe every police officer from here to France." He seemed hurried and desperate, almost terrified. "Paris, correct? You said you have family there."

"I have no one." I continued to stare at him, searching for some hint as to why he would order me away, after all we had been through. My heart was a tangle of hurt and confusion. "Why now? I don't understand."

"You cannot be serious," he said, incredulous. "You could have ridden the horse off the cliff today! No, you must go. If you stay any longer, this place will claim you as well."

"I haven't gone mad."

"That's what Audra said too." He stepped closer and took my hands in his own. "Please, Miss Timmons," he said.

Hadn't this been all I wanted, not so long ago? A chance to run away and start again. But now, the thought of leaving tore painfully at my soul.

"If you could have seen your face today," he continued. "You weren't screaming, or trying to get control of the horse. You were staring straight ahead, intent on racing toward something invisible. You were in a trance. And when I finally got you off the horse, all you kept saying was, 'It was her,' over and over until you fainted in my arms. I had never felt so helpless."

The chill washed over me as the memory resurfaced. Audra's image came through the mist as if she had been standing there, waiting for me. I could no longer deny what I believed to be true. But admitting it would mean two things: everything Maman told me was wrong, and now she was punishing me from beyond the grave.

All the unexplained occurrences that had been happening to me were not tricks played by someone living in the manor. The handwriting in the ghost book, the upside-down picture, the voice in the night, and finally the undeniable evidence in front of my own eyes today were the work of one person. Even her own horse sensed her.

"I saw Audra's ghost," I told him.

He let go of my hands and gave me one of his scrutinizing looks. "How can you say that? I thought we were beyond such games."

"Trust me," I said. Then I told him everything, starting with the ghost book and ending with the voice leading me to the dungeon. "I found the diary this morning, and I went to the stables with the intention of telling you right away."

He said nothing, only walked to the wardrobe and opened the door. He crouched down and ran his finger along the message scratched into the wood. I let out a sigh, somewhat worried it wouldn't have been there.

"And there's a secret dungeon as well?" He laughed, but it sounded wounded. "Where's the diary, then? I must see it with my own eyes."

Placing the candle on the vanity, I opened the top drawer, conscious of the fact that he had moved closer to stand behind me. This diary would reveal Dr. Barnaby's affair, but I could not bear the weight of one more secret. "You may find a few entries shocking," I began. "But remember, her heart ruled her, and whatever you might read . . ." I stopped and stared at the drawer. My stomach dropped; this was what it must have felt like to plummet from a cliff's edge.

The diary was not there. But the tiara was. Its stones caught the candlelight and winked at me wickedly.

CHAPTER FIFTY-ONE

Mr. Pemberton reached around me and lifted the tiara, examining it. "I'm ashamed to admit my surprise," he said dryly.

I had no words. I was certain no one had seen me moving the tiara to the library. But I couldn't tell Mr. Pemberton that without admitting I had once intended to steal it after the séance. That plan—that earlier version of myself—felt lifetimes ago, though it had only been a few days. Humiliation burned across my face as I confessed a half-truth. "I tried it on for a laugh to see what it would be like to be beautiful. Then I came back to my room, and I'd forgotten to take it off!" My words tumbled out quickly. "I was going to return it, but I was afraid you'd assume the worst of me."

One blond eyebrow arched. "You can hardly blame me."

"If I wanted to steal the tiara, why would I open the drawer and show you?" The headdress's reappearing was unsettling, but more than that, I couldn't bear him thinking badly of me. Had our connection only been my own wistful fantasy?

"It's been a strange day." He seemed to compose himself. "Where is the diary?" he asked again, using the voice he usually reserved for ordering the staff.

"I . . . I don't know," I stammered, pushing the petticoats off to the side and back again. "It was here! Just this morning!" I looked around the room, as if an explanation might leap out at me.

He stayed silent. It was worse than any cutting remark.

When he eventually spoke, he sounded more defeated than stern. "After what happened with Sadie, I was considering calling off the séance. I told myself I should finally let Audra's memory and Somerset Park have some peace. I was considering starting a new life." He held my stare for only a matter of seconds.

I couldn't stand this. The thought of leaving, disgraced forever in his eyes, was unendurable. "So much has changed since we first devised this scheme. I want . . . I *must* do this séance for her. Audra's spirit has been begging for my help all along. Someone in this house is responsible for her death." I took a deep breath and raised my chin to look him in the eye. "I may know how she left her room. I need to look. One last time."

He closed his eyes, pained. Then he nodded. "All right, then," he said. "One last time."

As we made our way down the hall, his last three words clung to my skin like morning frost. It felt so final. Somerset Park would forever be etched into my very soul, but my time here was running out.

We silently gained entry to Audra's room. I went to the fireplace and lit a few candles. Mr. Pemberton gave the area a wary once-over. He seemed uncomfortable here, and I wondered when he'd last stepped foot in this room, or even if he ever had.

"May I?" I said, holding out my hand. After he passed me the tiara, I returned it to the top drawer of the dresser. I had hoped the diary might have somehow returned to this place too, but the secret compartment remained empty.

Regardless, I had a notion that Audra still had one more secret to share. Now I had to put it to the test. I motioned to the towering image of Lady Chadwick. "Audra's father had this portrait brought up from the Gallery Hall after her mother died." I went to the large armoire against the opposite wall. "They must have moved her wardrobe to accommodate the painting." I opened both doors and looked inside. The dresses were still parted as I'd left them, Audra's unworn wedding gown exposed in all its macabre glory.

Mr. Pemberton groaned, glancing away from it. "Miss Timmons, please," he said. "Is this necessary?"

I pushed the garment aside and showed him the back paneling. "See the mismatched cedar wood? The new boards are not as aged as the darker ones. This made me wonder why the wardrobe needed a new back."

He squinted and leaned forward, inspecting the wood.

I returned to the portrait. "In her diary Audra referenced a confidant she named Dearest, someone with sad brown eyes who looked down on her. It was someone who shared her secret—a secret way to escape."

"Escape?" He took the lamp and held it up to the portrait, Lady Chadwick's angular face frowning back as us disapprovingly. "But Audra's mother had blue eyes."

I moved his hand down until the light shone on the dog. "Meet Dearest," I said.

He stood there, examining it, mouth open in awe.

I ran my hands along the length of the frame, silently praying this was the answer. Then I felt a series of protruding bolts—hidden hinges. "Pull here," I told him.

Mr. Pemberton fixed his fingers into the grooves of the frame and pulled back. With an echoing creak, the portrait swung open, revealing a gaping hole in the wall looking down into a black passage. A plume of stale air blew into our faces.

"This must have been here since the manor was first built," he said.

"A way to spy on the staff?" I offered.

"This is how she got out!" He turned to me with an expression that somehow encompassed both relief and amazement.

I smiled at him. We were finally at the threshold of discovering what had truly happened to Audra that night. But more important, we were doing it together.

"My deepest apologies for doubting you, Miss Timmons," he said. "You're nothing less than remarkable. Do you know where it leads?"

I beamed. "Only one way to find out."

The narrow passageway could only fit the width of one person. I insisted on going in first with the lamp while Mr. Pemberton followed close behind. We made our way past massive cobwebs thick as cotton and cracked stone walls that seemed they might crumble at the slightest pressure. The tunnel soon came to a dead end, but there was a ladder nailed to the wall that went through a hole in the floor.

"Wait." Mr. Pemberton reached down and gave the ladder a good tug. His arm brushed mine, and I had a faint memory of being carried in his arms up the staircase. The ladder held fast. "I'll go first," he said.

"Be careful," I told him, holding the lamp above his head.

He made his way down, hand under hand. Before he disappeared completely, he paused with his face looking up at me from the floor. "I stand by my offer to give you enough money to start over anywhere you like," he said earnestly.

"I appreciate that," I replied, smiling a little. "No matter; I think you'll agree it's impossible for me to walk away at this point."

"Well, yes. But I wanted you to know, in case."

"In case there's a murderer waiting for you at the bottom of this ladder?"

He rolled his eyes at my response and disappeared downward. The thud of something heavy hitting the floor echoed from below. He grunted and called up that the bottom few rungs were missing, so I'd have to jump the last part, but it was safe.

With the lamp in one hand, I descended. Once I came to the bottom rung, I passed the light to him, which he placed on the floor. I was still a few feet over his head.

"Let go," he said. "I'll catch you."

I hardly had time to gasp before I felt his hands on my waist and my feet lightly landing on the floor.

"Good?" he asked. I nodded and picked up the lamp, glad he couldn't see my blush. My second rescue in one day. I was learning the secret to getting Mr. Pemberton's attention.

We cleared another long hallway until we spotted a pinprick of light cutting through the darkness up ahead. Familiar voices echoed through the walls. I came to the source of the light and saw someone had drilled a small peephole.

I looked through the opening and saw the library below. The room appeared rounded on the edges. I must have been spying through the glass eye of one of the mounted animals.

Flora stood by the circular table I had planned to use at the séance. She was twisting the dust rag in her hands. William paced in front of her, a glass in one hand and a bottle in the other.

"I warned you this would happen," he said. "I told you she had to be taken care of, but you couldn't do it. Now the whole house is feeling sorry for her." He took a drink.

Flora winced and took a step backward. "But it's not that easy, William. She's too smart for me to fool. She'd know in a second somethin' was wrong."

Mr. Pemberton came closer, angling his face toward mine as we listened together.

William laughed at this. "I know you've done it before. Don't give me that innocent, wide-eyed act. You couldn't do it because you think she likes you."

"No." Her voice trembled. "I wasn't sure of how much to use. I'd never forgive me'self if the same thing happened again. I've been havin' dreams! I've been hearin' her call out to me at night!" She made a move to step around him, but he cut her off.

"Don't be stupid," he hissed. He looked at the closed door of the library. "And keep your voice down."

"I'm scared." She clutched the rag to her chest. "I hates this room. I think the ghosts know, William. Maybe I should just tell someone. It was a mistake. And everyone will finally know the truth."

I turned briefly to Mr. Pemberton. Our stunned expressions mirrored each other.

Choking down a mouthful of wine, William set the bottle on the table and went to Flora. "No. What's done is done. We can't change the past." He gripped her shoulders. "As long as you do what I tell you to, everything will work out."

Flora stiffened, but she gave him a weak smile. "And we'll be in charge of Somerset Park?"

He snorted. "How can you doubt me? I'm the one who made sure you didn't end up going to jail the first time, remember? I kept you safe for a reason."

"Because you love me?"

"Because I know you are the only one clever enough to help win back what is rightfully mine." He leaned closer, laying a hand on her waist. "And you only have to do one thing for me. Can you do it? Can you give us our happily ever after?"

She hesitated. Her eyes glanced cautiously at the grandfather's portrait.

"Flora?" His voice was hard, a threat disguised as a prompt.

She nodded. "Yes."

"Good." He let her go, returning to the wine bottle once more. "I expect Miss Timmons won't feel a thing."

My chest rose and fell as if I'd been running. A hand cradled my elbow. In the faint light of the lamp, Mr. Pemberton's face was paler than the moon, yet there was an intensity in his eyes.

"I can't believe it," I whispered. "All this time I imagined it was William who had something to do with Audra's death, but it was Flora!" I licked my dry lips, unwilling to acknowledge how stupid I'd been to trust her.

Maman was right. I was the only one I could depend on. And yet Mr. Pemberton was still beside me.

"We must make her part of the séance," I said. "She's superstitious. I can target her. We're sure to get a confession."

"Have you an ounce of sense? We just overheard two people plotting what I'm most certain is your murder, and all you can think about is the schematics for the séance. The obvious course of action would be to call the police and have them both arrested."

"The coppers are champing at the bit to get me back in a cell. And what kind of proof do we have? All we heard was William say I won't feel a thing. No one mentioned murder."

"How can you be so stubborn?" he fumed, his whispered voice slowly rising in volume. "Give me one reason why I shouldn't go after them this very minute. If you don't want the police, I'll accept that, but I won't have you share the same roof with those two!"

"Shh." I pointed to the wall. "William was secretly in love with Audra," I whispered, watching the storm brewing in his eyes. "He confessed to her on the eve of your wedding, and he provided her with information that confirmed he was the heir to Somerset Park. He wanted her to call off your marriage and be with him instead."

"He what?!"

I put a finger to my lips in warning. Then I leaned closer and whispered the story of William's heritage. "Mrs. Donovan is the only other person who knew," I said. "She could be in on this too, but there's only one way to find out for certain."

His brow pinched together. "If William is the rightful heir I can understand his hatred of me, but the danger he poses can't be ignored. He may have been involved in Audra's death, and I certainly don't excuse his threats on your life."

"We have to go through with the séance." I was surprised by my fervor. Not only because I finally knew who to target, but because I was finally doing what Audra's ghost had been asking of me from the beginning.

Help me.

And I was the only one who could. This wouldn't be a con. This would be justice.

Mr. Pemberton leaned even closer, his anger diminishing. "I've never met anyone as determined to give me so much strife," he said with affection.

It was tempting to stay here with him, standing so close in the dark. For a moment I considered taking another step toward him. But time was not on our side. "Let's see where this passageway ends up," I said.

I led the way with the lamp, moving slowly. Still, the next dead end came upon us without warning, and I nearly tumbled through the hole in the floor. The top of the ladder barely peeked over the edge.

"Miss Timmons," Mr. Pemberton managed to say, looping an

arm around my waist to pull me back. "How have you managed to stay alive this long?"

"You should lead," I said, handing over the light.

He took the lamp, and then my hand, pulling me behind him. "I don't want to lose you in the dark," he said.

I smiled at his back.

After another series of turns, and one more trek down another ladder, we came through a door that led into the hallway just off the kitchen.

It was quiet this time of night. The door swung shut behind us, blending in perfectly with the wainscoting. I would never have known it was there. How many of these passageways extended through the house?

We entered the empty kitchen. Mr. Pemberton stirred the embers of the fireplace with the poker, both of us trying to digest all we'd seen and heard. We were standing in the same spot where we'd first met.

He blinked at the dying flames. "I can't help but feel responsible. If I had known, I could have protected her from William. I should have tried harder to earn her trust."

His guilt was palpable. I knew more than anyone the destructive force of self-proclaimed blame. I was unsure when Dr. Barnaby would confess, but I decided Mr. Pemberton shouldn't have to go another day blaming himself for something he wasn't responsible for. "It wouldn't have mattered," I said. "Even if you had declared your adoration and thrown yourself at her feet. She was in love with someone else. They were going to leave Somerset together, in secret."

"You're certain?" The surprise in his voice was evident, but also, interestingly, relief.

I nodded. I considered telling him the name, but I didn't want to add to his suffering.

"I wonder if William found out," he said. "He could have been mad enough to kill her."

"It's possible," I agreed.

He let out a sigh as he shook his head. There was a bewildered expression about him, but one free of the previous burden. I was glad to have given him that reprieve. "Thank you," he said. "That information means a lot to me."

"You're not upset she was in love with someone else?"

"Our arrangement was financial. Any feelings that might have developed out of the union would have been slow, but cordial I suppose." He paused and locked his gaze on me. "Not like real love. I'm beginning to appreciate what she was willing to do for a love like that."

His stare held me in place. Any thoughts I'd had were stolen from my mind. I couldn't come up with a reply. What did I know of real love? I knew what the men who came to Miss Crane's desired, but that thirst was easily quenched. Any girl would do.

But this look from Mr. Pemberton was different. It held a promise. A promise that thrilled and saddened me, for it was one I knew I didn't deserve. But I couldn't tell him this. I replied, "My mother always told me love brought heartache."

He seemed to consider that. Then he asked, "Are you looking forward to beginning a new life?"

A hollowness sat in my chest that I couldn't explain. I wanted to turn back time, to ask him more about what he thought of love. The conflict must have shown on my face.

"I thought that would make you happy. You could be in Paris in a few days," he continued. "In time for your birthday." He looked rather sheepish. "It was in your police file."

The ocean's icy breath crept across the back of my neck. My nineteenth birthday—the one I was fated not to celebrate.

"Yes," I replied, but Paris was the last thing on my mind. There was a growing sense that I would never leave Somerset Park.

Mr. Pemberton angled his head, maybe sensing I was losing confidence. "Have you changed your mind?"

"No." I shook my head. "I'll target William and Flora for Audra's death. We both saw how close she was to breaking under pressure." For the first time, I would be conducting a séance with a real ghost. Be that as it may, it wasn't something I could count on. "All the usual tricks and gimmicks will be in place," I said.

As if answering, the back door suddenly swung open, bringing in a gust of salty air, blown wide by an unseen force.

CHAPTER FIFTY-TWO

Once everyone has sat down, I'll add the candles, putting the special ones in front of Flora and William. They will be the first to extinguish." I was in the library, crouched under the round table, making sure the slim piece of wood was jimmied in place under the pedestal.

"How will that work?" Mr. Pemberton asked. I watched his shoes walk around the table. Then he crouched down, his blue eyes coming into view. "You promised me a few more trade secrets." He held out his hand, helping me to my feet. My finger brushed against the gold pinkie ring. This time I didn't bother to keep my smile hidden. I had resolved to enjoy what little time we had left. I knew his straightforward nature well enough by now that if he intended to progress our relationship any further, he would have said so, rather than mentioning my eventual departure so often.

"I cut the wicks." I brushed my hands down the front of the dress, smoothing out the wrinkles. I had chosen a simple one, knowing I wouldn't have any assistance from Flora. "They vary in length, so I manipulate which candle goes out first."

He picked one up and held it up to the light. "Impressive," he said.

With his head tilted back, I could see the scar under his jaw. I would miss that scar. The door was closed, but the sounds of the staff preparing for tonight's party echoed throughout. Everyone was under strict orders not to disturb the library.

I yawned into my hand. All night I kept imagining Flora coming into my room with a knife behind her back.

"Likewise, Miss Timmons," Mr. Pemberton replied, fighting off his own yawn. His red-rimmed eyes were evidence of lack of sleep. He'd stayed outside my room again last night.

I opened the ghost book to the message page and wrote in my practised cursive *William* and then *Flora*. I hesitated, bothered by a small needling of guilt. William could go to jail—I had no problem with that—but Flora seemed more of an unwilling accomplice. Maman would call me foolish.

"Here's the key to lock up when you're finished." He placed it on the table, but then stood in place, making no motion to leave. "One more thing." He reached into his vest pocket again and pulled out a small velvet box. He held it out to me. "An early birthday present, Miss Timmons."

"Oh." I worked to keep my hands from shaking as I opened the lid. It was a cameo brooch, set in silver. My fingertips felt along the silhouette carved from ivory.

"It was my mother's. I'm not sure if women in Paris wear such ornamentation, but I wanted you to have something to remember me—or rather, Somerset Park—by. Perhaps you'll only wear it for special occasions, or maybe you'll leave it in the box. It's up to you."

"I won't leave it in the box," I said, still staring down at the delicate profile.

The two of us bowed over the brooch, not daring to look up at each other.

He said, "You admitted you tried on the tiara because you wanted to see what it would be like to be beautiful. I can assure you the tiara is unwarranted. You only need to see yourself as others do."

I lifted my gaze. His eyes were a warm, cloudless summer sky. How could Audra not have fallen in love with him? "Thank you, Mr. Pemberton," I said. "I will always treasure it." And although I didn't say it out loud, I knew I needed no token to remember him forever.

His lips curled up, mischievous. "I wonder if you might at last consider calling me Gareth, at least once before you leave. I would like to think we are parting ways as more than a formal acquaintance." Then he added with a whisper, "Miss Timmons."

I felt the whisper all the way to my toes. There was nothing I wanted more than to reach up and trace the scar with my finger, even place a kiss there. I almost told him everything then, all the secrets that weren't in the police report the night Maman died. But I knew that would change everything. It was better to leave him with this image of me.

"I have always found friendship difficult," I said. "But you are the one thing I will remember fondly about Somerset Park." Then I took a step back. "However, I believe calling each other by our first names will only cloud an already complicated situation."

His smile eased into a conciliatory expression. He bowed his chin. "I suppose I must accept your decision. I cannot find fault with you keeping me as a pleasant memory. I will do the same."

A knock at the door made both of us step apart. I hadn't realized how close we still were.

"Come in," Mr. Pemberton said.

The door opened and Bramwell stood in place, tall and austere. "Forgive me, my lord, but there is an issue with the wine cellar."

Mr. Pemberton put his attention back on me.

"Go, I'm almost finished here," I said.

He lingered long enough to give me a reassuring smile, then turned and left the room with Bramwell.

The space felt empty without him. I glanced up at the stag's head, reasoning that's where the peephole was located. I wondered how many times Lord Chadwick had stood there, spying on his family and servants.

It was time to refocus; I closed the ghost book and checked over all the props once more. The grandfather clock chimed, reminding me that in a few hours this room would be filled with guests. All that remained was ensuring Flora would be among them.

Returning to my room, I lit several of my candles. Then I pulled the servants' cord and paced the floor until a light knock came at the door.

"Come in," I said.

Flora stood there with a tray in her hands. "Mrs. Galloway thought you'd want some refreshments before the party, miss." She wouldn't meet my gaze.

"I'm sorry for what I said about Mr. Sutterly. It's none of my business." I took the tray from her and placed it on the small table, eyeing the teapot suspiciously. "I hope you'll forgive me. And I hope you'll consider being part of the séance tonight."

"Me?" Her voice rose an octave.

"Absolutely," I continued, pretending not to notice her nerves. "Having you there will be an important addition. I've already gained permission from Mr. Pemberton. And don't forget, Mr. Sutterly will be there too."

Her bottom lip started to tremble. "No, miss. I don't think so."

I glanced at the candle nearest to the window. Then I rubbed my arms. "Do you feel that?" I asked. "Check the window, please. There must be a draft."

With a stiff manner, Flora checked the window. "It's closed, miss. There's no dr—"

The candle went out. We watched a wisp of smoke rise up from the glass chimney.

"How odd," I said. "I sense a spirit is with us. And yet I haven't called to anyone. That's never happened before."

Flora stepped away from the window, edging closer to the fireplace. The horror on her face was unbridled. The two candles on the mantel extinguished one right after the other. She let out a yelp, a hand flying to her throat.

I pointed at her. "It's you!" I called out. "The spirit is connected to you. Wait!" I raised my chin, as if looking at something just over Flora's shoulders. "It's Maisie! She's trying to say something."

Flora shook her head, skittering backward. "You're just tryin' to be spooky."

In reply, the remaining candles burned out. Only the lamp remained lit on the bedside table. This time she screamed in earnest.

Walking toward her, I said, "Maisie is desperate to send you a message. It's costing her a great deal of strength."

"No!" Flora cried. "I don't trust you!"

The lamp slid off the bedside table and tumbled to the rug as if hit by an invisible hand.

I curled up the string I'd just yanked and let it drop to the floor. The top of my boot gave it a nudge, kicking it under the bed. "She says you're troubled by a secret. A secret you're too afraid to tell anyone."

Flora chewed on her lower lip.

I reached for her hands. "Maisie says once you tell the truth, it will release you from your nightmares and your correct path will reveal itself."

"Does she forgive me?" Flora clutched my hands tightly, her fingernails digging into my skin.

That was unexpected. Still, I continued. "Yes. She loves you."

She collapsed into my arms, heaving great sobs into my shoulder. "It was an accident!"

A bit stunned, I patted her back and soothed her with whispers. "There, there," I said.

"All I wanted was to make her better," Flora sputtered. "Auntie Lil said there was nothin' we could do, but I had to try somethin'. I didn't know enough, though. The tea leaves looked the same to me. I thought I was givin' her a tonic to help with fever. Instead, it stopped her heart!"

My own heart practically faltered at this. Flora's guilt was for Maisie, and not Audra?

Flora's wet face pressed into my shoulder. "Oh, Maisie," she bellowed. "I'm so sorry."

"You gave Maisie one of Auntie Lil's concoctions?"

"And she died the next day!" Flora pulled back. Her face was streaked with tears. "I only wanted to make her better, honestly. But William told me he overheard the doctor say it was unexplained how her heart stopped. But I know it was me! I killed Maisie!"

My heart went out to her. An accident, an act with consequences you could never erase—this I understood. But then I remembered what Barnaby had told me. "The doctor said she had a weak heart already, and was susceptible to the illness. He would know; he was with her all night."

She sniffed. "But William told me what he heard." A myriad of expressions swept across her face. I watched her struggle to puzzle the pieces together.

A little nudge was in order. I went to the table and poured a cup of tea, then offered it to her. "Here, a spot of this will help."

Flora took the cup. It rattled on the saucer. She stared at it for an eternity before dissolving into tears again. "Oh, miss! I'm so sorry. It was all William's idea. He wanted me to put one of Auntie Lil's sleeping potions in your tea. He wanted you to be so drowsy for the séance everyone would think you were drunk. He wanted the lord to kick you out. He hates you, miss. And I didn't want to do it—I likes you, I really do. But he said he'd tell the lord about how I hurt Maisie. And if I hurt Maisie, I might have had somethin' to do with Lady Audra's death. I can't go to jail! I can't have Auntie Lil thinkin' I'm so terrible."

At last. I breathed a sigh. "He's trying to sabotage the séance on purpose, Flora. And there's only one reason."

Flora lowered her head, accepting this truth. "Do you still needs me for the séance?" she whispered. "I don't want to see him."

"No," I assured her. "Don't fret. After tonight you won't have to contend with William anymore. I'll see to that."

Her devastation was heartbreaking. For so long she had been burdened with this grief. I hoped I could offer her one morsel of cheer. "Maisie also said you have a genuine beau in your midst. You just have to open your eyes to see him."

She wiped at her nose with her sleeve. "Oh, Jenny. I'm a right mess. Let's not speak of this any longer. And my heavens, look outside! The sun's goin' down. We've got to get you ready."

Flora was true to her word. In no time I was fitted into the crimson dress overlaid with black lace. My hair was carefully pinned back, a few curls left to skim my cheeks. When I looked in the mirror, I hardly recognized myself. For the first time, I looked entirely like the sort of creature who belonged among the finery of Somerset Park.

"Too bad you ain't got no necklace, Jenny," Flora said, touching my collar. "The neckline is elegant for sure, but plain."

I reached for the velvet box on the vanity.

CHAPTER FIFTY-THREE

With every candle lit, Somerset Park was luminous. Garlands of evergreen boughs studded with blooms from the greenhouse decorated the main foyer. I stood at the railing overlooking the main hall and watched the couples twirl below. Long tables of refreshments lined the back wall: punch in sparkling crystal glasses, silver bowls of nuts, tiers of brightly colored tarts. The celebration had been going on for some time. I had grown weary watching the revelers, and had no intentions of joining them. This was not my world.

As it turned out, Mr. Pemberton was an excellent dancer and was never long without a partner. Even so, as he effortlessly stepped in time with each new song, his eyes searched the balcony and found mine. It would have been easy to feel jealous of the various women whom he held in his arms, but I could no longer afford to indulge such romantic desires. This would be our last evening together. I made myself recall his reply when I told him I couldn't dance.

Then you should hope no one asks you.

It would have been much easier to leave Somerset Park if Mr. Pemberton had remained proud and cruel.

I hadn't spoken to him since our time in the library that afternoon, but he sent me a note; a horse would wait for me at the stables with a satchel of money, to make use of if I so chose. The fact he thought I wouldn't fulfill my promise of making William confess to Audra's murder left me with a faint sense of foreboding.

I spied William a few times in the crowd. He was sullen and distracted, keeping mostly to himself in the corners. I could practically read his mind, knowing that everything he saw was rightfully his. Each time Harry swept past him, he took a full glass from the tray.

I was glad. The more inebriated he was, the more careless he would be later.

Mr. Lockhart occupied one of the settees pushed off to the side. He nodded appreciatively at the dancers while his cane tapped in time with the music. A heavy layer of guilt settled inside my chest. He had plucked me from inevitable doom and asked only that I give Mr. Pemberton peace. A peaceful séance was the opposite of what I would be delivering. I would be denying a dying man his last wish. I hoped he would understand.

One person was oddly absent. Perhaps Dr. Barnaby's grief would be too difficult to hide among all this festivity. Or maybe he was preserving any emotional fortitude for the séance.

Finally, the musicians announced they would play the last song. I took my time descending the grand staircase. Mr. Pemberton began a speech, thanking everyone for coming to pay tribute to Audra. I admit, I had visions of our eyes meeting across the room, hoping he would notice the brooch.

Instead, it was Mr. Lockhart who made his way to me. The guests quietly melted away for him as he limped forward. "My dear." He smiled. "You look lovely. I know your talents will shine tonight." There was a faint bruise on his left cheek. I imagined him bending over to tie his shoes only to bang his head on the bedside table.

Mr. Lockhart touched my hand and leaned forward. "After-ward," he whispered, "we can discuss your trial. I'm encouraged by a discrepancy I found in your file. I plan on putting a team into investigating the coroner who signed the death certificate. The first cause of death had been scratched out and written over. Most un-usual."

"Cause of death?" I echoed. I flexed my hands, remembering how the shawl felt in my grip. The partygoers jostled us about, taking all the air with them.

I stammered an excuse and left Mr. Lockhart, eager to escape the crowd. It wasn't until I'd rushed into the library, closing the door behind me, that I could breathe again. I put my back against it, resisting the urge to sink to my knees. Mr. Lockhart had to have been misinformed. I had the cause of death—myself.

I went to the table, my silk dress rustling in the quiet. There was a dampness to the air, like old mold. The fire had not been lit yet. I opened the ghost book to the secret page and completely wiped away Flora's name. I also removed her chair, leaving the other five in place.

Above the enormous mantel, Lord Chadwick's portrait had been replaced with Audra's. She smiled demurely down at me. She was still just as beautiful, but there seemed to be an added notion of revenge in her countenance. I hoped she approved of this plan. I hoped this was what she meant by all the messages, begging for help.

I had initially presumed her to be a wealthy heiress, a woman who never wanted for anything in her life. Now, though, I sensed our connection. I was the one she had reached out to, leading me to clues, and begging for my assistance. Both of us had lost our parents, and in a way both of us were fighting a prophecy of doom.

Hers was the family sickness. Mine was the fortune-teller's promise of a watery death.

And both of us had secrets.

This was mine: if Audra could reach out to me beyond the grave, then surely, my mother could. Maman's spiritual absence was a punishment for what I had done, a cold reminder I did not deserve happiness.

Cause of death.

No matter what was written or not written on the coroner's report, I knew I was responsible. Needing to focus, I double-checked the props, then made sure all the windows were locked.

"Miss Timmons." Bramwell had appeared at the door, holding a candelabra. "The others are waiting for you." There was no welcoming expression on his face. I wondered what the staff must be saying about me.

Locking the library door behind me, I followed him, nervously adjusting my dress. As we neared the drawing room, I heard a voice that made my blood run cold. I halted on the spot, fighting the urge to flee in the opposite direction.

Bramwell stood at the open door and announced my name.

A hush fell over the men. I searched the faces, and when our eyes met, his crooked grin was identical to the one he had given me as I was leaving the police station.

"Constable Rigby," I said.

He bowed. "Evening, Miss Timmons." He didn't bother to conceal the anticipation in his voice. His uniform buttons were polished and glinted in the candlelight, as did the pistol holstered to his side. "I'm looking forward to the séance. Can't wait to see how this one turns out."

My throat grew tight. I stood there, unable to move.

Mr. Pemberton left his drink on the mantel and came to my side. His eyes paused on the cameo brooch. He looked toward the constable. "Your attendance is contingent on your honor, sir," he said. "I hope you will acknowledge truthfully what happens this evening."

"With all due respect, m'lord, the law doesn't need an invitation to arrest a known felon. I've orders to take Miss Timmons back to London as soon as the séance is over." Constable Rigby smirked, which was his best effort at being professional. He could hardly keep from gloating.

Mr. Pemberton offered me his arm. I couldn't feel my legs, but somehow I managed to walk with him. "Did you know?" I whispered as quietly as I could.

"No. He only arrived shortly before you."

The first time I had entered this drawing room, the golden wall-paper caused everything to shimmer. Tonight, though, I could see the small cracks in the seams where the paper had peeled back, and where mold had set in the corners of the windowpanes. The house itself had begun to rapidly decay, an omen to my own miserable misfortune. Ghosts blew whispers of death in my ear while spiders spun crowns of webbing atop the chandeliers.

Mr. Lockhart hobbled over.

"You used me," I said. I tried to keep the anger from my voice. "From the very beginning."

"It was the only way they would allow you to come with me. I will still give you my services," he offered. Then he coughed into his handkerchief. I saw spots of blood before he hastily put it away.

His offer was pointless. He may not live that long.

Dr. Barnaby was on the settee. Now I saw a rip in the material, and one of its feet was badly scuffed. I had been so much in awe of Somerset, my mind had been impervious to its imperfections. What else had I been blind against?

"This woman is one of my patients," Dr. Barnaby said, looking toward the constable. An empty wineglass sat beside him, and his cheeks were flushed. "And I'll determine if she's well enough to travel back to London."

I was too shocked to acknowledge his coming to my defense. I also suspected he'd been hiding in here drinking all evening. Everything had turned on its head. No matter how prepared I had been, fate stepped in and spun the wheel of fortune, or in my case, misfortune. There was no way out.

William snorted from across the room. He lounged in a chair, his black dinner jacket unbuttoned. He held up his glass for a refill, practically celebrating my arrest already. In that moment, I wanted to blurt out how Audra had hated him in the end. I wanted to watch his frail ego char to ash under the glare of the truth. I wanted Flora to see him for the deceitful pig he was.

Bramwell opened another bottle of wine.

The air felt thick in my lungs. Constable Rigby looked as if he wanted to string me up from the closest tree. He probably had plans to murder me on the way back to London to ensure I saw no trial. Maybe he'd toss me off the cliff himself.

There was only one thing I was in control of now. "It's time," I announced. "Please follow me to the library."

With my hand on Mr. Pemberton's arm, we walked ahead of everyone. He leaned close and whispered, "I have every confidence in you. Having the police here will serve us better and make it impossible for William to escape. Tonight, someone will go to London in handcuffs, but it won't be you."

I stayed quiet. Handcuffs or not, the fortune-teller's promise crept over me. My time was coming to an end.

CHAPTER FIFTY-FOUR

Once we were all inside the library, Bramwell closed the doors. He and Harry lit the candles and started the fire. Slowly, the room came into full grisly view. Bloodred curtains with gold fringe covered each window. Along the walls, the eyes of the mounted kills leered with menacing stares, while Audra's portrait looked down on the entire room from above the massive fireplace.

Only Mr. Pemberton and I knew the painting had been moved purposely for tonight. Each man stopped and stared up at her, their lips opening slightly.

The effect was significant.

Constable Rigby stood between the door and the table. "Have her take out her fancy hairpins," he said to Mr. Pemberton, as if I weren't in the room. Then he held up a pair of handcuffs. "Can't have her picking the lock and escaping."

My ears flamed with anger and embarrassment. He'd said it on purpose, to remind everyone I was a criminal. I'm surprised he didn't insist on me wearing them for the séance.

"Do not forget where you are, Constable Rigby," Mr. Pemberton said. "You have no right to give orders under my roof."

"Your roof," William sneered under his breath. He plunked down at the round table, spilling some of the brandy he'd taken from the sitting room. Although he was dressed properly, there was an odd odor about him. I wondered what drink he had chosen to indulge in this evening.

I placed a candle in front of each chair, covering them with the chimneys. I pointed to William's glass of liquor. "You have to remove it from the table," I told him. "It can interfere."

He glared at me, probably figuring out by this point that Flora had not kept her promise to drug me. But he stayed quiet and drank the entire contents. Then he turned and threw the glass into the fireplace. There was a hiss followed by a small explosion in the flames.

We all jumped. Mr. Lockhart put a hand to his chest. I could hardly feel guilty now about not giving him his séance of peace, since he'd been lying to me all along.

Next, Dr. Barnaby and Mr. Pemberton took their chairs, leaving me the empty one between them.

I went around the library and blew out the other candles set around the room until the only illumination was from the ones under the glass chimneys. Harry and Bramwell stood at the doors like well-dressed sentries.

I took my place at the table. Reaching for the ghost book, I opened it up, showing everyone the blank surface. I faced Mr. Pemberton. "Do you have a message for Lady Audra?" I asked.

He reached inside his dinner jacket and pulled out a neatly folded piece of paper. "Please read it out loud, Miss Timmons," he instructed.

Mr. Lockhart sniffed, tears emerging from his lower lids. "She loved you so much." He'd propped his cane against his chair. One ruby eye stared at me.

I darted a glance toward Dr. Barnaby. He was staring at the ghost book. His pained expression would have been interpreted by anyone as casual grief, but I knew better.

I unfolded the note. It was a question. But unlike Mrs. Hartford's query of love, this one was grim. I read, "'Who betrayed you?'"

Mr. Lockhart gasped. He looked at Mr. Pemberton with an expression of disgust. "What is this trickery?" he asked. Then he turned to me and realized I was not shocked. His mouth turned down in a disappointed betrayal. "I see," he said.

I found his disapproval bothered me more than I expected. I pictured the bloodstains on his handkerchief. The miserable weight of the guilt resurfaced, and I dropped my gaze.

I refolded the note and placed it in the ghost book. Dr. Barnaby let out a quivering sigh as I closed the cover, keeping the note between the slates. The die had been cast. There was no turning back now.

"Lay your hands on the table," I instructed. "Palms down, fingers splayed wide."

My eye caught the gold ring on Mr. Pemberton's finger. I thought about his scar and how he'd suffered at the hands of his father. My heart was conflicted. He seemed so sure he could save me, but how could I escape Constable Rigby this time? It seemed the people I thought I could trust were not who they were at all. Was there even a horse waiting for me at the stables? I imagined more constables lined up with horses of their own. I swallowed the paranoia and set to task.

"Hold hands," I told them, both of mine reaching for Mr. Pemberton and Dr. Barnaby. I was bridging the span between Audra's lover and fiancé. The room grew quiet—too quiet. The only sound came from the occasional pops and hisses of the fireplace. I realized the grandfather clock had stopped ticking, yet again. Its pendulum hung, unmoving.

The floor creaked as Constable Rigby shifted his weight, bringing me back to the moment. I began, "Our beloved Audra, who grew up in this very house, we bring you gifts of love from our hearts to reach you in death. Commune with us, Audra, and move among us." I repeated the phrase and then added, "Let us know what happened to you that night. Who took you from us far too early?"

The bookcase ladder creaked on its rusty hinges. I took that as my cue. "She is here," I declared. I worked the shimmied piece of wood with the toe of my shoe, making the table rock awkwardly.

There was a whimper from the doors. I suspected it was Harry.

My voice dropped lower. "With whom do you wish to speak?" I said.

The candle in front of Mr. Lockhart went out. He gasped.

I frowned at William's candle. It was still burning. How could I have made that mistake? Only one candle had the wick cut.

Without warning, the long windows at the other end of the room flung open at the same time. The curtains blew inward as if lifted by invisible hands. Impossible! I had checked their locks only moments ago.

"Our beloved Audra," I started again, this time unsure. "Who took you from us that night? Who killed you?"

"Please," Mr. Lockhart cried. "Don't defame her memory. I beg you, stop this!"

Mr. Pemberton's candle went out next. We exchanged confused glances.

There was an echo of a scream from somewhere outside the door.

She was here. For the very first time, I was speaking these words to something real. And I wanted her answer.

I repeated, "Who took you from us that night? Who killed you? Tell us! Please, Audra."

"Enough!" Mr. Lockhart cried out. He reached forward and opened the book. We all leaned forward. There, in Audra's handwriting, was one name—*Gareth*.

CHAPTER FIFTY-FIVE

Mr. Pemberton stared at me, aghast. "What is this?" he asked me.

Before I could answer, my candle went out next, then William's, and, then last, Dr. Barnaby's. The only light was from the fireplace.

"Ha! You see? There's your pr—" William coughed and wheezed. "There's your proof." He suddenly stood, making the chair fall back. His fingers pulled at his necktie as blood trickled from his nose. The wheezing intensified. "Audra," he croaked. Then he collapsed to the floor.

Dr. Barnaby rushed from his chair. He crouched beside William, slapping his face and calling his name. He loosened the necktie and the first few buttons to help him breathe.

Everyone left the table and huddled over them. William looked almost like he was asleep, except for the bulging eyes and spittle about the mouth.

"Oh dear." Mr. Lockhart winced.

Mr. Pemberton's jaw dropped. He stared at his adversary, now splayed on the floor, unmoving.

Harry and Bramwell edged closer from the periphery.

Dr. Barnaby took out his pocket watch and pressed his fingers to William's neck. The room was quiet; only the curtains flapped in the breeze. Dr. Barnaby shut his watch. "He's dead," he said.

Great sparks came from the fire. Constable Rigby pushed me to the side. He knelt by William's body and leaned close, taking a deep sniff. "This man has been poisoned." He glared up at me.

I put a hand to my chest as I stepped backward. I knew there was nothing I could say to prove my innocence. The fire began to smoke heavily, blowing out thick clouds into the room.

"I heard them," Harry said, pointing a shaking finger at me. "She and the lord were in the kitchen the other night. I heard them talk about the séance and how they were going to frame Mr. Sutterly for Lady Audra's murder!"

A full smile took over Constable Rigby's face. He pulled out the set of handcuffs.

I looked up at Audra's portrait. She was my last chance at salvation; I had reached my most extreme measure of desperation, hoping that a ghost would save me.

The door burst open. Flora ran in, pale and out of breath. "Bramwell, Henry! Mrs. Donovan's gotten outside! We think she's by the cliff. Please, come help look. Mrs. Galloway asked me . . ." She stopped when she saw William on the floor. "What?" She ran to his side and dropped to her knees, cradling his head in her lap. "No, no, no," she sobbed.

Dr. Barnaby put a hand on her shoulder.

Flora tore away from his touch. When she looked at me, her red eyes were ablaze with accusation. "You told me I wouldn't have to worry about William after tonight. Look what you done!"

"No!" I shook my head furiously. "I didn't mean like this!"

I heard a swift click of metal. Something cold as ice clamped around my wrist.

I looked and saw a handcuff. "That's all the proof I need," Constable Rigby said, fastening my wrists together in front of me.

"That's hardly proof," Mr. Pemberton said, moving to stand between us. "Release her at once."

In a flash, Constable Rigby had Mr. Pemberton cuffed too. "And I suppose you're the innocent accomplice?" He snorted. "You two can keep each other company on the way back to London."

Even though there was a dead man on the floor, Constable Rigby couldn't help but celebrate his success.

The smoke from the fireplace grew thicker. By this time everyone was coughing, and my eyes had started watering. Bramwell whooshed past with a hand over his mouth. Dr. Barnaby yelled for everyone to calm down. A queer ache in my stomach turned to nausea.

There was another scream from Flora as she pointed to the far end of the room. Everyone froze.

It was her. Audra. She hardly resembled her portrait above the fireplace. Her nightdress was caked with dirt, while a curtain of matted hair framed her bloodied face. A pool of seaweed lay at her bare feet. This was no parlour trick. Her standing corpse reeked of death, the putrid scent scratching at our throats and making us gag.

I blinked a few times. The floor seemed to tilt at an alarming angle. I imagined myself on the deck of the sinking schooner in my painting. Maybe that was the real message all along: *Save yourself.*

Too late.

She raised a skeletal hand and pointed a bony finger at Mr. Pemberton. "Murderer!" she hissed.

Harry let out a garbled scream and clambered through the smoke toward the door.

Audra took a step closer, the seaweed dragging behind her like a rancid wedding train. She nailed her gaze onto Mr. Pemberton.

His face had turned ashen as he raised his cuffed hands protectively. I watched his chest rise and fall rapidly.

She repeated the word over and over, raising her raspy voice each time. Soon, her screams filled the room. "Murderer! Murderer! Murderer!"

"No!" he cried out. I had only heard him use that tone once before, when I was about to go over the cliff. He was truly terrified.

Constable Rigby's gun shook. He pointed it at Audra, his eyes wild. The smoke grew thicker, obscuring the scene.

Flora shrieked as the blaze from the fireplace trailed out onto the rug. Flames licked the bottom of her skirt as she tried to pull William's body away from the fire.

Mr. Lockhart let out a forsaken wail and fell on the floor, puffing out of breath and thrashing. His extended cane made Constable Rigby stumble and drop the gun.

Mayhem ensued. Dr. Barnaby took off his jacket and beat at the flames, screaming for water. Coughing fits broke out. I heard gagging and had to swallow hard not to follow with the same.

I looked for Audra again, but her ghost had disappeared. Then I noticed the smoke had drawn toward the grandfather clock. I'd dealt with enough candles to know what that meant.

"Miss Timmons!" Mr. Pemberton warned.

I turned and saw the end of Constable Rigby's pistol pointed straight at me. There was a shout as Mr. Pemberton launched himself into the officer's side, sending them both into the nearest shelf. Books tumbled on top of them.

"Run!" Mr. Pemberton yelled to me.

A shot cracked through the air. The wood beside me exploded. Constable Rigby hollered for me to freeze. Another shot rang out.

I dropped to the floor, where the air was less hazy, and scrambled to the clock. I saw where one side had come away from the wall. Just as I suspected, there was an opening behind it. I slipped through the slim space and discovered another passageway.

The clock's door swung shut behind me, immediately cutting off the chaos. I leaned against it and heaved, coughing as the remnants of smoke left my lungs. My hands chafed against the cuffs. Pulling out a hairpin, I had them picked and was tossing them to the side faster than you could say, *Rest in peace*.

I looked down. Fresh wax pooled on the floor from a lit candle stub. I glanced back up just in time to see a white nightgown disappearing around the corner. She had been watching me.

Without hesitating, I gave chase. A ghost wouldn't have need for a secret passage.

I ran through the maze of thin hallways, playing a macabre game of hide-and-seek as she led me along. Finally, I reached a ladder that dropped into the familiar passageway. I found the secret door that led to the hallway from the kitchen.

Slowly, I peeked around the corner. "Fire upstairs!" Mrs. Galloway was shouting. "Everyone out!" A stream of staff vacated quickly, leaving the kitchen empty.

I stepped into the hallway. To my left, a faint trail of muddied footsteps led into the pantry. To my right was the door to the back garden. And beyond it, the path to the stables, where a horse with a satchel full of money waited for me. Hopefully.

But my feet wouldn't move.

Maman's mantra came to me. *You can only depend on yourself, ma petite chérie.*

I ran to the garden door and reached for the knob. There was still a red mark on my wrist from the handcuff. I knew Mr. Pemberton couldn't pick his lock. Constable Rigby had come all the way to Somerset Park because he was assured of an arrest. He wouldn't leave unless he had someone—anyone—in handcuffs.

There was only one way to prove Mr. Pemberton's innocence. And I was the only one who knew the truth.

My own words mocked me. *My choices are made only with regard to my own self-preservation.*

"Damn!" I turned around and made my way through the pantry. Unsurprisingly, I found the door to the wine cellar wide open. I took one of the candles from the wall as I pushed my way through. I winced at the rancid air as I stood at the top of the steps that led to the dungeon. I had vowed never to return, and yet here I was.

"I know you're down there, Mrs. Donovan," I hollered. My voice echoed back. "Time to confess."

The door slammed behind me.

I turned in time to see the serpent's ruby eye just before it struck.

CHAPTER FIFTY-SIX

Despite the rain I had just walked through, the bag of roasted chestnuts I carried were still warm. Each Friday afternoon, Maman sent me out to get a special treat for us to share. However, the weather had been so miserable that I was forced to return earlier than usual.

The cold had permeated my thin cloak. As I climbed the stairs to our room, all I could think about was falling into our small bed and wrapping myself in its blankets. I hoped Maman would let me burn a bit of coal in the grate.

When I rounded the landing, my squeaking boots announced my arrival. There were other noises in Miss Crane's boardinghouse too, so I began to hum, trying to drown them out.

I tried the doorknob, but it held fast. I silently cursed and adjusted my hand to get a better grip. I was struck with the horrible thought that Maman had gone out and locked the door behind her. I hated spending time in the parlour downstairs. Too many of the guests assumed I was available, and more than once I had come close to getting a black eye from a client who thought I was rejecting his company.

I was about to try the knob again when I heard voices on the other side of the door. Maman's tone was urgent. The other was gruff and much deeper.

My shivering stopped, but a new coldness crept over me.

I stepped back as the door swung open. A man I had never seen before came out with a jacket over his arm, holding a pair of shoes in his hands. Maman followed, wrapped in her shawl and with only a slip underneath.

"You're back early, *ma petite chérie.*" She gave me a quivering smile.

The bag of chestnuts dropped from my hand and hit the floor. A few escaped, rolling across the uneven surface.

"You must be freezing," she said, taking me by the hand and pulling me into our room. The bed I had been dreaming about crawling into was unmade, the blankets shoved to the bottom. A sour taste sat at the back of my throat.

Maman moved about, talking quickly in both French and English, the way she always did when she was nervous. Her dress was slung over a chair; she took it and pulled it over her head, then went to straighten the bed, all the while still prattling. I couldn't tell what she was saying over the roar of rushing blood in my ears. I could only make out a few words at a time. "Money . . . he's the only one . . . so you don't have to . . ."

She didn't look at me as she said any of this, but I couldn't take my eyes off her. Her hair had streaks of grey starting at the temples. The beautiful shawl she had once prized was tattered and threadbare. Her boots sitting by the door were lined with newspaper.

She continued to tidy, assuring all of our few items were neatly in place. I grabbed my copy of *The Hunchback of Notre Dame* off the bedside table. I didn't want her touching anything of mine.

When she finally looked at me, her gaze did not hold the fiery spark I was used to. She was defeated, and—something I didn't recognize at first—shameful.

She sniffed. "I had no choice, *ma petite chérie*. We cannot live on what the séances pay."

I looked at the bed. I was sure I could never sleep there again. A horror swept through me as I realized what this meant. Why Maman made me run errands on certain days. How even though we were doing less and less business, Miss Crane still let us keep a room.

Maman took a step closer. "The police are more invasive than ever. We can't keep pushing our luck! This is my only option to keep our home."

"How can you call this a home? How can you do this?" I motioned to the bed, unable to say the words.

Her face crumbled. "What I do is not real love, *ma petite chérie*. I am only comforting someone who is lonely. Not so different from our séances."

I couldn't breathe. I had burst into tears, unable to understand the person in front of me. How could she even make such a comparison? I wrenched the door open. "I hate you," I cried. "And I hate this place! I wish we'd never met Miss Crane."

She pushed the door shut before I could leave; the slam was so sharp it made me jump back.

"Genevieve! Be quiet."

I snorted at the absurdity of her request.

Her eyes flashed a warning. "You remember the man who died in this room?"

I nodded, still too angry to allow her the satisfaction of a verbal answer.

"I saw his name in the paper the next day. He was very important—a judge." Maman leaned closer, her voice an urgent whisper. "I listen when the other girls talk among themselves. They say

Miss Crane poisoned him as a favour for the police. That's the real reason Drusilla didn't want this room anymore. She worried his ghost was out for revenge. But he's not the first man to die here. Miss Crane will ally with whoever is willing to pay."

I frowned at her, unconvinced. "I don't see what this has to do with us."

Maman clutched my shoulders. "You are best to stay invisible and give her what she asks."

"And what if she asks me to be her next girl, Maman? What then?"

She flinched as if my words had struck her. "You will never be one of her girls." She slunk back, her body slouched with hurt. "I do this to protect you. Please, why can't you understand?"

Time halted. I saw myself, clutching the doorknob, shivering in my wet boots and eager for an escape. Trapped in a room where death and despair still lingered on the sheets. Captive in a house supported by thin crooked walls, and full of dark secrets. Standing in front of a woman who I couldn't bear to look at a second longer because all I could see was my future self.

"No." I opened the door and ran, but Maman was faster than I realized. Her grip on my elbow was like iron. I would not give in as I pulled away from her, half dragging us both. The chestnuts I had dropped scattered and bounced down the stairs. A door at the end of the hallway creaked open, and a head peeked out.

Maman was an anchor, in every sense, and I craved to be free. All my resentment rushed to the surface. Her actions and choices had brought us both to this battleground. "You can't take care of me properly anymore," I screamed. "You're a horrible mother." A few more doors opened, more faces peering out to watch us.

Then I said the thing I thought about late at night, when my eyes were shut tight, and the pillow was pushed against my ears. "I wish I'd never been born. I wish you'd jumped into the harbour the day my father died."

I knew I'd said the one thing that would break her heart. But a part of me felt relief, a warped victory. I steadied myself for her to finally pull away, to give up trying to convince me.

Instead, she pulled me into a hug. "You saved me that day," she whimpered. "And have been keeping me alive ever since. Please don't hate me. You were meant to live, *ma petite chérie*."

I didn't hear the plea in her voice; I only heard anguish. I had taken her word as the perfect truth for as long as I'd been breathing—until then.

"No!" I ripped myself from her embrace. I wanted her to disappear; I couldn't stand to be next to her. I wanted her to know she couldn't solve everything with a simple hug.

When she reached out for me again, I recoiled. I edged closer to the top of the stairs, clutching my book in front of me like a shield.

She snatched it from my grip. "This is not real," she said. Her tone was firm, more controlled than how I felt. "It's a story about people who never existed. Why do you care so much for them?"

I grabbed the book and tried to tug it out of her grip, but she had decided she would not lose. She stepped backward, yanking fiercely. The spine was fragile from years of being reread. Our struggle was enough to rip it in half. I watched my only treasure in the world come apart. Pages erupted. The momentum made Maman fall back. She slipped on a chestnut and her feet came out from under her.

Instinctively, I reached forward, but I only caught her shawl. It took just seconds. Then she was at the bottom of the stairs, motionless. I thought I saw her chest rise. I prayed for her to lift her head.

The girls rushed around me, some descending the stairs to reach Maman. Miss Crane appeared from the parlour. Her eyes swept over my mother's limp form. She knelt over her, calling her name. Book pages lazily drifted down from above like large snowflakes. I started to clamber down the stairs, but someone ordered Drusilla to hold me in place. Miss Crane's back blocked my view. I couldn't see my mother.

Someone went to fetch an ambulance, but instead they returned with a constable. His black beard matched his beady eyes as he looked me up and down. Maman's shawl was pulled from my grip as handcuffs encircled my wrists.

They didn't let me look at Maman, but it didn't matter. I already knew the truth. I knew she was dead because half of my heart had suddenly gone dark.

At the police station, someone kind put a blanket around me, but I couldn't stop shaking. Several of the girls had attested that I'd pushed Maman.

Miss Crane took an officer to the side. Money exchanged hands. Then she was in front of me, helping me stand. "Come home, Jenny. Your room is waiting for you." I could tell from her tone that I had no choice. She owned me now.

Maman was dead, and I would never be the same.

CHAPTER FIFTY-SEVEN

I woke with a pounding headache, shivering and slumped against something hard. I blinked, trying to focus through the dimness, but there were only vague shadows. Nothing looked familiar. Then I realized my dress was floating around my waist.

I screamed and flailed in the water until my feet found purchase and I could stand. Heavy cuffs encircled my wrists; their rusted chains were attached to the rock wall behind me. I tugged sharply, but the chains held. Hot pain inflamed both arms where the skin was already rubbed raw. Another wave came in, reaching my knees. The air reeked of seaweed and rot. There was a single torch attached to the wall. I tried to focus on its flame as my heart pounded a panicked rhythm.

The water ebbed and flowed like the very sea was breathing. My foot slipped on the rocks, and I felt a crush of glass under my shoe. Squinting down at the water, I could make out the glint of a shattered lamp, the very one I had dropped the last time I came here.

I was at the bottom of the dungeon.

I thought of the bone I saw that night; I wasn't the first to be in these chains. The water reached higher with the next wave.

My hand went to the wall, crusted with barnacles. I looked up and saw the high-tide line was a few feet above my head. I knew the chains would not reach that far. I pictured myself standing on tiptoe, chin pointed to the roof, nostrils flared, hoping for one last sip of air until I had nothing to breathe but the sea.

A sob escaped my shivering lips. I cried a bit, but that only added more salt to my grave. I became angry with myself. I couldn't give up so easily. "Pretend they're Constable Rigby's cuffs," I said.

I pulled out a handful of hairpins from my curls. There was a throbbing twinge as I rubbed my thumb over a large bump. It was covered in a thick layer of crust I believed to be my own dried blood. I remembered seeing the snake head of Mr. Lockhart's cane.

The waves nudged me off balance again, reminding me I had to work fast. Luckily, the chains were long enough for me to reach across and hold the pin with one hand while I worked on the lock of the other.

My fingers were practically numb, but desperation kept the blood pumping. My sobs were close to the surface, but I swallowed them down. The first pin broke after one twist, the second couldn't advance, and the third and fourth bent like dried grass. The iron was so rusted over, even if I'd had a key, it probably wouldn't have worked.

I had to think!

I bent down and picked up a rock and pounded the chain with all the strength I had. It did nothing more than send jolts of pain up my arm.

"That won't work, Jenny," a woman said.

I turned around, searching the dark. There was the swish of water as she walked closer. Then she stepped into the circle of torchlight. Her nightdress was still dirty, and her matted hair hung past her shoulders, but her face was clean of the blood. At that moment I knew exactly how the Hartford family must have felt when I ran from the séance with a bag of their jewelry. I had been conned.

Ghosts were not real, but people pretending to be dead were.

"Lady Audra," I said, weary.

"I hope you don't mind that I called you by your nickname," she said. "Even though this is our first meeting, I already consider us friends. I'm so pleased to finally make your acquaintance." Then she gave me the slightest of curtsies. I noticed she was holding Mr. Lockhart's cane. "Although I wish it were under different circumstances."

"Me as well. You don't have the key, do you?" I asked, raising one cuff.

"I can give you a hand." She tossed the skeletal arm I'd seen her point toward Mr. Pemberton. She laughed again. The sound echoed off the rocks and resounded inside my skull. "A dungeon affords a lady all kinds of props," she said. "Something I'm sure you can appreciate in your line of work."

She lit another two torches along the wall, bringing more of the space into view. There were other sets of handcuffs fixed to the rocks. How long had they been here?

Audra seemed impervious to the bitter temperature of the water. "Tonight went much better than I expected," she said. "How much have you figured out?"

"None," I said. "Other than you're still alive."

"Come now," she said, pointing the cane at me. "You know half the story already. You met all the main players in my little mystery. And you read my diary. It was so exciting to watch you discover it."

"It was a fake?" I asked. The water level had risen to my hips, swirling around me like a fatal embrace.

She looked insulted. "No! Every word was the absolute truth. I'm glad I made a record. Anyone reading it would be able to see how I was wronged. You understand now."

It wasn't a question, but I answered her. "I'm not sure what I understand at the moment." I was confused and horrified by this flesh-and-blood version of Audra. Where was the selfless young woman who was so kind to everyone, who only wished to be safe and loved? Where was the woman I had been determined to seek justice for?

Her head turned with a snap. "Stop it!" she yelled to the wall. She kept staring, then sighed and returned her attention to me. "Grandfather would be proud. Apparently, nerve skipped my father's generation. He couldn't stand up to Mother. I would never forsake my child the way he did with poor William. Oh, I know I shouldn't feel too badly for him, but he had such a difficult start, didn't he?" Her tone was relaxed, as if we were old friends sharing tea in the library. "It was my father's cowardice that set this in motion. So if you want to blame anyone for your being in those handcuffs, it should be him."

"That's fair," I said, sensing I would need to appeal to her pride. "I can see how much stronger you are than your father ever was." I tried to make it a compliment, but all I could think of was how wrong the version of Audra I had created in my mind was compared to the real woman in front of me, dressed in a bloodstained nightgown and devoid of remorse.

Her expression softened. "It's been enjoyable watching you this past week. I have a fondness for your plucky spirit." Then she wrinkled her nose at my cuffs. "Shame I had to use those, though."

A tremor rattled all the way up my body; my hair stood on end. "What happened after you left your room that night?" I asked, hoping to keep her talking. If she was willing to stay with me, I still had a chance to get out of this.

"The very thing everyone thinks happened, my sweet. I heard

the voice again! It drew me out of the house and right to the cliff." Audra looked at a space over my head, her tone becoming dreamlike. "I couldn't fight the lure of her pleas. I left through the secret passageway and made my way to the cliff—that's where her voice is the strongest. I don't remember for certain if I jumped or if I fell, but one moment the muddy cliff was under my feet, and the next I was in the water."

I was stunned. "That's it? You fell? No one pushed you?"

"You think I'm lying?" She narrowed her eyes. "Sometimes the simplest explanation is the right one."

I looked at my cuffs, realizing nothing about this was simple.

"The high tide saved my life. I have no doubt it was divine intervention." Her voice took on a rushed excitement, and she clamoured closer to me. "I made it to the shore and clung to the rocks, looking for the opening. You see, Somerset has more than one secret. The passageways inside the walls are one, and this cave is the other."

She tapped her temple. "I knew the secret, and that's what saved me. Grandfather showed me, but I was too young at the time to comprehend its importance. He understood I deserved to know everything because I am the rightful heir! Me. Not my own father, not even William, and certainly not Gareth." Then she let out a tired laugh. "Even the ghosts know, Jenny. It was her voice that led me to this dungeon from the outside. I can hear them because I'm the true Linwood heir—curse and all."

"Of course you're the heir," I said. I could no longer feel my legs. "And the voices led you here?"

"When I reached the dungeon, I passed out on the bottom stairs." Her eyes were lit with a fiery evil, similar to the expression of Lord Chadwick's portrait in the library.

The library.

A tug pulled behind my ribs, imagining the fate of those I'd left behind.

Run! Mr. Pemberton had said. Two gunshots followed immediately. I didn't remember him shouting after that.

"I was too weak to climb to the top, though," Audra continued. She put a hand to her stomach. "And I had bled. I was losing my baby. The cramping began right after William caused me to fall."

Audra waded to another part of the wall, where there was a small pile of rocks on a ledge. "I was alone," she said. Her voice was soft now, tragic. "I had to bury it, poor thing. The voices stopped after that . . . for a while." She kissed her finger, then touched the top stone. "It was a boy. He would have been the new heir."

I motioned to the staircase. "But you're not alone anymore. You can go up now," I gently proposed. "We both can. It will thrill everyone. You have no idea the joy you'll bring back to Somerset!" I tried to smile at the last part, but my teeth were chattering.

Audra returned to me, swishing through the waist-high water. She used the gold tip of the cane to lift my chin. "I know very well. There's more than one secret passageway in this house. When I finally dragged myself up to the wine cellar, I waited until the kitchen was empty. I couldn't let anyone see me. My skirts were covered in the blood of my infant son. And I had to find out what had become of Barnaby. What if our secret had been discovered once I went missing? What if he'd told Gareth the truth out of unbearable guilt? I didn't survive a drop off the cliff to become a disgrace. I went through the secret passage off the kitchen and back to my room."

Then she hit me with a murderous stare. "And do you know what I learned, staying hidden and watching them through the peepholes?" She leaned in close; her breath was sour. "There were tears, yes, but they didn't last long. And my love? He merely dropped his voice when he spoke of me. He had more sympathy for his best friend."

I had seen myself how well the doctor disguised his pain. "Barnaby couldn't show his true remorse. He had to keep your relationship a secret."

"Enough!" Audra raised the cane above her head like she was going to hit me again. I flinched, and it made her laugh. "I now see him for what he is: unscrupulous and conniving. Doing whatever he fancied, no matter what I truly wanted. Not only had he convinced me to give up Somerset Park and my child's rightful claim to the title of earl, but he was going to make me live a lie. What would Grandfather have said?"

I could hear the insanity creeping into her voice more and more. I had to calm her paranoia and make her feel comfortable enough to trust me. "You've been wronged," I said. "And you deserve Somerset."

She tilted her head at me, as if trying to detect a lie. "Gareth's devotion, on the other hand, was a surprise. Don't misunderstand, I realize obligation motivates him, not love."

Gareth. Audra obviously wrote his name in the ghost book. But why? It still didn't make any sense.

"And William?" I prompted. If she was upset with the men in her life, she might be willing to save me.

She reached out and squeezed my shoulder. "Such a betrayal. It wasn't enough that he attacked me and caused my miscarriage. He used my memory as an excuse to slip further into the bottle. How dare he assume to claim himself a Linwood! Even if he had Father's blood in his veins, Somerset belongs to me. He and that conniving Mrs. Donovan thought they could take everything for themselves. Laughable." She rolled her eyes. "And for all his talk of undying love, he cozied up to Flora quickly enough! I will tell you this, Jenny. Once I saw how everyone had moved on after my death, I was ready to jump off the cliff again and make sure the job was finished."

There was a resounding creak from above. I recognized the groan of the hinges from the wine cellar door.

I almost fainted with relief. "Down here!" I yelled as loudly as I could, but my voice was swallowed up by the crashing of the waves.

The light of a small lantern swiftly made its way down the steps.

"But someone found me before I could go through with it," Audra said. "The one person I could trust. The only one who had my interest at heart this whole time, who never gave up on me."

She touched the side of her hair as if fixing a curl, except it was matted and stiff with dried blood. "I'd been watching him for days. He was the only one who truly mourned me. He was sitting in the library with the family estate papers strewn about the table. I can still remember the expression on his face when I slipped out from behind the grandfather clock!"

The footsteps grew louder on the stone steps and then stopped. They lifted the lantern. I looked up at the kind face. "You," I whispered.

CHAPTER FIFTY-EIGHT

Mr. Lockhart frowned down at me. "Miss Timmons? What are you doing here? You were supposed to escape to the stables!"

I could only raise my bound wrists as an answer, temporarily stunned at his presence in the dungeon. And how did he know about the horse?

His eyes grew large, reflecting the lantern's light as he took in my handcuffs. His voice cracked as he spoke. "How old are those? Thirty, forty, fifty years?" He finally looked at Audra. "Do you have any idea what you've done?" he reprimanded. "Is there even a key?"

Audra reached up and tried to twirl a strand of crusted hair around her finger. "She followed me. I had to make sure she didn't run off and ruin our secret."

I shivered in silence, observing their dynamic.

Mr. Lockhart put a hand on the wall to steady himself. "After all the careful preparation I've done . . ." His sentence fell away as he noticed the water mark on the rock wall I was chained against. He must have come to the same conclusion I had; I wouldn't survive high tide. The water level had already reached the middle of my chest.

"You can hardly be mad at me," Audra replied, her voice rising. "If you had just used two herbal bundles on the fire instead of one, she wouldn't have seen me slip behind the clock."

I thought of the thick smoke in the library. "That was you?" I asked Mr. Lockhart.

His expression caved. It took him a moment before he could answer. "Auntie Lil has a soft place in her heart for me. Please believe me, Miss Timmons: I wish you no harm. We all must make difficult choices for those we love. Lady Audra and I have been planning this for months."

Audra nodded in eager agreement. She searched his face while smiling widely, as if imploring him to match the expression. "And the séance went splendidly! Especially the constable's reaction. He was blubbering on the floor and crying the last I saw of him." She slipped out of the water and joined him on the bottom step. The tide still covered their feet.

Mr. Lockhart blinked back a tear. He sniffed, then held up a finger to her. "We must not take pleasure in the pain of others. That is not our motive, remember?"

Audra jutted out her chin. "You said you cared for me as if I was your own daughter. You promised to help me get my revenge. You promised I could keep Somerset." Her words came out faster with each rushed breath. "You promised me the voices would stop! You promised me! You promised me!" She raised the cane, but he was faster and held her hands in his.

"Audra," he said firmly. His voice cut through her hysterical echoes. "Close your eyes and take a breath. Five, four, three, two, one. And again."

I watched as Audra took another long inhale and exhale.

"Good," he praised. He then put his dinner jacket over her shoulders. I took in Mr. Lockhart's stooped posture and furrowed brow. Surely, someone saw him hobble down to the wine cellar. Constable Rigby was more bloodhound than human, and while

I'd always cursed his cunning, I wished with all my might he'd find me this time. But I was determined to be found alive and with the real villains behind the murders, so that Mr. Pemberton would not be convicted. I had to keep them with me.

One thing was certain. Audra was mad. Perhaps I could use that to my advantage.

"What is your motive, then?" I asked. "Whether intended or not, pain has been caused."

He sighed heavily, like he wanted nothing more than to wake from this weary dream. "When I learned of William's actions the night before the wedding, I knew I had to come up with a plan to make sure he'd never hurt her again. Audra had destroyed the only proof of his claim to Somerset. He was already unstable; his dark descent was only a matter of time. I feared if Audra resurfaced, he'd do something even more desperate."

I thought that seemed unlikely. I said, "There must be another reason to warrant this elaborate plan."

Audra stiffened. "It wasn't as if Barnaby was worth coming back from the dead for. That was clear." Then her voice took on a grim quality. "But I wanted more than Somerset—I wanted revenge. They would not forget me so easily this time."

Mr. Lockhart winced. He reeked of regret and weakness.

I sensed an advantage, but only if I kept them talking.

"But there was a body," I said. Then I remembered what Flora had told me about her friend being able to wear Audra's gowns and how they had the same hair. "Maisie," I said.

Mr. Lockhart nodded solemnly. "An unfortunate death that served a greater purpose. I knew a body would solidify Audra's death and afford us the time we needed to put a plan in place. With my regular contributions to the church, I was trusted enough to buy the silence of a few workmen to dig up Maisie's coffin. After that was settled . . ." He paused as if the words were a struggle.

"We needed William and Gareth removed," Audra finished. She was no longer looking at me, but at the small pile of stones on the other side of the dungeon. "It had to be severe enough to warrant my vindication."

Mr. Lockhart patted her arm. "With all the gossip about ghosts and family curses, I came up with the idea for a séance. We needed someone who had nothing to lose, but who had enough skill to convince the others. After all, who would doubt the spiritualist who actually believed Audra's ghost was real?" He gave me the saddest of smiles.

"You've been conning me from the very beginning," I said to him. I remembered reading in the diary about how he always touched his beard when he lied. How had I missed such an obvious thing? Had I really been so desperate for his approval? The water level inched higher, relentless. "You're an impressive trickster, Mr. Lockhart. I even thought you were dying."

He shook his head at me. "Only because I told you. To everyone else, I had a cold and a bad limp."

"You coughed up blood, though. I saw it."

Rather than pride, his expression was full of regret, void of any self-congratulations. "Chicken blood. It was already on my handkerchief. I used your preconceived idea to complete the lie."

Maman would have been impressed with his technique. I, on the other hand, was silently raging but, more important, running out of time. "Of course no one was suspicious," I said, working to keep my voice calm. "You're the elderly solicitor with decades of loyalty to the family, so kind and giving." Mr. Lockhart didn't acknowledge my praise, and I hoped I could still manipulate him with his guilt. Then I realized he hadn't thought of everything. There was one fact that could save me. I focused my gaze on him. "Who poisoned William?"

Audra giggled. I noticed a clump of hair in her hand. She bent over and gently placed it on the surface of the water and watched it drift away.

Mr. Lockhart regarded her with an increasingly pale complexion. "I've been poisoning him for some time," he confessed. "Auntie Lil considers me a valuable customer. There's no love lost between her and this family." The corners of his mouth turned down. "I knew the effects of the poison were slowly accumulating in William, but not fast enough for our needs, so I added the largest dose to his brandy tonight."

"Having him die during the séance was very effective," I replied. A tangle of seaweed swirled around my ankles, almost tugging my feet out from under me, but I managed to keep myself straight as I looked at him. "It's as if you had been planning to take over Somerset for years."

Audra's eyes lit with a new attentiveness.

I continued, "You had to act quickly. You were worried Mr. Pemberton was going to sell the estate and use the money to relocate to Spain. You'd no longer be needed and out of a job. This scheme worked out well for you too."

"No," he said sternly, showing a lively defiance for the first time since discovering me chained to the rocks. "It was the only way to make William pay."

"But why frame Gareth?" I asked. "He did nothing to Audra. He's the one who's pursued justice for her death."

"Is it Gareth now?" Audra teased, but her smile was all teeth, a grinning shark. "I did sense a growing attraction between the two of you. He talks in his sleep, you know. He whispered your name more than once. To be truthful, I'm a little jealous." She started pulling at the back of her hair. "A little jealous," she repeated, louder.

Mr. Lockhart steadied her hand. "Take a deep breath," he instructed. However, there was a new impatience in his tone. He counted her down from five again. She slowly lowered her grip. He turned to me and explained, "Audra wanted to frame Barnaby for her murder, but I assured her that he would suffer more knowing that his best friend may have killed his true love and unborn child."

Audra gave him a pout that bordered on suspicion.

I pressed my point further. "If Gareth is convicted, who gets Somerset?" I asked.

The corner of Mr. Lockhart's mustache twitched. "Somerset Park will be bequeathed to the family solicitor."

"You," I clarified.

He nodded. "Audra will slip away with me for a lengthy holiday as father and daughter. Once Mr. Pemberton has been convicted and sentenced, I'll become the rightful caretaker of Somerset. I'll hire all new staff, and then Audra can return as my niece." His words sounded heavy, bloated with regret.

Audra stared at him the entire time, her frown growing deeper as he spoke.

Mr. Lockhart continued, "I'm not proud of the things I've done, Miss Timmons, but it was the only way to give Audra what was rightfully hers. Her father trusted me more than anyone. And he was right to do so."

"Was he?" Audra pulled away from him. "Or was that just another example of why Father was such a disappointment? He didn't even know the dungeon existed! Grandfather only told me."

She gave the area a sweeping glance with a look of sinister adoration. She held the cane like a scepter. The one ruby eye caught the lantern's light.

I raised a hand to the large bump on my head. "You're the one who hit Mrs. Donovan," I said, remembering how Dr. Barnaby described the odd shape to the wound on her scalp—that must have been when the other ruby eye fell out. "But she's fiercely loyal. Why did you attack her?"

Audra regarded me with disgust. "Her loyalty lies with William. And she'd been snooping around the third floor, where I'd been hiding all these months. I muddied your boots to make you think you did it." A sly smile slipped into place. "The wardrobe in my room isn't the only one that leads to a secret passageway."

Her eyes gave no hint of remorse. Whether it was the curse or the family sickness to blame, or even the prolonged effects of an unwavering revenge, this was not the Audra I was determined to give justice. She had warped into the horrible creature before me, morals disintegrated and teeming with vitriol.

Mr. Lockhart stood by Audra's side, unmoving like a snared shadow. He put his hand over hers, slipping the cane out of her grasp.

The next wave washed over my shoulders, licking at my chin before it swept back out.

"Do you really think you can both live at Somerset and no one will suspect?" I asked. My hands shook uncontrollably as I clutched them to my chest. I paused, feeling the cameo brooch. My frozen fingers worked the clasp.

"What other choice do I have?" Mr. Lockhart practically cried. "We have no options, and now you're . . ." He pressed his lips together.

The pin came unclasped. I lowered my hands out of sight. I nudged the pin into one of the locks, slowly coaxing it through the chamber. "You won't get away with this," I said. "Gareth won't give up until he figures out what happened."

Audra glared across the dungeon, clenching her fists.

Mr. Lockhart made a sound at the back of his throat. Then he murmured, "He's handcuffed and halfway to London by now."

At least he's still alive, I thought, relieved I hadn't been responsible for his death. It was time to use my last weapon. "He knows about the dungeon," I said. "And he's wealthy enough to hire the best investigators. When they find my body chained to this rock wall, it will prove he was framed. He won't stop hunting you until you're exposed for the murderer you are."

Mr. Lockhart calmly put down the lantern. "They won't find your body."

"What?" Audra's head snapped in his direction.

A thousand angels sang in my ears as energy bounded through my frozen limbs. He was letting me go! I'd done it, I'd convinced him to save me. Then I paused. "You had the key the whole time?"

"There's no key," Mr. Lockhart said. He began to weep. "They won't find your body because I'll remove it. If they search the dungeon, they'll only find decade-old skeletons."

"No!" Audra growled and jumped into the water beside me. She stared defiantly up at Mr. Lockhart. "You can't take her."

He held his arms out wide, palms up, pleading with her. "You cannot have it both ways, Audra. We can't let her live. The only way you can have Somerset back is if Mr. Pemberton is arrested for your murder."

"I'll be silent as a mouse," I lied. "I'm completely selfish; I have no qualms letting him spend a lifetime in jail."

"Let her live?" Audra called out, as if answering someone else. Then she started to laugh. It grated the air like a piercing scream.

Mr. Lockhart ignored her and looked at me. Two tears rolled down his cheeks, disappearing into his mustache. "And what if he's sentenced to hang?" He paused, giving me a chance to refute his claim, but he already knew the truth. "You would not remain silent. No, don't bother arguing. I know he had a horse ready with a satchel full of money for you; I saw the note he'd slipped under your door. I've been watching you two through the passageways. The very fact that you decided to follow Audra instead of securing your own escape proves you are not as selfish as you claim."

I tried to keep my expression blank, but I felt my resolve give way as he continued to cry. I stared at my hands, manacled in rusted bands under the water. I thought I had been clever, keeping them talking, giving myself time to be found. But there was only one reason Mr. Lockhart hadn't left me.

"That's why you're still here," I said. "You have to make sure I drown."

Leaving the lantern on the upper stair, Mr. Lockhart descended the last steps into the water. The cane dragged behind him, useless. The sea reached nearly to the knot of his necktie. "Your grave will be unmarked, but I'll ensure you have a proper burial." He waded toward me. "I am to blame, but at least I can make sure you don't suffer." He pulled off the top of the cane, revealing the small dagger. "It will be quick, and you won't die alone."

Before I could react, Audra leapt forward, coming between us. She punched a fist into his jaw, making him stumble backward and lose his balance in the waves. With a murderous scream, she lunged, trying to grab the cane.

He cursed at her, holding the dagger above his head. "You caused this!" he yelled at her. "You're making me do this!"

Her fingernails scraped the side of his face as he tried to fend her off with one hand. I kept my eyes on the dagger as I feverishly worked the brooch. I felt the pin advance a bit more.

Audra seemed to be gaining strength. She pounded his chest, and they both disappeared under the waves in a swirling mass.

The dungeon became eerily quiet. Only my quickening breaths and the splash of the tide echoed around me. Mr. Lockhart surfaced first, his mouth opened in a silent scream. The hilt of the dagger was sticking out of the side of his neck.

Stunned, he pressed a hand to his wound as blood gushed between his fingers. A gurgling came from his throat. He stared at me in terrified awe, silently pleading. But it was too late. He'd condemned us both to this watery grave. *I'm sorry*, he mouthed. Then his eyes rolled back, and his body crumpled into the waves.

CHAPTER FIFTY-NINE

Audra sputtered a million apologies as her shaking hands reached for Mr. Lockhart's lifeless body, now floating faceup. "What am I to do without you?" She cradled him in her arms as the blood swirled with the seawater around them.

A complicated sorrow rushed over me, making me want to scream at the absurd cruelty of it all, or at least cry like Audra, but I couldn't give in; I had to keep my wits. I knew how to package away grief. Any remorse I had for Mr. Lockhart had to be pushed down and ignored. My fingers should have been numb from the water, but all my concentration was focused on working that tiny pin through the rusted lock.

Audra looked up from Mr. Lockhart, still in her arms. She'd stopped crying, but her eyes were puffy and red. "I couldn't let you die in vain." She smiled at me demurely, and it was more unsettling than any sneer. "The voices want us to suffer as they did. It's the only way they'll be quiet."

I fought to keep balance as the water continued to ebb and flow around me. "I'm a spiritualist. I can contact the ghosts and learn what they want for certain. Then they'll finally give you peace."

"I can hear them fine." She stared at me unblinking, her eyes as cold and hard as the cuffs that encircled my wrists. "Somerset is more than a home. It's a part of me, surely as if I were made of its stones. I could never leave and then return pretending to be someone else." She looked back down at Mr. Lockhart's face, then gently pulled his eyelids closed. "But he has finally shown me the answer. Now I know death is the only true way to claim Somerset forever. That's what the voices have been trying to tell me all along."

I licked my lips and tasted salt. "Don't give up, Audra. You were meant to be head of Somerset." My fingers worked underwater. I felt the pin move again. "All your sacrifices won't be for nothing. There's always a way. I can help you."

She kissed Mr. Lockhart on the forehead, then let go of his body. The waves pushed him to the other side of the dungeon, leaving a trail of blood through the water. "I've spent many hours down here, staring at the skeletons, wondering how they must have felt. Screaming for help until the last breaths left their chests." She lowered her voice like she was telling me a secret. "I only heard them after they died. Still do." A note of fear had crept into her voice. She looked over her shoulder at the shadows. "No matter how far I travel, their screams for help will still find me. Somerset will never be free of their tortured spirits until we pay the price."

The pin suddenly stopped. I held my breath and twisted the brooch, testing the tumblers. I could sense the pressure. All I needed was one more turn. Then there was a snap, and I felt the brooch break off and slip from my fingers. I watched it sink out of sight.

There was a moment of dumb shock, then a surge of furious misery that made me scream out loud. The dam that I'd been working so hard to keep intact fell apart. The grief, the anger, and all the horrible guilt exploded from my very heart.

I pounded the water with my fists and pulled with all my might, ignoring how the iron wore at my flesh. I continued to thrash around until weakness set in. Gasping, I pressed my back up against the rock wall. I had no more ideas, no more tricks. An unrelenting wretchedness took over.

Audra watched me with a knowing expression. "Death is the only way to escape those cuffs, Jenny. You know I'm right. Death is your old friend, yes? How can you be afraid of something you've known your entire life?"

There was a dullness in my ears, giving her words a muffled quality. I said nothing because part of me had always known it was going to end this way.

I wish I'd never been born. I wish you'd jumped into the harbour the day my father died.

My final, cruel words to Maman came back to haunt me. It was fitting. I knew I didn't deserve any better before I took my last breath.

"This is how we all get what we want," she said calmly. "They will find the dungeon, see our bodies, and know that Gareth is innocent. You can give him his freedom. And we get Somerset. Think of it! We'll live on as legends, much better than anything we could have done in our lifetime. We will never get old. We'll always be beautiful. A famous artist will paint your portrait and they'll hang it beside mine in the Gallery Hall. Imagine how grand! And we'll haunt Somerset forever. Like sisters."

Audra took my shivering hands in hers. "The ghosts of Somerset are girls, like you and me, and they will not release their claim until we give them what they ask for. They want us to join them in death. This will be my last act of love for my dear home. Tonight, we will become part of Somerset's history."

The last of my energy surrendered in that moment. Hadn't I already accepted this as my fate since I heard the fortune-teller? This was my punishment for causing Maman's death, for not seeing the sacrifices she was making for us, and for not realizing that without her, I was nothing.

A heavy calmness enveloped me.

I didn't deserve a second chance. Fate kept putting me on this road to the ocean, despite the choices I made. Gareth was wrong. Destiny was not malleable by the choices you made. It was set in stone, and mine would never alter to a course that led to Paris, and family laughter, and riding horses. It had always ended here.

"All right, my sweet?" Audra nodded encouragingly. "We'll do it together."

I dropped my chin, defeated.

I watched as she ducked under, the matted blond hair sinking beneath the surface. Then she pulled on my chains, taking me with her. I felt her arms wrap around me tightly. I pictured our bodies locked in an eternal embrace.

Darkness crept in from the edges. My lungs burned, but I ignored the impulse to take a breath. There was almost a sense of relief. Death had been courting me all my life; I was ready to accept him with open arms. I didn't know how to waltz, but I would dance with death tonight.

There was a violent jolt from somewhere deep inside me. Maman's voice was angry. *You were meant to live*, ma petite chérie.

She spoke again, louder this time. It was coming from my heart. *You were meant to live!*

Maman taught me to be independent so I could be strong. But being strong included trusting my heart too.

The heart sees.

Images of Gareth, and long summer afternoons with the wind in my hair and his lips on mine, played behind my eyelids.

I pushed Audra away and stood tall, my mouth cresting above the water for a gulp of air. She grabbed my hair and dragged me down again. Bubbles exploded from my mouth as her entire weight pushed me to the bottom. Pain streaked across my hand. A piece of glass from the lamp had cut into my palm. I clutched it and blindly stabbed at her grip.

Even beneath the waves, I heard her shriek. Her weight shifted enough that I could push myself back up to stand. I searched for another mouthful of air.

Audra's face rose to meet me above the water, distorted with pure anger. "No!" she screamed, coming at me again. I thought of the bruises and cuts Mr. Lockhart claimed were the result of clumsiness and old age. She wouldn't let me go; this would be a fight to the death.

My iron cuff grazed her jaw. She cried out, then made another grab for my hair. I swung at her with the other hand, and this time the contact was heavy. Her head whipped back and hit the rock wall with a sickening thud. Her eyes went still. Then her limbs went slack.

Her body eased into the water, the dirty nightgown billowing around her like the petals of a *Helleborus orientalis*.

I tilted back my head and screamed, "Help me!" The next wave pushed me off my feet. Water smoothed over my face as my boots scrambled for another inch, but the chains were already stretched their full length.

"Help me!" My voice echoed in the empty dungeon. "Help me!"

Those two words were destined to chase me to the grave. Maybe it was my own screams for help I'd been hearing all along. I pictured Flora as an old woman in Auntie Lil's rocking chair, telling the tale of how my ghost haunts the dungeon. Would anyone find us at all?

I called out, knowing his name would be the last thing from my lips. "Gareth!"

Water filled my mouth. The waves came again, but this time the water level didn't recede. I kept screaming, prepared to use my dying breath as proof I wanted to live.

I want to live, I thought. *I want to live.*

I was meant to live. I deserve to live.

There was a massive splash beside me. I thought Audra had come back to life and was ready to kill me for good.

Strong hands were under my arms, tugging roughly. Then a mouth was pressed over mine, blowing air into my lungs. I accepted the breath gratefully. The next wave rolled over us, and the hold on me loosened. I tried to call out for them not to leave me, but only a stream of bubbles left my lips.

I glanced up at the water's surface above me and could just make out the distorted silhouette of his face. Then he dipped beneath the water again and his mouth pressed against mine a second time, giving me air, keeping me alive.

I felt the water stir as someone else jumped into the surf beside me. There was a shuddering clang of steel followed by the sudden release of the heavy chain from one wrist. To my other cuff, the same sensation of tremendous vibration, and then I was free.

Together we rose. I took in a desperate lungful of air, clinging to him. My stomach heaved as I brought up seawater. I dared not look behind me, where I knew the bodies must be floating. The moment felt too large to grasp or even try to understand. I could only react. Tears came next as I started to violently shake.

Joseph clambered out of the water. The stable hatchet was in his grip, dripping.

Gareth helped me up the stairs until we were completely out of the water. We collapsed into each other's arms, shivering.

"Miss Timmons," he finally said, breathless. "You missed the stables entirely."

"Call me Genevieve," I replied.

CHAPTER SIXTY

It was so quiet in the graveyard. I could hear the melting snow drip from the oak branches above me. I replaced the dead flowers from Maisie's headstone with a new posy. Her actual remains had been retrieved from the Linwood family crypt and brought back to where they rightfully belonged. I promised Flora before she left for her new placement at a grand house several counties over that I would take up the task of leaving flowers for her best friend.

Auntie Lil's cottage had become my newly adopted home. There was always cake to eat and soothing tea when I couldn't sleep. Her gentle companionship and maternal goodness made for the perfect place to recuperate after the séance, and a soothing escape from the trials.

I had carried the guilt for causing Maman's death all this time, but her murder had not been by my hand. My séance had indeed driven someone to confession: Constable Rigby.

The night my mother fell down the stairs, he was the first copper to arrive, and by no coincidence. He was already on his way for a meeting with Miss Crane. She had ordered one of the girls to fetch him instead of an ambulance. And while I was held back at the top of the stairs, clutching her shawl, she had purposely bent over Maman's body, blocking my view. She pretended to tend to her injuries, while all along she had been covering her nose and mouth, ensuring she'd never breathe again. The coroner was convinced, through bribery and blackmail, to change the death certificate from suffocation to a broken neck.

Miss Crane knew the secrets of many a powerful Londoner, but her power over others could only reach so far.

A new cause of death was enough to reopen the case. Constable Rigby made a plea deal, and the word of a copper, even a crooked one, would always outweigh that of a woman who ran a brothel. Although she was only responsible for my mother's death, Miss Crane's trial was the last chapter of the Somerset Slayings, as the press had dubbed them. News of the triple murders at the grand estate made the headlines of every paper. It was too salacious not to.

I stood up from Maisie's grave and made my way to the rock wall that surrounded the church. Winter was losing its grip as new shoots poked through the hard ground. Gareth was waiting for me, standing beside his horse. With the February morning mist swirling about, he looked like an angel I'd conjured from my imagination.

I reached into my basket and handed him two smaller posies. He took them with a cheerless expression and slipped them into the horse's satchel.

"I know you don't approve," I said, "but Mr. Lockhart was repentant at the end, and Audra was a victim, in some ways. It's only right to leave tokens at their graves as well."

He let out a sigh. "You may have exonerated them in your soul, but I will never forgive either of them for nearly taking your life."

I stayed silent. Even though it had been several months since that horrible night, I still had nightmares about being down in the dungeon, trapped under the water. It had been Mrs. Donovan who heard me calling for help, while the rest of the staff had evacuated due to the fire.

As Constable Rigby had somewhat of a breakdown at the sight of Audra's ghost, Gareth was able to escape during the commotion in the library. He ran to the stables. First, to see if I had made a clean getaway, and second, to have Joseph use the hatchet to free him from the handcuffs. When Joseph told him I'd never arrived, they both ran back to the manor. As they entered the back door to the kitchen, Mrs. Donovan told them someone was crying out from the pantry. They didn't believe her until they heard me call out his name.

Poor Mrs. Donovan never fully recovered from her injuries. News of William's death was worse than any blow to the head, and she took to bed, dying a few weeks after.

The charges of theft against me were dropped after the police received a letter of apology from the Hartford family. Apparently, when Mrs. Hartford learned of my tragic misfortune at the hands of Miss Crane, she forgave my attempt to steal her jewels. In addition, Gareth paid a small fortune to one of the top solicitors in London. They reviewed the coroner's report in my police file and deemed suffocation to be the true cause of Maman's death. I wondered if Mr. Lockhart had mentioned it during the party on purpose. I like to think he was offering me a chance to save myself, in case I was sent back in jail.

"Enough of the past," Gareth said, offering me his arm. "I don't want our last few hours spoiled."

I slipped my gloved hand into the bend of his elbow. We continued our walk down the village road, fresh with the recent dusting of snow. Gareth was leaving for Spain to interview prospective buyers for Somerset Park. The library had been slightly damaged from the smoke the night of the séance, but the grounds were still spectacular. He wanted to find someone who would maintain the stables to his standards.

He turned to me with a sly grin in place. "I may take advantage of my time there to tour some properties for my own use. Any requests?"

"Requests?" I teased. "Not suggestions?"

"How else am I to tempt you?"

I blushed, imagining all the ways. "Rolling hills," I answered.

"Very well."

"And a forest of trees," I added. "Perhaps a river or creek—but far away from the ocean."

He cleared his throat. "Indeed."

We rounded the turn and paused. Somerset rose from a sea of mist in the distance, hauntingly beautiful. But I could never set foot on the grounds again. The moment grew serious, our flirtation dissipated by the grim memories.

Gareth took my hands in his, then very slowly removed one of my gloves. "Will you permit me to leave you with a token so you won't forget me?"

"Impossible."

Then he slipped off his family ring from his pinkie and put it on my index finger—it fit perfectly. "Are you certain?" I asked, flexing my hand to look at it. "I lost the last piece of jewelry you gave me."

The smile vanished from his face. "I have nightmares about not saving you in time."

"You sound in need of Auntie Lil's tea." She'd had an uptake in business since Dr. Barnaby left. He went to London, intent on becoming a surgeon. I suspected he was no longer interested in bedside medicine. He left a long apology letter for Gareth and hoped they could reconcile their friendship, although a stint of time was required for a full recovery.

"No, thank you." Gareth chuckled. "I see how she leers at me when I visit the cottage."

"It's not you. It's your connection to Somerset and its curse."

"She's partly right. I am under a spell." He reached out and twirled the ring on my finger. "One I don't mind, actually."

Warmth filled my stomach, and I smiled, lost in images of us, together. Blissful wishes of moments to come. How could I ever have doubted his sincerity? He was the person I trusted most implicitly now.

He leaned closer. "Are you sure you don't want me to stay for the trial?" he asked once again, for what seemed like the hundredth time.

The day they arrested Miss Crane, I made sure to be waiting across the street for a front-row seat. But if she was ashamed, it didn't show. Her posture was straight, and her large ridiculous hat was in place. I wasn't prepared for the fear that tightened my throat, or the paralysis that made it impossible for me to do anything but stare uselessly as she disappeared into the paddy wagon. The clever speech I'd prepared for weeks was lost between the beats of my thudding heart.

I was still no more than the quiet girl she'd first met. The frustration and anger boiled over, and I spent the entire carriage ride back to Wrendale in tears. When I expressed disappointment in myself for not being strong enough to face Miss Crane, Auntie Lil told me being brave meant listening to your instincts instead of your pride.

"No," I told Gareth. "I'll follow the trial through the papers. I'm anxious for it to be over, honestly. I'm ready for my new life to start."

He smiled and kissed my hand. "As am I."

OVER THE NEXT week, Miss Crane made the front page each day, and it was clear from the reporter's account that she was determined to control the narrative of her time in the spotlight. She told the packed courtroom that Maman and I had a stormy relationship and were seen fighting the night she died.

Even though Constable Rigby had given a statement implicating her, she would never confess the truth. I made a promise to myself that no matter how much it bothered me, I would be present the day of her verdict.

I would do it for Maman.

THE ONLY NOISE in the courtroom was the artist's pencil a few rows back, sketching madly to capture the moment. The newspapers had runners waiting in the hall outside to take the headline to their offices for tomorrow's front page.

My hands shook in my lap, knowing I could have easily been the one in the defendant's box. I started to turn the gold ring on my index finger, matching each rotation with a breath.

The judge stared down his glasses at the defendant's box. "Guilty," he finally said.

There was an explosion of creaks from the wooden benches as the press jumped from their spots. I closed my eyes and sent a prayer to Maman, trying to imagine what she would say.

I looked up in time to see Miss Crane being taken away in handcuffs.

Ignoring the reporters' requests for a quote, I went directly to the police station. As luck would have it, the young constable whom I had met the last time I was here allowed me to sneak back and visit the prisoner. I smoothed out my silk dress and adjusted my hat, making sure the peacock feather was just right. The hallway to the cells seemed especially cold and dark.

Good.

My boots tapped my arrival like a soldier's victory march.

She sat with her head bowed over her hands. I cleared my throat.

Even though she didn't have the garish lipstick or bright-colored dress, her cold eyes were hard and merciless. She stood and made her way over, resting her elbows on the bars.

I was glad the long skirt hid my trembling knees.

"Think you're fooling anyone in those fancy clothes?" she asked. "A new hat won't change what people think of you." She gave me a pitiful expression, as if I were on the wrong side of the bars. "One day you'll realize everything I did was for your own good."

Not only had she killed my mother, but she'd let me think it was my fault. She'd lied in court, to no avail of course, but now that I was finally facing her, I had to press her for the truth.

"You won't find any sympathetic ears in jail," I said, working to keep my voice steady. "There is no audience, only me. This is your chance to confess."

She made a tsking noise and shook her head. "The second I laid eyes on you, I knew you'd be worth the time and effort, no matter if it took a few years. I would have molded you into my most valuable girl. But your mother wouldn't let me get close to you."

To hear her calmly discuss Maman's murder as nothing more than a business venture set my blood on fire. I fought the urge to reach through the bars and hit her, but I had to hold back and let her finish.

She nodded with a slight smile on her chapped lips. "I was going to make you into something special. Something amazing and unforgettable. With your beauty and my brains, we'd never want for anything London could offer. We could've owned the city." Then her expression crumbled, aging her a million years.

"Instead, you're going to rot in jail." I took a step closer, nailing her in place with my stare.

I had never talked back to Miss Crane in such a way. She growled like a cornered dog. "I'm the only one who took care of you when all the other girls wanted you out! Your own grandmother couldn't be bothered. She refused to send a pound even though she's stinking rich."

I shook my head at her and began to turn away, unwilling to hear this slander.

"Wait!" Her face molded itself into an expression of exaggerated sadness. She began to sob uncontrollably, clutching the bars with both hands. "It was only me who cared, Jenny. It was always me."

I was tired of her cruel lies and manipulation. I replied with her own words. "Oh, now, don't give me them dark pools of fake tears. You'd sooner cheat a dying man than give him a drink of water."

With that, I left, content to let my last image of her be a pitiful, wilting creature, stripped bare of all rouge and finery, staring after me in utter despair.

As I walked outside, a gust of cold air sobered me. Miss Crane's words echoed through my mind. Then I stopped in my tracks before reaching the carriage. Grandmother? Maman's family had never known I existed. So how would Miss Crane know they were wealthy? I turned the corner in the direction of the boardinghouse, though the thought of returning there curdled my stomach. Was she only using this last opportunity to torture me?

Being brave meant listening to my instinct. I had to at least check before returning to Wrendale.

When I reached the boardinghouse, I tentatively knocked on the door. I smoothed out the front of my dress self-consciously, worried it might be too much for this part of London.

Drusilla answered. "Jenny?" She looked me up and down with the same surprise I felt.

I almost didn't recognize her fresh face and bright smile. She still favoured a low neckline, but the dress was new and clean.

She welcomed me inside and led me to the parlour. The furniture was the same, but the cobwebs were gone, and a vase of flowers brightened the area considerably. The three-legged settee wobbled on the stack of books propping it up as we sat.

We discussed the trial and Miss Crane's conviction. She told me that the girls would keep the boardinghouse running for their own profit.

"It's completely different when you get to choose the blokes," she explained.

Eventually, I told her about my meeting with Miss Crane and her mention of my grandmother. "Do you know of any ledgers she would have kept?" I asked. "Any records of correspondence?"

Drusilla shook her head. "The police went through all her papers," she said. "Her office wasn't anything more than a tiny desk, and it's completely empty. Sorry."

I hadn't realized how foolishly optimistic I'd become. I was embarrassed by how easily I'd been duped. Maman hadn't contacted her family in decades; I was certain they didn't know of my existence. "Thank you anyway," I said. "I'm sure she was lying."

There was a curious knock at the door—four quick raps. Drusilla smiled as she checked the clock on the wall. "That's Fred. He's me afternoon appointment." She hurried to the foyer. There were hushed words exchanged as she ushered him quickly past the archway and up the stairs. "Be right there, love," she called out to him.

I stood to take my leave and thank Drusilla for the visit. The settee wobbled. I regarded the stack of books. They'd been here holding up this settee since I first arrived with Maman. What other use did a boardinghouse have for books? My skin prickled as an idea swept over me.

With Drusilla's help, I lifted one end of the settee, freeing the stack. I held the first novel upside down, fanning it open. Money floated to the rug. Drusilla squealed and tucked the bills into her cleavage. The second book had nothing but moths.

The third novel held an envelope.

Shaking, I unfolded the letter. It was entirely in French, but I recognized Maman's name. I could understand and speak a bit of my mother's language, but translating it properly would need Gareth's help. Was this written by my grandmother? Did she indeed know about me? I wasn't sure if I could bear any more rejection, but I needed to know for certain.

"Oy." Drusilla leaned over my shoulder. "Good or bad?"

I refolded the letter and slipped it back into the envelope. "I'm not sure, but at least I know where it came from," I said, pointing to the return address.

Drusilla winked. "Bring me back a croissant."

EPILOGUE

Paris, April 1853

The trees were blossoming, the length of the avenue stretching out beneath an unending canopy of white flowers. The carriage ride had been smooth, but my stomach was a nest of bees. Gareth had offered to accompany me, but I told him I needed to do this on my own.

We agreed to meet at Notre Dame afterward.

Somerset Park had been sold to Miss Gibbons's American cousin. Unfortunately, news reached us that a large part of the estate had been destroyed by a fire a few weeks ago. Joseph confided he was certain Audra's ghost was responsible.

But I knew better. Ghosts did not exist.

My nightmares of drowning were becoming less frequent. The fortune-teller may have been right, after all. I did die in the water that night. A new woman emerged from the dungeon, one who would fight for the happiness she deserved.

With a gentle jolt, my ride came to a stop. I looked up at the elegant house. "Oh," I whispered, feeling what little resolve I had crumble. The carriage door opened, and the footman stood there, waiting for me. I stepped out into the sunlit street, smoothing out my dress and touching the ribbon at my neck, worried the knot might have loosened.

The front door opened, but unlike at Somerset Park, it was a young maid who answered. *"Bonjour, mademoiselle."*

I handed her my card. Her eyes grew wide as she read my name.

I hoped my new dress and bonnet were the right style. I hoped she couldn't tell I was shaking in my shoes. I hoped they would like me.

"This way, please, Miss Timmons," she said in her thick French accent. She led me through the foyer and down a hallway. We stopped at a yellow door, which she knocked on and then opened.

Each nervous face turned toward me as I waited at the entrance to the parlour. This time I wasn't holding a bag of séance props. It was only me.

An elderly woman in fine silk with eyes like Maman's stood and inched her way toward me. She was slightly hunched, with a white head of hair, elegantly fashioned. She reached out and took my hands in her wrinkled ones. She seemed to drink me up, studying every bit of me. She spoke at length, but I couldn't understand her quick French. She smiled at me with her whole face.

Warmth grew inside my chest.

A younger woman was at my side in an instant, smiling and touching my shoulder. "She said you look just like her Justine. Same hair, same eyes."

Justine—Maman.

The heart sees.

My chest swelled. I nodded. *"Merci, Grand-mère,"* I said, hoping I hadn't ruined the pronunciation too badly.

She touched my cheek. *"Ma petite chérie."* Then she pulled me into a hug.

There was laughter all around us; the room brightened, as if every lamp had been lit. Everyone came closer to greet me. I had cousins and aunts and uncles, and they all wanted to know me.

Food and wine came next. After a while, I sat on the settee with Grand-mère, and we looked at portraits of Maman she'd sat for over the years. I did look like her, so very much. We both wiped tears from our cheeks when she described her despair after Maman ran away. At first, pride had held her back from seeking Maman out, but the longer she did not return, the more her heart cracked. It made Grand-mère realize nothing was worth losing family.

Then one day they received news that Maman's husband had died, but no one knew what had become of Maman. They all thought she had perished in the accident too. None of them had any idea of my existence until they received a letter from Maman. Grand-mère handed me the note, which had been neatly folded three times.

I lightly touched the faded script, knowing Maman's handwriting instantly. I was pulled into a memory of sitting on the bed while she did my braids. I could almost feel her fingers combing through my hair.

She translated for me, moving her finger along the words. According to the date at the top, Maman had written the letter a few months before she died, asking her family for money, not for herself but for her daughter. However, she never mentioned my name, only that I was wonderful and beautiful and deserved a better life.

"She thought you never wrote back," I told them. Maman started sending me out for errands shortly after that. Her last hope had been to beg her family for assistance. When they didn't respond, she had no choice but to become one of Miss Crane's girls. I grew ashamed, remembering the last words I had spoken to her, not knowing how much of her soul she'd already sacrificed for me.

Then it was my turn to take out the letter I'd found at Miss Crane's, explaining she had kept it from Maman. The young woman translated as Grand-mère spoke quickly. She said, "When we didn't receive a reply, we sent an investigator to the address from Justine's letter. A woman said Mrs. Timmons was murdered, her own daughter hung for the crime."

Miss Crane's vindictiveness had no bounds.

"Darkness settled over the house," she continued. "It only lifted when we received your letter."

After a promise to return for dinner, I politely declined the offer of a carriage, and instead decided to walk to my next appointment. The stroll was more than pleasant, and my new shoes with perfectly intact soles hardly touched the ground.

Love had infused me with a lightness.

I paused in front of the cathedral, attempting to take it all in at once. Notre Dame was massive in all its splendor. I thought of the sketch of Maman, the one I had found hidden at the bottom of the jewelry box. I was standing in almost the same spot. I knew she was with me—not because I felt her spirit, but because she was a part of me and always would be.

I turned and found his familiar gait among the bustle of the street. He tipped his hat as he neared, giving me the smile that had sealed my fate the first time I saw it.

I ran to him, eager to share the news of my new family. But once I was in his embrace, I forgot about talking, and kissed him instead.

Maman used to say that love meant heartbreak, but I had learned that love was also the cure.

Gareth lifted me in his arms and swung me around. My eyes were closed tight, but I could see my entire future.

The heart sees.

ACKNOWLEDGMENTS

I am indebted to my agent, Jill Marr, for her enthusiasm, unfailing support, and expertise. I will be forever grateful that she picked this story out of the slush pile.

This novel exists because of the passion and brilliant insight of my editors: Julia Elliott at William Morrow in New York, and Iris Tupholme at HarperCollins Canada. They embraced *A Dreadful Splendor* and were essential in helping me further develop Genevieve's story to create the most satisfying version. Working with them has been a privilege and a delight. As well, Julia McDowell's editorial input was valuable and I'm grateful for her acuity and thoughtful attention. This novel also benefited from Janet Robbins Rosenberg, with her meticulous and perceptive copyediting.

Thank you to the superb team of HarperCollins Canada and William Morrow for their dedication and talent. I couldn't have found a better group to champion this story.

A large slice of gratitude to Kate Forrester for creating this stylishly fabulous cover.

Thank you again to my parents, Eric and Ethel Bishop. Especially my mom for introducing me to Vincent Price long ago and passing on her love of mysteries.

Finally, a note to thank all my family and friends who continue to cheer on my writing from the sidelines. I'm continually grateful and extremely lucky to have in my life my husband, Ken, and our children, Ruth and Adam. And lastly a thank-you to Oscar, the best dog ever.

ABOUT THE AUTHOR

Always in the mood for a good scare, B. R. Myers spent most of her teen years behind the covers of Lois Duncan, Ray Bradbury, and Stephen King. When she's not putting her characters in precarious situations, she works as a registered nurse. A member of the Writers' Federation of Nova Scotia, she lives in Halifax with her family—and there is still a stack of books on her bedside table.

She is the author of nine young adult novels. Her contemporary coming-of-age novel *Girl on the Run* was a CCBC Best Book for Teens pick of the year. Her publication *Rogue Princess* was chosen as a Top Ten Best Audiobook from *School Library Journal*.